A Secret Kept

Also by Tatiana de Rosnay

Sarah's Key

A Secret Kept

Tatiana de Rosnay

St. Martin's Griffin
New York

This is a work of fiction. All of the characters, organizations, and events portrayed in this novel are either products of the author's imagination or are used fictitiously.

 Printed in the United States of America. For information, address St. Martin's Press, 175 Fifth Avenue, New York, N.Y. 10010.

www.stmartins.com

The Library of Congress has cataloged the hardcover edition as follows:

Rosnay, Tatiana de, 1961–
A secret kept / Tatiana de Rosnay.—1st ed.
p. cm.
ISBN 978-0-312-59331-5
1. Brothers and sisters—Fiction. 2. Family secrets—Fiction. 3. Noirmoutier Island (France)—Fiction. 4. Psychological fiction. I. Title.
PR9105.9.R66S43 2010
823'.914—dc22
2010022062

ISBN 978-0-312-55349-4 (trade paperback)

First published under the title *Boomerang* in France by Editions Héloïse d'Ormesson

10 9 8 7 6

This book is for

Cecilia and Alexis, my wonderful sister and brother,
and for Cedric and Caroline, their loved ones.

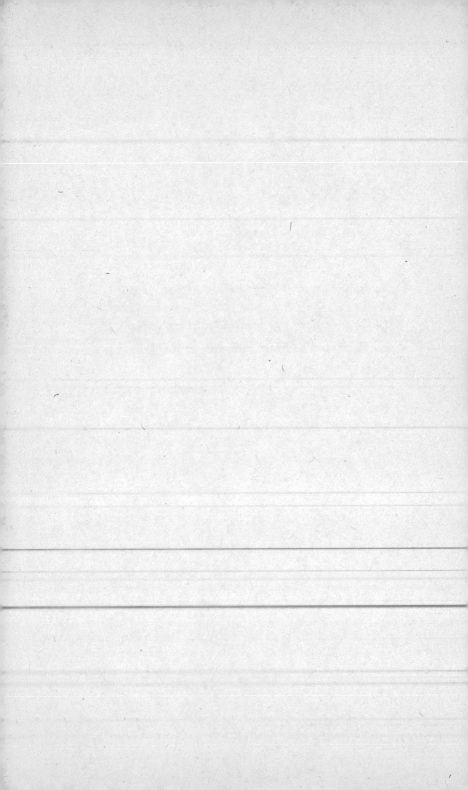

In loving memory of Pierre-Emmanuel (1989–2006)

Let my name be ever the household word that it always was. Let it be spoken without an effort, without the ghost of a shadow upon it.

—HENRY SCOTT HOLLAND

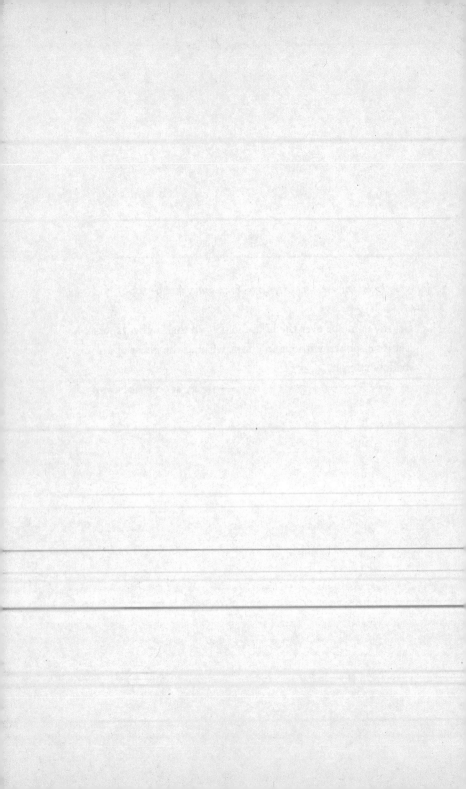

“Manderley was no more.”
—DAPHNE DU MAURIER, *Rebecca*

A Secret Kept

I AM SHOWN INTO a small, drab room, told to sit down and wait. Six empty brown plastic chairs face each other on tired linoleum. In a corner, a fake green plant, shiny leaves coated with dust. I do as I am told. I sit down. My thighs tremble. My palms feel clammy, my throat parched. My head throbs. I think, I should call our father now, I should call him before it gets too late. But my hand makes no effort to grab the phone in the pocket of my jeans. Call our father and tell him what? Tell him how?

The lighting is harsh, glaring strips of neon barring the ceiling. The walls are yellowish and cracked. I sit there, numb. Helpless. Lost. I long for a cigarette. I wonder if I am going to retch, bring up the bitter coffee and stale brioche I had a couple of hours ago.

I can still hear the screech of the wheels, feel the sudden lurch of the car as it veered sharply to the right, careening into the railing. And her scream. I can still hear her scream.

How many people have waited here? I think. How many people have sat where I am sitting now and waited for news of their loved ones? I cannot help imagining what these jaundiced walls have seen. What they know. What they remember. Tears, shouts, or relief. Hope, pain, or joy.

The minutes click by. I watch the round face of a grimy clock above the door. There is nothing else for me to do but wait.

After half an hour or so, a nurse comes in. She has a long, horsey face, skinny white arms.

"Monsieur Rey?"

"Yes," I say, my heart in my mouth.

"You need to fill out these papers. With her details."

She hands me a couple of sheets and a pen.

"Is she all right?" I mumble.

My voice seems thin and strained.

She flickers watery, lashless eyes over me.

"The doctor will tell you. The doctor will come."

She leaves. She has a sad, flat ass.

I spread the sheets of paper over my knees with trembling fingers.

Name, birth date and place, marital status, address, social security number, health insurance number. My hand still shakes as I print out "Mélanie Rey, born August 15, 1967, at Boulogne-Billancourt, single, 49 rue de la Roquette, Paris 75011."

I have no idea what my sister's social security number is. Or her health insurance number for that matter. All that stuff must be in her bag. Where is her bag? I can't remember anything about her bag. Just the way her body slumped forward when they hauled her out of the car. The way her limp arms hung down to the ground from the stretcher. And there I was, not a hair out of place, not a bruise on my skin, and I had been sitting right next to her. I flinch. I keep thinking I am going to wake up.

The nurse comes back with a glass of water. I gulp it down. It has a metallic, stale taste. I thank her. I tell her I don't have Mélanie's social security number. She nods, takes the sheets, and leaves.

The minutes inch by. The room is silent. It is a small hospital. A small town, I guess. In the suburbs of Nantes. I'm not quite sure where. I stink. No air-conditioning. I can smell the sweat trickling under my armpits, gathering around my groin. The sweaty, meaty smell of despair and panic. My head still throbs. I try breathing calmly. I manage to do this for a couple of minutes. Then the helpless, awful feeling takes over and swamps me.

Paris is more than three hours away. I wonder again if I should call my father. I tell myself I need to wait. I don't even know what the doctor has to say. I glance down at my watch. Ten thirty. Where would our father be now? I wonder. At some dinner party? Or watching cable TV in his study, with Régine in the next room, on the phone, painting her nails?

I decide to wait a little longer. I am tempted to call my ex-wife. Astrid's name is still the first one that pops up in times of stress or despair. But the thought of her with Serge, in Malakoff, in our old house, in our old bed, with him invariably answering the phone, even her mobile, for Christ's sake—"Oh, hi, Antoine, what's up, man?"—is just too much. So I don't call Astrid, although I long to.

I stay in the small, stuffy room and try once more to remain calm. Try to stop the panic rising within me. I think of my kids. Arno in all his teenage glory and rebellion. Margaux, a creature of mystery at fourteen. Lucas, still a baby at eleven, compared with the other two and their raging hormones. I simply cannot imagine myself telling them, "Your aunt is dead. Mélanie is dead. My sister is dead." The words make no sense. I push them away.

Another hour creeps by. I sit there, my head in my hands. I try to sort out the mess building up in my mind. I start thinking about the deadlines I need to keep. Tomorrow is Monday, and after this long weekend, there are many urgent things to be done—that unpleasant Rabagny and his god-awful day-care center I should not have taken on; Florence, that hopeless assistant I know I have to fire. But how can I possibly think of this? I realize, appalled at myself. How can I think of my job now, at this precise moment when Mélanie is somewhere between life and death? I say to myself with a sinking heart, Why Mélanie? Why her? Why not me? This trip had been my idea. My present for her birthday. That fortieth birthday she was so upset about.

A woman of my age comes in at last. A green operating blouse and one of those funny little paper hats surgeons wear. Shrewd hazel eyes, short chestnut hair touched with silver. She smiles. My heart leaps. I rush to my feet.

"That was a close call, Monsieur Rey," she says.

I notice small brown stains on the front of her uniform. I wonder with dread whether those stains are Mélanie's blood.

"Your sister is going to be all right."

To my horror, my face crumples up, tears spill out. My nose runs. I am acutely embarrassed to be crying in front of this woman, but I can't prevent it.

"It's okay," the doctor says. She grips my arm. She has small, square hands. She pushes me back down into the chair, sits beside me. I bawl the way I used to when I was a kid, deep sobs that come from the gut.

"She was driving, right?"

I nod, try to tidy up my damp nostrils with the back of my hand.

"We know she wasn't drinking. We checked that. Can you tell me what happened?"

I manage to repeat what I told the police and the ambulance people earlier on. That my sister wanted to drive the rest of the way home. That she was a reliable driver. That I had never been nervous with her at the wheel.

"Did she black out?" asks the doctor. The name on her badge reads: DR. BÉNÉDICTE BESSON.

"No, she didn't."

And then it comes back to me. Something I had not told the ambulance people, because I only remember it just now.

I look down at the doctor's small, tanned face. My own face is still twitching with the crying. I catch my breath.

"My sister was in the middle of telling me something. . . . She turned to me. And then it happened. The car drove off the highway. It happened so fast."

The doctor urges me on.

"What was she telling you?"

Mélanie's eyes. Her hands clasping the wheel. *Antoine, there's something I need to say. I've kept it back all day. Last night, at the hotel, I remembered something. Something about . . .* Her eyes, troubled, worried. And then the car driving off the road.

SHE FELL ASLEEP AS SOON as they were able to make their way through the sluggish suburban gridlock that circled Paris. Antoine smiled as her head dropped back against the car window. Her mouth opened, and he thought he heard a tiny snore. She had been irritable that morning when he came to pick her up just after dawn. She hated surprises and always had. He knew that, didn't he? Why the hell was he organizing a surprise trip? Honestly! Wasn't it bad enough turning forty? Getting over an agonizing breakup? Never having been married, not having any kids, and people mentioning biological clocks every five minutes? "If somebody utters that word one more time, I'll hit them," she hissed between gritted teeth. But the idea of facing the long weekend alone was unbearable for her. He knew that. He knew she couldn't stand thinking about her hot, empty apartment above the noisy rue de la Roquette, and all her friends out of town leaving joyful messages on her voice mail: "Hey, Mel, you're *forty*!" Forty. He glanced across at her. Mélanie, his little sister, was going to be forty. He couldn't quite believe it. Which made him forty-three. He couldn't quite believe that either.

Yet the crinkled eyes in the rearview mirror were those of a man in early middle age. Thick salt-and-pepper hair, a long, lean face. He noticed that Mélanie dyed her hair brown. Her roots were unmistakably gray. There was something touching about her dyeing her hair. Why? he mused. So many women dyed their hair. Maybe it was because she was his kid sister. He simply could not imagine her growing old. Her face was still lovely. Perhaps it was even lovelier than it had been in her twenties or thirties, because her bone structure had such class. He never tired of gazing at Mélanie. Everything about her was small, feminine, delicate. Everything about her—the dark green eyes, the beautiful curve of a nose, the startling white smile, the slim wrists and ankles—reminded him of their mother. She didn't like being told that she looked like Clarisse. She had never liked it. But to Antoine it was like their mother peeping out from Mélanie's eyes.

The Peugeot gathered speed, and Antoine guessed they'd probably be there in less than four hours. They had left early enough to beat the traffic. Despite her questions, he hadn't breathed a word about their destination. He had just grinned. "Pack enough for a couple of days. We're going to celebrate your birthday in style."

There had been a minor problem with Astrid, his ex-wife. A little smoothing out to do. That long weekend was normally "his." The kids were supposed to be leaving Astrid's parents' place in the Dordogne to come to him. He had been firm on the phone. It was Mel's birthday, she was forty, he wanted to make it special for her, she still wasn't over Olivier, she was going through a bad patch. Astrid's voice: "Oh, *merde*, Antoine. I've had the kids for the past two weeks. Serge and I really need some time for ourselves."

Serge. Even the mere name made him cringe. A photographer in his early thirties. The muscular, rugged outdoor type. He specialized in food. *Natures mortes* for luxurious cookbooks. He spent hours trying to get pasta to glisten, veal to look savory, fruit to look luscious. Serge. Every time Antoine shook his hand when he came to pick up the children, he was confronted with the hideous recollection of Astrid's digital camera and what he had discovered in its memory card while she was out shopping that fateful Saturday. At first, puzzled, he had seen only a pair of hairy buttocks clenching and unclenching. And then he had realized with horror that the buttocks were actually pumping a penis into what looked extraordinarily like Astrid's body. That was how he had found out. He had confronted Astrid, laden with shopping bags, on that doomed Saturday afternoon, and she had burst into tears and admitted that she loved Serge, that the affair had been going on ever since that trip to Turkey with the kids, and that she felt so relieved that he now knew.

Antoine felt tempted to light a cigarette to ward off unpleasant memories. But he knew the smoke would wake his sister and she would make some cantankerous comment about his "filthy habit." Instead, he concentrated on the highway opening up before him.

Astrid still felt guilty about Serge—he felt it—about how he, Antoine, had found out about their affair. About the divorce. About the aftermath of it all. And she loved Mélanie dearly. They had been friends for a long time, and they worked in the same field, publishing. She hadn't had the heart to say no. Astrid had sighed, "Okay, then. The kids can come to you later. Give Mel a hell of a birthday."

When Antoine stopped at a gas station for a refill, Mélanie at last yawned and rolled the car window down.

"*Hé*, Tonio," she drawled, "where the hell are we?"

"You really have no idea?"

She shrugged.

"Nope."

"You've been asleep for the past two hours."

"Well, you did turn up at dawn, you bastard."

After a quick coffee (for her) and a quick cigarette (for him), they got back into the car. She seemed less petulant, Antoine noticed.

"It's cute of you to do this," she said.

"Thanks."

"You're a cute brother."

"I know."

"You didn't have to. Maybe you had other plans?"

"No other plans."

"Like a girlfriend?"

He sighed.

"No girlfriend."

The thought of his recent affairs made him want to stop the car, get out, and weep. Since the divorce there had been a string of women. And a string of disillusion. Women he had met via the Internet on those infamous websites. Women of his age, married women, divorced women, younger women. He had thrown himself into the dating process with gusto, determined to find it exhilarating. But after the first couple of sexually acrobatic stunts, coming back heavy-hearted and drained to his new empty apartment and his new empty bed, he found the truth staring him in the face. He had shied away from it long enough. He still loved Astrid. He had finally admitted that to himself. He still loved his ex-wife. He loved her so desperately it made him feel sick to his stomach.

Mélanie was saying, "Probably had better, more exciting things to do than to take your spinster of a sister on a long weekend."

"Don't be silly, Mel. This is what I want to do. I want to do this for you."

She glanced at a signpost on the highway.

"Hey, we're heading west!"

"Clever girl!"

"What's west?" she asked, ignoring the affectionate irony in his voice.

"Think," he said.

"Um, Normandy? Brittany? Vendée?"

"You're on the right track."

She said nothing, listening to the old Beatles CD Antoine had turned on. As they drove on, she uttered a little scream. "I know! You're taking me to Noirmoutier!"

"Bingo," he said.

But her face had sobered up. She looked down at her hands in her lap, her lips tightening.

"What's wrong?" he said, concerned. He had been expecting laughter, whoops, smiles, anything but her static face.

"I haven't been back there."

"So?" he said. "Neither have I."

"It's been"—she paused to count on her slim fingers—"1973, right? It's been thirty-four years. I won't remember a thing! I was six years old."

Antoine slowed the car.

"It doesn't matter. It's just, you know, to celebrate your birthday. We did your sixth birthday there, remember?"

"No," she said slowly. "I don't remember a thing about Noirmoutier."

She must have realized that she was acting like a spoiled child, because she swiftly put a hand on her brother's arm.

"Oh, but it doesn't matter, Tonio. I'm happy. I am, really. And the weather is beautiful. It's so nice to be alone with you and to get away from everything!"

By "everything," Antoine knew she meant Olivier and the wreckage their breakup had left behind. And her fiercely competitive job as a publisher at one of France's most famous publishing companies.

"I booked us into the Hotel Saint-Pierre. You remember that, don't you?"

"Yes!" she exclaimed. "Yes, I do! The old, lovely hotel in the woods! With Grand-père and Grand-mère . . . Oh, God, so long ago . . ."

The Beatles sang on. Mélanie hummed along. Antoine felt relieved, at peace. She liked his surprise. She was happy to go back. But one little thing niggled at him. One little thing he hadn't taken into account when the idea of going back had occurred to him.

Noirmoutier 1973 had been their last summer with Clarisse.

WHY NOIRMOUTIER? HE WONDERED as the car sped on and Mélanie hummed to "Let It Be." He had never considered himself a nostalgic person. He had never looked back. But since his divorce he had changed. Relentlessly he had found himself thinking more about the past than the present or the future. The weight of the past year, his first year alone, that dreary, solitary year, had sparked off pangs of regret, longing for his childhood, striving for happy memories. That was how the island had come back to him, timidly at first, then more powerfully and more precisely as the memories came tumbling in like mail gathering in a box.

His grandparents, regal and white-haired—Blanche with her parasol and Robert with his silver cigarette box that never left him, sitting on the shadowy hotel veranda and drinking their coffee. He would wave at them from the garden. His father's sister, Solange, plump and sunburned, reading fashion magazines in her deck chair. Mélanie, small and wiry, a floppy sun hat framing her cheeks. And Clarisse raising her heart-shaped face to the sun. And their father turning up on weekends smelling of cigar smoke and the city. And the cobbled submersible road that fascinated him as a child and still did. The Gois passage. You could only use it at low tide. Before the bridge was built, in 1971, it was the only way to get onto the island.

He wanted to do something special for Mélanie's birthday. He had been thinking about it since April. Not just another surprise birthday party with giggling friends hiding in the bathroom and laden with bottles of champagne. No, something different. Something she would remember. He needed to shift her out of the rut she was stuck in, her job that was eating up her life, her obsession with her age, and, above all, her not getting over Olivier.

He had never liked Olivier. Stuck-up, pompous snob. He cooked superbly. Made his own sushi. Specialized in Oriental arts. Listened to Lully. Spoke four languages fluently. Knew how to waltz. And couldn't live up to commitment, even after six years with Mélanie. Olivier wasn't ready to settle down. Despite being forty-one. So he had left Mélanie only to promptly get a twenty-five-year-old manicurist pregnant. He was now the proud father of twins. Mélanie never forgave him.

Why Noirmoutier? Because they had spent unforgettable summers there. Because Noirmoutier was the symbol of the perfection of youth, of those happy-go-lucky days when the summer vacation seemed endless, when you felt you were nine years old forever. When there was nothing more promising than a perfect day on the beach with friends. When school was a century away. Why hadn't he ever taken Astrid and the children to the island? he wondered. Of course, he had told them all about it. But Noirmoutier was his private past, he realized, his and Mélanie's, pure and untouched.

And he had wanted to spend time with his sister, just to be with her. On their own. They didn't see that much of each other in Paris, he reflected. She was always busy, lunching or dining with some author or on a book tour. He was often off visiting a building site out of town or taken up with a last-minute deadline for a job. Sometimes she came over for brunch on Sunday mornings when the children were there. She made the creamiest scrambled eggs. Yes, he found he needed to be with her, alone with her at this fragile, complicated moment of his life. His friends were important to him, he needed their mirth, their entertainment, but what he craved now was Mélanie's support, her presence, the fact that she was the only tie that linked him to his past.

He had forgotten what a long drive it was from Paris. He recalled the two cars—Robert, Blanche, and Solange in the lethargic black DS Citroën with Clarisse and Mélanie, and the nervous Triumph, their father at the wheel smoking his cigar and Antoine sitting in the back feeling nauseous. It took six or seven hours, including the leisurely lunch at the little auberge near Nantes. Grand-père was particularly picky about food, wine, and waiters.

Antoine wondered what Mélanie remembered of the endless drive. She was after all three years younger than he. She had said she didn't remember anything. He glanced across at her. She had stopped humming and was studying her hands with that intent, stern expression that sometimes frightened him.

Was this a good idea? he pondered. Was she truly happy about coming back here all these years later, coming back to a place where forgotten childhood memories lingered, motionless for the moment, like the surface of untroubled water?

"Do you remember all this?" Antoine asked as the car climbed the broad curve of the bridge. On their right, along the mainland, rows of gigantic rotating silver windmills.

"No," she said. "Just sitting in the car and waiting for the tide. And riding in along the Gois passage. It was fun. And our father getting so impatient because Grand-père got the tide schedule wrong again."

He too remembered waiting for the tide. Waiting for hours for the Gois causeway to appear beneath the slowly receding waves. And there it was at last, cobbles glistening with seawater, a four-kilometer amphibian road dotted with high rescue poles with little platforms for unfortunate drivers and pedestrians stranded by the upcoming flood.

She put a quick hand on his knee.

"Antoine, can we go back to the Gois? I really want to see it again."

"Of course!"

He felt elated that she had at last remembered something. And something as important and mysterious as the Passage du Gois. *Gois.* Even the word fascinated him. Pronounced like *Boa.* It was an old name for an old road.

Grand-père never took the new bridge. He grumbled about the excessive toll and how the concrete structure's gigantic sweep scarred the landscape. So he stuck to the Gois passage despite his son's jeering at him and the long wait.

As they drove onto the island, Antoine realized that his memories of the Gois causeway were intact. He could play them back in his mind like a movie. He wondered if Mélanie felt the same. The large austere cross at the beginning of the causeway came back to him. *To protect and cherish,* Clarisse used to whisper, holding his hand tight. He remembered sitting on the island shore and watching the waves dwindle into nothingness until the vast gray bank appeared like magic. Once the sea hissed away, the bank crowded over with shell searchers wielding shrimp nets. He recalled Mélanie's little legs rushing along the sand and Clarisse's plastic bucket soon overflowing with cockles, clams, and periwinkles. He remembered the sharp, tangy smell of seaweed, the bite of salty wind. His grandparents looking on, benign and weathered, arm in arm. And Clarisse's long black hair aflutter. The cars would drone past along the causeway. Noirmoutier was no longer an island. He liked that idea. But the thought of the sea inching back up again, inexorable, was both thrilling and terrifying.

He had never tired of listening to gruesome Gois disaster stories. Back at the Hotel Saint-Pierre, the gardener, old *père* Benoît, layered on all the gory details. Antoine's favorite story was the one about the June 1968 accident when three people of the same family drowned. Their car got stuck as the tide came up. They didn't think of climbing one of the nearby rescue poles. The tragedy triggered headlines. Antoine couldn't understand how a car could possibly be swept away by water and how people were unable to escape. So old *père* Benoît had taken him to watch the tide creeping in along the Gois passage.

For a long time, nothing had happened. Antoine had felt bored. Old *père* Benoît reeked of Gitanes and red wine. Then the boy noticed more and more people gathering around them. "Look, boy," the old man whispered. "They've come to watch the Gois close over. Every day, at high tide, people come from far away to watch this."

Antoine saw that there were no more cars making their way down the causeway. To his left, the immense bay filled slowly, in complete silence, like a huge transparent lake. The water seemed deeper and darker, trickling over the muddy ridges of sand. Toward the right, sudden swollen waves that had appeared from nowhere were already impatiently licking the causeway. The two separate fluxes of water came together in a strange and startling embrace that surprised him, casting a long ribbon of foam above the cobbled road. The Gois passage disappeared in a couple of seconds, engulfed by the tide. It was impossible to imagine a road had ever lain there. Now there was only the blue sea and nine rescue poles emerging from its swirling surface. Noirmoutier was an island once more. Triumphant seagulls shrieked and circled overhead. Antoine marveled.

"You see, boy," said *père* Benoît. "That's how fast it goes. Some fellas think they can make it inland before the tide, only four little kilometers. But you saw that wave, didn't you? Never mess with the Gois. Remember that."

Antoine was aware that every Noirmoutrin had a copy of the tide schedule stuffed into a pocket or a glove compartment. He knew the folks here never said "When can you cross?" but "When can you pass?" He knew they didn't measure the Gois metrically, but by its rescue poles: *The Parisian got stuck by the second rescue pole. His engine was swamped.* As a boy, he had hungrily read all the Gois books he could get his hands on.

Before this trip for Mélanie's birthday he had hunted those books down. It had taken him a while to remember that they were in a jumble of cardboard boxes in his cellar, boxes he'd never bothered to unpack since his recent divorce and move. His best-loved book was there: *The Extraordinary History of the Gois Passage.* He had opened it, smiling, remembering how he would spend hours poring over the old black-and-white photographs of wrecked cars poking their bumpers out of seawater under a rescue pole. He decided to take the book with him, and as he closed it, a white card came fluttering out. Intrigued, he picked it up.

> To Antoine, for his birthday, so that the Gois passage no longer holds any mysteries for you. Your loving *Maman*. January 7, 1972.

He hadn't seen his mother's handwriting for a long time. Something pricked the back of his throat. He had quickly put the card away.

Mélanie's voice bought him back.

"Why didn't we ride in on the Gois?" she asked.

He smiled apologetically. "Sorry. Forgot to check the tide schedule."

The first thing they noticed was how Barbâtre had thrived. It was no longer the small village overlooking the beach that they remembered, but a bustling place boasting modern bungalows and malls. The island roads were thick with traffic, another nasty surprise. The summer season was at its peak for the long weekend of August 15, but when they reached the north end of the island, they saw to their relief that nothing much had changed. They entered the Bois de la Chaise, a green stretch of pine trees and holm oaks strewn with curiously different styled houses that used to amuse Antoine so as a child: nineteenth-century Gothic villas, logwood summer chalets, Basque-like farms, English manors, all bearing names that came back to Antoine like old friends' faces: Le Gaillardin, Les Balises, La Maison du Pêcheur.

Mélanie suddenly exclaimed, "I do remember this!" She swept her hand toward the windshield. "All this!"

Antoine could not make out whether she was happy or nervous. He felt a little anxious. They turned into the hotel gates, wheels crunching on white gravel. Strawberry bushes and mimosas lined the alley. It hadn't changed, he thought, slamming the car door. No, it hadn't changed at all, but it looked a good deal smaller. The same thatch of ivy creeping up the façade. The same dark green door, the same blue-carpeted entrance, the stairs on the right.

They went to stand by the large bay window that looked out to the garden. The same hollyhocks, the same fruit trees, pomegranate trees, eucalypti, and oleanders. It was shockingly familiar. Even the smell lingering in the entrance was familiar. A musty, humid odor enhanced with beeswax and lavender, with fresh, clean linen and vestiges of good, rich food. The particular smell that old, large houses by the sea carry year after year. Before Antoine could mention the wonderfully recognizable smell to his sister, they were greeted by a buxom young lady sitting behind the reception desk. Rooms 22 and 26. Second floor.

On their way up, they peeped into the dining room. It had been repainted. Neither of them recalled that lurid pink, but the rest was exactly the same. Faded sepia photographs of the Gois, watercolors of Noirmoutier castle, of the salt marshes, of the Bois de la Chaise regatta. Same wicker chairs, same square tables covered with starched white tablecloths. Nothing had changed.

Mélanie whispered, "We used to come down the stairs for dinner. You had your hair plastered down with eau de cologne, and you wore a navy blue jacket and a yellow Lacoste shirt . . ."

"Yes!" He laughed and pointed to the largest table in the room, the one in the middle. "We used to sit there. That was our table. And you wore pink and white smocked dresses from that posh shop on the avenue Victor-Hugo and a matching ribbon in your hair."

How proud and important he used to feel as he came down those blue-carpeted stairs in his blazer, his hair combed like a *petit monsieur*, and from their table, Robert and Blanche looking on fondly, a martini for Blanche, a whiskey on the rocks for Robert. Solange, sipping her champagne with her little finger in the air. And everybody used to look up from their dinner and admire the entrance of these beautifully groomed children, cheeks pink from the sun, hair smoothed back. Yes, they were the Rey family. The wealthy, respectable, impeccable, proper Rey family. They had the best table. Blanche gave the biggest tips. She had seemingly endless supplies of rolled-up ten-franc bills in her Hermès purse. The Rey table demanded constant, careful attention from the staff. Robert's glass always had to be half full. Blanche wanted no salt whatsoever because of her blood pressure. Solange's sole meunière had to be perfectly prepared, without the slightest, smallest fish bone, or she'd make a fuss.

Antoine wondered if anybody here remembered the Rey family. The girl at the reception desk was too young. Who recalled the patrician grandparents, the officious daughter, the gifted son who only came on weekends, the well-behaved children?

And the beautiful daughter-in-law.

All of a sudden, the precise memory of his mother coming down those stairs in a black strapless dress hit him in the chest like a blow. Her long black hair, still damp from the shower, twisted up into a chignon, her tiny, slim feet in suede slippers. Everybody watching as she glided into the room with that dancer's step she had passed on to Mélanie. He could see her so clearly it hurt. The freckles on the bridge of her nose. The pearls in her earlobes.

"What's wrong?" Mélanie asked. "You look peculiar."

"Nothing," he said. "Let's go to the beach."

A FEW MOMENTS LATER they were heading on foot toward the Plage des Dames, a couple of minutes away from the hotel. He remembered this little jaunt too—the thrill of getting to the beach, and how slowly the adults used to walk, and how aggravating it was to have to linger behind with them.

The path was packed with joggers, cyclists, teenagers on scooters, families with dogs, children, babies. He pointed out the large brown red-shuttered villa that Robert and Blanche nearly bought one summer. An Audi van was parked in front of it. A man his age and two teenagers were hauling groceries out of the trunk.

"I wonder why they didn't buy it in the end," said Mélanie.

"After Clarisse died, I don't think anyone came back to the island," he said.

"I wonder why," said Mélanie again.

Antoine pointed one more time across the road.

"There used to be a little grocery shop right there. Blanche would buy us candy. It's gone."

They walked on in silence for a while. Then the beach appeared at the end of the road, and they both grinned, memories rolling in like waves. Mélanie pointed to the long wooden pier on the left while Antoine gestured to the uneven row of beach cabins.

"Remember our cabin—that rubbery, woody, salty smell?" Mélanie laughed. And then she cried out, "Oh, look, Tonio, the Plantier lighthouse! It looks tiny all of a sudden!"

Antoine couldn't help smiling at her enthusiasm. But she was right. The lighthouse he had so admired as a child, which used to tower over the pine trees, seemed to have shrunk. That's because you've grown up, buster, he thought to himself. Yup, you've grown up. But how he longed, all of a sudden, to be that kid on the beach again, that kid building sand castles, running along the pier and getting splinters in his feet, pulling on his mother's arm for another *glace à la fraise.*

No, he wasn't that kid anymore. He was a divorced, lonely middle-aged man whose life had never seemed emptier, never seemed sadder than today. His wife had left him, he despised his job, and his adorable kids had morphed into sullen teenagers. He was pulled away from his reminiscences by a bloodcurdling whoop. Mélanie, no longer by his side, had stripped to a daringly brief bikini and was flinging herself into the sea. He looked at her, flabbergasted. She seemed incandescent with joy, her long hair hanging like a black curtain down her back.

"Come on in, you noodle!" she yelled. "It's divine!"

She pronounced *divine* the way Blanche used to, *dee-vine.* He hadn't seen his sister in a bathing suit for years. She looked good, taut and firm. Certainly better than he did. He had put on weight in that initial dreary year of his divorce. Those lonely evenings in front of the computer or the DVD player had taken their toll. Gone was Astrid's healthy, wholesome cooking, a perfect balance of protein, vitamins, and roughage. He now lived on frozen food and takeout, rich stuff you could heat up fast in the microwave, and it had nicely added on pounds during that first, unbearable winter. His long, lanky build had grown a potbelly, like his father's, like his grandfather's. Going on a diet had been too much of an effort. It was bad enough getting up in the mornings, gearing up to try to keep up with the workload piling up. Bad enough living alone, when he had just spent the last eighteen years married and raising a family. Bad enough trying to convince everyone, most of all himself, that he was happy.

The thought of Mélanie's eyes on his pale, flabby stomach made him wince.

"I left my bathing suit at the hotel!" he yelled back.

"You dope!"

He went to stand on the wooden pier that reached far into the water. The beach was filling up steadily with families, old people, sulky teenagers. It had not changed. Time had not altered a thing. It made him smile, but it also made tears come to his eyes. He brushed them away angrily.

Boats of all shapes and sizes churned along the choppy sea. He walked to the end of the rickety pier and looked back at the beach and then out to sea. He had forgotten how beautiful the island was. He breathed in great, wolfish gulps of sea air.

He watched his sister come out of the water and shake her hair dry, like a dog. Despite her small size, she had long legs. Like Clarisse. From afar, she seemed much taller than she actually was. She came up to the pier shivering, her sweatshirt tied around her.

"That was fabulous," she said, putting an arm across his shoulders. "Do you remember that old gardener at the hotel? *Père* Benoît?"

"No, I don't . . ."

"An old fellow with a white beard. He used to tell us horrible stories about people drowning on the Gois."

"Oh! Awful breath, right? A mixture of Camembert and cheap red wine. And Gitanes."

"That's him." Antoine chuckled. "He once took me here, to this pier, and he told me all about the *Saint Philibert* disaster."

"What happened to poor Saint Phili? Isn't he the Noirmoutrin monk the church here is named after?"

"He's been dead since the seventh century, Mel." Antoine smiled. "No, this is a more recent story. I loved it. It was so Gothic."

"So what happened?"

"A ship named after the monk. It went down in 1931, I think, just over there." Antoine pointed ahead to Bourgneuf Bay. "It was quite a tragedy. A mini *Titanic*. I believe the boat was heading back to Saint-Nazaire. Her passengers had just enjoyed a picnic here on the Plage des Dames. Nice weather and everything. And then, when she had barely left this very pier, a storm blew up, a huge one. A wave knocked the ship over. About five hundred people drowned. A lot of women and kids. Hardly any survivors."

Mélanie gasped. "How could that old man tell you things like that? How perverse of him! You were only a little boy."

"No, it wasn't perverse. It was magnificently romantic. I remember being heartbroken. He said the graveyard in Nantes was full of bodies from the *Saint Philibert* tragedy. He said he would take me there one day."

"Thank God he didn't and that he's pushing up daisies now."

They laughed and continued looking out to sea.

"You know, I thought I wouldn't remember a thing," she murmured. "All this is making me feel so emotional. I hope I don't break down and cry."

He pressed her arm. "I feel like that too. Don't worry."

"What a pair of soppy dummies!"

They laughed again, walking back to the beach where Mélanie had left her jeans and sandals in a little pile on the sand. They sat down.

"I'm going to have a cigarette," said Antoine, "whether you like it or not."

"Your lungs, not mine. Smoke away from me."

He turned his back to her. She leaned against him. They had to shout against the wind.

"So many things are coming back . . . About her."

"About Clarisse?"

"Yes," Mélanie said. "I can see her here. I can see her on this beach. She had an orange bathing suit. A fuzzy material. And she used to chase us into the water. She taught us to swim, you remember that."

"Yes, I do. We both learned the same summer. Solange kept scoffing that you were far too young to swim at six."

"She was already that bossy, wasn't she?"

"Bossy and husbandless, like she is now. Do you ever see her in Paris?"

Mélanie shook her head. "No. I don't think she sees Father much either, you know. I think they had a falling-out when Grand-père died. Money matters, inheritance stuff. And she doesn't get on with Régine. She looks after Blanche a lot. Hires the medical team for her, makes sure the apartment is well kept, and all that."

"She had a soft spot for me in the old days," said Antoine. "She was always buying me ice cream, taking me for long walks along the beach, holding me by the hand. She even used to come sailing with me, with those boys from the boating club."

"Robert and Blanche never swam. They would sit up there at that café."

"They were too old to swim."

"Antoine!" she scoffed. "This was more than thirty years ago. They were in their sixties."

He whistled. "You're right. Younger than Father! They acted so old. Careful about everything. Fussy. Picky."

"Blanche is still like that," Mélanie said. "Going to see her has been tough lately."

"I hardly go anymore," admitted Antoine. "Last time I went, it was awful. She was in a bad mood, complaining about everything. I didn't stay long. I couldn't stand being there. That huge, dark apartment."

"Never gets the sun," said Mélanie. "Wrong side of the avenue Henri-Martin. Remember Odette? Shuffling around on those felt slippers to make the floorboards shine. Always telling us to shut up."

Antoine laughed.

"Her son Gaspard looks so much like her. I'm glad he's still there, looking after the place. Putting up with those nurses Solange hires. Putting up with Blanche's temper."

"Blanche was an affectionate granny with us, wasn't she?" he said. "Now she's a tyrant."

"I don't know about that," said Mélanie slowly. "She was sweet to us, but only when we did what we were told. Which is what we did."

"What do you mean?"

"Well, we were ideally silent, polite, meek grandchildren. We never had tantrums or fits."

"Because we were brought up that way," said Antoine.

"Yes," said Mélanie, turning to face her brother and plucking the half-smoked cigarette from his fingers, then burying it into the sand, heedless of his protests. "We were brought up that way."

"What are you getting at?" he asked.

She screwed up her eyes. "How did Clarisse get on with Blanche and Robert? Did she approve of the fact that we had to be meek and polite all the time?"

He scratched the back of his head.

"I don't remember," he said flatly.

She looked across at him and smiled.

"You'll see. You will. If I'm starting to, then you will too."

TONIGHT I WAITED FOR you on the pier, but you did not come. It grew cold, and after a while I left, thinking maybe it was difficult for you to get away this time. I told them I just needed a quick walk on the beach after dinner, and I wonder if they believed me. She always looks at me like she knows something, although I am sure, perfectly sure, that nobody knows. Nobody knows. How could they know? How could anyone guess anything? When they see me, they see a nice, timid, proper mother with her polite, charming son and daughter. When they see you . . . Ah, but when anyone sees you, they see temptation. How can anyone resist you? How could I have resisted you? You know that, don't you? You knew that the minute you laid your eyes on me that first day at the beach, last year. You are the devil in disguise.

There was a rainbow earlier on, a lovely one, and now the night is coming fast, gathering darkness and clouds. I miss you.

THEY HAD A LATE lunch at the Café Noir in Noirmoutier-en-l'Île, the largest town on the island. It was a crowded, noisy place, obviously a favorite hangout for the locals. Antoine ordered grilled sardines and a glass of white wine. Mélanie had a plate of *bonnottes*—the famous little round potatoes of the area—sautéed with bacon, butter, and coarse salt. The weather had grown hot, but a fresh wind kept the heat at bay. The café's terrace gave onto the small harbor and the thin strip of a murky canal lined with old salt warehouses and jammed with rusty fishing boats and small sailboats.

"We didn't come here much, did we?" asked Mélanie, her mouth full.

"No," Antoine said. "Blanche and Robert liked to stick to the hotel. They never got farther than the beach."

"We didn't come here with Solange or Clarisse either, right?"

"Solange took us to visit the Noirmoutier château once or twice, and the church. Clarisse was supposed to come, but she had one of her migraines."

"The château is a blank," said Mélanie. "But I do remember Clarisse's migraines."

He watched the nearby table fill up with tanned teenagers. Most of the girls were wearing tiny bikinis. Barely older than his daughter, Margaux. He had never been attracted to women considerably younger than he, but the ones he had met since his divorce, through the Internet or via friends, had amazed him with the unabashed boldness of their sexual behavior. The younger they were, the cruder and more violent they proved to be in bed. At first he had been terrifically aroused. But then, very quickly, the novelty had worn off. Where was the romance? Where was the emotion, the pang, the sharing, the charming awkwardness? These girls flaunted the smooth, knowing moves of porn queens and gave head with such blasé nonchalance it repelled him.

"What are you thinking about?" asked Mélanie, rubbing sunblock on the tip of her nose.

"Are you seeing someone right now?" he asked in return. "I mean, do you have a boyfriend?"

"Nothing serious. What about you?"

He looked across at the group of loud teens again. One girl was rather spectacular. Long, dark blond hair, an Egyptian-like build: large shoulders, narrow hips. A little too skinny, he decided. And a little too full of herself.

"I already told you in the car. No one."

"Not even one-night stands?"

He sighed, ordered some more wine. Not at all good for his paunch, he thought fleetingly. Too bad.

"I've had enough of one-night stands."

"Yeah, so have I."

He was surprised. He didn't think Mélanie would go for that sort of thing.

She snorted. "You see me as some kind of prude, don't you?"

"Of course not," he said.

"Yes, you do, I can tell. Well, for your information, dear brother, I'm having an affair with a married man."

He stared at her.

"And?"

She shrugged. "And I hate it."

"So why are you having this affair?"

"Because I can't stand being alone. The empty bed. The lonely nights. That's why."

She said it savagely, almost menacingly. They ate and drank in silence for a moment. Then she went on.

"He's far older than I am, in his sixties. I guess that makes me feel young." A wry smile. "His wife despises sex. She's the intellectual type, so he says. He sleeps around. He's a powerful businessman. Works in finance. He has a lot of money. Buys me presents." She showed him a heavy gold bracelet. "He's a sex addict. He throws himself on me and sucks me all over. Like a crazy vampire. In bed, he's ten times more of a man than Olivier ever was—or any of my recent flings, for that matter."

The thought of Mélanie cavorting with a lecherous sexagenarian was definitely unappealing. She giggled at the sight of Antoine's face.

"I guess it's hard imagining your little sister having sex. Like it's hard imagining your parents having sex."

"Or your kids," he added grimly.

She caught her breath.

"Oh! I hadn't thought about that. You're right."

She didn't ask him to go into detail, and he felt relieved. He thought of the condoms he had found in his sports bag a couple of months ago. Arno had borrowed that bag for a while. He had handed them back, and Arno had grinned sheepishly. Antoine ended up feeling more embarrassed than his son.

There had been no warning. The cute little boy had sprouted overnight into a tall, thin fuzzy-faced giant who merely grunted when he needed to communicate. Antoine had been expecting this. He had witnessed friends' sons go through the same brutal transformation. But that didn't make it any easier when it actually happened. Especially as Arno's blatant forage into puberty had coincided with Astrid's betrayal. The most unfortunate timing. This meant that Antoine had to deal with the unavoidable weekend clashes about coming home before midnight, finishing homework, taking at least one shower. Astrid no doubt had to deal with those issues too, but on her end, there was another man in the house. Which probably made her less crabby and impatient than her ex-husband. Antoine felt pulled down and depressed by his isolation. Bearing the brunt of the increasingly numerous stormy situations with Arno alone made him feel even worse. Astrid and he had been a team. They had always done things together. Made decisions together. Faced the enemy together. That was over. Antoine was on his own now. And when Friday night came around and he heard his children's key in the lock, he had to brace himself, to square his shoulders like a soldier going into battle.

Margaux was at the brink of her full-fledged debut into adolescence. Antoine found hers even harder. He had no idea how to deal with it. She was like a cat—mute, sinuous, and withdrawn. She would spend hours chatting on the computer or riveted to her cell phone. A "bad" text message could bring on tears or total silence. She shied away from her father, avoiding body contact with him. He missed her hugs, her affection. The chatterbox with the lopsided smile and pigtails was gone forever. In her place was a willowy *femme-enfant* with budding breasts, shiny, pimply skin, and garish eye makeup he longed to wipe away with his fingers. And the fact that Astrid was no longer around made Margaux's complex budding out even trickier to assess on his own.

THANK YOU FOR YOUR sweet note. I know I cannot keep your letters, though I long to, as you cannot keep mine. I cannot believe the summer will soon be over and that you will be leaving again. You seem calm and confident, but I am afraid. Maybe it is because you are wiser than I am. You are not worried. You feel there is hope for us. You think it will work out for you and me. I don't know. It frightens me. You have taken such a hold over my life this past year. You are like the tide, sweeping relentlessly over the Gois. I surrender time and time again. But fear soon replaces the ecstasy.

She often looks at me curiously, like she knows what is going on, and I feel we must be so careful. But how could she know? How could she guess? Could anyone? I don't feel guilty, because what I have for you is pure. Don't smile as you read this, please. Don't make fun of me. I am thirty-five years old, a mother of two, and with you I feel like a child. You know that. You know what you have started up within me. You have set me alive. Don't laugh.

You come from a modern country, you are sophisticated and well read, you have a degree, a job, a status. I am only a housewife. I grew up in a sunny village that reeked of lavender and goat cheese. My parents sold fruit and olive oil in the market. When they died, my sister and I worked at the stalls in Le Vigan. I had never taken a train before I met my husband. I was twenty-five years old, and I discovered another world. I had gone to Paris for a little holiday. But I never came back. I met him in a restaurant on the *grands boulevards,* where I was having a drink with a girlfriend. And that's how it started, him and me.

I sometimes wonder what you see in me. But more and more I feel you reaching out to me, even in the way you look at me, silently. Your eyes reach out for me.

Tomorrow brings you to me, my love.

AFTER LUNCH THEY WENT swimming in the hotel pool. Antoine was so hot he decided to face Mélanie in a bathing suit. She made no comment about the shape his body was in. He felt thankful. How he hated himself. And to think that when Astrid was still his wife, he weighed at least eight kilos less. He was going to have to do something about it. And something about the smoking.

The pool was a bright artificial blue and full of screaming children. It didn't exist back in the seventies. Robert and Blanche would have hated it, thought Antoine. They loathed vulgarity, loud people, anything nouveau riche. Their huge, chilly apartment on the quiet avenue Henri-Martin, not far from the Bois de Boulogne, was a haven of elegance, refinement, and silence. Odette, the chinless *bonne*, hobbled about, opening and shutting doors noiselessly. Even the telephone rang in a muffled way. Meals lasted for hours, and the worst thing, he recalled, was having to be put to bed on Christmas Eve just after dinner and being woken up at midnight for the presents. He would never forget that groggy, jet-lagged feeling, stumbling back into the living room, bleary-eyed. Why weren't they allowed to stay up to wait for *Père Noël*? Christmas came only once a year.

"I keep thinking about what you said," Antoine said.

"What?"

"About Clarisse and our grandparents. I think you're right. I think they gave her a hard time."

"What do you remember?"

"Nothing much." He shrugged. "Nothing in particular, but just how uptight they were about everything."

"Ah, so it's coming back . . ."

"Something is coming back."

"Like what?"

He squinted across to her against the sun.

"I remember a fight. During our last summer here."

Mélanie sat up.

"A fight? No one ever fought. Everything was always smooth, unruffled."

Antoine sat up too. The pool was teeming with writhing, glistening bodies, stoic parents looking on.

"One night they quarreled. Blanche and Clarisse. In Blanche's room. I heard them."

"What did you hear?"

"I heard Clarisse crying."

Mélanie said nothing.

He went on. "Blanche had a cold, stony voice. I couldn't hear what she was saying, but it sounded like she was very angry. And then Clarisse came out and saw me there. She hugged me and wiped her tears away. She smiled and said she'd had a little argument with Grand-mère. And what was I doing out of bed, she said, and she shooed me back to my room."

"What do you think it meant?" mused Mélanie.

"I don't know. I have no idea. Maybe it's nothing."

"Do you think they were happy together?"

"She and Father? Yes, they were. I think so. Clarisse made people happy. You remember that, don't you?"

She nodded. A pause.

Then she whispered, "I miss her."

He heard the stifled sob in her voice and reached over to grasp her hand.

"Coming back here is like coming back to her," she said.

He squeezed her hand, relieved that she couldn't see his eyes behind his dark glasses.

"I know. I'm sorry. I didn't think about that when I thought of this trip."

She smiled at him. "Don't be sorry. On the contrary. It's a lovely present. It's bringing her back to me. Thank you."

He wanted to let tears run down his cheeks, but he held them back in silence, reining in his emotions, the way he'd done all his life, the way he'd been taught to do.

They lay back again, their pale Parisian faces turned to the sun. She was right. Their mother was coming back to them slowly, like the seawater gliding over the Gois. Fragments of memories, like butterflies escaping from a net. Nothing chronological, nothing precise, but more like a nebulous, lazy dream. Images of her on the beach in her orange bathing suit, her smile, her pale green eyes.

He remembered that Blanche was adamant about the children having to wait at least two hours after lunch before they could swim. It was terribly bad to swim right after a meal, she said over and over again. So they would build endless sand castles and wait. Such a long wait. But sometimes Blanche fell asleep. There she was, open-mouthed under her parasol, sweltering in her long skirt and tricot vest, her city shoes dusty with sand, her knitting askew in her lap. Solange was off on one of her shopping sprees and would later come back to the hotel laden with goodies for everyone. Robert had strolled back to the hotel, smoking his Gitanes, his straw hat tilted far back over his head. Clarisse would whistle to the children, jerk her chin toward the sea. "But we've got to wait another half hour!" Antoine would whisper. And Clarisse would flaunt a devilish smile at him. "Oh yes? Who says?" And they would all three of them tear off silently to the water, leaving Blanche snoring in the shade.

"Do you have any photos of her?" asked Antoine. "I only have a couple."

"Very few," said Mélanie.

"I can't believe we don't have more photos of our mother."

"We don't," she said.

A toddler next to them wailed as it was dragged out of the water by a red-faced woman.

"There are no photographs of her anymore in the avenue Kléber apartment."

"But there used to be," he replied, getting agitated. "The one of you, me, and her at the Jardin d'Acclimatation, on the little train. What happened to that one? And the one of their wedding?"

"I don't remember those."

"They were in the entrance and on Father's desk. But they all disappeared after her death. The albums as well."

He wondered where those photos and albums were now. What could their father have done with them?

There was nothing to prove that Clarisse had lived at avenue Kléber for ten years, that this had been her home.

Régine, their stepmother, had taken over, had redesigned the place and erased every single trace of François Rey's first wife, Clarisse. And it was only now that Antoine fully realized all this.

I SOMETIMES WONDER, WHEN I lie in your arms, if I was ever happy before. I mean, before I met you, a year ago. I must have felt happy, seemed happy, always considered myself a happy person, and yet everything I have experienced before you seems stale and flat. I can imagine your perfect left eyebrow riding up the way it does when you flash that ironic smile. I don't care, these letters will be destroyed anyway, torn to a thousand pieces, so I can write what I want.

I was a happy child in my village overlooking the river, and we spoke with that coarse southern accent that my husband's family disapprove of because it is not Parisian, not chic. I am not stupid, you know. If I didn't look the way I do, they would never have accepted me. They put up with the accent because I look pretty in a cocktail dress. Because I am pretty. No, I am not vain, and you know that. You know soon enough that you are pretty. You can tell by the way people look at you. That will happen to my daughter. She is so young still, only six, but she will be beautiful. Why am I telling you all this? You don't care if I come from the south and if I have the wrong accent. You love me the way I am.

THEY HAD DINNER IN the pink dining room. Antoine had wanted to reserve "their" table, but they were told by the buxom young lady that the table was for large *familles.* The room filled up with children, couples, old people. Mélanie and Antoine sat back and watched. Nothing had changed. They smiled as they looked over the menu.

"Remember the Grand Marnier soufflé?" whispered Antoine. "We had it once, only once."

Mélanie laughed. "How could I ever forget the Grand Marnier soufflé?"

The waiter bringing it, solemn, ceremonious, the other diners mesmerized by the orange and blue flames. A hush falling over the room. The dish was placed in front of the children. Everybody holding their breath.

"We were such a perfect family," said Mélanie ironically. "Perfect in every way."

"Too perfect, you think?" he said.

She nodded. "Yes. Boringly perfect. Look at your family. That's what I call a real family—kids with personalities, tempers, kids who are sometimes outspoken—but that's what I like about them. Your family is what I call perfect."

He felt his face sag and tried to smile. "Mel, I'm no longer a family."

She put a hand in front of her mouth.

"Tonio, I'm so sorry. I guess I still can't quite accept the divorce."

"Neither can I," he said.

"How are you bearing up?"

"Let's talk about something else."

"Sorry."

She hurriedly patted his sleeve. They ordered and ate in silence. Antoine felt the emptiness of his life taking over again. He wondered whether this void was the onslaught of a midlife crisis. Probably. A man with just about everything in his life gone to pot. A wife who had left him for another guy. A job as an architect that he no longer found any pleasure in. How did that happen? he thought. He had fought so hard to create his own company. It had taken him so long to get his foot in the door, had demanded such relentless effort. And now it was as if all his juices had dried up. It all seemed stale, flat. He no longer even wanted to work with his team, give the orders, get on with the building sites, do all the stuff that his position demanded. He no longer had the energy. It had withered away.

He remembered that party he had gone to last month where he had been confronted with the friends of his past, people he hadn't seen since he was fifteen years old, all from his old school, the rigorous Collège Stanislas, notorious for the excellence of its results, its grueling religious education, and the inhumanity of its professors ("French without fear and Christian without reproach" was the grim school motto). He had been found on the Internet by Jean-Charles de Rodon, a greasy teacher's pet he had never liked, and had meant to turn down the invitation to a dinner party with "all the gang," but the sight of his forlorn living room had coerced him into saying yes. And he found himself seated at a round table in an overheated apartment near the Parc Monceau, surrounded by long-married couples who appeared to be steadfastly producing heirs and had raised pitying eyebrows at the mention of his divorce. Never had he felt more left out. His school friends had turned into balding, self-satisfied well-to-do bores, all in finance, insurance, and banking, and their high-maintenance wives were perhaps even worse, ensconced in Parisian finery and engrossed in detailed conversations that invariably concerned the upbringing of children.

How he had missed Astrid that evening, Astrid and her unconventional clothes: her dark red velvet redingote that made her look like a Brontë heroine, her flea market trinkets, her leggings. How he missed her jokes, her earthy laugh. In order to get away as fast as possible, he had mumbled something about an early start. Relief swamped him as he drove through the deserted streets of the seventeenth arrondissement. He far preferred his empty rooms to another half hour with Monsieur de Rodon and his crowd.

As he had drawn near Montparnasse, an old Stones song that he loved was played on Radio Nostalgie. "Angie." He sang along.

He had almost felt happy.

ANTOINE HAD TROUBLE FALLING asleep that first night at the Hotel Saint-Pierre. Yet there was no noise. The old place was silent, calm. His first night here since 1973. The last time he slept under this very roof, he thought, he was nine years old and his mother was still alive. There was something disquieting about that.

The rooms had changed very little. The same thick, mossy carpet, blue wallpaper, old-fashioned photographs of bathing beauties. The bathroom had been refurbished, he noticed. The bidet had been replaced by a toilet. In the old days, one had to go pee in the toilet on the landing. He peered out from behind the faded blue curtains to the dark garden below. No one was about. It was late. The boisterous children had at last been put to bed.

He had been in front of her old room, on the first floor. He remembered it well, the one facing the stairs. Number 9. He had only a hazy recollection of his father in that room. His father rarely came to the island. Too busy. For the entire two weeks of the Rey family's stay, he probably made one or two brief appearances.

But when his father did turn up, it was like an emperor returning to his kingdom. Blanche made sure fresh flowers were sent to her son's room, and she drove the hotel staff frantic with fastidious details concerning François's preferred wines and desserts. Robert checked his watch every five minutes, puffing away at his Gitanes with impatience and making continuous comments on where François should most probably be at that very moment on his drive over. *Papa is coming, Papa is coming,* Mélanie would chant feverishly, hopping from room to room. And Clarisse would wear the black dress he preferred, the short one, the one that showed off her knees. Only Solange, sunbathing on the terrace, seemed impervious to the return of the prodigal son, her parents' favorite child. Antoine loved watching his father get out of the Triumph with a victorious roar and stretch his arms and legs. The first person he reached out for was always Clarisse. There was something about the way his father looked at his mother at that very moment that made Antoine want to glance away. There was raw, naked love in his father's eyes, and his father's lingering hands on his mother's hips embarrassed the boy.

On his way up, Antoine had stopped in front of Blanche's room as well. His grandmother never showed herself before at least ten o'clock. She had breakfast in bed while he, Solange, Mélanie, and Clarisse had breakfast with Robert on the veranda, near the mangrove plant. Later, Blanche would make her grand appearance, her little parasol hooked over her arm, heady wafts of Heure Bleue preceding her down the stairs.

When Antoine got up the next morning, tired after a restless night, it was still early and Mélanie wasn't awake yet. The hotel seemed vacant. He enjoyed his coffee, marveling that the little round *pains* were the same ones he used to gulp down thirty-odd years ago. What a slow, tidy life they had led. Those endless, lazy summers.

The highlight of the season was the fireworks on the Plage des Dames for August 15, a national holiday, which also coincided with Mélanie's birthday. When she was very small, she used to think the fireworks were for her, that all those people on the beach were gathered specially for her birthday. He recalled a miserably wet August 15 one year when the fireworks were canceled and everybody stayed in, sullenly cramping the hotel. There had been a violent storm. He wondered if Mélanie remembered. She had been frightened. But then so had Clarisse. Yes, Clarisse was frightened of storms—it was all coming back to him—she would cower down and bury her head in her arms and tremble. Like a little girl.

He finished his breakfast and waited a little while for Mélanie. A lady in her fifties was seated behind the reception desk. She put down the telephone and beamed at him as he walked past.

"You don't remember me, do you?" she cooed.

He looked at her closely. There was something vaguely familiar about her eyes.

"I'm Bernadette."

Bernadette! Bernadette had been such a pretty wisp of a girl, dark and fetching, a far cry from the matronly woman facing him. When he was a boy, he had a crush on Bernadette and her long, glossy braids. She knew it, and she always gave him the best piece of meat or an extra bread roll or more tarte Tatin.

"I recognized you right away, Monsieur Antoine. And Mademoiselle Mélanie too!"

Bernadette and her white teeth and her lissome figure. Her cheerful smile.

"How wonderful to see you," he mumbled, embarrassed that he hadn't recognized her.

"You haven't changed," she gushed, clasping her hands together. "What a family you made. Your grandparents, your aunt, your mother."

"You remember them?" he asked, smiling.

"Well, of course, Monsieur Antoine. Your grandmother gave us the biggest tips of the season! Your aunt too! How could a little waitress forget that? And your mother, so lovely and kind. Believe me, we were all crushed when your family never came back."

Antoine looked down at her. She did have the same eyes, black and glowing.

"Never came back?" he echoed.

"Well, yes," she said, nodding. "Your family had come here several summers running, and then suddenly, one summer, none of you returned. The owner, old Madame Jacquot, do you remember her, she was most upset. She wondered whether your grandparents were unhappy about the hotel, if there was something they were displeased with. Year after year we waited, but the Rey family never came back. Until you, today."

Antoine swallowed. "The last summer we came, I think it was 1973."

Bernadette nodded, and leaning down, after a moment's hesitation, she pulled an old black book from a large drawer. She opened it, turned a couple of yellowed pages. Her finger halted over a penciled name in a column.

"Yes, that's right, 1973. The last summer."

"Well, you see"—he faltered—"our mother died the following year. That's why no one came back."

Bernadette's face flushed bright red. She gasped, pressed a fluttering hand to her collarbone.

There was an awkward silence.

"Your mother died? I did not know, we did not know . . . I'm so sorry . . ."

"It's all right," murmured Antoine. "You didn't know. It happened a long time ago."

"I can't believe it," she whispered. "Such a lovely young woman . . ."

He wished Mélanie would hurry up. He could not bear the idea of Bernadette's asking him about his mother's death. He waited in stony silence, his hand on the reception desk, his eyes cast down.

But Bernadette said nothing. She remained motionless, the crimson slowly ebbing from her cheeks, her eyes mournful.

I LOVE OUR SECRET. I love our secret love. But for how long? How long will we let our secret last? It has already been a year. I run my hand along your silken skin and I wonder if I really want this to come out into the open. I can guess what this will bring. It is like smelling rain on the incoming wind. I know what this entails, what this means for you, what this means for me. But I know too, so deeply, so intimately that it hurts me, that I need you. You are the one. It frightens me so, but you are the one.

How will this ever work out? What about my children? What will this do to them? How will we find a way to live together, you and I, and the little ones? Where? When? You say you are not afraid to tell the world. But surely you see how this is easier for you. You are independent, you earn your own money, you are your own boss. You are not married. You have no children. You are free. Look at me. The housewife from the Cévennes. The one who looks the part in a little black dress.

I have not been back to my native town for so long now. To the old stone house tucked away in the hills. Memories of the bleating goats in the parched yard, the olive trees, my mother hanging the sheets out to dry. The view of Mont Aigoual. The peaches and apricots my father used to fondle with his callused hands. If they were still alive now, if they knew, or my sister, who has become a stranger since I went north to marry a Parisian, I wonder what they'd have to say. If they could ever understand.

Love you and love you and love you.

MÉLANIE HAD SLEPT WELL and late. Her eyes were puffy, he noticed, but her face was glowing, smoothed out by a good night's rest and pink from yesterday's sun. He decided not to tell her about Bernadette. Why mention that conversation? It was useless. It would pain her, as it had pained him. She had breakfast in peaceful silence while he read the local newspaper and drank fresh coffee. The weather was going to hold, he announced. She smiled.

"I slept like a log," she said, putting her napkin down. "That hasn't happened for a long time. How about you?"

"Slept very well," he lied. For some reason he didn't want to tell her that he had been kept awake just thinking about their last summer here. Again and again, images from the past had imprinted themselves upon his closed eyelids.

A young woman and her small boy came in and sat at a nearby table. The child's voice was whiny and high, his entire being hermetically closed to his mother's admonishing.

"Aren't you glad your kids are over that age?" Mélanie whispered.

He raised his eyebrows. "At the moment, I feel like my children are strangers."

"What do you mean?"

"They have their own separate lives I know nothing about. When they come and spend time with me, they are either in front of the computer or the TV or sending text messages."

"I can't believe that," she said.

"It's true. We meet at meals, and these take place in silence. Sometimes Margaux even comes to the table with her iPod. Thank God Lucas isn't at that stage yet. But he soon will be."

Mélanie stared at him.

"Why don't you tell her to stop it? Why don't you get Arno and Margaux to talk to you?"

He looked across the table at his sister. What could he tell her? What did she know about kids, and teenagers in particular? Their silences, their outbursts, their inner rage? How could he tell her that sometimes he felt his children's contempt so harshly it made him recoil?

"You have to get them to respect you, Antoine."

Respect. Oh yes, and how he had respected his father as a teenager. How he had never crossed the line. Never rebelled. Never shouted back. Never slammed a door.

"I think that what they are going through is healthy and normal," he mumbled. "It's normal to be rude and difficult at that age. It has to come out."

She said nothing, sipping her tea. He continued, his face a trifle redder. The little boy at the next table went on bawling.

"What is difficult is that I have to face all this alone. Without Astrid. It all happened so suddenly. Overnight. They are your children, but they are strangers. And you know nothing about their lives, who they see, where they go."

"How is that possible?"

"Because of the Internet, because of mobile phones. When we were that age, our friends had to call home, talk to Father or Régine, ask to speak to us. That's finished. Now you don't know who your kid is seeing. You never speak to their friends directly."

"Unless they bring them home."

"Which they don't always do."

The little boy had at last stopped whining and was busy munching a croissant the size of his plate.

"Does Margaux still see Pauline?" asked Mélanie.

"Yes, of course. But Pauline is the exception. They've been in the same school since they were six years old. You wouldn't recognize Pauline."

"Why?"

"Pauline has the figure of Marilyn Monroe."

"Are you kidding? Skinny little Pauline with her buck teeth and freckles?"

"The very same skinny little Pauline."

"My God," said Mélanie, awed. Then she put out her hand and patted his gently. "You're doing fine, Antoine. I'm proud of you. Must be a heck of a job raising two teenagers."

He felt his eyes going wet. He hurriedly stood up.

"What about a morning dip?" He smiled down at her.

After their swim and, later, lunch, Mélanie went up to her room to finish reading a manuscript and Antoine decided to go rest in the shade. The heat was less fierce than he had expected, but he would probably end up in the pool at one point, he guessed. He installed himself on the terrace in a wooden deck chair beneath the large parasol and tried to read a couple of pages of a novel Mélanie had given him. One of her star authors—a brash young man, barely twenty, with peroxide hair and an attitude. Antoine's interest soon waned.

Around the pool, families came and went. It was far more amusing watching them. There were a couple of forty-year-olds who could have been Astrid and him, he mused. The guy was in fine shape, tight abdomen and muscular arms, but she was not as good, running to fat. Their two teenagers were the exact replica of his. The girl had a perpetual moue, earphones screwed in tight, and black nail polish. The boy, younger, more like Lucas, he decided, was enthralled by a

Nintendo. When their parents spoke to them, they were answered by shrugs and grunts. Welcome to the club, thought Antoine. But at least this couple were in it together. They were a team. They could deal with the oncoming storms. He had to face the storms alone.

When was the last time he had a conversation with Astrid about their kids? He couldn't remember. And what were they like with her, with Serge? Were they just as bad? Worse? Better? How did she cope with it? Did she ever lose her temper? Scream back? And what about Serge? How did he deal with three children who weren't even his own?

Antoine noticed another family, younger, with their toddlers. Late twenties, early thirties, two small children. The mother sat with the little girl on the grass, patiently helping her daughter to put a large plastic puzzle together. Every time the girl got it right, her mother clapped and cooed. He used to do that too, he remembered. That blissful period when children were small and sweet. You could hug them and tickle them. Play hide-and-seek. Play the monster. Run after them, scoop them up in your arms, swing them over your shoulder. Their shrieks and screams in your ears. You could sing them to sleep and gaze at them for hours, marveling at the perfection of their features.

He watched the father giving the baby a bottle, cautiously tying the bib, fitting the rubber nipple into his son's mouth. He felt overwhelmed by sadness, for what was gone and no longer, for a cherished time in his life when Astrid and he were still going strong, when he enjoyed his job, felt he was doing well, felt at peace with himself, felt young. He remembered walking through Malakoff with his family on Sunday mornings at the market, Lucas still in the stroller pushed by Astrid, and the other two sauntering along, their hot, sticky hands in his. The neighbors, the shopkeepers would wave and nod. He had felt so proud. So secure in his own world. As if nothing could ever destroy it. As if nothing would ever change.

When did it all start? He hadn't seen it coming. And if he had, if he had been warned, would it have made all this easier? Was this about growing old? Was this what was in store for him now? He felt he could no longer bear the sight of the happy little family that reminded him of his past, so he got up, sucked in his stomach, and slithered down into the pool. The cool water did him good, and he swam laps for a while, till his arms and legs ached and he felt breathless. He went back to his chair and spread his towel over the lawn.

The sun beat down on him, fierce and strong. Just what he needed. The intoxicating smell of roses floated over to his nostrils, and with a pang he remembered having afternoon tea with his grandparents on this very lawn, by the roses. He recalled the slim, spongy madeleines he would dip into his milky Darjeeling, the acrid smoke from his grandfather's cigarette, his grandmother's velvety, soprano-like intonations, his aunt's abrupt, hoarse laughter. And he remembered his mother and her smile, and the way her eyes lit up when she looked at her children.

Gone. All gone. He wondered what the year ahead would bring. And how he could possibly shake off this overpowering sadness. Never had he felt it more intensely than since his return to Noirmoutier. He could travel. He could take time off and go somewhere very far away, somewhere he had not been back to for years—China or India. But the thought of doing that alone put him off. He could ask one of his close friends, Hélène or Emmanuel or Didier. Nonsense. Who could take off a couple of weeks or a month in this day and age? Hélène was mother to three demanding children. Emmanuel worked in advertising and had the worst hours ever. Didier was a fellow architect and never seemed to stop working. Nobody could rush off to Asia at the drop of a hat.

Tomorrow was Mélanie's birthday. He had made reservations at one of the best restaurants in Noirmoutier, L'Hostellerie du Château. One they had never been to, not even in the heyday of Blanche and Robert.

As he turned from his back to his stomach, he thought of the week ahead. People coming back to town after their vacation. Visions of bronzed faces in Parisian streets. The workload he had to face. The new assistant he had to find. The children starting school again. August slipping into September. And how on earth was he going to face another winter on his own?

DURING THAT TERRIBLE STORM on the little one's birthday I was afraid, as usual, but while they were all huddled in the candlelit dining room, you came to me in the dark, my love. The lights had gone out, but we did not need them. Your hands were like beams shining into me, glaring into me, almost white with their passion, and you took me to yet another level, where I had never been before, where my husband had never taken me, no one, do you hear, no one. I went back to them when the lights went on, and the cake came. I went back to my role as perfect wife and mother, but I was shining with your desire, coated with it, and she looked at me again, as if she suspected something, as if she knew. Listen, I am not afraid. I am not afraid of them anymore. I know that soon I will have to leave, go back to Paris, resume my everyday life, the avenue Kléber and its quiet, well-to-do atmosphere, the children . . .

I talk to you too much about my children, don't I? But they are my little treasures. They mean the world to me. You know that expression, the apple of her eye? That's what they are, my precious little angels, the apples of my eye. If life is to be with you, which is what I want more than anything else in the world, my love, then life is to be with you and them. The four of us. Like a little family. But is that at all possible? Is it?

My husband has canceled his trip here this weekend. Which means you can come to my room again, in the dead of the night. I shall be waiting. It gives me shivers, just imagining what you are going to do to me and how I shall take you.

Destroy this.

His sister was stunning tonight, her hair swept back, held by a black bow, her slender figure outlined by a simple black dress. His mother looking straight out at him from her eyes. But he didn't tell her. That was his own private memory. He was pleased about the choice of the restaurant. A stone's throw from Noirmoutier castle, it had looked deceptively simple from the outside, with its narrow porch and olive green shutters. The main room was vast, with a high, pointed ceiling, cream-colored walls, wooden tables, and a large fireplace, but he had reserved outside, on the small, intimate tented *terrasse*, where their table awaited them beneath a fragrant fig tree growing against a crumbling wall. There were no noisy families here, he noted, no squealing babies, no temperamental teenagers. The perfect place to celebrate Mélanie's fortieth birthday. He ordered two flutes of rosé champagne, her favorite, and they quietly looked over the menu.

Foie gras poêlé au vinaigre de framboises et au melon.
Huîtres chaudes au caviar d'Aquitaine et à la crème de poireaux.
Homard bleu à l'Armagnac.
Turbot de pleine mer sur galette de pommes de terre ailées.

"This is really nice, Tonio," Mélanie said finally when they had clicked their glasses together. "Thank you."

He smiled. This was exactly what he had in mind when he planned this trip a couple of months ago.

"So how does it feel being forty?"

She grimaced. "Awful. Hate it."

She gulped down her champagne.

"You look pretty damn good for forty, Mel."

She shrugged. "Doesn't make me any less lonely, Tonio."

"Maybe this year . . ."

She sneered. "Yeah, maybe this year. Maybe this year I'll meet a nice guy. I say that each year. The problem is, as we all know, guys my age aren't looking for forty-year-old women. Either they're divorced and they want a younger wife, or they're single—which makes them even more suspicious—and they also shy away from women their age."

He smiled.

"Well, *I'm* not into younger women. I've had my share of those. All they want to do is go to nightclubs, go shopping, or get married."

"Aha," she said. "Get married. That's the core of the problem. Can you explain to me why nobody wants to marry me? Am I going to end up like Solange? A fat, bossy old lady?"

Her green eyes teared up. He couldn't bear having the lovely evening spoiled by her sadness. He put down his cigarette and grabbed her wrist gently but firmly. Their orders came, and he paused till the waitress had left.

"Mel, you just haven't met the right guy. Olivier was a mistake, and it lasted too long. You were always hoping he'd propose. He never did, and I'm glad he didn't, as he would have been wrong for you. You know that."

She wiped her eyes slowly and smiled at him.

"Yes, I know that. He took six years of my life, and what a mess he left behind. I sometimes wonder if I'm in the right field to meet men. Maybe publishing is not the right place. A lot of writers and journalists are either gay or complicated and neurotic. And I'm fed up with having affairs with married men, like my horny old lover. Maybe I should come and work with you. You see men all day long, don't you?"

He laughed ironically. Yes, he did, he saw men all day long, and few women, actually. Men like Rabagny, who had so little charm it was almost unfair, men like the surly foremen he had to deal with constantly, with whom he sometimes had less patience than with his own children, men like the plumbers, carpenters, painters, and electricians he had known for years and whose crude jokes he had learned to put up with.

"You wouldn't like those kinds of men," he remarked, gulping down an oyster.

"How would you know? Try me! Take me to one of your building sites."

"All right, then." He grinned. "I'll introduce you to Régis Rabagny. Don't tell me I didn't warn you."

"Who the hell is Régis Rabagny?"

"The bane of my existence. A young, ambitious entrepreneur. He's bosom buddies with the mayor at the town hall in the twelfth arrondissement. Thinks he's God's gift to Parisian parents because he's created a line of avant-garde bilingual day-care centers. They're actually quite spectacular, but he's having a hard time getting them accepted by the safety board, and no matter how I try to tell him that we have to stick to rules and not take risks where children are involved, he won't listen to me. He thinks I don't understand his 'art,' his 'creations.'"

He was hoping to make Mélanie laugh with a couple of witty examples concerning Rabagny's notorious tantrums, but he noticed that his sister was no longer listening to him. She was looking beyond his shoulder.

A couple had walked onto the terrace and were shown to a nearby table. A man and a woman in their fifties, tall, fantastically elegant. They both had silver hair—hers was whiter, his more salt-and-pepper—and tanned faces, the kind of tan that comes from sailing or riding, not just lying around on deck chairs. They were so astoundingly beautiful that a hush had come over the terrace. All the diners had turned to look at the couple. Impervious to the attention they were getting, they sat down, and soon champagne was on its way to them, brought by the waitress. Antoine and Mélanie watched as they smiled at each other, made a toast, and clasped hands.

"Wow," said Mélanie quietly.

"Beauty and harmony."

"True love."

"So it does exist."

Mélanie leaned forward. "Maybe they're phonies. Just a couple of actors playing a part."

Antoine laughed. "You mean, to make us jealous?"

Her face lit up. "No! To make us hope. To make us believe it is possible."

His heart went out to her as she sat there in her black dress, clasping her champagne, the lovely line of her shoulders and arms etched against the fig tree in the background. There had to be a man, he thought, a good man, a nice, intelligent man, a man who could fall for a woman like Mélanie. He didn't have to be as perfect as that man sitting at the next table, he didn't have to look half as handsome, but he could be strong and true and he could make her happy. He wondered where that man was right now. Thousands of miles away, or just around the corner? He could not bear the idea of Mélanie growing old alone.

"What are you thinking about?" she said.

"I want you to be happy," he answered.

Her mouth twitched. "I want the same for you."

They sat in silence for a while and ate their meal, trying not to stare at the perfect couple.

At last she said, "You have to get over Astrid."

He sighed. "I don't know how to do that, Mel."

"I want you to, so much."

"I want to as well."

"I sometimes hate her for what she's done to you," she muttered.

He winced. "Don't. Don't hate her."

Melanie played with his lighter. She said, "I can't. You can't hate Astrid. It's impossible to hate Astrid."

How right she was. It was impossible to hate Astrid. Astrid was like sunshine. Her smile, her laugh, her perky walk, her chuckle, her singsong voice held light and movement. She hugged, she kissed, she crooned, she took your hand and held it tight, she was always there for her friends, for her family. You could call Astrid anytime. She would listen, nod her head, give advice, try to help. She never lost her temper, or if she did, it was for your own good.

The cake came, its candles lighting up the dusk. Everybody clapped, and the beautiful couple raised their champagne flutes to Mélanie, as did all the other diners. Antoine smiled and clapped.

Behind his smile, the old pain was still there. It seared into him so precisely he nearly gasped. He had let Astrid go. He hadn't even realized she was slipping away. He had seen nothing coming. It had been like a head-on collision.

As they were having coffee and herbal tea, the chef came out to greet his guests table by table to ask whether they had enjoyed their meal. When he turned to them and saw Mélanie in her black dress, he suddenly cried out, startling them. "Madame Rey!"

Mélanie's face flushed scarlet. So did Antoine's. This sixty-year-old man clearly thought he was looking at Clarisse.

He snatched up Mélanie's hand, kissed it rapturously.

"It has been such a long time, Madame Rey. Over thirty years, I'd say! But I've never forgotten you. Never! You used to dine here with your friends from the Hotel Saint-Pierre. It seems like merely yesterday. I was just starting out in those days."

There was a tight silence. The chef glanced from Mélanie to Antoine, his eyes dancing. Then he slowly began to understand. He gently released her hand.

Mélanie still said nothing, a small, embarrassed smile floating around her lips.

"*Mon Dieu*, what an old fool I am! You cannot be Madame Rey, you are far too young . . ."

Antoine cleared his throat.

"Yet you look so much like her . . . You can only be—"

"Her daughter," Mélanie said at last, calmly. She smoothed down a lock of hair escaping from her ponytail.

"Her daughter! Of course! And you must be—"

"Her son," said Antoine laboriously, wishing this man would go away. He probably didn't even know their mother was dead. Antoine couldn't bear telling him. He hoped Mélanie wouldn't say anything either, and she did not. She held her tongue as the man rambled on. Antoine concentrated on the bill and left a good tip. He and Mélanie stood up to leave. The chef insisted on shaking their hands.

"Please give my respects to Madame Rey. Tell her how honored I am to meet her children, although her coming back to see me would be the most splendid surprise."

They both nodded, murmured their thanks, and fled.

"Do I look *that* much like her?" whispered Mélanie.

"Well, yes. You do."

YOU HAVE JUST LEFT your room, and I am slipping this under your door, not leaving it in our usual hiding place, and I pray you get it before you catch your train back to Paris. I slept with your roses, and it was like sleeping with you. They are soft and precious, like your skin, like the secret places of your body where I love to go, those places that are mine now because I want to imprint myself upon them so that you may never forget me, never forget our time together, never forget how we met here last year, that first glance, that first smile, that first word, that first kiss. I am sure you are smiling as you read this, but I don't care, I don't care at all, because I know how strong our love is. You think sometimes I am young and very foolish. Soon we will find a way to face the world, you and I. Very soon.

Destroy this.

THEY SAT TOGETHER, SHOULDER to shoulder, watching the sea slide slowly over the Gois. Mélanie spoke very little, her dark hair moving about in the wind, her face glum. She hadn't slept well, she explained when she came down for breakfast, and her eyes were small slits this morning, giving her an almost Asian appearance. He hadn't bothered about it at first, but as the morning drew on and she became more and more silent, drawn up in herself, he'd gently asked her if something was wrong, and she'd shrugged away his question. She had turned off her phone, he noticed, something she rarely did. She was usually riveted to it, constantly checking for text messages or missed calls. He wondered whether this had something to do with Olivier. Maybe he had telephoned her for her birthday or left a message, and had reopened the old wound. Clumsy bastard, he thought. Or was it the aging beau who'd forgotten to call her yesterday?

With the same fascination he'd felt in his youth, he watched the water hungrily eat up the paved road. There. It was done. No more road. A small shooting pain went through him, as if a special moment had been lost forever, never to happen again. Maybe he preferred watching the Gois passage emerge from the sea, firm and gray—a long strip slicing the waters—rather than seeing it slip under the frothy waves, like witnessing a drowning. He wished they had chosen another moment to come here. There was something sinister about the place today, and Mélanie's strange mood did nothing to alleviate it.

This was their last morning here. Was that why she remained silent, heedless of what was going on around them—the gulls circling ahead, the wind biting at their ears, and people turning back inland now that the Gois had closed over? She had drawn her knees up to her body and was resting her chin on them, arms tight around her legs. Her green eyes looked dazed. He wondered whether she was getting a migraine, like their mother used to, those powerful, bad ones that would literally cripple her. He thought of the long drive back to Paris, the inevitable traffic jams. His empty apartment. Her empty apartment. Maybe she was thinking about that too. Going back to a still, silent place. No one waiting up for you. No one to greet you as you walked in, drained after hours behind the wheel, no one to hug you. There was of course the lecherous old lover, but he was probably with his wife during this long holiday weekend. Maybe she was thinking about tomorrow, Monday, going back to her office in Saint-Germain-des-Prés, and dealing with the neurotic, egotistic authors she had told him about, or her impatient, demanding boss and his depressed assistant.

The same sort of people Astrid dealt with in a rival publishing house. Antoine had never felt part of the publishing scene. He had never enjoyed the glittering literary parties where champagne flowed and writers mingled with journalists, publishers, editors, publicists. He used to watch Astrid flitter through the crowd in her pretty cocktail dress and high heels, a smile on her face, going from group to group with the same ease, the same graceful nod, while he stuck to the bar, chain-smoked, and felt miserable, out of place. After a while he had stopped going. Maybe that had been a bad idea, he now thought. Maybe his stepping out of his wife's professional life had been his first mistake. How blind he had been. How stupid.

Tomorrow, Monday. His sad little office on the avenue du Maine.

The dermatologist he shared it with, a silent, whey-faced woman whose only apparent pleasure was burning warts off her patients' feet.

Florence, his assistant. Her plump cheeks, shiny forehead, beady black eyes, and greasy brown hair. Her unfortunate calves, her stubby fingers. Florence had been a disaster from the start. She never got anything right—although she was firmly convinced she did and that *he* was the one who didn't explain things properly. She was overly susceptible, capable of suffragette-like tantrums that invariably ended with her sobbing over her keyboard.

Tomorrow, Monday, and the future dreary evenings lining up in his mind like a traffic jam on an endless highway. A replica of the past year, woven with solitude, sorrow, and self-loathing.

Had it been a good idea, coming back here? He stealthily glanced at his sister's drawn face. Being confronted with mementos from so long ago, bringing back their mother's eyes, her voice, her laugh, the way she flitted across this very beach. Maybe he should have left all that aside, whisked Mélanie off to Deauville, Saint-Tropez, Barcelona, or Amsterdam, anywhere, anyplace, as long as those family memories would not come back to trouble them.

He drew his arm around her shoulders and clumsily jiggled her, as if to say, "Hey, cheer up, don't ruin it all." She did not smile back. Instead she turned her head and looked at him searchingly, as if she were trying to decipher something behind his eyes. Then she parted her lips, about to speak, but she closed them again, shook her head with a grimace, and sighed.

"What's up, Mel?"

She smiled, and he didn't like that smile. It was a tight, unpleasant one. It merely stretched her lips and made her look older and sadder.

"Nothing," she murmured against the wind. "Nothing at all."

The morning inched by, and still she did not speak. It was only later, when they hauled their luggage into the car, that she seemed to ease up a little. When they were on their way, with him at the wheel, she made a few phone calls, even hummed along to an old Bee Gees song. He felt relief swamp him. She was all right, then. She was going to be fine, just a bad headache, just a tricky moment.

SOMEWHERE AFTER NANTES THEY stopped on the highway for a coffee and a snack. She said she felt like driving. She was a good driver, she always had been. He switched places with her, watching her slide the car seat forward, fasten her seat belt, and lower the rearview mirror to her level. So small, so dainty, her slim legs, her slender arms. So fragile too. He had always felt protective of her. Even before their mother died. During the somber, confusing years that had followed Clarisse's death, he remembered how frightened Mélanie had been of the dark, how she always had to keep a night-light on while she slept, like Scarlett O'Hara's little girl, Bonnie. He remembered that the constantly changing au pair girls, even the nicest ones, didn't know how to comfort her when she had a nightmare, and only he was able to do that, cuddling her, gently singing the same lullabies Clarisse sang to lull them to sleep. Their father seldom came. He didn't seem to be aware that Mélanie had nightmares even when the night-light was burning, and that night after night she cried out for her mother. Antoine remembered how Mélanie could not understand Clarisse's death. She had asked, over and over again, *Where is Maman? Where is Maman? When is Maman coming back?* And nobody answered her, not even Robert and Blanche, or their father or Solange, or the endless string of family friends who came to the avenue Kléber after their mother's death, who would smear lipstick on their cheeks and ruffle their hair. No one knew what to say to this desperate, frightened little girl. He knew, intuitively, at ten, what death was. He understood the finality of it, that their mother was never coming back.

Mélanie's small, delicate hands on the steering wheel. Only one ring, on her right hand, a simple, broad gold band that had belonged to their mother. The traffic ahead was growing dense toward Angers as they made their way back to Paris. They would probably end up in a mammoth jam, he thought, his lungs aching for a cigarette.

After a long silence Mélanie spoke.

"Antoine, there's something I need to say."

Her voice sounded so strained that he quickly swiveled to look at her. She had her eyes on the road, but there was something tight about her jaw.

She fell silent.

"You can tell me," he said softly. "Don't worry."

Her knuckles were white, he noticed. His heart started to pump a little faster.

"I've kept it back all day," she said hurriedly. "Last night, at the hotel, I remembered something. Something about—"

It happened so fast he scarcely had time to draw breath. First she turned her eyes to him, dark, troubled. Then she turned her face, and it seemed to him that the car was also turning, veering right, Mélanie's hands suddenly helpless on the wheel. Then came the sharp whine of screeching tires, the loud blast of a horn behind them, and the strange, sickening sensation of losing balance when Mélanie loomed overhead above him, her shriek thickening as they lurched to one side, the rush of air blocking his ears as the air bag bloomed painfully white into his face. Mélanie's scream was a strangled moan, lost in the splintering of glass and crumpled metal. Then only the muffled sound of his heartbeat.

ANTOINE, THERE'S SOMETHING I need to say. I've kept it back all day. Last night, at the hotel, I remembered something. Something about—

The doctor waits for me to speak. To answer her question: "What was she telling you?"

But how can I pronounce the words Mélanie uttered before the car veered off the highway? I don't want to bring this up with the doctor. I don't want to talk to anyone about what Mélanie said, not yet. My head aches, and my eyes feel itchy and red, still stinging with tears.

"Can I see her?" I ask Dr. Besson at last, breaking the silence between us. "I can't stand sitting here and not seeing her."

She shakes her head firmly. "You'll see her tomorrow."

I stare at her blankly.

"You mean we can't leave now?"

The doctor stares back at me.

"Your sister nearly died."

I swallow. I feel dizzy.

"What?"

"We had to operate. There was a problem with her spleen. And she broke a couple of vertebrae in her upper back."

"Which means—what?" I stammer.

"Which means she'll be staying here for a while. And when she can be moved, she'll be taken to Paris in an ambulance."

"For how long?"

"It could be a couple of weeks."

"But I thought you said she'd be all right!"

"She is, now. She will need time to get over this. And you were lucky, Monsieur. You got away unharmed. I need to examine you now. Can you come with me, please?"

In a sort of daze, I follow her to a nearby consulting room. The hospital seems empty, silent; I feel as if Dr. Besson and I are the only ones around. She tells me to sit down, rolls up my sleeve, checks my pulse. As she gets on with her work, I remember lifting myself out of the car, which was resting on its flank like a wounded animal. Mélanie was hunched up in the far left corner, motionless. I couldn't see her face. The air bag had blown up over it. I remember calling out to her, yelling her name at the top of my lungs.

After a while Dr. Besson tells me I am fine, with slightly high blood pressure. "You can stay here tonight. We have rooms for next of kin. The nurse will come."

I thank her and leave, heading back to the hospital entrance. I know I have to call our father. I have to tell him what happened. It cannot wait any longer. It is nearly midnight. I step out of the building and light a cigarette. The parking lot in front of me is deserted except for a couple of smokers. The town seems asleep. Above me, the sky stretches dark blue. Stars twinkle. I sit down on a wooden bench. I finish the cigarette and toss the butt away. I try the home number on the avenue Kléber. The answering machine with Régine's nasal whine comes on. I hang up and try his mobile phone.

"What is it?" he barks before I can pronounce a single word.

I relish the small power I now have, the tiny power I can at last wield over our aging, domineering, tyrannical father, my father who still makes me feel twelve years old and useless in every way, who disapproves of my job as a mediocre, unexciting architect, my recent divorce, my smoking, the way I bring up my kids, my haircut, which according to him always leaves my hair too long, the fact that I wear jeans and not suits and never ties, my non-French car, my sad new apartment on the rue Froidevaux overlooking the Montparnasse Cemetery. The pleasure I glean from this is as sharply sweet as a quick jerk-off under the shower.

"We had an accident. Mélanie's in the hospital. She's broken something in her back, and they had to operate on her spleen."

I savor the swift intake of his breath.

"Where are you?" he finally gasps.

"The hospital at Le Loroux-Bottereau."

"Where the hell is that?"

"Twenty kilometers from Nantes."

"What are you and Mélanie doing there?"

"We went on a little trip for her birthday."

A pause.

"Who was driving?"

"She was."

"What happened?"

"I don't know. The car just drove off the highway."

"I'll be there in the morning. I'll take care of everything. Don't worry. Goodbye."

He hangs up. I groan inwardly. Him, here, tomorrow. Bossing the nurses around. Being respected. Looking down at the doctor. Our father is no longer a tall man, but he still feels that he is. When he walks into a room, faces turn to him like sunflowers to the sun. Nor is he particularly good-looking: receding hairline, bulky nose, glaring dark eyes. He had been, in his youth. I'm often told I look like him, same height, same brown eyes. But there is nothing bossy about me. He has gotten stout. I noticed that the last time I saw him. Which was six months ago. We don't meet much anymore, and now that the children are old enough to visit their grandfather without me, I see him even less.

Our mother died in 1974. Since then, Mélanie and I have spoken of her by her first name. Clarisse. It seemed too hard to say Maman. Aneurysm. François—yes, that is our father's name, François Rey, does it not ring out with true authority and grandeur?—was only thirty-seven when his wife died. Six years younger than I am now. I cannot remember where and when he met the blond, thin-lipped, ambitious Régine (an interior decorator), but I do remember the pompous wedding in May 1977 at Robert and Blanche Rey's apartment overlooking the Bois de Boulogne, and how dismayed Mélanie and I had been. Our father did not seem in love at all. He never glanced at Régine, had no tender gestures toward her. So why was he marrying her? we wondered. Because he felt lonely? Because he needed a woman to look after his bereaved household? We felt betrayed. There Régine was, all of thirty, simpering in a beige Courrèges suit that did nothing for her behind. Oh, yes, she had made a good catch. A widower, but a wealthy widower. One of Paris's most brilliant lawyers. Heir to a well-known, respected family, his father a renowned lawyer, his mother the daughter of a famous pediatrician, granddaughter of a wealthy property owner, the crème de la crème of the demanding, conservative, Right Bank Parisian bourgeoisie from Passy. A superb apartment on the *bon chic bon genre* avenue Kléber. The only hitch was two children of thirteen and ten who were still stricken by their mother's death. She put up with us. She took it all in her stride. She redecorated the apartment, transformed its splendid Haussmanian proportions to ultramodern square white spaces, gutted the fireplaces and stucco, ripped up the old, creaking floorboards, and turned the whole thing into a maroon and ash decor that looked like an airport boarding gate. All their friends thought it was the most audacious and clever makeover they had ever seen. We hated it.

She raised us in that stiff, traditional bourgeois French way. *Bonjour, Madame. Au revoir, Monsieur.* Impeccable manners, excellent results at school, Mass every Sunday morning at Saint-Pierre de

Chaillot. Emotions of any sort were kept in check. Children were seen and not heard. Never talk about politics, sex, religion, money, or love. Our mother's name was never uttered. We soon understood that we were better off not pronouncing it. We never talked about her death either. Or anything whatsoever concerning her.

Our half sister, Joséphine, was born in 1982 and became our father's favorite. There was a fifteen-year difference between Mélanie and her. And I, at just eighteen, was sharing a place on the Left Bank with a couple of friends and studying political science at the rue Saint-Guillaume *faculté*.

I had left home—that is, if the avenue Kléber and what it had become since Clarisse died could ever be called home.

I WAKE UP THE next morning feeling stiff all over. The bumpy hospital bed is the most uncomfortable thing I've ever slept on. Had I even slept? The thought of my sister looms. Is she all right? Will she pull through? I look across the bare room at my suitcase and my laptop in its special bag. They got through the accident unscathed. Not even a tear or a scratch. I tried the computer before I went to bed last night, and it had switched on smoothly. How was that possible? I had seen the state of the car. I had been inside that car. And yet despite the wreckage, my suitcase, my computer, and myself are fine.

The nurse this morning is a different, plumper, dimpled one.

"You can see your sister now." She beams. I follow her down a couple of corridors where half-asleep old people shuffle by, then up a flight of stairs into a room where Mélanie is lying on a complicated bed with all sorts of contraptions around her. Her entire torso is plastered from shoulders to waist. Her neck emerges, long and thin, like a giraffe's. She seems taller and leaner than she actually is.

She is awake, her green eyes dark, smudged with shadows. Her skin is very pale. I have never seen her so pale. She looks different, I can't quite understand how or why.

"Tonio," she breathes.

I want to be strong, big brotherly, but the sight of her moistens my eyes. I daren't touch her. I am worried I may break something, harm her. I sit down in the chair by the side of the bed, feeling gauche.

"Are you okay?" she mouths.

"I'm fine. And you?" I whisper back.

"Can't move. This thing scratches like hell."

Fleetingly I wonder if she really is okay, if she really will be able to move one day, if Dr. Besson has told the entire truth.

"Does it hurt?" I ask.

She shakes her head. "I feel strange." Her voice is slow, weak. "Like I don't know who I am anymore."

I caress her hand.

"Antoine," she says. "Where are we?"

"In a town called Le Loroux-Bottereau. We had an accident on the highway after we left Nantes."

"An accident?"

I realize she doesn't remember anything at all.

I decide not to remind her. Not for the moment. I tell her I don't remember either. She seems pacified by this and squeezes my hand back.

Then I say, "He's coming."

She knows who I mean. She sighs and turns her head, and I watch as her lashes flutter down against her pale cheek. I go on looking at her. I feel like her guardian angel. I haven't watched a woman sleep since Astrid. I used to watch Astrid for hours. I'd never tire of gazing at her peaceful face, the quiver of her lips, the mother-of-pearl eyelids, and the slow heave of her bosom. In her sleep she seemed fragile and young, like Margaux now. I haven't watched Astrid sleep since our last summer together, a year ago.

The summer our marriage broke up, Astrid and I rented a square white house on the Greek island of Naxos. We had already decided to separate in June (or rather, Astrid had decided to leave me for Serge), but it was impossible to cancel the rental or the airline and boat tickets at such short notice. So we went ahead with the ordeal of our last summer as an official married couple. We hadn't told the children anything yet, and we tried to be their normal, everyday parents. We ended up acting so falsely enthusiastic that the children guessed something was amiss. Astrid spent most of her time reading on the sun deck in the nude. She developed a chocolaty tan that made me sick because I knew Serge would soon run his hamlike hands along it, not I.

For the entire three weeks of our grueling stay I felt like putting a bullet through my head. I would sit on the lower terrace overlooking Orkos and Plaka, chain-smoking between steady swipes of lukewarm ouzo. The view was stupendous, and I would admire it through a drunken haze of acute unhappiness. The brown, rounded island of Paros seemed a mere swim away, the sea shimmering ultramarine, dotted with foamy white specks caused by overpowering wind. When I got too desperate or too drunk, or both, I'd stagger down the steep, dusty path to the creek and fling myself into the water. A jellyfish once stung me, but I was so distraught I hardly felt it. Later, Arno had pointed at my chest, and looking down, I had discovered an angry red welt, as if someone had taken a whip to my skin.

The summer of hell. To add to my mental discomfort, the serenity of the early mornings was shattered by the grating sound of bulldozers and drills from higher up on the hill where an overambitious Italian was building a villa that looked like a set for a James Bond movie. Incessant lumbering trucks laden with dug-up earth toiled up and down the little path that passed right in front of our house. Impervious, I sprawled on the terrace, black exhaust fumes billowing in my face. The drivers were friendly, waving to me each time they shuddered past, their monstrous engines a couple of yards from my untouched breakfast.

To top it all, tank water was scarce, the electricity failed us each evening, the mosquitoes were bloodthirsty, and Arno broke the high-tech suspended marble toilet simply by sitting on it. Every night I'd share the bed with my soon to be ex-wife, watch her sleep, and silently cry. She had murmured again and again, like a patient mother with a reluctant child, *Antoine, I just don't love you the way I used to*, taking me into her arms with maternal gusto while I still shivered with desire at her touch. How is that possible? How can that happen? How can a man ever get over that?

I had introduced Astrid to Mélanie eighteen years ago. Astrid happened to be a junior publicist for a rival publishing company. They soon became good friends. I remember the interesting contrast they made: small, delicate, dark-haired Mélanie, and Astrid, with her fair hair, pale blue eyes. Astrid's mother, Bibi, is Swedish, from Uppsala, laid-back, artistic, and definitely odd. But charming. Astrid's father, Jean-Luc, is a famed nutritionist, one of those tanned, sickeningly fit men who make you feel like a cholesterol-riddled slob. Obsessed with regular bowel movements, he sprinkles bran over everything Bibi cooks.

Thinking of Astrid makes me want to call her and tell her what happened. I tiptoe out of the room. Her phone rings and rings. She doesn't pick up. The paranoia in me suggests that I should prevent my number from flashing on her screen so that she won't know who called. I leave her a short message. Nine o'clock. She is probably in her car right now, our old Audi. I know her schedule by heart. She has already dropped Lucas off at the local school, and Arno and Margaux at Port-Royal where their lycée is, and she is fighting morning traffic to get to Saint-Germain-des-Prés, to her office on the rue Bonaparte, across from Saint-Sulpice church. She is putting on her makeup at red lights, and men look at her from the next car and think, Pretty woman. Then I remember it's mid-August. She's still on vacation. With him. They are probably back in Malakoff with the children. They drove up from Dordogne this weekend.

When I turn back to Mélanie's room, there is an old man with a paunch standing in front of her door. I need a couple of seconds to understand who he is.

He takes me into his arms roughly. I am always startled by my father's abrupt hugs. I never hug my son like that. Arno is at an age where he loathes being hugged, so when I do hug him, I do it gently.

He steps back and squints up at me. Brown eyes protruding, full red lips, thinner now, turned down. His vein-ridden hands seem fragile, his shoulders droop. Yes, my father is an old man. This is something of a shock. Do our own parents see us getting older as well? Mélanie and I are no longer young, even if we are still his children. I recall one of our father's carefully nipped and tucked lady friends, Janine, saying to Mélanie and me, "It's so strange seeing your friends' children becoming middle-aged." And Mélanie had replied with a smooth smile, "It is even stranger seeing your parents' friends becoming old ladies."

My father may look decrepit, but he has not yet lost his spirit.

"Where the devil is the doctor?" he growls. "What the hell is going on? This is a useless hospital."

I say nothing. I am used to his outbursts. They don't impress me anymore. A young nurse scurries by like a frightened rabbit.

"Have you seen Mel?" I ask.

He shrugs. "She's asleep," he grunts.

"She's going to pull through," I say.

He glares at me, infuriated.

"I'm having her transferred to Paris. There is no point keeping her here. She needs the best doctors."

I think of Bénédicte Besson's patient hazel eyes, of the bloodstains on the front of her uniform, of what she did last night to save my sister's life. My father sits down heavily on a nearby chair. He looks at me, expecting an answer or a reaction. I give him neither.

"Tell me again what happened."

I do so.

"Had she been drinking?"

"No."

"How can you just drive off the highway?"

"That's what happened."

"Where's your car?"

"It's more or less wrecked."

He observes me, sullen, dubious.

"Why were you two in Noirmoutier?"

"It was a surprise for Mel's birthday."

"Some surprise," he mutters.

Anger rises. He still gets at me, I marvel. He can still do that, I still let him do that.

"She loved it," I say hotly. "We had three wonderful days. It was—"

I stop. I sound like an irate kid. Exactly what he wanted. His mouth twitches the way it does when he is amused. Is Mélanie pretending to be asleep? I somehow know she is listening to every word from behind the closed door.

Our father wasn't always like this. After Clarisse died, he closed up. He became tough, bitter, and always in a hurry. It was hard to remember the real father, the happy one, the one who smiled and laughed, the one who tweaked our hair and made us crêpes on Sunday morning. Even if he was busy, even if he came home late, he'd make time for us. He would play games with us, take us to the Bois de Boulogne, or drive us out to Versailles to walk in the park and fly Mélanie's kite.

He never shows us his love anymore. He hasn't done that since 1974.

"I've never been fond of Noirmoutier," he announces.

"Why not?"

He raises his bushy eyebrows.

"But Robert and Blanche liked it, didn't they?" I ask.

"Yes, they did. They nearly bought a place there. You remember?"

"Yes," I say. "A big house near the hotel. With red shutters. In the woods."

"Les Bruyères."

"Why didn't they?"

He shrugs. But again, he doesn't give me an answer. I knew he never got on well with his parents. Robert, my grandfather, hated being contradicted. And although Blanche had a softer disposition, she certainly wasn't the doting mother type. And he was never close to his sister, Solange.

Is my father such a hard man because his parents were everything but loving with him? Am I a soft and gentle father (*Too soft, way too gentle!* Astrid would complain after another fight with Arno) because I am afraid of breaking Arno's wings the way my father broke mine? In fact, I realize I don't mind coming across as weak, because there is no way I could ever reproduce my father's harshness with my own son.

"How's that good-for-nothing teenager of yours?" he asks. He never asks about Margaux or Lucas. Something about Arno being the heir to the name.

Arno's pale, pointed face comes to me. His spiky, gelled haircut, his sideburns, his pierced left eyebrow. His uneven stubble. Sixteen. A child in a man's body.

"He's fine," I say. "He's with Astrid now."

I instantly regret pronouncing her name. I know he will pounce on it and it will spark an endless monologue. How could I have let that woman leave me for another man? How could I have accepted the divorce? Didn't I know what it would do to me, to the children? Didn't I have any pride, any balls? *Des couilles.* With my father, it always boiled down to balls. As I brace myself while he launches into full swing, the doctor appears. His eyebrows come rushing down. His jaw bulges.

"You tell me exactly what the situation is, Mademoiselle. Now."

"Yes, sir," she replies very seriously.

And as he turns to open the door to Mélanie's room, her eyes meet mine. To my astonishment, she winks.

So he does come across as an exasperating little old man. No one is afraid of him. He is no longer the sharp-tongued, impressive lawyer. And somehow that makes me sad.

"I'm afraid your daughter cannot be moved for the moment," says Dr. Besson patiently, her eyes only barely tinted with impatience.

My father blusters on. "She needs to be in the best of hands, in Paris, with the best doctors. She can't possibly stay here."

Bénédicte Besson hardly stirs. But I can tell how deeply the blow strikes by the hardening of her mouth. She says nothing.

"I need to see your superior. The person who runs this place."

"There is no superior," says Dr. Besson quietly.

"What do you mean?"

"I mean this is my hospital. I run it. I am responsible for the hospital and for every patient here."

She says this with such quiet command that my father shuts up at last.

Mélanie has opened her eyes. Our father grabs her hand, hanging on to it for dear life, as if this were the last time he will ever touch her. He leans toward her, half of his body on the bed. The way he clasps her hand moves me. He is realizing he has nearly lost his daughter. His *petite Mélabelle.* Her nickname from long ago. He wipes his eyes with the cotton handkerchief he always keeps in his pocket. He cannot say a word, it seems. He can only sit there and breathe audibly.

Mélanie is disturbed by this display of emotion. She doesn't want to see his ravaged, wet face. So she looks at me. For so many years now, our father hasn't ever shown his feelings, only displeasure or anger. This is an unexpected flashback to the tender, caring father he used to be, before our mother died.

We sit in silence for a while. The doctor leaves, shutting the door behind her. My father's hand gripping his daughter's brings back all the times I'd been to an emergency room for my children. When Lucas fell from his bike and sliced his forehead open. When Margaux fell down the stairs and broke her tibia. When Arno had the highest fever I had ever seen. The rush. The panic. Astrid clinging to me. Her face as white as chalk. The clasping of hands.

I look at my father, and I am aware that I am silently sharing something with him for once, although he doesn't know it, although he can't see it. We are sharing that bottomless pit of fear you feel only when you have become a parent and something happens to your child.

My thoughts revert to this room and why we are here. What had Mélanie tried to tell me just before the accident? That she remembered something during her last night at the Hotel Saint-Pierre. That she had held it back all day. What could she have recalled? I mentally go back to our stay. So many memories had come flowing in. What could this one have been? Why had she held it back? Was that why she seemed strange since breakfast, almost dazed? Sitting next to her by the Gois, I had asked her what was wrong and she'd shrugged it off. Hadn't slept well, she'd mumbled. And all morning long, she had been remote. Her strange mood had only just started to wear off when we got into the car to drive back to Paris in the afternoon.

A bustling nurse enters, pushing a cart in front of her. Time to check Mélanie's blood pressure, make sure her stitches are okay. She asks my father and me to step out for a moment. Stitches? Then I remember. Her spleen was operated on. My father and I stand outside, awkward, tense. He seems to have regained his composure, although his nose is still red. I rack my brains to try to think of something to say to him. Nothing comes. I inwardly laugh at the irony of the situation. Father and son reunite by ailing daughter's bedside and are incapable of speaking to each other.

Thankfully, my phone buzzes in my back pocket. I quickly step out of the building to answer it. It's Astrid. Her voice is tearful. I tell her I think Mel is going to be fine. I tell her how lucky we were. She asks if I want her to come with the kids. I feel a surge of pure joy sear through me. If she says things like that, doesn't that mean she still cares? Doesn't that mean she still loves me somehow? Before I can say anything, Arno's raspy voice comes on. He too sounds upset. I know how fond of my sister he is. When he was small, she used to parade him around the Luxembourg Gardens, pretending he was her son. He loved it. So did she. I tell him Mel is going to be stuck here for a while, that she has a cast from her waist to her neck. He says he wants to come and see her. He says Astrid is bringing them. The thought of seeing my family again, all of us together, like the good old days—not just exchanging kids on doorsteps with harassed remarks like "Oh and don't forget her cough syrup, this time" or "Do remember to sign the report cards, will you?"—makes me want to burst out into a song and dance. Astrid takes the phone again and asks for directions. I try to keep my voice cool and collected. Then she puts Margaux on. Soft, whispery, feminine. "Papa, tell Mel we love her and we are on our way." She hangs up before I get a chance to speak to rambunctious number three, Lucas. *We are on our way,* she said.

I light a cigarette and smoke it with relish. I can't bear the idea of going back inside and having to talk to my father. So I smoke another one and enjoy it just as much. They are on their way. With or without Serge? I wonder.

When I come back to Mélanie's room, I find our half sister, Joséphine, lolling against the wall. She must have come with our father. I am surprised to see her there. She isn't particularly close to Mélanie. Or to me. I hadn't seen her for months, probably since last Christmas at the avenue Kléber. We go to the empty cafeteria on the ground floor. Mélanie is apparently resting, and our father is sitting in his car, on the phone.

Joséphine is fashionably thin, wearing low-hipped, faded jeans, Converse Star sneakers, and a khaki tank top. Her blond hair is cut short like a boy's. She has Régine's sallow skin and thin mouth and our father's brown eyes.

We light our cigarettes. That is probably the only thing we have in common. Smoking.

"Can we smoke in here?" she whispers, leaning toward me.

"There's no one around," I reply, shrugging.

"What were you and Mel doing in Noirmoutier?" she asks, inhaling deeply.

She never beats around the bush. She gets straight to the point. I like that about her.

"Mel's birthday. A surprise."

She nods, sipping her coffee.

"You used to go there when you were kids, right? With your mother."

The way she says that makes me look at her closely.

"Yes. Our mother, father, and grandparents," I say.

"You never talk about your mother," she says.

Twenty-five years old. Not dumb. A little vain, although to me her gamine looks are nothing to write home about. The fact that she and I share our father's blood has never made me feel brotherly toward her.

"We don't talk about anything much, you and I," she goes on.

"Does that bother you?" I ask.

She twists her rings around her fingers, her cigarette hanging mannishly from her mouth.

"Yes, it does. I don't know a thing about you."

People come into the cafeteria and give us outraged looks because we are smoking. We stub out our Marlboros.

"Don't forget I had already left the avenue Kléber when you were born," I say.

"Perhaps. But you are still my half brother. I'm here because I do care. I care about Mel. I care about you."

This is so out of character coming from her that I can only gape.

She smirks. "Close your mouth, Antoine."

I chortle.

She says, "Tell me about your mother. No one ever talks about her."

"What do you want to know?"

She lifts an eyebrow. "Anything."

"She died in 1974. She had a brain aneurysm. She was thirty-six years old. It happened very fast. We came home from school and she had been taken to the hospital. She was dead." I glance at her. "Hasn't Régine or Papa told you all this?"

"No," she says. "Go on."

"That's it."

"No, I mean what was she like?"

"Mélanie looks like her. Petite, dark, green eyes. She laughed a lot. She made us all happy."

It seemed to me that our father stopped smiling after Clarisse died and that he smiles even less since his marriage to Régine. I don't want to say this to Joséphine, so I shut up. But I'm sure she knows as well as I do that her parents lead two different lives. My father meets his retired lawyer friends, spends hours in his study reading or writing, complains a lot, and Régine patiently puts up with his grumbling, goes out to play bridge at her ladies' club, and tries to pretend all is well at avenue Kléber.

"And her family? Do you ever see them?"

"They died when she was young. They were from a modest rural background. I remember she had a sister, older than she, who she never saw much. And after her death that sister fizzled out of our lives. I don't even know where she lives."

"What was her name?"

"Clarisse Elzyère."

"Where was she from?"

"The Cévennes."

"Are you okay?" she asks suddenly. "You look awful."

I grin. "Thanks."

Then I say, after a slight pause, "Actually, you're right. To tell the truth, I'm exhausted. And then *him* turning up."

"Yeah," she says. "You don't get on with him, do you?"

"Not much."

Which is a half lie, because I did get on with him when Clarisse was still alive. He was the first one to call me Tonio. We had a quiet complicity that suited the calm little boy I used to be. No rushing about playing football. No sweaty, manly activities on weekends, but contemplative strolls through our neighborhood and frequent visits to the Louvre, to the Egyptian wing, my favorite. Sometimes, among the sarcophagi and mummies, I'd catch a whisper. *Isn't that the lawyer François Rey?* And I was proud to be seen holding his hand, proud to be his son. But that was more than thirty years ago.

"His bark is worse than his bite."

"Easy for you, you're his little *chouchou*, his favorite."

She had the good grace to acknowledge this with a certain elegance.

"Well, it isn't always easy being the *chouchou*," she mutters. Then she says, "How's your family?"

"They're on their way. You'll see them if you stick around for a bit."

"Great," she says a little too brightly. "And your job, how's that going?"

I wonder why she is doing her best to keep up this falsely concerned questionnaire. Joséphine has never asked me for anything except cigarettes. The last thing I want to talk about is my job. Even thinking about it brings back something stale. "Well, I'm still working as an architect and I'm still as unhappy about it."

Before she can ask why, I throw her one of my own questions.

"And what about you? Boyfriend, job, all that? Where are you at? Are you still seeing the guy who owns a nightclub? And are you still working for that designer in the Marais?"

I don't bring up the married man she had an affair with last year, or the long stint without a job when she appeared to be spending most of her time watching DVDs in her father's study or shopping in her mother's shiny black Mini.

All of a sudden she flashes a smile at me. It looks more like a grimace. She smooths her hair back and clears her throat.

"Actually, Antoine, I would really appreciate it if you could . . ." She pauses, clears her throat again. "If you could lend me some money."

Her brown eyes, both pleading and brazen, stare back at me.

"How much?" I ask.

"Well, say, a thousand euros."

"Are you in trouble?" I ask, using the Daddy voice I use with Arno.

She shakes her head. "No, of course not! I just need some cash. And, you know, I'd rather not ask them for anything."

I assume that "them" means her parents.

"I haven't got that kind of money on me."

"There's a cash machine right across the street," she says helpfully.

She waits.

"I take it you need it now?"

She nods.

"Joséphine, I don't mind lending you this, but I will need it back. Since my divorce, it hasn't exactly been the lap of luxury."

"Sure, no problem. Promise."

"And I don't think I can withdraw that amount."

"Well, what about whatever the machine gives you in cash and the rest by check?"

She gets up and sashays out, swinging her scrawny hips triumphantly. As we leave the hospital to go to the bank, lighting up cigarettes on the way, I can't help feeling conned. So much for her new sisterly attitude.

After handing the bills and a check to Joséphine, who pecks me on the cheek and saunters off, I stroll into town, not wanting to go back to the hospital for the moment. It is one of those provincial boroughs, with nothing remarkable about it. A little town hall, sporting a withered tricolor flag, facing an austere church. A *bar-tabac* and a *boulangerie*. An unpretentious-looking hotel called L'Auberge du Dauphin. I see no one around. The *bar-tabac* is deserted. Too early for lunch. A glum young man lifts his chin to me as I walk in. I order a coffee and sit down. An invisible radio blares out the news on Europe 1. The plastic-topped tables are greasy to the touch. Should I make a couple of phone calls, tell my close friends what happened? Call Emmanuel, Hélène, Didier? I keep putting it off. Is it because I don't want to pronounce those words again? To describe the accident over and over? And what about Mélanie's friends? And her boss? Who is going to tell him? Probably me. Next week is a big week for Mélanie—with the beginning of the fall literary season. The busiest time of year for anyone who works in publishing, and this includes my ex-wife. And then there is my own workload, Rabagny and his fits of temper, the layouts he wants to alter yet again, the assistant I need to find after I manage to fire Florence.

I light a cigarette.

"You won't be able to do that next year," sneers the young man with a churlish smile. "Everybody will be going outside to smoke. Or not coming here at all. Bad business ahead. Real bad business. Might as well close up the place."

He looks so worked up that I decide, in a cowardly fashion, not to venture into the conversation. Instead, I smile, nod my head, shrug, and plunge myself into the blithe study of my mobile phone.

I took up smoking again when Astrid told me she loved Serge. I had stopped for ten years. And in the flick of a lighter I became a smoker again. Everybody gave me hell about it. I didn't care. Astrid, a true health freak, had been appalled. I still didn't care. Smoking was the one thing no one could take away from me. It was the only part of my present life that gave me some kind of satisfaction. I knew I was a bad example for my children, especially at Arno's and Margaux's fragile, impressionable ages, when smoking is considered a risqué, hip thing to do. The apartment at the rue Froidevaux smells of stale smoke. When I get home, that's what greets me. And the view over the cemetery. Looking over death. Of course, I can't complain, my deceased neighbors are a prestigious bunch: Baudelaire, de Maupassant, Beckett, Sartre, de Beauvoir. But I soon learn to look away from the living-room window. Or I only look out at night, when the austere crucifixes and stone monuments are no longer visible, when the long stretch to the Tour Montparnasse is just a mysterious black space full of nothingness.

I had spent time trying to make that apartment look and feel like home. In vain. I had pilfered Astrid's photo albums, ruthlessly tearing out my favorite photos of the children, of us, plastering them all over my walls. Arno at birth in my bewildered arms, Margaux in her first dress, Lucas triumphant on the top of the Eiffel Tower, brandishing a sticky lollypop. Ski vacations, summer vacations, Loire châteaux visits, birthdays, school plays, Christmases: an endless, desperate exhibition of what our happy family once was.

Despite the photos, despite the colorful curtains (Mélanie had helped choose those), the cheerful kitchen, the comfortable Habitat sofas, the clever lighting, there is something heart-wrenchingly empty about the place. It seems to come to life only when the kids turn up on their allotted weekends. I still wake up in the new bed, scratch my head, and wonder where I am. I can't stand going back to Malakoff, being confronted with Astrid and her new life in our old house. Why are people so attached to houses? Why does it hurt so much to let a house go?

We bought that house together, twelve years ago. It was an unfashionable area then, considered unglamorous and working class, and our move to that "grotty little suburb" south of Paris had sprouted raised eyebrows. And there had been so much to be done. The high and narrow *pavillon de banlieue* was crumbling, damp and run-down. That was why it was cheap. We took it on as a challenge. We loved every minute of it, even the setbacks, the problems with the bank, with a fellow architect, with the plumber, the mason, the carpenter. We worked on it day in, day out. And it finally became perfect. Malakoff, our little *paradis*. Our envious Parisian friends realized how close it was to the city, how easy it was to get to, just beyond the Porte de Vanves. And we even had a garden—who can boast of a garden in Paris?—which meant we had our meals outside in the summer, despite the muffled roar of the nearby *périphérique* that we soon got used to. A garden, which I tenderly looked after, and a dog, a clumsy old Labrador who still couldn't understand why I had moved out and who this new guy in Astrid's bed was. Good old Titus.

My heart still aches for that house. The winters, and the cozy fireplace. The big living room, shabby with the wear and tear of three children and the dog. Lucas's drawings. Astrid's incense sticks that gave me headaches. Margaux's homework. Arno's size twelve sneakers. The dark red sofa that had seen better days but remained comfortable enough to sleep on. The sagging armchairs that embraced you like old friends.

Our home. The day I had to leave it. The day I stood on the doorstep and turned around and looked at it for the last time. The last time as my home. The children weren't there. Astrid watched me, her eyes wistful. *You'll be okay, Antoine. The kids will come and see you every other weekend. You'll see, it'll be fine.* And I had nodded, not wanting her to see tears welling up. She had said, *Take what you want. Take what you think is yours.* I had started to fill up cardboard boxes with all my junk, savagely, angrily; then I had slowed down. I didn't want any memories, except the photos. I didn't want anything except the photos. I didn't want anything from this house except for her to love me again.

I used to have my office on the top floor. The ideal office. Space, light, and silence. I had planned it myself. When I was up there, overlooking the reddish roofs and the gray strip of the ring road always cluttered by traffic, I felt like Leo DiCaprio when he gloats, "I'm the king of the world!" on the doomed *Titanic*'s deck, arms outstretched to the horizon. My doomed office. It was my lair, my den. In the good old days, Astrid used to creep up when the children were asleep, and we'd make love on the carpet, listening to Cat Stevens sing "Sad Lisa. Lisa Lisa, sad Lisa Lisa." Serge has his office up there now, I guess. I don't want to think about what they do on the carpet.

As I sit there in that dingy café, waiting for my family to turn up, listening to a corny song by Michel Sardou, I wonder if my father wasn't right after all.

I never fought for her. I never kicked up a fuss. I never let all hell loose. I let her go. I was meek and well-behaved, like the little boy I used to be. The one with the combed-back hair and the navy blue jacket. The one who said *s'il vous plaît*, *merci*, and *pardon*.

At last I glimpse the familiar Audi, coated with dust. I watch my family get out of the car. They don't know I'm there, they can't see me yet. I leave the café and hide behind a large tree near the parking lot. My heart swells. I haven't seen them for a while. Arno's hair is blonder, bleached by the sun. He wears it down to his shoulders. I see he is trying to grow a straggly goatee, which oddly enough suits him. Margaux has a bandanna around her head. She has filled out, she is no longer so skinny. She walks clumsily, not comfortable with herself. Lucas is the one who surprises me the most. The plump kid is now all arms and legs. I can see the future teen inside him struggling to get out, like the Incredible Hulk.

I don't want to look at Astrid right away, but I can't hold out much longer. She is wearing a long, faded jean dress that I love, buttoned up in the front and close-fitting. Her blond hair, a little more silvery I notice, is tied back. She looks wan. But still so beautiful. Serge is not there. I breathe a sigh of relief.

I watch them leave the parking lot and head to the hospital. I make my appearance. Lucas howls and flings himself on me, his arms and legs wrapping themselves around me. Arno grabs my head and kisses me on the forehead. He is definitely taller than I am now. Margaux stands apart, on one leg, like a flamingo, then comes forward and buries her head in my shoulder. I discern that under the bandanna her hair is dyed bright orange. I recoil, but say nothing.

I save Astrid for last. I wait till the children have had their fill of me, and I reach out for her and hug her with a sort of feverish hunger she probably mistakes for anguish concerning my sister. It is unbelievably good holding her close again. Her scent, her softness, the velvet touch of her naked arms make me reel. She doesn't push me away. She hugs me back, hard. I want to kiss her and nearly do. Then I remember they haven't come here for me. They've come for Mel.

I take them in to see her. On our way, we bump into my father and Joséphine. My father greets everybody with his brutal hugs. He pulls on Arno's goatee. "What is this, for God's sake?" he roars. He slaps Arno on the back. "Stand up straight, you good-for-nothing nincompoop. Doesn't your father ever tell you that? He's as bad as you, honestly."

I know he is joking, but as always, there is a bite to his jesting. Ever since Arno was a small child, my father has been on me about the way I raise him—always the wrong way, in his eyes. We all tiptoe into Mélanie's room. She is still sleeping. Her face is even paler than it was in the morning. She looks frail, all of a sudden older than her forty years. Margaux's eyes well up, and I see tears glisten. She seems horrified by her aunt's appearance. I wrap my arm around her shoulder and draw her close to me. She has a sweaty, salty smell. No longer the little-girl cinnamon smell. Arno stares, his mouth open. Lucas fidgets, looking from me to his mother, then back to Mélanie.

Then Mélanie turns her head and slowly opens her eyes. She sees the children, and her whole face lights up. She gives a weak smile. Margaux bursts into tears. I see that Astrid's eyes are wet too, that her mouth is trembling, and all this is too much for me. I back away discreetly and slip out into the corridor. I take a cigarette out and just hold it.

"No smoking!" booms a matronly nurse, waving an irate finger at me.

"I'm just holding it," I explain. "Holding, not smoking."

She glares at me as if I were a shoplifter caught red-handed. I put the cigarette back in the pack. I suddenly think of Clarisse. She is the only one missing here. If she were still alive, she would be here now, in that room, with her daughter and her grandchildren. Her husband. She would be nearly seventy. Even if I try as hard as I can, I cannot imagine my mother at sixty-nine years old. She will always be a young woman. I am the middle-aged man. She never knew middle age. She never knew what it was like to raise teenage children. She died before all that. I wonder what kind of mother she would have been to us when we were in our teens. It would have been different had she been alive. Everything would have been different. Mélanie and I had kept our puberty in check. We had been coerced into submission. No outbursts, no screams, no slamming doors, no insults. No healthy teenage rebellion. Uptight Régine had muzzled us. Blanche and Robert had looked on in approval. It was the done thing, in their eyes. Seen and not heard. And our father had overnight turned into someone else. Someone who wasn't really interested in his children, nor in whom they would end up being one day.

We had not been allowed to be teenagers.

As I accompany my family back outside, a tall woman wearing a pale blue uniform walks past me and smiles. She has a badge, but I can't make out whether she is a nurse or a doctor. I smile back. I wonder fleetingly who she is and think how nice it is in these provincial hospitals that people actually greet you, which is never the case in Paris. Astrid still seems tired, and I begin to think the drive back to the city in the grueling heat is not a good idea. Can't they stay a little longer? She hesitates, then mumbles something about Serge waiting for her. I add that I have checked into a nearby hotel, as Mélanie can't be moved yet. Why doesn't she go and rest there for a while? The room is small, but cool. She can even have a shower. She tilts her head and seems to like the idea. I hand over the key and point out the hotel to her, just beyond the town hall. I watch her and Margaux walk away.

Arno and I go back to the hospital and sit on the wooden bench in front of the entrance.

"She's going to make it, right?" he says.

I nod at him. "Mel? You bet. She's going to be fine."

But even to me my voice seems strained.

"You said the car drove off the highway, Dad."

"Yes. Mel was driving. And it happened."

"But how? How did it happen?"

I decide to tell him the truth. Recently Arno has been closed up, remote, only answering my questions with short grunts. I can't even remember the last time we had a decent conversation. Hearing his voice again, having him look me in the eyes and not somewhere near my feet makes me long to keep this unexpected contact going, no matter how.

"She was in the middle of telling me about something that upset her. And then it happened."

His blue eyes, so like Astrid's, zoom into mine.

"What was she telling you?" he whispers.

"She only had time to say she recalled something. It bothered her. But since the accident, she doesn't remember."

Arno remains silent. He has such big hands now. A man's hands.

"What do you think it was?"

I take a deep breath.

"I think it was about our mother."

He looks surprised. "Your mother? You never talk about your mother."

"No. But being in Noirmoutier for those three days brought back old memories."

"Why do you think Mel remembered something about your mother?"

I like the way he questions me—simple, fast questions, no fuss, no stalling.

"Because we spent a lot of time during our stay talking about her. Remembering all sorts of things."

I stop. How can I explain all this to my sixteen-year-old son? What will he make of it? Why does he care?

"Go on," he urges. "What things?"

"Like who she was."

"You forgot that?"

"That's not what I mean. The day she died was the worst day of my life. Imagine saying goodbye to your mother, going to school with the au pair girl, living your normal school day, and coming back in the afternoon with the au pair again, like every afternoon, with your *pain au chocolat* in your hand. Except that when you get home, your father is there, your grandparents are there, and they have this dreadful expression on their faces. And then they tell you your mother is dead. That something happened in her brain, and she died. And then, at the hospital, you are shown a body under a sheet and you're told it's your mother. The sheet is pulled back, but you close your eyes. That's what I did."

He stares at me, shocked.

"Why didn't you ever tell me all this?"

I shrug. "Because you never asked."

His eyebrows, one of them pierced with a silver stud that I find repulsive, come down.

"That's a dumb excuse."

"I didn't know how to talk to you about it."

"Why?" he asks.

Now his questions are starting to bother me. But I want to keep on answering them. I feel a strong urge to get this off my chest and tell my son about it for the first time.

"Because when she died, everything changed for Mel and me. No one explained to us what happened. Those were the seventies, remember. People are careful with kids now, they take them to shrinks when stuff like that happens. But no one helped us. Our mother flew out of our lives. Our father remarried. Our mother's name was never mentioned. All her photos disappeared."

"Really?" Arno mutters.

I shake my head. "She was erased from our lives. And we let that happen because we were dazed by grief, we were kids, we were helpless. And by the time we were old enough to fend for ourselves, it was time to leave our father's house. So that's what we did, Mélanie and

I. And somewhere along the way we let everything concerning our mother be boxed up and locked away. And I'm not talking about her clothes, her books, her objects. I mean our memories of her."

I find it hard to breathe all of a sudden.

"What was she like?" he asks.

"Physically, like Mel. Same coloring, same silhouette. She was bubbly, joyful. Full of life."

I stop. Something too close to my heart hurts. I cannot speak. The words don't come.

"Sorry," mumbles Arno. "We'll talk about it another day. No prob, Dad."

He stretches his long legs and pats my back affectionately. He seems embarrassed by my emotion and doesn't know how to deal with it.

The tall woman in the blue uniform I noticed earlier walks past us again and smiles once more. Pretty legs. Pretty smile. I smile back at her.

Arno's mobile phone goes off, and he heaves up to answer it. He lowers his voice and moves away from me. I can't make out what he is saying. I have no inkling whatsoever about my son's intimate life. He rarely brings friends home, except a goth-type girl with dyed black hair and purple lips that disturb me, giving her a drowned Ophelia-like look. They sit around his room and listen to music full blast. I don't like questioning him. Once, my seemingly cheerful interrogations were greeted with an icy "Are you from the Gestapo, or what?" Since then, I keep my mouth shut. I remember hating my father prying when I was Arno's age. Except I would never have dared answer him that way.

I light a cigarette and get up to take a few steps. I keep thinking about what I should do now, how to organize things around Mélanie's hospital stay. What to start with.

I feel a presence next to me, and when I turn, I see it is the tall woman in the pale blue uniform.

"Could I have a cigarette?"'

My hands fumble as I offer her my packet. Another fumble with the unwilling lighter.

"Do you work here?"

She has interesting gold eyes. Early forties, but I'm bad at guessing ages. She could be younger. All I know is that she's nice to look at.

"Yes," she says.

We stand there, a little self-conscious. I look down at her badge. ANGÈLE ROUVATIER.

"Are you a doctor?" I ask.

She smiles. "No, not exactly."

Before I can ask another question, she says, "Is that young man your son?"

"Yes. We are here because—"

"I know why you are here," she says. "This is a small hospital."

Her voice is low, friendly. But there is something strange about her, something slightly aloof. I can't quite pinpoint it.

"Your sister was lucky. That was a bad crash. You were lucky too."

"Yes," I say. "Very lucky."

We puff away in silence.

"So you work with Dr. Besson?" I ask.

"She's the boss."

I nod. I notice she wears no wedding band. That's the kind of thing I notice now. I never used to, before.

"I have to go. Thanks for the cigarette."

She takes off. I admire her long, slim calves. I can't even remember the last woman I had sex with. Probably some girl I met on the Internet. Some dismal fling that lasted a couple of hours. A used condom, a hurried goodbye, and that was it.

The only nice girl I had met since my divorce was a married one. Hélène. One of her daughters was in Margaux's art class. But she wasn't interested in having an affair. She only wanted to be friends. That was fine with me. She became a close and precious ally. She would take me out to dinner at some noisy brasserie in the Latin Quarter and hold my hand and listen to me mope. Her husband didn't seem to mind. Not that I'd make any husband jealous. Hélène lives on boulevard de Sébastopol in a rambling apartment she inherited from her grandfather and did up with great audacity. Her building has a crumbling old façade in an area squashed between the Halles and the Pompidou Centre, two symbols of overt presidential vanity. Going to visit Hélène never ceases to bring back pangs of my childhood, when my father and I roamed through the odorous market stalls that no longer exist. He was fond of getting me out of the sixteenth arrondissement and showing me the *vieux* Paris and its Zola-like reminiscences. I remember ogling the garishly dressed hookers lined up and down the rue Saint-Denis until my father sternly told me to stop.

I watch Astrid and Margaux come back from the hotel, refreshed after their shower. Astrid's face has smoothed out; she seems less tired. She is holding Margaux's hand and swinging it the way she did when Margaux was a little girl.

I know it will soon be time for them to leave. I know I need to get ready for that moment. It always takes me a while.

At the end of the day Mélanie's face seems a little pinker against the white pillow—or perhaps it is my hopeful imagination. Our families have left, and we are alone now in the slowly abating August heat, with the whirring noise of the fan in our ears. This afternoon I called her boss, Thierry Drancourt, her assistant, Lucie, her close friends, Valérie, Agnès, Victor. I tried to explain the situation in the best way possible, with the smoothest, most reassuring voice—accident, broken back, hospital, rest, will be okay—but they had all sounded worried. Could they send something, could they be of any help, was she suffering? I briefly calmed them down with a confident tone. She was going to be fine, just fine. On Mel's phone, which I had gotten hold of, I found a couple of messages from the old beau, but I did not call him back.

Then, in the privacy of the men's toilets down the hall, I phoned my own close friends, Hélène, Didier, and Emmanuel, and told them with a very different, trembling voice how afraid I had been, how afraid I still was, looking at her lying there in her cast, motionless, a dead look in her eyes. Hélène sounded tearful, and Didier could hardly speak. Only Emmanuel managed to comfort me with his deafening baritone voice and warm chuckle. He offered to come down to be with me, and I toyed with the idea for a while.

"I don't think I want to drive ever again," Mélanie says feebly.

"Forget it. It's too early, anyway."

She shrugs, or tries to, and winces. "The kids have grown. Lucas is a young man. Margaux with her orange hair. Arno and his goatee." She stretches her parched lips and smiles. "And Astrid . . ." she says.

"Yeah . . ." I sigh. "And Astrid."

She slowly reaches out and takes my hand. She squeezes it. "Whatshisname didn't show up, huh?"

"Thank God."

The doctor comes in with a nurse for the evening checkup, and I leave the room after having kissed my sister goodbye. I walk up and down the corridors, the rubbery soles of my tennis shoes making squeaky noises. As I head out to the main entrance, I see her again, just outside.

Angèle Rouvatier. She is wearing black jeans and a sleeveless black T-shirt. She is sitting astride a magnificent vintage black Harley-Davidson, helmet tucked under one arm. With the other hand she is holding a phone to her ear. Her brown hair falls against her face, and I cannot make out her expression. I stand there and watch her for a while, my eyes running down the slim length of her thighs, down the tapered back, along the round, feminine shoulders. Her forearms are tanned; she must have spent some time in the sun recently. I wonder what she looks like in a bathing suit. I wonder what her life is, whether she is married, single, a mother, childless. I wonder what she smells like, just there, under the glossy curtain of hair. She must have sensed something because she whips around and sees me checking her out. I step back fast, my heart thumping with discomfiture. She smiles at me, pockets her phone, and makes a little gesture with her finger: come here. I plod toward her, feeling idiotic.

"How is your sister this evening?" she asks.

Her eyes are gold, even in this light.

"She seems better," I mumble. "Thank you."

"You have a beautiful family. Your wife and daughter and son."

"Thank you."

"They've gone?"

"Yes."

A silence.

"I'm divorced." I don't know why I say that. It sounds pathetic.

"So you're stuck here for a bit, it seems?"

"Yes. She can't be moved."

She nods, gets up from the Harley. I admire the lithe way she swings her leg over the saddle.

"You have time for a drink?" she says.

She looks straight at me.

"Sure," I say, trying to sound like this happens to me every day. "Any idea where?"

"Not much choice. There's a bar over there, near the town hall. But it's probably closed at this hour. Or there's the bar at the Dauphin Hotel."

"That's where I'm staying," I say.

She nods. "There's no other place to stay. It's the only hotel open at this time of year."

She walks faster than I do, and I get breathless trying to keep up with her. We are silent, but the silence is not heavy. When we get to the hotel, there is no one in the bar. We wait around for a while. The place seems totally empty.

"You must have a minibar in your room," she says.

Again that direct look, straight at me. There is something both terrifying and exhilarating about her. She follows me to my room. I fumble with my keys. The door slides open, clicks shut, and there she is in my arms, the glossy hair against my cheek. She kisses me deeply, thoroughly. She tastes of mint and tobacco. She is stronger, taller than Astrid or any other woman I've held in my arms recently.

I feel stupid, standing there being kissed, like a clumsy teenager, swamped by my own inertia. My hands suddenly come to life. I grasp her. Like a drowning man clasping a life jacket, I clasp her to me feverishly, my palms flat against the small of her back. She melts into me, makes small, crooning sighs that come from deep within her. We fall onto the bed, and she straddles me with the same easy movement she used on her motorbike. Her eyes seem to glow like a cat's. She smiles slowly, then unbuckles my belt, unzips my fly. She touches me with a precise yet gentle sensuality that has me rock hard in seconds. She never stops looking at me, smiling at me, even as I enter her. She immediately slows me down, masterfully, stops my hips from bucking, and I know this will not be one of those rapid, rudimentary fucks that is over in minutes. This is something else.

She rides me, and I watch the tawny lines of her body. She leans down to clasp my face between her hands, and she kisses me with a tenderness that surprises me. She takes her time, revels in it. What happens is something slow, unhurried, but the buildup is so powerful that I can feel it searing up through my toes to my tailbone and spine, scorching me, almost like pain. She lies flat out on me, breathless. Beneath my palm, the skin of her back is damp.

"Thank you," she whispers. "I needed that."

I manage a dry chuckle. "I beg to differ. I needed that as well."

She reaches across to the table, grabs a cigarette, lights it, and hands it to me.

"The moment I laid eyes on you, I knew."

"Knew what?" I ask.

"That I'd have you."

She takes the cigarette from my fingers.

I suddenly notice I am wearing a condom. I have no recollection of her putting one on me. She must have slipped it on with a dexterity that I had not even fathomed.

"You still love her, don't you?"

"Who?" I say that, but I know exactly who she means.

"Your wife."

Why bother hiding anything from this unusual, beautiful stranger?

"Yes. I still love her. She left me for another man a year ago. I feel like shit."

Angèle stubs the cigarette out. Then she turns to face me again.

"I could tell. Just by the way you looked at her. It must hurt."

"It does."

"What do you do? Your job, I mean."

"I'm an architect. But the boring kind. I refurbish offices and warehouses. Hospitals, libraries, labs. Nothing exciting. I don't create."

"You like putting yourself down, don't you?"

"No," I say, stung.

"Then stop it."

I remain silent, discreetly sliding the condom off. I get up to throw it away in the bathroom. I avoid looking at myself in the mirror, as always.

"And what about you, Madame Rouvatier? What do you do?" I say, coming back to the bed, keeping my stomach in.

She looks at me coolly.

"I'm a mortician."

I swallow.

She smiles. Perfect white, square teeth.

"I handle dead people all day long. With the same hands that were stroking your dick a few moments ago."

I glance at her hands. Strong and capable. Yet so feminine.

"Some men are turned off by my job. I don't tell them. If I do, they lose their hard-on. Are you upset?"

"No," I say truthfully. "Surprised, I guess. Tell me about your job. I've never met a mortician."

"My job is about learning to respect death. That's all. If your sister had died last night in that accident—and thank God, she didn't—it would have been my job to make her look peaceful. So that you and your family could lay eyes on her one last time and not be afraid."

"How do you do that?"

She shrugs. "It's a job. The same way you do up offices, I do up death."

"It is tough?"

"Yes. When you get children. Or babies. Or pregnant women."

I shiver.

"Do you have any of your own? Children or babies?"

"No," she says. "I'm not a family person. That's why I admire other people's."

"Are you married?"

"You sound like a cop. I'm not the marrying kind either. Anything else?"

I smile. "Nope."

"Good. Because I need to go now. My boyfriend will be wondering where I am."

"Your boyfriend?" I cannot keep the bewilderment out of my voice.

She flashes her teeth at me. "Yes. I do have a couple of those."

She gets up, passes into the bathroom. I hear the shower run briefly. She appears wrapped up in a towel. I watch her. I cannot help but find her fascinating. She knows it. She slips on her underwear, jeans, T-shirt.

"I'll be seeing you again. You know that, don't you?"

"Yes," I breathe.

She leans over and kisses me full on the mouth, hungrily.

"I'll be back for more, Monsieur Parisian. You don't have to suck your tummy in like that. You're hot enough as it is."

The door clicks. She is gone. I try to get myself together. I still feel wiped out, as if a tidal wave has hit me. I cannot help chuckling as I shower, recalling her boldness. But behind the audacity, there is something incredibly appealing about her, a warmth, an irresistible charm. She has achieved something excellent, I decide as I change into a T-shirt and a pair of jeans. She made me feel good about myself, and this has not happened for ages. I catch myself humming and nearly laugh out loud.

I look at myself straight on in the mirror. I haven't done that for a long time. My longish face. Thick eyebrows. Lean limbs apart from the big belly. I grin. The man facing me no longer looks like Droopy. No, he's even rather sexy, I think, with his ruffled salt-and-pepper hair and a devilish glint in his chestnut eyes.

If only Astrid could see me now, I think. If only Astrid could want me as much as Angèle Rouvatier-who-is-coming-back-for-more did. I groan. When am I going to stop pining for my ex-wife? When am I going to be able to turn that page and move on?

I think of Angèle's work. I have no idea what morticians do, exactly. Do I want to know? It fascinates me in some obscure way I do not want to delve into. I remember a TV documentary about what was done to bodies after death. Serums being pumped into them, crumpled-up faces smoothed out, wounds stitched together, limbs rearranged, special makeup applied. A grim job, I had remarked to Astrid, who was watching it with me. Here in this provincial hospital, what kind of deaths does Angèle Rouvatier get every day? Old people passing away. Car accidents. Cancer. Heart attacks. I wonder all of a sudden if a mortician tended to my mother's body all those years ago. I remember the day we were taken to the hospital. I had closed my eyes. I wonder if Mélanie had too. The funeral took place at Saint-Pierre de Chaillot church, ten minutes away from the avenue Kléber. My mother was buried in the nearby Passy cemetery, at the Trocadéro. In the Rey family grave. I had taken the children there years ago to show them her grave, the grave of a grandmother they never knew. How is it that I have such little recollection of her funeral? Only short flashes of the dark church, few people, whispers, white lilies and their overpowering perfume, strangers hugging us over and over. I need to talk to my sister about this, to see what she remembers, if she remembers our mother's dead face, but I know this is not the moment.

I think again about what Mélanie wanted to tell me when the car drove off the highway. This has not left my mind since the accident.

It has been with me since, at the back of my mind, like a dead weight pressing down on me. I wonder whether I should talk to Dr. Besson, how I should put it to her, what she might think. What she would suggest. But the only person I want to talk to about this right now is my ex-wife, and she is not here.

I turn on my mobile phone and listen to messages. One from Florence about a new contract. Three from Rabagny. I had accepted his state-of-the-art day-care center project near the Bastille only because the pay was good and I couldn't afford being fussy these days. The alimony I transfer to Astrid each month is considerable. Our lawyers had worked it out. There was nothing I could do about it. I had always earned more money than she had, and I suppose it was a fair deal. But by the end of the month I feel the pinch.

Rabagny can't understand where I am and why I am not calling him back, although I did send him a text message yesterday explaining the accident on my way back to Paris, not going into any more detail. I hate the sound of his voice. High-pitched and whiny, like a spoiled kid's. There is a problem with the playground surfaces. The color is wrong. The consistency is wrong. He rants on and on, spits out his words. I can almost see his ratlike face, protruding eyes, oversize ears. I didn't like him from the start. He is barely thirty, as arrogant as he is unpleasant to look at. I glance at my watch: seven o'clock. I could still get back to him. I don't. I erase all his messages with satisfying savagery.

The next message is from Hélène. Her soft, dovelike voice. She wants to know how Mélanie is, how I am since our last talk a few hours back. She is still in Honfleur with her family. Since my divorce I have often been to that house. It overlooks the sea, and it is a happy, untidy, cozy house I feel good in. Hélène is a precious friend because she knows exactly how to make me feel better about myself and my life. For a short while, anyway. What I loathed about the divorce was the split between our friends. Some of them chose Astrid, others chose me. Why? I never knew. Do they not find it strange to go have dinner at the house in Malakoff with him sitting at my place? Do they find it sad to visit me in the empty rue Froidevaux apartment, where it is obvious that I can't get myself together? Some of those friends chose Astrid over me because she exudes happiness. It's easier to socialize with someone happy, I guess. No one wants to sit around and brood with the loser. No one wants to hear about my lonesomeness, about how all at sea I felt those first months when I found myself without a family after eighteen years of being a paterfamilias. How silent those early mornings seemed in my IKEA kitchen, with just the smell of burned baguette and the jingle of the RTL News on the radio to keep me company. I used to stand there, numbed by the lack of noise: Astrid yelling for the kids to hurry up, the tremendous sound of Arno thundering down the stairs, Titus barking in excitement, Lucas shrieking because he couldn't find his gym bag. A year later, I admit that I have become used to the new morning silence. But I still miss the noise.

There are also a couple of messages from other clients. Some of them are urgent. The summer break is over. People are now back at work, into the swing of things. I start thinking about how long I should be staying here. How much longer I can stay here. It will soon be three days. And Mel can't be moved yet. Dr. Besson is not giving me more details. I think she wants to wait to see how Mélanie is doing before she gets precise. More messages from the insurance company about the wrecked car and paperwork I need to fill out. I diligently write all this down in my little notebook.

I turn on my computer and use the phone line by the bed to check my e-mail. A couple from Emmanuel and a few business ones. I answer them swiftly. I then open AutoCAD files concerning projects I should be working on. I am almost amused at how uninterested I am by the sight of them. There was a time when imagining new office spaces, a library, a hospital, a sports center, a lab, gave me a thrill. Now it turns me off. Worse still, it makes me feel as if I've wasted most of my life and my energy in a field that simply does not fuel me.

How did this happen? When did it all fizzle out? Probably when Astrid left me. Maybe I am going through a depression, maybe it really is a midlife crisis. I just didn't see it coming. But do you ever see these things coming?

I close the computer and lie down on the bed. The sheets still smell of Angèle Rouvatier, which pleases me. The room is a small modern one, devoid of charm, comfortable enough. The walls are pearl gray, the thinning carpet a faded beige. The window looks out onto a parking lot. By this time Mélanie has had her dinner, served ridiculously early, as always in hospitals. I have the choice between a McDonald's on the town's outskirts or a little *pension de famille* on the main avenue, where I have already been twice. The service is slow-moving, the room full of toothless octogenarians, but the meals are wholesome. Tonight I decide I shall fast. It will do me good.

I switch on the television and try to concentrate on the news. Political unrest in the Middle East, bombs, riots, death, violence. I flick from channel to channel, sickened by what I see, till I finally end up in the middle of *Singing in the Rain*. As ever, I am mesmerized by Cyd Charisse's sculptural legs and her tight-fitting emerald corset as she gyrates around a gawky, bespectacled Gene Kelly.

As I lie there marveling at those long, rounded, firm thighs, I feel a sort of peace come over me. I go on watching the movie with the placidity of a drowsy child. It is a quiet happiness that I have not felt for a long time. Why? I wonder. What on earth do I have to feel happy about tonight? My sister is in a cast from the waist up and will not be able to walk till God knows when, I'm still in love with my ex-wife, and I hate my job.

But the potent, peaceful feeling sweeps through me, stronger than all those negative thoughts. It wipes away the pain of the Astrid memories that keep popping back up like a jack-in-the-box, it soothes the worry about Mélanie, it erases the anger and frustration of the job issues. I lie there and surrender to it. How beautiful Charisse is with that white veil wrapped around her, arms outstretched beseechingly against the purple stage set. Her legs are so long that even when she is barefoot, they seem endless. I feel I could lie there forever, comforted by Angèle Rouvatier's musky smell and Cyd Charisse's thighs.

My phone bleeps, telling me a text message has come through. Regretfully I tear my eyes away from Charisse to pick up my phone.

Dream a little dream of me.

The phone number belonging to the text message is an unknown one. I smile. I know who this is. It can only be Angèle Rouvatier. She probably got my number from Mélanie's file, which she has access to as part of the hospital staff.

The quiet, content feeling slowly wraps itself around me like a purring cat. I want to make the most of it because somehow, somewhere, I can see that it is not going to last. It is like taking shelter in the eye of a hurricane.

No matter how hard I try, I can never prevent myself, again and again, from going back in my mind to that fateful trip when Astrid met Serge. This was four years ago. The kids had not yet entered the turbulence of adolescence. We had booked a vacation in Turkey, at the Club Med at Palmiye. This had been my idea. We usually spent most of the summer with Astrid's parents, Bibi and Jean-Luc, in their house in the Dordogne region, near Sarlat. My father and Régine had a place in the Loire Valley, a presbytery Régine had transformed into another glaringly modern horror, where we were rarely invited and seldom felt welcome.

The summers with Bibi and Jean-Luc had begun to take their toll. Despite the grandiose beauty of Black Périgord, cohabiting with my in-laws grew tough. There was something fastidious about Jean-Luc's obsession with bowel movements, consistency of stools, frugal menus, calorie counting, and perpetual exercise. Bibi put up with all this, as busy as a bee in the kitchen, her moonlike pink face dimpling, her snow-white hair tied back in a bun, indulging in happy humming and plenty of good-natured shrugs. Every morning as I drank my black, sugared coffee—"So *bad* for you!" barked Jean-Luc, "you'll be *dead* by the time you're fifty!"—and hid behind a hydrangea bush to hurriedly smoke a cigarette—"A cigarette will reduce your lifetime *by five minutes*, did you know that?"—Bibi would walk briskly around the garden entirely swathed in plastic in order to perspire as much as possible, brandishing two ski poles. This was called the Nordic walk, and as she was Swedish, I supposed it suited her, although she did look ridiculous.

My in-laws' throwback to 1960s nudity around the swimming pool and in the house had also begun to tire me. They pranced about like aging fauns, impervious to the fact that their sagging behinds inspired nothing but pity. But I had not dared bring this up with Astrid, who was also into summer nudism on a more moderate scale. The alarm went off when Arno, just twelve, mumbled something at dinner about being embarrassed having friends over to the pool because of his grandparents' flaunting their genitals. By then we had decided to spend our summers elsewhere, although we did come back to visit.

So we swapped oak-dotted, forested Dordogne, bichermuesli, and nudist in-laws for the teeming-hot, overly cheerful, and calorific Club Med. I had not noticed Serge at first. I didn't pick up any sign of danger whatsoever. Astrid went off to her aqua gym classes and tennis lessons, the kids went to the Mini Club, and I spent hours on the beach or in the sea, snoozing, swimming, tanning, or reading. I read a lot that summer, I remember, novels that Mélanie passed on from her publishing house, talented new authors, confirmed authors, foreign authors. I read them breezily, easily, not completely concentrating. Everything I did that summer, I did lazily. I should have kept my guard up. Instead, I lolled in the sun, convinced that all was right in my small world.

I think she met him on the tennis courts. They had the same teacher, a smarmy Italian who wore tight white shorts and strutted his stuff like Travolta on the dance floor. I didn't sense anything was odd till later, during a trip to Istanbul. Serge was part of our group, fifteen of us from the Club Med, with a guide, an odd Turk who was educated in Europe and spoke with a surprising Belgian accent. Dazed with heat and exhaustion, we traipsed through Topkapi, the

Blue Mosque, Saint Sophia, the ancient cisterns with the strange upside-down Medusa heads, the bazaar. Lucas was only seven and did a lot of complaining. He was the smallest child there.

What I noticed first was Astrid laughing. We were on a boat cruising up the Bosphorus, the guide pointing out the sights on the Asian bank, when I heard her laugh again and again. Serge was standing with his back to me, he had his arm around a girl, and they were all laughing together. The girl was young, fresh-faced, her hair tied back in a ponytail. "Hey, Tonio, come and meet Serge and Nadia." So I ambled over and shook hands, screwing my eyes up against the sun to be able to see his face. Nothing special about him. Smaller than I am, beefy. Unremarkable features. Except I noticed that Astrid kept looking at him. And he at her. He was there with his girlfriend, and he couldn't take his eyes off my wife. I felt like shoving him overboard.

What I also noticed, with rising anguish, was that when we got back to Palmiye, we kept bumping into him at every corner. Lo and behold, there was Serge in the hammam, there was Serge doing the customary Club Med Crazy Signs, dancing with the kids by the pool, there was Serge at the dinner table next to ours. Sometimes Nadia was there, sometimes she wasn't. "They're a modern couple," Astrid had explained. I had no idea what that meant, but I didn't like it one bit.

During the aqua gym classes, he was inevitably there, treading water next to my wife, kneading the back of her neck and shoulders during the mutual massage relaxing session at the end. There was nothing I could do to get rid of him. I began to understand with a dull hopelessness that I would have to wait till the end of our stay to see the last of him. I had no idea that their affair began just after we all returned to France. For me, Serge was an unpleasant part of our otherwise successful vacation. How blind I had been.

It was then that Astrid began to show signs of strain. She was often tired, short-tempered. We never seemed to make love anymore. She fell asleep early, cuddled up on her side of the bed, her back to me. Once or twice at night, after the kids had gone to bed, I caught her crying alone in the kitchen. She always managed to convince me that it was just sheer exhaustion or a problem at the office, nothing serious. And I believed her.

It was so easy, believing her. Not asking her any questions. Not asking myself any questions.

She was crying because she loved him and she didn't know how to tell me.

The next day, Mélanie's closest friend, Valérie, turns up with her four-year-old daughter, Léa (Mélanie's goddaughter), her husband, Marc, and their Jack Russell terrier, Rose. I had to wait outside with the child and the dog while they went in to spend some time with Mélanie. The dog is the snappy kind that cannot keep still, seems to be built on springs, and barks persistently. The little girl is just as bad, despite her angelic looks. In order to try to pacify them both, I walk them round and round the hospital, holding one on the lead and the other by the hand, much to Angèle Rouvatier's amusement as she watches me from a first-floor window. I feel a slow heat irradiate my pelvis as her eyes flicker over me. But it's hard to look sexy with a howling child and a yelping dog in tow. Rose inelegantly straddles and pees on anything she can, including the front wheel of Angèle's Harley, and Léa wants her *maman* and can't think why she has to be lumped with me in the heat of an August afternoon in some worthless place where there isn't even anywhere decent to play or any ice cream to be bought. I realize how lost I am, confronted with a child of that age. I have forgotten how tyrannical they can be, how obtuse, how noisy. I find myself longing for the nebulous silences of adolescence I have become accustomed to, which I think I know how to deal with. Why in God's name do people have children? I muse, as the combination of Léa's wails and Rose's growls is now causing nurses to open windows and glance at me with despair or disdain.

Valérie finally emerges from the building and takes over the screaming pair, much to my relief. I wait till Marc comes out and whisks Rose and Léa off for a walk, and I sit down with Valérie under the shade of a chestnut tree. The heat is worse today, the white-hot, drying-out kind that makes you long for icy, bottomless fjords. Valérie is majestic and tanned, just back from a vacation in Spain. She and Mélanie have been friends for years, through the Sainte-Marie de l'Assomption school they both went to on the rue de Lubeck. I suddenly wonder if Valérie remembers my mother. I want to ask her but don't. Valérie is a sculptor, quite well known. I find her work good, although overtly sexual and far too explicit to have hanging about a house full of kids, but I guess that's because I'm a "bourgeois, uptight boy from the sixteenth arrondissement." I can almost hear Mel's voice poking fun at me.

Valérie looks upset. In the past couple of days I have become used to Mélanie's state and have to keep reminding myself that the first time is inevitably a shock. I reach out and take her hand.

"She looks so fragile," she whispers.

"Yes," I say, "but she is looking better than she did on the first day."

"You're not hiding anything from me, are you?" she asks sharply.

"What do you mean?"

"Well, like is she going to be paralyzed—or something hideous?"

"Of course not. But the truth is, the doctor is not telling me much. I have no idea how long Mel is going to have to stay here, when she is going to be up on her feet again."

Valérie scratches the top of her head. "We saw her doctor while she was in there. Nice woman, I thought."

"Yes, she is."

She turns to look at me. "What about you, Tonio? How are you bearing up?"

I smile and shrug. "I feel like I'm in a sort of daze."

"It must have been awful, especially after such a nice weekend. I spoke to Mel on her birthday. She sounded like you were having a great time."

"Yes," I said lamely, "we were."

"I keep wondering why this happened."

She looks at me again. I don't know what to answer, so I look away.

I finally sigh. "She just drove off the road, Valérie. That's all there is to it. That's how it happened."

She puts a tanned arm around me. "Tell you what, why don't you let me stay here a couple of days. You can drive up with Marc to Paris and I'll stay and look after Mel for a while."

I toy with the idea in silence.

She goes on: "There's nothing much for you to do here for the moment. She can't be moved, so why don't you go back home, let me take over, and we'll see how it goes. You need to get back to your job, see your kids over the weekend, and then you can come back with your dad, for instance."

"I feel bad leaving her."

She scoffs. "Oh, come on. I'm her oldest, closest friend. I'm doing this for her, and for you too. For both of you."

I squeeze her arm. I pause. Then I say, "Valérie, do you remember my mother?"

"Your mother?"

"You've been friends with Mel for so long, I thought maybe you remembered her."

"We met just after she died. We were eight, I think. I do recall my parents telling me I should never ask Mel about it. But Mel showed me photos of her, letters, little things that belonged to her. And then your father remarried. And then we grew into frivolous teenagers, and we became interested in boys and all that. We didn't talk about your mother much. But I felt so sorry for both of you. You were the only children I knew whose mother had died. It made me feel guilty and sad."

Guilty and sad. I remember friends at school acting that way too. Some friends were so shocked that they couldn't talk to me normally anymore. They ignored me or blushed when I spoke to them. The headmistress had made an awkward speech, I remember, and there had been a special Mass for Clarisse. The teachers were all very nice to me for a couple of months. I became the boy whose mother died. Whispers behind my back, nudges, the thrust of chins. Look, that's him, his mother died.

I see Marc coming back with the little girl and the dog. I know I can trust Valérie to look after my sister. She explains that she has a bag with her stuff, she can stay for a couple of days, it is easy and necessary, and she wants to do it.

So I make up my mind quite quickly. I decide to leave with Marc, Rose, and Léa. I just need time to pack, tell the hotel that Valérie will be needing a room, and say goodbye to my sister, who is so happy to see her best friend that she doesn't seem upset by my taking off.

I hover outside what I believe is Angèle's office, hoping to catch her. She doesn't seem to be around. I think about what she is doing right now, what corpse she is attending to at that very moment. As I step away, I see Dr. Besson and explain to her that I will be leaving my sister in the care of a close friend and that I will soon be back.

She reassures me, tells me Mélanie will be in the best of hands, and then she has this strange sentence.

"Keep an eye out for your father."

I nod and walk away, but I can't help wondering what she means. Does she think my father looks ill? Did she notice something I didn't? I have half a mind to turn back and ask her to explain, but Marc is waiting for me and the child has already begun to make a fuss, so we take off fast, waving to Valérie's tall, comforting figure at the hospital entrance.

The drive is long and hot but miraculously quiet, as both dog and child fall asleep. Marc is the silent type. We listen to classical music and don't engage in much talking, which I feel relieved about.

The first thing I do when I get home is to fling open all the windows. The rooms are stuffy and stale. Paris has that dusty, heavy, broiling summer smell, laden with exhaust fumes and dog shit. The noisy rue Froidevaux, three floors down, spews up its incessant roar of traffic. I can never leave the windows open long, the noise is too horrendous.

The fridge is empty. I can't face the idea of a lonely meal. I call Emmanuel, get his answering machine, beg him to cross teeming-hot, jammed Paris all the way from the Marais to give me some moral support and company over dinner, which he will no doubt end up making. My phone beeps a few minutes later, and I expect a text message from Emmanuel. But no.

That's called taking French leave. When are you back?

My blood races around my chest, making me even sweatier. Angèle Rouvatier. I can't help grinning. I cradle the phone in my hand like a sentimental teenager. I text back fast:

I miss you. Will call you soon.

I immediately feel foolish. Should I have sent that? Should I have admitted I miss her? I rush down to the Monoprix on the avenue du Général Leclerc and buy wine, cheese, ham, and bread. The phone beeps again as I leave the shop. It's Emmanuel texting to say he is on his way.

As I wait for him, I choose an old Aretha Franklin CD and turn it up loud. The old lady above is stone deaf, and the couple below are still on vacation. I pour myself a glass of Chardonnay and walk through my empty apartment, humming along to "Think." My children will be turning up this weekend. I peer into their rooms. Once the divorce was in full swing, they liked the idea of having rooms in two different houses, I remember. That helped. I let them decorate each room their own special way. Lucas's walls are plastered with Jedi and Darth Vaders. Arno painted his dark blue, which looks incongruously aquatic. Margaux pinned up a poster of Marilyn Manson at his worst. I look at it only if I have to. There is another upsetting photograph of Margaux and Pauline, her best friend, both heavily made up and exhibiting their middle fingers. My cleaning lady, the energetic and talkative Mme Georges, complains about the state of Arno's room. She says she can't get the door open, there's so much stuff lying around on the floor. Margaux's is just as bad. Only Lucas makes a small effort at cleaning things up. I let them live with their mess. They spend so little time with me, and the idea of telling them to clean up again and again does not appeal to me at all. I leave that to Astrid. And to Serge.

I notice that Lucas has a family tree above his desk. I'd never seen it. I put my wineglass down to have a look. Astrid's parents, French on one side, Swedish on the other, going back to her grandparents. On our side, the Rey family, and a question mark beside my father's photograph. I realize that Lucas knows very little about my mother. I even wonder if he knows her name. What have I told my children about her? Hardly anything.

I grab a pencil on his desk and meticulously print out "Clarisse Elzyère, 1938–1974" in the little box next to "François Rey, 1937."

There are photographs of every single parent on that tree except for my mother. A strange frustration works through me.

THE DOORBELL ANNOUNCES EMMANUEL'S arrival. I am suddenly glad to see him, very glad not to be alone, and I eagerly wrap my arms around his stocky, burly body. He pats me on the back in a comforting, fatherly fashion.

I've known Emmanuel for more than ten years. We met when I refurbished his advertising company's offices with my team. He is my age, but looks older, I guess, because of his entirely bald pate. He makes up for his lack of hair with a bushy ginger beard he likes to finger. Emmanuel wears bright, outlandish colors I would never dare try, and he carries them off with a certain panache. Tonight his Ralph Lauren shirt is a tropical orange. His eyes sparkle at me, baby blue from behind his rimless glasses.

I want to tell him how happy I am that he is here, how thankful I am for his presence, but as usual, in true Rey fashion, the words fizzle out on my tongue and I keep them bottled up within me.

I grab the plastic bag he is carrying, and he follows me to the kitchen. He gets to work at once, and I watch him, offering to help although I know this is perfectly useless. He takes over the place as if it were his, and I let him.

"You still don't have a proper apron, do you?" he grumbles.

I point to Margaux's pink Mickey Mouse one hanging on a peg

near the door. She's had it since she was ten. He sighs and manages to tie it around his fleshy loins. I try not to laugh.

Emmanuel's personal life is a mystery to me. He is more or less involved with a woebegone, complicated creature called Monique who has two teenage children by a previous marriage. I'm not sure what he sees in her. And I'm pretty sure he has affairs whenever she's not around, like now, as she is still on vacation in Normandy with her kids. I can tell he's up to something, because he's whistling as he chops up the avocados and he flaunts that naughty boy expression I usually see on his face at this time of year.

Despite his extra padding, Emmanuel never seems to suffer from the heat. As I sit there sipping my wine, I feel sweat glistening at my temples and on my upper lip while he remains as cool as a cucumber. The kitchen window is open and gives onto a typically Parisian courtyard, as dark as a cave even at noon, facing the neighbor's grimy windowpane and damp kitchen cloths hanging over the ledge. Not a breath of air sneaks into the room. I hate Paris in this heat. I miss Malakoff and the small, fresh garden, the rickety table and chair under the old poplar tree. Emmanuel bustles about, complaining about my lack of good knives and a pepper grinder.

I have never been a cook. Astrid was the cook in our couple. She rustled up the most delicious, original stuff that never ceased to impress our friends. I wonder suddenly if my mother was a good cook. I have no recollection of appetizing kitchen smells at the avenue Kléber. Before our father married Régine, a governess was hired to look after the household and us. Madame Tulard. A thin, hairy-chinned woman. Watery soup. Halfhearted brussels sprouts. Leathery veal. Soggy *riz-au-lait*. Suddenly I remember piping-hot goat cheese on whole wheat bread. That came from our mother. The acrid tang of the melted cheese, the wheatlike, floury sensation of the bread, the sweet hint of fresh thyme and basil, the drop of olive oil. I remember her telling me she used to eat goat cheese as a child in the Cévennes. They had a name, those little round cheeses . . . Pélardons . . . Picadons . . .

Emmanuel asks me how Mel is doing. I tell him Valérie turned up to take over for a couple of days. I tell him I don't really know how my sister is, but I like and trust her surgeon, Bénédicte Besson, how earnest and kind she is, how she comforted me the night of the accident, how she put up with our father. He then asks how the children are, neatly producing two plates of finely chopped fresh vegetables, sliced Gouda, tangy yogurt sauce, and Italian ham. This is merely our hors d'oeuvre, as I know his robust appetite well. As we both start to eat, I tell him that my children will be turning up this weekend. I glance at him as he wolfs down his food. Like Mélanie, what does Emmanuel know about raising children? What does he know about teenagers? Nothing. Lucky man. I hide a wry smile. Try as I might, I can't imagine Emmanuel as a father.

I wait till he has finished his plate and is up again cooking our salmon. This is fast and deft. I watch him, marveling at his skill. He sprinkles dill over the fish and hands me my share and a half lemon. I then say, "Mélanie drove off the highway because something about our mother came back to her."

He looks up at me, startled. A small piece of dill is caught between his teeth. He picks at it.

"She doesn't remember anything now," I go on, eating the salmon steadily.

He eats too, his eyes on me. "But she will," he says. "You know that."

"Yes," I say. "She will. For the moment she hasn't, and I just can't stop thinking about it. It's driving me crazy."

I wait till he has finished his salmon. Then I light up a cigarette. I know he hates it, but I am, after all, in my own house.

"What do you think it was?"

"Something that upset her tremendously. Enough to lose control of the car."

I smoke in silence as he has another go at trying to dislodge the piece of dill.

"And then, I met this *woman*," I say.

His face perks up. He raises an eyebrow.

"She's a mortician."

He guffaws. "You're kidding."

I smile. "She's the sexiest thing."

He rubs his chin, eyes beaming.

"And?" he eggs me on. Emmanuel loves this sort of conversation.

"Well, she made a beeline for me. She's amazing. Magnificent."

"Blond?"

"No. Brunette. Yellowy green eyes. Great body. Great sense of humor."

"Where does she live?"

"Clisson."

"Where's that?"

"Somewhere near Nantes."

He chuckles.

"Well, you should see her again because she's done you good, my boy. You haven't looked this full of beans since—"

"Since Astrid took off."

"No, since before that. You haven't looked this good for years."

I raise my glass of Chardonnay. "Here's to Angèle Rouvatier."

Our glasses tinkle.

I think about her in that provincial hospital. I think about her slow smile and her smooth skin and the taste of her. And I want her so badly I almost burst. Emmanuel is right. I haven't felt this way in years.

On Friday afternoon I leave my office to see my father. The heat has not faded. Paris is ablaze. Tourists troop here and there, drained. Trees hang limp; dust and dirt gather in gray, billowing clouds. I decide to walk the distance from the avenue du Maine to the avenue Kléber, which should take me roughly forty-five minutes. It's too hot to cycle, and I feel like some sort of exercise.

The latest news from the hospital is good. Dr. Besson and Valérie have both called to say that Mélanie is gaining strength. (There have also been several text messages from Angèle Rouvatier, but they were of a more erotic nature, which naturally thrilled me. I have stored each and every one of them on my phone.)

As I turn left after passing the Invalides, my phone vibrates in my pocket. I glance at the number flashing up on the screen. Rabagny. I pick up, although I instantly wish I hadn't.

He doesn't even bother to greet me. He never does. He is fifteen years younger than I am, at least, and he has absolutely no respect for me whatsoever.

"I've just been to the day-care center," he barks. "And all I can say is that I am appalled by your lack of professionalism. I hired you because you had a good reputation and some people seemed impressed by your work."

I let him ramble on. This is not new. It happens nearly every time we speak to each other. I had often tried reminding him, as calmly as possible, that in France during the month of August it is impossible to get work done fast and equally difficult to expect speedy deliveries.

"I don't think the mayor is going to like the fact that the day-care center won't be ready to open at the beginning of September, as planned. Have you given any thought to this? I know you've been having family problems, but I sometimes wonder if you have not been using these problems as an excuse."

Without turning it off, I slip the phone into my shirt pocket and walk faster, gathering speed as I near the Seine. There has been a series of unfortunate mishaps concerning the day-care center: the wrong woodwork and a painter (not on my team) who didn't get the colors right. None of these events had anything to do with me. But Rabagny was impervious to that. He was out to get me. From the start he had never liked me. No matter what I did or said. I could tell just by the way he looked at me. Sometimes he stared at my shoes in a pointed manner. I wonder how much longer I am going to put up with his behavior. The job was well paid, above the usual standard. I know I have to stick it out. The question is, how?

After the place de l'Alma and hordes of tearful tourists peering down into the tunnel where Lady Di died, I begin the slow ascent on the avenue du Président-Wilson. The cars are scarcer here; it is a more residential area. My neighborhood, as a child. The quiet, placid, wealthy, uptight, gloomy sixteenth arrondissement. If you admit to a Parisian that you live in the sixteenth arrondissement, he or she at once thinks, Money. This is where the wealthy live, and this is where they flaunt it. There is old money here, and there is nouveau riche. Both cohabit with more or less grace. I don't miss the sixteenth arrondissement. I'm glad I live on the Left Bank of the Seine, in noisy, colorful, trendy Montparnasse, even if my apartment gives onto a cemetery. In the summer this district empties alarmingly. Everyone is away, in Normandy, in Brittany, on the Riviera.

As I head toward the avenue Kléber, cutting across to it via the rue de Longchamp, my childhood comes back to me, and it does not feel good. I see the quiet, earnest little boy I used to be, with my gray flannel shorts and navy blue sweater. Why, I wonder, is there something sad and sinister about these empty streets lined with regal, Haussmanian buildings? Why do I find it hard to breathe as I walk along them?

When I get to the avenue Kléber, I check my watch and find that I'm early. I pursue my walk farther, down the rue des Belles-Feuilles. I haven't been here for years. I remember a bustling, lively place. I came here often as a child. It was the shopping street. You got the freshest fish here, the juiciest meat, crisp baguettes straight from the oven. This is where my mother did her shopping every morning, wicker basket over her arm, Mel and me in tow, breathing in mouthwatering whiffs of roasting chicken and hot croissants. Today the street is deserted. A triumphant McDonald's reigns where a fine restaurant used to be, and a frozen-food store now replaces a movie theater. Most of the food stalls have been traded for chic clothing and shoe shops. The enticing smells have gone.

I get to the end of the street. If I turn left, down the rue de la Pompe, it would lead me straight to my grandmother's place on the avenue Henri-Martin. I toy with the idea of going to visit her now. Slow, gentle Gaspard would let me in, beaming, so happy to see "Monsieur Antoine." I put it off for another day and head back toward my father's.

In the mid-seventies, I remember, after our mother died, the Galerie Saint-Didier was built just beyond, an unsightly, gigantic triangle that ate up part of the exquisite *hôtels particuliers* of the area and sprouted malls and supermarkets in their wake. As I walk past, I notice that the huge construction has not aged well, its surface marred by rust and stains. I hurry along. Somebody has left two messages on my voice mail. I don't listen to them, because I know it has to be Rabagny.

MY STEPMOTHER OPENS the door and pecks me on the cheek. Régine sports a dark, toasty tan that makes her look older and more withered than she actually is. As usual, she is wearing one of her Courrèges revival outfits and exudes Chanel No. 5. She asks me how Mel is. I answer, following her into the living room. I have never liked coming back here. It is like going back in time, back to a place where I was unhappy. My body remembers it, and I can feel every part of me clenching up in self-defense. The apartment, like the Galerie Saint-Didier, has not aged well either. Its daring modernity has faded and now looks impossibly unfashionable. The maroon and gray decor, the fluffy wall-to-wall carpet have lost both brightness and texture. Everything seems scruffy, spotted.

My father comes shuffling in. I am taken aback by his wizened appearance, although I saw him barely a week ago. He looks exhausted. His lips are colorless. His skin has an odd, yellowish hue. I can hardly believe this is the formidable lawyer who had his opponents quaking as soon as he marched into the courtroom.

The infamous Vallombreux affair, in the early seventies, launched my father's career as an eminent lawyer. Edgar Vallombreux, an influential political counselor, had been found half dead in his country house near Bordeaux after a presumed suicide following a disastrous result for his party in recent elections. Paralyzed, unable to speak, depressed, he was confined to a hospital bed for the rest of his life. His wife, Marguerite, never bought the suicide story. It was clear to her that her husband had been assaulted because he was aware of fiscal indiscretions concerning a couple of highly placed ministers.

I remember when *Le Figaro* printed an entire page about François Rey, the young, impudent lawyer who dared take on the Ministry of Finance without a qualm, and who, after weeks of a palpitating trial that had the entire country holding its breath, proved that Vallombreux had indeed been the victim of a substantial financial scandal that left several heads tumbling in its aftermath. In my adolescence I was often asked if I had anything to do with "the legendary lawyer." Sometimes, embarrassed or annoyed, I used to say I didn't. Mélanie and I were kept out of our father's professional life. We had seldom seen him in action in the courtroom. We simply knew that he was respected and feared.

My father pats me on the shoulder, makes his way to the bar, and hands me a whiskey poured out with a shaking hand. I dislike whiskey, but I don't have the heart to remind him. I pretend to sip at it. He sits down with a groan and rubs his kneecaps. He is retired now and not happy about it. Younger lawyers have stepped into his shoes, and he is no longer part of the legal scene. What does he do all day long? I wonder. Does he read, see friends? Talk to his wife? I know nothing about my father's life. He knows nothing about mine. And what he thinks he knows, he disapproves of.

Joséphine appears, mumbling into the mobile phone caught between her cheek and shoulder. She smiles at me and hands me something. I glance down to see a folded five-hundred-euro bill. She winks at me and makes a sort of gesture explaining that the rest will come later.

My father talks to me, something about plumbing problems in their country house, but I don't listen. I look around the room and try to remember what it was like when my mother was still alive. There were plants by the windows; the floorboards glistened a lustrous chestnut. There were books in one corner and a chintz-covered sofa, and a desk where she used to sit and write in the morning sun. What did she write? I wonder. And where did all her stuff go? All her books, her photos, her letters? I want to ask my father, but I don't. I know I cannot. He is now complaining about the new gardener Régine hired.

No one ever talks about my mother. Especially here. She died here. Her body was carried out through that very entrance, down those red-carpeted stairs. Where did she die, exactly? I was never told. In her room, which was just beyond the entrance? Here, in the kitchen, all the way down the endless corridor? How did it happen? Who was there? Who found her?

Aneurysm. I had looked it up recently on the Internet. It happened. Like a bolt of lightning. It happened to people at any age. Just like that.

Thirty-three years ago my mother died in the very apartment I am sitting in now. I don't remember the last time I kissed her. And it hurts me, not remembering.

"Are you listening to me at all, Antoine?" asks my father sarcastically.

WHEN I GET HOME, my children are already there. I can hear the din of their presence as I toil up the stairs. Music, footsteps, loud voices. Lucas is watching TV, dirty shoes on the sofa. As I come in, he rushes up to greet me. Margaux appears in the doorway. I still can't get used to the orange hair, but I don't say anything.

"Hey, Dad . . ." she drawls.

There is a movement behind her, and I see Pauline appear over her shoulder. Her best friend since they were small. Except that Pauline now looks like a twenty-year-old. A minute ago she was a scraggy little thing. Now it is impossible not to notice her full bosom and womanly hips. I don't hug her the way I used to when she was a kid. In fact I don't even kiss her on the cheek. We sort of wave at each other from a polite distance.

"Is it okay if Pauline sleeps over?"

My heart sinks. I know that if Pauline spends the night, I will not see my daughter, except at dinner. They will then retire to Margaux's room, giggle and whisper all night long, and there will be no "quality time" with my child.

"Sure," I say halfheartedly. "Is it all right with your parents?"

Pauline shrugs. "Yeah, no problem."

She has grown even more, it seems, during the summer, looming over Margaux. She is wearing a short jean skirt and a tight purple

T-shirt. Fourteen years old. Nobody would believe it just looking at her. She probably has her period. I know Margaux has not started yet. Astrid told me not very long ago. With a body like that, Pauline attracts all sorts of men, I realize. Kids from school, and older. Guys my age. I wonder how her parents deal with those issues. What they tell her. What she knows. Maybe she has a regular boyfriend, maybe she has sex, is already on the pill. Fourteen years old.

Arno comes breezing in, clapping me on the back. His phone chimes, and he answers it, saying, "Hold on a sec." He disappears. Lucas turns to the TV and the girls take off. I am left alone in the entrance. I feel like a fool.

I go into the kitchen, my feet making a lot of noise on the creaky floorboards. There is nothing else to do but to cook them dinner. A pasta salad, with mozzarella, cherry tomatoes, fresh basil, and ham cubes. As I stand there chopping up the cheese, my life feels so empty, I almost laugh. I do. Later, when the food is ready, it seems to take ages to get them to come and sit. They all have something better to do.

"No iPods, Nintendos, or cell phones at the table, please," I say firmly, plunking the food down.

My words are greeted with shrugs and sighs. Then silence punctuated by slurps and munches as they tuck in. I look at our little group as from a distance. My first summer without Astrid. Yes, I hate every minute of it.

The evening stretches out in front of me like a parched meadow. The girls are closeted up in Margaux's room, Lucas is glued to his Nintendo, and Arno is riveted to the Internet in his own room. It was a mistake, I now realize, to have Wi-Fi installed here and computers for each of them. They revert to their personal spaces, and I end up hardly seeing them. Nobody watches TV anymore *en famille.* The Internet has taken over, silent and predatory.

I lie down on the couch and watch a DVD. A Bruce Willis action movie. At one point I press pause to call Valérie and Mélanie and to text Angèle about our next rendezvous. The evening wears on. Muffled giggles come from Margaux's room, little pings and pongs from Lucas's Nintendo, and from Arno's I can just make out the brassy beat emanating from his headphones. The heat gets to me, and I doze off.

When I open my eyes, groggy, it is nearly two in the morning. I stagger up. Lucas is fast asleep, his cheek squashing his Nintendo. I gently put him to bed, doing all I can not to wake him. I decide not to knock on Arno's door. After all, he is still on vacation, and I can't face another altercation about how late it is, that he should be asleep at this hour. As I walk to my daughter's room, the unmistakable whiff of a cigarette tickles my nose. I pause, my hand on the doorknob. More stifled laughs. I knock. The laughter ceases. Margaux opens the door. The room is hazy with smoke.

"Are you girls smoking in here?" My voice comes out strangled, almost humble, and I cringe, hearing myself.

Margaux shrugs. Pauline is flat out on the bed wearing nothing but flimsy blue panties and a frilly bra. I avert my eyes from the roundness of her breasts, which seem to leap out at me.

"Just a couple of cigarettes, Dad," says Margaux, rolling her eyes.

"But you're only fourteen," I bluster. "This is such a dumb thing to do . . ."

"Well, if it's so dumb, why do you do it, Dad?" she sneers.

She closes the door in my face.

I am left there, arms akimbo. I lift my hand to tentatively knock again. I don't. I retreat to my room and sit on my bed. What would Astrid have done in this very situation? I wonder. Shouted at her? Punished her? Threatened her? Does Margaux dare smoke under her mother's roof? Why do I feel so useless? It can't get any worse than this. Or can it?

Even in her severe blue hospital uniform, Angèle is sexy. She wraps her arms around me, heedless of the fact that we are in the hospital morgue, that corpses lurk on the other side of the door, that bereaved families sit stricken in the nearby waiting room.

Her touch electrifies me.

"When are you free?" I whisper. I haven't seen her for more than three weeks. The last time I came to see Mélanie, I was with my father, and there wasn't the slightest possibility of spending time with Angèle. My father was tired and needed to be driven back home.

She sighs. "Pileup on the highway, couple of heart attacks, one cancer, one aneurysm—everybody seems to have chosen the same time to die."

"Aneurysm . . ." I murmur.

"A young woman in her thirties."

I keep her close to me, stroking her smooth, glossy hair.

"My mother died of an aneurysm in her mid-thirties."

She looks up at me.

"You were a kid."

"Yes."

"Did you see her in death?"

"No. I closed my eyes at the last moment."

"Aneurysm deaths usually look good. This young lady is lovely in death. I hardly had to work on her."

The place where we are standing is cool, quiet, a little corridor off the waiting room.

"Have you checked on your sister yet?" she asks.

"I just arrived. She is with the nurses. I'm going back there now."

"Okay. Give me a couple of hours. I should be done by then."

She kisses me on the mouth, a warm, wet kiss. I make my way back up to Mélanie's ward. The hospital seems fuller, busier than usual. My sister's face is less pale, almost pink. Her eyes light up when she sees me.

"I can't wait to get out of here," she whispers. "They're all very nice, but I just want to go home."

"What is Dr. Besson saying?"

"She says it could be quite soon."

She asks how my week was. I grin, not quite knowing how to begin. A wretched week, in every way. Tiresome paperwork for the car insurance. Another argument with Rabagny about the day-care center. More exasperation with Florence. Our father and his aging, tired face, his short temper. A difficult weekend with the kids. School had just started and everyone was tense. Never had I felt more relieved to drop them off at Malakoff. I just tell Mélanie it was one of those crappy weeks where everything goes wrong.

I sit with her for a while. We talk about the letters she has been getting, flowers, phone calls. The old beau has sent a ruby ring from a place Vendôme jeweler. Sometimes I think she is going to talk about the crash, but she doesn't. Nothing is coming back to her yet. I need to be patient.

"I can't wait for fall, for winter." Mélanie sighs. "I hate the end of summer. I hate the heat, I hate everything about it. I can't wait for chilly winter mornings and hot-water bottles."

Dr. Besson comes in, shakes my hand. She tells us that Mélanie can be driven back to Paris by ambulance within the next weeks, probably after the middle of September. She will be allowed to convalesce in her own home for at least two months, under the care of a physiotherapist and with regular visits to her doctor.

"Your sister has been very brave," she says later, as we fill out paperwork in her office. She hands me a stack of social security papers and insurance forms. Then she looks right at me. "How is your father?"

"You think he's ill, don't you?"

She nods.

I say, "He hasn't told me or my sister what's wrong with him. I notice how tired he is, but that's all I can tell you."

"What about your mother?" she asks. "Does she know something?"

"Our mother died when we were young."

"Oh, I'm sorry," she says quickly.

"Our father is remarried. But I'm not sure what my stepmother can tell me about his health. We aren't very close."

She nods. Pauses awhile. Then says, "I just want to make sure he's under medical supervision."

"Why are you worried?"

She looks at me. Shrewd hazel irises. "I just want to make sure."

"Do you want me to talk to him?"

"Yes," she says. "Just ask him if he's been seeing his doctor."

"All right," I say. "I will."

As I make my way back to Angèle's office, I wonder what it was about my father that Dr. Besson noticed. What did her expert medical eye see that I didn't? I feel annoyed, concerned. I haven't seen my father since my last visit. Nor have I spoken to him. But I have dreamed of him in the past few weeks, as I have dreamed of my mother. Noirmoutier coming back to me, like the tide rising over the Gois passage and the gulls circling over the rescue poles. Dreams of my father, my mother, when they were young, on the beach. My mother's smile, my father's laugh. Dreams of my recent stay with

Mélanie. The night of her birthday, how beautiful she looked in her black dress. The elegant couple next to us, raising their glasses of champagne in our direction. The chef exclaiming, "Madame Rey!" Room number 9. My mother's room. Since the night of the accident, I have dreamed of Noirmoutier again and again. Noirmoutier has never left me.

HOSPITAL MORGUE, reads the sign. I knock once, then twice. No answer. I stand outside Angèle's door for a long time. I guess she isn't done yet. I go and sit in the small waiting room reserved for the bereaved. It is empty right now, and I feel relieved that I'm the only one there. Time creeps by. I check my phone. No missed calls. No voice messages. No texts.

A small noise makes me look up. A person wearing goggles, a mask, a paper skullcap, latex gloves, and light blue overalls tucked into rubber boots is standing in front of me. I rush to my feet. A gloved hand takes off the goggles and the mask. Angèle's beautiful, chiseled features appear.

"Hell of a day," she says. "Sorry I kept you waiting."

She looks tired, her face drawn.

Behind her, the door to her offices is partially open. I glance into the space I can see from here. A small blue room. Completely bare. Linoleum. Beyond that, another door, open as well. White walls, white tiled floors. Gurneys. Vials and various tools I can't make out. A strange, powerful smell floats in the air. She smells of it too. I can pick it up on her overalls. Is it the smell of death? Of formaldehyde? All I know is that this is the first time I ever smell it and the first time I smell it on her.

"Are you afraid?" she asks gently.

"No," I say.

"Do you want to go in?"

I don't hesitate. "Yes, I do."

She takes off her gloves, and the warm flesh of her hand meets mine.

"Come into Morticia's lair," she whispers. She closes the heavy door behind her. We are standing in the first room. "This is where the bodies are wheeled in so that their families can see them for the last time. The viewing room."

I try to imagine what goes on here. Was it in a place like this that Mélanie and I were shown our mother's body? It must have been. Something in my mind goes blank, and I can't imagine or remember anything. If I had seen her in death all those years ago, if I hadn't closed my eyes, it would have been in a room like this one. I follow Angèle into the larger room beyond. The odor here is stronger, almost overpowering. Like sulfur. There is a body covered with a white hospital sheet, on a gurney. The place is very clean. Pristine surfaces. Shining instruments. No stains. Light pouring through the blinds. I can hear the hum of air-conditioning. It is cooler in here, cooler than anywhere else in the hospital.

"What do you want to know?" Angèle says.

"What you can tell me."

She smiles. "Let me introduce you to this afternoon's patient."

She gently moves the sheet back from the form on the gurney. I feel myself stiffening, as I had all those years ago when the sheet was removed from my mother's body, but the face that appears is a peaceful, tranquil one. An old man with a bushy white beard. He is wearing a gray suit, a white shirt, a navy blue tie, and patent leather shoes. His hands are crossed on his chest.

"Come closer," she says. "He won't bite."

He looks asleep, but as I come near, I can see the utter stillness of death.

"This is Monsieur B. He had a heart attack. He was eighty-five."

"Did he come in looking this good?"

"When he came in, he was wearing stained pajamas, his face was crumpled up, and he was bright purple."

I flinch.

"I start by washing my patients. I take my time. I wash them from head to toe. I use this special hose here." She points to a nearby sink and faucet. "I use a sponge and detergent. While I do this, I bend and flex arms and legs, so that rigor mortis doesn't set in too fast. I close the eyes with special little caps, and I suture the mouth, but I hate that word, so I'd rather say I *close* the mouth, and sometimes I use an adhesive because it looks more natural. I hate those small-stitched mouths some morticians make. If there has been trauma to the face or body, I work on those areas with wax or other methods. Sometimes that takes a while. Then I start the embalming process. Do you know what that is?"

"Not exactly," I say truthfully.

"I inject the embalming fluid via the carotid artery. Right here." She points to Monsieur B.'s neck. "I pump it in. Slowly. And I pump the blood out from the jugular vein. Do you know what the embalming fluid does?"

"No."

"It restores natural color. It delays decomposition, at least for a while. When I pumped up Monsieur B., for instance, it took all the purple out of his face. After the arterial embalming, I use an aspirator to suck all bodily fluids away. Stomach, abdomen, heart, lungs, bladder." She pauses. "Are you okay?"

"Yes," I say, and again, I am truthful. This is the first time I've seen a dead body, apart from the shape under the sheet that was my mother. I am forty-three years old and I have never laid eyes on death. I inwardly thank Monsieur B. for looking so peachy pink and content. Did my mother look like this? I wonder.

"Then what do you do?"

"I fill all the cavities with concentrated chemicals and then I suture all incisions and orifices. That takes a while too. I won't go into details. You wouldn't like it. And then I dress my patients."

I love the way she says "my patients." They are stone dead, but they are still her patients. I notice that during the entire time she has been talking to me, her gloveless hand is on Monsieur B.'s shoulder.

"The last thing I do, which is what I was working on when you knocked, is makeup. It has to be natural. Sometimes I ask for recent photos of my patients so I can see what they looked like when they were alive. I try to stick to that."

"Has Monsieur B.'s family been to see him yet?"

She looks at her watch.

"Tomorrow. I'm very happy with Monsieur B. That's why I showed him to you. I'm less happy . . . with my other patients of the day."

"Why?" I ask.

She moves away from the gurney and stands by the window. She is silent for a while.

"Death can be very ugly. No matter what you do, no matter how hard you try, you can't get a body looking peaceful enough for the family to see it."

I shiver, thinking about what she sees every day.

"How does this not get to you?"

She turns to look at me.

"Oh, but it does." She sighs, puts the sheet back over Monsieur B.'s face. "I do this job because of my father. He committed suicide. I was thirteen years old. I'm the one who found him. I came home from school, and there he was, slumped over on the kitchen table with his brains splattered over the walls."

"Jesus," I breathe.

"My mother was in such a state that I had to make all the calls, do everything, organize the funeral. My older sister collapsed. I grew up that day. Became the tough cookie I am now. The mortician who worked on him did an incredible job. He reconstructed my father's head with wax. My mother and family could look at the body and not faint. But I was the only one who had seen my father in death. I was the only one who could compare. I was so impressed by the mortician's craft that I knew I wanted to do that later on. I passed my exam and became a mortician at twenty-two."

"Was it hard?"

"At first, yes. But I know how important it is, when you've lost someone, to be able to have a last, peaceful look at that loved one's body."

"Are there many female morticians?"

"More than you think. When I get babies, or children, the parents are relieved that I'm a woman. I guess they feel a woman will care more, will have a gentler touch, will pay more attention to detail and dignity."

She turns to me, takes my hand. Smiles that slow smile.

"Let me have a quick shower and I'll whiz you away. Let's go to my place."

We go into the adjoining office. Beyond is a white tiled bathroom.

"I won't be a minute," she says. She leaves the room.

I notice photographs on her desk. Black-and-white ones of a man in his forties. He looks so much like her, it has to be her father. The same eyes, the same chin. I sit at her desk looking at the paperwork, calendar, computer, letters. Paraphernalia. The usual clutter of a day's work. There is a small date book by her mobile phone. I feel tempted to reach out and pick it up. Leaf through it. I want to know everything about the fascinating Angèle Rouvatier. Her dates, her rendezvous, her secrets. But I don't in the end. I feel content just sitting here and waiting for her, even if I am most probably just another boyfriend she keeps dangling on a string. I can hear the shower running in the next room. Water on her bare skin. I keep thinking about my hands on that skin and that smooth body. I keep thinking about her warm, wet mouth. About what I am going to do to her when I get to her house. I think about that very precisely. I begin to get the most monumental erection. Is this fitting, I wonder, in a morgue?

For the first time in a long while I feel as if my life has brightened up at last. Like that fragile, fresh sunshine right after the rain. Like the Gois passage emerging from the receding tide.

I want to make the most of it.

In late September, Mélanie goes back home for the first time since the accident. I stand with her at the threshold of her apartment and cannot help noticing how frail and white she is. She still walks haltingly, with crutches, and I know the next weeks will be taken up with physiotherapy. She is so happy to be back home, and her smile lights up her face as she sees all her friends gathered for her return, laden with gifts and flowers.

Every time I turn up at the rue de la Roquette, she has somebody over, someone preparing tea or cooking, listening to music with her, or making her laugh. If all goes well, she tells us, she could be back at work in the spring. Whether she wants to or not is another matter. "I don't know if the publishing scene is as exciting," she admits to Valérie and me one evening over dinner. "I find reading difficult. I simply can't concentrate. I never was like that before."

The accident has changed my sister. She appears quieter, more thoughtful, less stressed. She has stopped dyeing her hair, and the silver strands shining through her dark locks suit her, giving her even greater class. A friend gave her a cat as a present, a black, golden-eyed creature called Mina.

When I'm talking to my sister, I often long to burst out with "Mel, do you remember what you were telling me just before we crashed?" But I don't dare. Her fragility still awes me. I have more or less given up waiting for her to recall what she was trying to tell me. But the thought never leaves me.

"What about your elderly, salacious admirer?" I ask her one day, teasingly, as Mina purrs on my knees.

We are in her large, bright sitting room. Rows and rows of books, pale olive walls, a large white sofa, a round marble table, a fireplace. Mélanie did wonders with this apartment. She bought it fifteen years ago, without borrowing any money from our father, when it was still a row of poky service rooms on the top floor of an unpretentious building in a then unfashionable arrondissement. She had walls knocked down, parquet floors rehabilitated, a fireplace installed. She did all this without my help or suggestions, which in those days I found rather insulting. But eventually I understood that it was Mélanie's way of standing up for herself. And I admired it.

She tosses her head. "Oh, him . . . He still writes to me and sends roses, and he even offered to take me to Venice for a long weekend. Can you imagine Venice on crutches?" We laugh. "God, when's the last time I had sex?" She looks at me blankly. "I can't even remember. Probably with him, poor old fellow." She shoots an inquisitive look in my direction. "And what about *your* sex life, Tonio? You're being most mysterious, and I haven't seen you look that perky in years."

I smile, thinking of Angèle's smooth, creamy thighs. I'm not quite sure when I will be seeing her again, but the anxious wait somehow makes it all the more exciting. We talk on the phone every day, several times a day, and there are texts and e-mails as well, and in the evenings I can see her naked on my webcam, locking myself up in my bedroom like a guilty teenager. I more or less admit to my sister that I'm having a long-distance online relationship with a terrifically sexy mortician.

"Wow," she breathes. "Eros and Thanatos. What a Freudian brew. When can I meet this lady?"

I say I don't even know when I will be seeing her properly again. After a while, the webcam excitement will wear off, I am sure, and

I will need to touch her in the flesh, to have her. To really have her. I don't say this to Mélanie in those exact terms, but she gets my drift.

Later, in a particularly bold text message, I admit this to Angèle. I get an instantaneous text message from her with the schedule of the next train from Montparnasse to Nantes. I can't make that train because of an important meeting for a new contract. Bank offices to be built in the twelfth arrondissement, near Bercy. Another tedious job, but yet again nothing I can afford to turn down.

My yearning for Angèle thrives day after day. The next time I see her, I know it will be like fireworks. And just thinking about that keeps me going.

DOWN IN MY CELLAR one evening in October, I come across a treasure. I am looking for a good bottle of wine to offer to Hélène, Emmanuel, and Didier at dinner, something they'd like and remember. But instead of coming back up with a bottle of Croizet-Bages, I triumphantly traipse upstairs with an old photo album. I didn't even remember that I had it. It was stuck in a cardboard box I hadn't bothered to open since the divorce, lost in a heap of report cards, maps, crumpled pillowcases, and moldy Disney beach towels. I fell upon it. How has this ended up in my possession, and how is it that I had no recollection of it? Old black-and-white photographs of Mélanie and me. My first Communion. Seven years old. Long white robe. Serious face. New watch on my proud wrist. Mélanie at four, plump cheeks and frilly smocked dress. The get-together at the avenue Henri-Martin apartment. Champagne, orange juice, and *macarons* from the nearby tearoom Carette. My grandparents gazing down at me benignly. Solange. My father. My mother. I have to sit down. There she is. Dark hair. Lovely smile. Her hand on my shoulder. So young. She had only three more years to live. It is difficult to believe, looking at that photograph. She is the very image of youth.

I turn the pages slowly, taking care not to get cigarette ash on them. They are musty from their stay in the cellar. Noirmoutier. The last summer, 1973. My mother must have stuck all these photos into this album, I realize. This is her handwriting, round and childish. I can almost see her, sitting at her desk at avenue Kléber, bent over the pages, concentrating. Glue and scissors. The special pen that wrote on black paper. Mélanie standing on the Gois at low tide with her shovel and pail. Solange smoking a cigarette and posing on the pier. Did my mother take these photos? Did she have a camera? I can't remember. Mélanie on the pier at the beach. Me in front of the casino. My father basking in the sun. All of us on the hotel terrace. Who took that one? I wonder. Bernadette? Another waitress? The perfect Rey family at their very best.

I close the album. As I do so, something white comes fluttering out of it. I bend to the floor to pick it up. It is an old boarding pass. I stare at it, perplexed. A flight to Biarritz back in the spring of 1989. In Astrid's maiden name. Of course. This is the flight I'd met Astrid on. She was attending a friend's wedding and I was renovating offices in a new mall for the architect I worked for. I remember being secretly thrilled that such a pretty young woman was seated next to me.

She had a wholesome, outdoor Scandinavian look that immediately appealed to me. This was not your manicured, mincing Parisian. During the flight I racked my brains for something to say, but she had a Walkman clamped to her ears and appeared to be riveted by *Elle* magazine. The landing became suddenly atrociously bumpy. It seemed we had arrived in the Basque country as the mother of all storms was brewing. The pilot attempted to land the plane twice before backing off each time, engines whining and shuddering. Winds howled around us, and the sky blackened to an inky dusk although it was only two in the afternoon. Astrid and I exchanged apprehensive smiles. The plane wobbled to and fro, wrenching our guts mercilessly with each swoop.

The bearded man sitting across the aisle seemed to have turned green. With a neat gesture he reached for the paper bag tucked into the seat pocket, opened it deftly, and, with a monstrous, greasy belch, threw up into it for what seemed to be an eternity. A sour stench of garlic and vomit wafted toward Astrid and me. She glanced at me helplessly. I could tell she was scared. I was not. What frightened me was not the chance that we might crash, but that I might spew my *spaghetti bolognaise* over this beautiful girl's knees. All we could hear was the sound of passengers being sick. As the plane spun dizzyingly round and round and I fought with all my might not to look at the bearded man, who had now filled a second bag with purple puke, her trembling hand came creeping into mine.

That was how I met my wife. And the fact that she had kept that ticket for all those years warmed my heart. The fifteen years between my mother's death and Astrid seem like a blur, a drive down a dark tunnel. I don't like thinking about those years. I was like a field horse with blinders, overcome by a frozen loneliness that ate at me, that I could not get rid of. Once I left the avenue Kléber and went to live on the Left Bank with two fellow students, my existence seemed slightly less dreary. There had been a girlfriend or two, trips abroad, discovering Asia, America. But when Astrid came into my life, all of a sudden there was light. And happiness. And laughter. And joy.

When my marriage broke down, when it finally hit me that Astrid no longer loved me, that she loved him, Serge, the bottom fell out of my world. I was back in the long, dark tunnel. Fragments of my life with Astrid came whirling back to me in my dreams and during the day. As we moved relentlessly toward the divorce, I incredulous, she determined, I frantically grasped at every memory I had to keep me going. One kept coming back to haunt me. Our first trip together as a couple. San Francisco. We were all of twenty-six, the year before Arno was born. We were young and carefree, as they say. Madly in love. There is a flock of memories I can conjure from that trip—driving across the Golden Gate in a convertible with Astrid's hair blowing into my face, the little hotel in Pacific Heights where we made love with mad frenzy, the riotous rides in cable cars.

But it is Alcatraz that comes back to me. We had taken a boat to visit the island and were given a guided tour. You could glimpse the city in all its glittering, hilly glory, barely three kilometers away, across cold and treacherous water. So close, yet so far away. Because the sun came pouring through the windows, the cells on "Seedy Block" were the desirable ones. The prisoners preferred being on this side, explained the guide. These cells were warmer, less chilly, even on cold winter nights. And on some nights, he went on, like on New Year's Eve, for instance, if the wind was coming from the right direction, the prisoners could hear the sound of parties drifting in from the St. Francis Yacht Club across the bay.

For a long time I have felt like an Alcatraz inmate, desperately feeding on the scraps the wind sends my way—laughter, singing, and music, the hubbub of a crowd I can hear but will never see.

AFTERNOON OF A DREARY November day. Four weeks to Christmas. Paris is decked out in scintillating tinsel, like a gaudy courtesan. I am sitting at my desk, working on a complicated layout for the Bercy bank offices for the fifth time that morning. I keep having to reprint it. The printer makes a moaning noise like a woman in labor. Florence has a cold. I still have not had the heart to fire her. There is something profoundly pitiful about her. Today, she never seems to stop blowing her nose. Every time she does so, she thrusts sturdy Kleenex-covered index fingers up her nostrils and rotates them like propellers. I itch to reach out and swipe her across the face.

The past two months have been a whirlwind of conflicts and fights. Arno is in serious trouble at school. Astrid and I have been called in twice to talk with the teachers. If he goes on like this, we are warned, he will not only be held back, he'll be expelled. Low grades, insolence, vandalization of school property, cutting class—we discover to our horror the extent of Arno's dark deeds. How did our charming, easygoing son morph into this rebellious thug? As quiet as her brother is boisterous, Margaux is wrapped up in a cool world of silence and contempt. She hardly talks to us, wears her iPod day in and day out. The only way to communicate with her is to send her a text message, even if she is in the next room. Only Lucas remains reasonably agreeable. For the moment.

The only positive news around me right now, beside Angèle, is Mélanie's speedy recovery. She now walks at a normal pace, with no hesitation, and regular exercise and physiotherapy have given her the extra strength she lacked. Getting back to work is not her priority. I guess she is making the most of her sick leave. She finally did go to Venice with the old beau, but there are new, younger men around her who seem never to stop taking her out to dinner, concerts, and openings.

I turn my back to the plastic Christmas tree squatting in the entrance, flashing green and red lights. Our second Christmas as a divorced couple is coming up. Astrid is in Tokyo with Serge, who has an "important sushi shoot" (the expression made Emmanuel hoot with laughter) for a glossy food catalog. She won't be back for another week. The children are spending the entire week with me, and so far their stay has been a grueling one.

My mobile phone buzzes. Mélanie. We stay awhile on the phone, reviewing Christmas presents, who needs what, who would like what. We discuss our father. We both are convinced that he is ill in some sort of way, but he's not telling us anything. When confronted, Régine replies flatly that she knows nothing. I once tried to get something out of Joséphine, but she admitted sheepishly that she hadn't even noticed our father was looking that bad.

Mélanie teases me about Angèle. "Your Morticia" she calls her. I've already admitted to Mel, not that I have anything to hide, that this woman is what keeps me going right now. Even if I've managed to see her only a couple of times since the summer, Angèle is a new energy in my life. Yes, she is exasperatingly independent, yes, she probably sees other men, yes, she sees me only when she wants to, but she keeps my mind off my ex-wife. She has resuscitated my manhood in every sense of the word. All my friends have noticed a change. Since Angèle Rouvatier has waltzed into my life, I've lost weight, I'm cheerful, I've stopped complaining. I'm more careful about my clothes. I like my shirts very white, very crisp, my jeans, black now, like hers, perfectly cut. I wear a long black coat that Arno finds "cool" and that even Margaux looks upon with approval. And every morning I splash on the eau de cologne Angèle gave me, a zesty Italian fragrance that always makes me think of her, of us.

During my long conversation with Mel, a beep goes off in my phone. Call-waiting. I quip, "Hold on!" and glance at the screen. It is Margaux's number. Margaux calls me so rarely that I tell my sister I need to take this call and I'll get back to her later.

"Hi, this is your dad!" I say breezily to my daughter.

The only thing I hear in return is silence.

"You there, Margaux?"

A strangled sob. My heart starts to pump.

"Honey, what is it?"

Florence's inquisitive, ferretlike face turns to me. I get up, walk briskly to the entrance of the office.

"Dad . . ."

Margaux seems to be miles away. Her voice is faint.

"Speak up, sweetie!"

"Dad!" Now she is screaming. The sound of it rips through my skull.

"What is it?"

My fingers tremble so much I almost drop the phone.

She is sobbing, the words tumbling out helter-skelter. I can't make heads or tails of them. I say, "Margaux, honey, please calm down, I can't understand you!"

Behind me, floorboards groan as Florence stealthily moves forward, not wanting to miss a word of this. I swivel around, confronting her with a glacial look. She freezes in midstep and cowers back to her desk.

"Margaux, talk to me. Please!"

I retreat to the entrance, finding shelter behind a large storage closet.

"Pauline is dead."

"What?" I gasp.

"Pauline died."

"But how?" I stutter. "Where are you? What happened?"

Her voice is flat now, devoid of all emotion.

"It happened during gym class just after lunch. She collapsed."

My mind races. I feel helpless, confused. I scramble back to my desk, grab my coat, my scarf, my keys.

"Are you still at the gym?"

"No. We're back at school. They took Pauline to the hospital. But it's too late."

"Have they called Patrick and Suzanne?"

"I guess so."

I almost wish she would start crying again. I can't stand her robotic voice. I tell her I will be right there. I don't look at Florence as I rush out. I run to the school in a frantic daze.

In the back of my mind, I think, with utmost dread, *Astrid is not here, Astrid is away, you are going to have to deal with this alone—you, the father, you, Daddy. You, the guy your daughter has hardly talked to for the past month, you, the guy she won't even look at.*

I don't feel the cold. I run as fast as I can. My legs are like lead. My breath billows around me. My tar-filled lungs throb. Port Royal is twenty minutes away. When I get to the school, there are groups of teenagers and adults standing outside the building. Everybody has bleary, puffy eyes, upset expressions. I finally see Margaux. Her face is ashen, glistening with tears. People are queuing up to hug her, to cry with her, and at first I wonder why. Then it hits me. She was Pauline's best friend. They've been going to this school since they were toddlers. That means more than ten years. Ten years in a fourteen-year-old life. A couple of teachers I know come up to talk to me. I mutter something, making my way through the crowd to my daughter. When I get to her, when I take her in my arms, she feels waiflike and fragile. I haven't hugged her for such a long time.

"What do you want to do?" I ask her.

"I want to go home," she replies very quietly.

I assume that given the circumstances, classes have been canceled. It is already four o'clock and dusk is setting in. She says goodbye to her friends, and we trudge along the avenue de l'Observatoire. The traffic is noisy, horns blaring, engines rumbling, but between us is only silence. What can I say to her? The words aren't coming. I can only wrap my arm around her and hold her tight as we walk on. I suddenly notice that she is burdened with a couple of different bags. I try to pry one from her, to ease her load, but she savagely hisses, "No!" She hands another one to me, one I recognize, her familiar battered Eastpak. She holds on to the other one for dear life. It must be Pauline's.

We pass the Saint-Vincent de Paul Hospital. This is where my children were born. And Pauline too. Pauline was born here fourteen years ago. That was how we met Patrick and Suzanne, as the girls were born two days apart. Astrid and Suzanne were in the same ward. When I first laid eyes on Pauline, it was in this very hospital, in the small plastic crib next to my daughter's.

Pauline is dead. I cannot take it in. The words make no sense. I want to make sure, I want to bombard Margaux with questions, but her haggard face puts me off. We walk on. It's getting darker. It is freezing. The way back seems endless. I finally glimpse the enormous bronze rump of the Denfert-Rochereau lion. Only a few minutes now.

As soon as we walk into the apartment, I make tea. Margaux sits on the sofa, her face in her hands, Pauline's bag on her lap. When she glances up at me as I come in with the tray, she has the hard, closed face of an adult. I place the tray down on the coffee table, pour out a mug for her, add milk and sugar, hand it to her. She takes it in silence. I fight the strong need for a cigarette. I could do with one, but it seems wrong to smoke now.

"Can you tell me what happened?"

She sips slowly. Then she says in a low, tense voice, "No."

Suddenly the cup clatters to the floor, making me jump, spilling milky tea into a star-shaped stain. Margaux chokes, and tears well up. I draw her to me, but she pushes me away furiously. Never have I seen her so angry, her features contorted, crimson, swollen with rage. She screams at the top of her voice, spitting specks of saliva into my face.

"Why did this happen, Dad? Why Pauline? She was only fourteen!"

I don't know how to calm her. No soothing words come to my lips. I feel useless. Nothing comes to mind. I am stranded, lost. What can I say to my daughter? How can I be of any help? Why don't I know how? If only Astrid were here, I think. She would know what to do, what to say. Mothers always know. Fathers don't. At least not this one.

"Let's call your mother," I mumble ineffectually, trying to calculate the time difference with Japan. "Why don't we give her a call."

My daughter stares at me with disdain. She stands facing me, clutching Pauline's bag to her.

"Is that all you can come up with?'" she whispers, outraged. *"Let's call your mother?* Is this how you think you are helping me right now?"

"Margaux, please . . ." I mumble.

"You're pathetic," she hisses. "This is the worst day of my life. And you don't even know how to fucking help me. I hate you. I hate you."

She turns away and strides into her room. The door slams shut. Her words bite into me. They sting. I don't care what time it is in Japan. I go and find the piece of paper with the hotel number in Tokyo. I dial the number with fumbling fingers. *I hate you. I hate you.* I can't get those words out of my head.

The front door bangs, and the boys walk in, Arno on his phone, as usual. Lucas starts to say something to me as the hotel picks up in Tokyo. I raise my hand to silence him. I ask for Astrid, using her maiden name, then suddenly remember that she is registered under Serge's name. The receptionist informs me flatly that it is nearly one a.m. local time. I say it is an emergency. The boys glance at me, surprised. Serge's droning voice comes on. He starts to complain about being woken up, but I snap at him and ask for Astrid. Then her voice, thin with alarm.

"What is it, Antoine?"

"Pauline is dead."

"What?" she breathes, all those miles away.

The boys stare at me, horrified.

"I don't know what happened. Margaux is in shock. Pauline collapsed during gym class. I only just found out. "

Silence. I imagine her sitting up in the bed, her hair tousled, him beside her, one of those high-tech, sleek hotel rooms in a skyscraper, the ultramodern bathroom, the view, the blackness of the middle of the night. The "sushi" catalog laid out on a large table with his photo gear. An open computer. A spiraling screen saver glowing in the dark.

"Are you there?" I say as the silence stretches on.

"Yes," she finally replies, calm, almost cold. "Can I speak to Margaux?"

The boys, openmouthed and gawky, stumble back to let me pass, phone in hand. I knock on my daughter's closed door. No answer.

"It's your mother."

The door opens a crack as the phone is plucked from my hand, then slams shut again. I make out a stifled sob, Margaux's fearful voice. I go back to the living room, where the boys await me, petrified. Lucas has gone white. He is fighting back tears.

"Dad," he murmurs, "why did Pauline die?"

Before I can answer him, my mobile phone buzzes. Patrick's number shows up. Pauline's father. With a sinking heart I take the call. My mouth goes dry. I've known this man ever since the day his daughter was born. For the past fourteen years we have had endless conversations about kindergartens, schools, vacations, trips, bad teachers, good ones, who picks up who and when, Disneyland, birthday parties, slumber parties, summer camps. I can only utter his name as I press the phone to my ear.

"Hi, Antoine . . ." His voice is exhausted, barely audible. "Listen . . ." He sighs. I wonder where he is. Probably still at the hospital. "I need your help."

"Yes, of course! Anything . . ."

"I think Margaux has Pauline's stuff. Her schoolbag and her clothes."

"That's right. What do you want me to do?"

"Just hang on to them. Pauline . . . has her ID card, keys, and her phone in there. Her wallet—I guess. Just hang on to them, okay? Just keep them, for the moment . . ."

His voice breaks. His tears immediately bring out the wet in my own eyes.

"God, Patrick—" I blurt out.

"I know. I know," he says, fighting to keep the tremor out of his voice. "Thank you. Thank you, pal."

He hangs up abruptly.

Tears gush. Huge, fat tears. There is no way I can hold them back. It is odd because there are no sobs, no hiccuping, as when I cried the night of the accident. Just a thick stream of tears pouring out of me.

Very slowly I set the phone down, collapse onto the sofa, my face in my hands. My sons stand there for a moment, unsure of what to do. Lucas comes to me first, pushing his head under my arms to fit against me, his wet cheeks slippery against mine. Arno lands at my feet, his bony arms encircling my calves.

This is the first time in their lives my boys have ever seen me cry. It's too late now. I can't stop it. I give in to it.

We stay like that for a long time.

PAULINE'S BAG IS IN the entrance, a pile of clothes neatly folded next to it. My eyes turn back to the bag and the clothes again and again. It is late, two or three in the morning. The night feels like a bottomless pit. I am emptied of all tears. Dried out. I have smoked half a pack. My face is a puffy mess. My limbs ache. But the thought of going to bed scares me.

Margaux's light is still on. I can hear regular breathing when I stick my ear to her door. She has passed out. The boys have too. The apartment is silent. There is hardly any traffic on the rue Froidevaux. I try not to look at the bag, but it seems to be calling out to me. After a while I give in. I tiptoe over to it, pick it up gingerly. I sit down, the bag and clothes on my lap. How is this possible? I wonder. Pauline is dead. And yet her stuff is here, on my lap. I zip the bag open. Fish around. A hairbrush. Long blond hairs still trapped in it. Pauline is dead, and strands of her hair are right here, shimmering between my fingers. I cannot understand it. Her phone is on silent mode. Thirty-two missed calls. Had her friends called her phone today just to hear her voice? Maybe I would have done just the same if my best friend had died. Schoolbooks. Neat handwriting. She was a good student. Better than Margaux. She wanted to be a doctor. Patrick was proud of that. Fourteen years old, and she already knew what she wanted to do. Her wallet. A purple diamanté affair. ID card. It was two years old. The photo was the Pauline I knew. The skinny kid I used to play hide-and-seek with. Makeup, lip gloss, a deodorant. Her date book. Homework for the next two weeks. I flip the pages. "Dallad on Sunday." A pink heart. Dallad was Margaux's nickname. Pauline was Pitou. Ever since they were small. Her clothes. The ones she had taken off to put her sport gear on. A white sweater and jeans. I put the sweater gently to my face. A mixture of cigarette smoke and fruity perfume. Pauline is dead, and her smell is still on that sweater.

I think of Patrick and Suzanne. Where are they now? With their daughter's body? At home, where no sleep will come? Could Pauline have been saved? Perhaps she had a heart condition. Did anyone know? If she hadn't been playing basketball, would she still be alive? The questions run round and round in my head. I feel a horrible panic grow. Getting up, I go to the window, wrench it open, letting the icy air seep through me. The cemetery stretches out in front of me, vast and dark. I keep thinking of Pauline, her dead body. Her braces. What will they do about her braces? Will she be buried with them? Will some dentist need to pry them out? Or is that a mortician's job? My hand reaches out to grab my phone. I need to talk. I need to talk to Angèle.

A couple of rings, and she picks up. Warm, sleepy voice.

"Hello there, Monsieur Parisian. Are you that lonely?"

I am so relieved to hear her voice in the middle of the night, at this abominable moment, that I nearly cry out. I tell her quickly what happened.

"Ouch," she says. "Your poor daughter. She saw her friend die. That's bad. How is she doing?"

"Not so good," I admit.

"And your wife is not there, right?"

"Yes."

Silence.

"Do you want me to come?"

This is so blunt that I gasp.

"Would you?"

"If you want me to."

Of course, yes, of course, please come, do come, get onto that Harley right now and drive like a bat out of hell, yes, please, please come, Angèle, I need you, come. Come! What would she think of me if I said that, if I beseeched her to come right now? Would she find me weak? Would she pity me? Does she pity me?

"I wouldn't want to be a pain. It's such a long drive."

She sighs. "You men. You just can't say things outright, can you? I'll come if you need me. Just let me know. Bye now. Early start tomorrow."

She hangs up. I feel like calling her back, but I don't. I tuck the phone into my pocket and lie back on the sofa. I finally doze off. When I wake up, the boys are making their breakfast. I glance in the mirror. I look like a rumpled cross between Mr. Magoo and Boris Yeltsin. Margaux is already in the bathroom and will probably stay there for a while. I hear the shower running.

As I pass in front of her room, I glance in. Her bedsheets are thrown back. Strange, I think, new sheets. I have never seen these before. Large red flowers. I come closer. These are not large red flowers. They are bloodstains. Margaux has had her period during the night. And from what Astrid has told me, this is her first time.

Is she all right? Is she shocked? How does she feel? Is she afraid, relieved, disgusted, embarrassed, in pain, all of these things? Margaux has her period. My little girl. She can have babies. She is ovulating. Producing eggs. I don't know if I like the thought of it. I don't know if I'm ready for it. But Astrid is not here, and I need to take this in my stride. Of course I knew my daughter would have her period one day. But I believed, in a cowardly and obscure fashion, that this was Astrid's feminine realm, not anything to do with me. How on earth do fathers deal with this? What I am supposed to do? Let her know that I know? That I'm proud? That I'm here to help, if she needs me, with a sort of burly John Wayne swagger, because, yes, of course, I know all about tampons (with or without applicators) and sanitary pads (light and heavy flow) and the throes of PMS. I'm a modern man, right? How can I talk to my daughter about her period? Especially today, after what happened last night. It seems impossible. The only thing that jumps to mind is calling Mélanie. I have no memory about Mel's period and how old she was when she got it, but in Astrid's absence, she is the only feminine ally I can think of.

I hear the bathroom bolt unlock and furtively step out of her room. Margaux appears, her hair gathered up in a towel. Purple circles under her eyes. She mumbles good morning and brushes past me. I reach out and graze her shoulder. She moves away.

"How are you, sweetie?" I ask tentatively. "How—are you feeling?"

She shrugs. The door closes with a loud click. Does she know what to do? I wonder. About her period. Sanitary pads and tampons. Of course she does. Astrid probably explained all this to her, her friends did. Pauline probably did. I go and make myself a coffee. The boys are on their way to school. They both hug me clumsily. As they leave, the doorbell rings.

It is Suzanne, Pauline's mother. There is a painful, emotional moment as we face each other on the doorstep. Her hands find mine as the boys peck her cheeks and slip away, overwhelmed.

Her face is bloated, her eyes little slits. Yet she bravely smiles at me. I take her into my arms. She smells of the hospital, of pain, of fear, of loss. We stand together, rocking slowly. She is a small woman. Her daughter used to tower above her. She looks up at me. Watery irises.

"I could do with some coffee."

"Sure! Right away."

I lead her into the kitchen. She sits down, taking off her coat and scarf. I pour out a cup for her, my hands unsteady. I sit down to face her.

"I'm here for you, Suzanne" is all I can come up with.

But she seems to like that, however feeble it must sound, for she nods and takes a trembling sip of the coffee. She says, "I keep thinking I'm going to wake up. That this thing is just a nightmare."

"Yes," I say softly.

She is wearing a green cardigan. White blouse. Black trousers. Low-cut boots. Was she wearing those clothes when they called her yesterday to tell her her daughter was dead? What was she doing when they called her? Was she at her office? In her car? What did she think when she saw the school's number show up—that Pauline had cut class, or that there had been a problem with a teacher? I want to tell her how ghastly I have felt since Margaux's call.

I want to express all my sympathy, all my sadness, all my wretchedness, yet nothing comes out. I can only take her hand and hold on to it for dear life. That's all I can do.

"The funeral is on Tuesday. Out in the country. At Tilly. Where my dad is buried."

"We'll be there. Of course."

"Thank you," she murmurs. "I came by to pick up Pauline's things. Her bag, I think, and some clothes."

"It's all here."

As I get up to fetch the bag and clothes, Margaux comes in. She sees Suzanne, and with a sharp little yelp that hurts me, she flings herself on Suzanne, burying her head in her shoulder, sobs racking her slim frame. I watch Suzanne comfort her, patting her hair. Margaux cries, and words come gushing out, the words she wouldn't say to me yesterday.

"We were in gym class, like every Thursday. We were playing basketball. Pitou sort of crumpled up on the floor. When the teacher turned her over, I knew. Her eyes had rolled up. You could only see the whites. The teacher tried to resuscitate her, did all the stuff you see on TV. It lasted forever. Somebody called an ambulance. But by the time they got there, it was over."

"There was no pain," Suzanne whispers, stroking Margaux's damp hair. "She felt no pain. It was over in seconds. The doctors told me."

"Why did she die?" asks Margaux simply, leaning back on her heels to look up at Suzanne.

"They believe there was a problem with Pauline's heart. A problem that none of us knew about. Her little brother is being tested this week to find out if he has the same problem."

"I want to see her," says Margaux. "I want to say goodbye to her."

Suzanne's eyes meet mine.

"Don't stop me, Dad," Margaux says quickly, not looking at me. "I want to see her."

"I'm not stopping you, sweetie. I understand."

Suzanne finishes her coffee. "Of course you can see her. She is still at the hospital. I can take you there, or your mother can later."

"My mother is in Japan," says Margaux.

"Your father can take you," says Suzanne, getting up. "I have to go now. So many things to do. Paperwork. The funeral. I want it to be a lovely funeral." She pauses and bites her lip. Her mouth twitches. "For my lovely daughter."

She quickly turns away, but I see her face crumble. She scoops up the bag and clothes and heads out. When she gets to the door, she squares her shoulders, like a soldier getting ready for battle. My admiration for her is immense.

"See you later," she whispers, not looking up, opening the front door and fumbling with the handle.

I SEEM TO BE spending a lot of time in hospital morgues, I reflect, as Margaux and I wait at la Pitié-Salpêtrière to see Pauline's body. This Parisian one is a tenebrous, depressing affair compared with the luminous place Angèle works in. No windows, the paint is flaking, the linoleum scratched, and no effort seems to have been made to cheer up the room. We are alone, and the only sounds we hear are footsteps clicking up and down the corridor and the murmur of low voices. The mortician is a portly man in his forties. He offers no words of condolence, not even a smile. He probably deals with so many deaths that he has become blasé. Even a fourteen-year-old dying of heart failure means little to him, I guess. But I am wrong. When he comes back to get us, he leans toward Margaux and says, "Your friend is ready. Are you going to be all right, miss?"

Margaux nods, her chin set.

"It's not easy seeing someone you love dead. Maybe your dad should come with you."

My daughter looks up at him, taking in his bad, florid skin.

"She was my best friend, and I saw her die," she says in a clenched, tight voice.

She will be saying that sentence for the rest of her life. The mortician nods.

"Your father and I will be just behind the door in case you need us, okay?"

She stands up, smoothing out her clothes, her hair. Her face once again looks years older. I want to hold her back, to protect her, to wrap her up in my arms. Will she be all right? Will she be strong enough? Will she collapse? Will this damage her forever? I fight the urge to grab her sleeve.

The mortician leads her to the next room, opens the door for her, and lets her in.

Suzanne and Patrick appear with their son. We hug and kiss in silence. The little boy is pale, tired. We wait some more.

Then Margaux's voice is heard. She says my name. Not Dad, but Antoine. She has never called me that before. She says my name twice.

I enter the room. It has the same proportions as the one in Angèle's hospital. I recognize the familiar, dominant smell. I allow my eyes to flicker toward the body laid out in front of us. Pauline seems very young. I come closer. So young, so frail. The shapely body appears to have shrunk. She is wearing a pink blouse and jeans. Converse sneakers. Her hands are crossed on her stomach. I glance finally at her face. No makeup. White, pure skin. Her blond hair combed back simply. Her closed mouth has a natural look to it. Angèle would approve.

Margaux hovers near me. I put my hand on the back of her head, as I did when she was small. She doesn't shrug me off the way she has been doing lately.

"This is something I don't understand," she says.

She slips out of the room. I stand in front of Pauline's body, alone. Astrid will not see this. She is still in Tokyo, flying back for the funeral on Tuesday. Serge and she could not change their reservations at the last minute. The last time she saw Pauline was probably at Malakoff, a week or so ago. When Astrid lands, Pauline will be in her coffin, ready for burial. She will never lay eyes on Pauline in death.

I don't know whether this is better for her or not. I have never faced this sort of situation with my ex-wife.

As I stand here, I think of my father. Like Pauline, my mother died in a couple of minutes. Had my father stood like this in the hospital morgue, contemplating his wife's body, trying to cope? Where was he when he was told his wife had died? Who had called him? No mobile phones in 1974. He was most likely at his office, which in those days was near the Champs-Élysées.

I stare at the dead face in front of me. So young. So fresh. Fourteen years old. I put my hand on her head, gently. Compared with Margaux's head, Margaux's living warmth, Pauline is stone-cold. I have never touched a dead person in my life. I leave my hand there. Goodbye, Pauline. Goodbye, little one.

The dread that I felt last night while I was holding Pauline's bag engulfs me. Her colorless face suddenly seems to melt into Margaux's face. I shiver. This could be my dead daughter. I could be looking at my daughter's dead body. Touching her corpse. I try to stop myself from trembling. I wish Angèle were by my side. I think of the comfort she could give me now, her common sense, her inner knowledge of death. I try to imagine that it was Angèle who tended to Pauline's body, with the care and respect I know she gives her "patients."

A hand on my shoulder. Patrick. He says nothing. We both stand there and look down at Pauline. He can feel me trembling. He squeezes my shoulder, in silence. I go on shaking and think of everything Pauline could have become. Everything that was in store for her that she will never know, that we will never know. Her studies. Traveling. Boyfriends. Independence. Her career. Love. Motherhood. Middle age. Growing old. Her entire life. What lay ahead and what is no more.

The dread in me abates, and anger takes over. Fourteen years old. For the love of God, fourteen years old. Why do these things happen? And when they do, how on earth do you pick yourself up and move on? Where do you find the courage, the strength? Is religion the answer? Is that where Patrick and Suzanne find solace? Is that what is helping them now?

"Suzanne dressed her. Alone. She didn't want anyone else to do it," says Patrick. "We chose her clothes together. Her favorite jeans, her favorite blouse."

He reaches out and softly strokes his daughter's cold cheek. I look at the pink blouse. The image of Suzanne's fingers painstakingly doing up that long line of buttons against Pauline's lifeless skin comes to me and weighs down on me with all its horrific might.

MARGAUX NEEDS TO BE with Suzanne and Patrick. I guess it's her way of staying close to Pauline. As I leave la Pitié, I check my phone. There is a voice message from my sister. "*Call me, urgent.*" I find Mélanie's voice strangely quiet, but I am so upset by what I have just seen, Pauline's body, that I don't mention it when I first get her on the phone. I then tell her hurriedly about Pauline's death, Margaux, the horror of it all. Astrid's absence. Margaux's period. Pauline's body. Patrick and Suzanne. Suzanne dressing Pauline—

"Antoine," says Mélanie pointedly, interrupting me. "Listen."

"What?" I say almost impatiently.

"I need to talk to you. You need to come now."

"I can't. I'm about to head back to the office."

"You have to come."

"Why? What's up?"

A short silence.

"Because I've remembered. I remembered why I had the accident."

A bizarre apprehension plucks at my heart. I've been waiting for this moment for the past three months. It is now here, it is at last here, and I don't know if I can face it. I don't know if I am strong enough. Pauline's death has drained me.

"Okay," I say weakly. "I'll be right over."

The ride from la Pitié to Bastille is a slow one, even though I am not far from Mel's place. The traffic inches on. I try to remain calm behind the wheel. I then spend ages looking for a parking place on busy rue de la Roquette. Mélanie is waiting for me with the cat in her arms.

"I'm so sorry about Pauline," she says, kissing me. "How awful it must be for Margaux . . . This is the worst timing . . . It's just that . . . It has come back to me. This morning. And I had to tell you."

The cat jumps down to come and rub itself against my legs.

"I don't know how to say this," she says simply. "I think it will be a shock to you."

"Try me."

We sit face-to-face. Her delicate fingers play with the bracelets around her wrist. A clicking sound that gets on my nerves.

"During our last night at the hotel, I woke up. I was thirsty, I couldn't get back to sleep. I tried to read, drank a glass of water, but nothing worked. So I slipped out of my room and went downstairs. The entire hotel was silent. No one was awake. I went through the reception area, the dining room, then finally back upstairs. That's when it happened."

She pauses.

"What happened?"

"You remember room number nine?"

"Yes," I say. "Clarisse's room."

"I passed that room on my way up. And then suddenly I had this flashback. It was so powerful I had to sit down on the stairs."

"What did you see?" I whisper.

"Our last summer—1973. I was frightened. There had been a storm. It was my birthday, do you remember?"

I nod.

"I couldn't sleep that night. I crept down the hotel stairs to our mother's room."

She pauses again. The cat purrs against me.

"The door was not locked, and I opened it very gently. The curtains were drawn back, and moonlight lit up the room. And then I saw that there was somebody in the bed with her."

"Our father?" I say, startled.

She shakes her head.

"No. I drew nearer. I could not understand. I was only six years old, remember. I could make out Clarisse's black hair. And she was holding somebody in her arms. Not our father."

"Who?" I gasp.

Our mother, with a lover . . . Our mother, with another man. With my grandparents and us, her children, sleeping only a couple of rooms away. Our mother. Her fuzzy orange bathing suit. Playing with us on the beach. Our mother at night with another man.

"I don't know who it was."

"What did he look like?" I say heatedly. "Had you ever seen him before? Was he staying at the hotel? Could you remember him?"

Mélanie bites her lip and averts her eyes. Then she says softly, "It was a woman, Antoine."

"What do you mean?"

"Our mother was holding a woman in her arms."

"A woman?" I repeat, stunned.

The cat jumps back up on her knees, and she hugs it fiercely.

"Yes, Antoine, a woman."

"Are you sure?"

"Yes. I came close to the bed. They were asleep. They had thrown the sheets back, and they were naked. I remember thinking that they were both beautiful, very feminine. The woman was tanned and slim, and she had long hair. I couldn't tell what color it was in the moonlight. It seemed a silvery blond. I stood there and looked at them for a while."

"Do you really think they were lovers?"

She smiles wryly. "Well, at six years old, I had no idea, of course.

But what I remember very distinctly is this: the woman's hand was cupped around one of Clarisse's breasts. It was a possessive, sexual gesture."

I get up, pace around the room, and stand by the window, looking down at the noisy rue de la Roquette. I find I can't speak for a minute or two.

"Are you shocked?" she asks.

"In a way."

Again the click of the bracelets.

"I tried to tell you. You knew something was wrong. And then I felt I just couldn't hold it back anymore, so on the way back—"

"And did you ever tell anyone about this the next day," I interrupt, "after it happened?"

"I tried, the very next morning, while we were playing on the beach with Solange. But you wouldn't listen. You shooed me away. I never spoke about this to anyone, and it slipped away from me little by little. I forgot about it. I had never thought about it again until that night at the hotel, thirty-four years later."

"Have you see this woman again? Any idea who she was?"

"No. I don't remember seeing her again. No idea who she was."

I come back to the chair facing Mélanie. "Do you think our mother was a lesbian?" I ask her, my voice low.

"I've been asking myself that very question," she says levelly.

"Do you think this was just one affair out of the blue, or do you think she'd been having affairs with women for a while?"

"I have not stopped thinking about all this. The same questions, and no answers."

"Do you think our father knew? And our grandparents?"

She gets up to go to the kitchen and boils some water, puts tea bags in mugs. I feel dazed, like after a sharp blow on the head.

"Remember that fight you witnessed between Clarisse and Blanche? You told me about it by the pool."

"Yes," I say. "Do you think it could have been about that?"

Mélanie shrugs. "Maybe. I don't think our bourgeois, respectable grandparents were very open concerning homosexuality. And this was back in 1973."

She hands me a mug of tea, sits down.

"And what about our father?" I say. "What does he know?"

"Maybe everybody in the Rey family knew. Maybe it made a scandal. But it wasn't talked about. No one talked about it."

"And then Clarisse died—"

"Yes," she says. "And then our mother died. And so no one talked about it ever again."

We are silent for a while, facing each other, sipping our tea.

"Do you know what upsets me most about all this?" she says finally. "And I know that's why I had the accident. Even just talking about it hurts me here." She lays a hand flat out on her collarbone.

"What upsets you?"

"Before I tell you, *you* tell me what you find upsetting."

I take a deep breath. "I feel like I have no idea who my mother was."

"Yes!" she exclaims, smiling for the first time, although it is not her usual, relaxed smile. "That's exactly it."

"And I have no idea how to find out who she was."

"I do," she says.

"How?"

"The first question is, do you want to know, Antoine? Do you really want to find out?"

"Of course! Why are you asking?"

The crooked smile, again.

"Because sometimes it's easier not to know. Sometimes truth hurts."

I remember the day I discovered the video on Astrid's camera of Serge and Astrid having sex. The shock of it. The shattering pain of it.

"I know what you mean," I say slowly. "I know about that pain."

"Are you ready to face that pain again, Antoine?"

"I don't know," I answer truthfully.

"I am," she says firmly. "And I will. I can't pretend nothing happened. I don't want to shut my eyes to this. I want to know who our mother really was."

Women are so much stronger than we men, I think, listening to her. Yet there is nothing physically powerful about her. In fact she appears more fragile than ever in her slim jeans and beige sweater, but such force exudes from her, such determination. Mélanie is not afraid, and I am. She takes my hand in an almost motherly gesture, as if she knows exactly what is going through my head.

"Don't let this get you down, Tonio. You go on home and tend to your daughter. She needs you. When you're ready, we can talk about this again. There is no hurry."

I nod, stand up, feeling light-headed. A lump in my throat. The idea of facing the office, Florence, the workload awaiting me seems impossible. I kiss my sister, head to the door, and as I'm about to step out, I turn around and say, "You say you know where to find out."

"Yes."

"Where?"

"Blanche."

Our grandmother. She is right, of course. Blanche must have answers. Some answers. But whether she will want to give us those answers is another matter.

INSTEAD OF GOING TO the office, I drive straight home. On my way there, I leave a message for Florence, stating briefly that I won't be coming in for the rest of the day. I make myself a cup of coffee, light up a cigarette, and sit down at the kitchen table. The lump in my throat is still there. My back aches. I realize how worn-out I am.

Pauline's dead face keeps wafting back to me. And the vision of what Mélanie revealed. The moonlit room that I did not see but I can all too well imagine. Our mother, her lover. A woman. Am I stunned because my mother was unfaithful, or am I even more shocked because she was bisexual? I'm not sure what upsets me more. And what does Mélanie feel about this, being a woman? Am I less shaken because I imagine a lesbian mother is a softer jolt for a man than having a gay father? A shrink would have a field day with this.

I think about my gay friends, both male and female, Mathilde, Milèna, David, Matthew, and what they told me about their coming out, how their parents reacted. Some parents accepted and understood, others went into total denial. But what do you do, I wonder, when you find out late in life that one of your parents is gay? No matter how open-minded you are, no matter how tolerant, it comes as a bolt from the blue. Especially if that parent is dead and is no longer around to answer your questions.

The front door bangs, and Arno comes loping in, followed by a sullen girl with black lipstick. I can't make out whether it's the usual girl or another. They all look the same—goth gear, metallic bracelets, long black clothes. He waves, grins. She barely says hello, stares down at the floor. They go straight to his room. Music blares. A couple of minutes later the door bangs again, and Lucas appears. His face lights up when he sees me. He comes rushing into my arms, nearly knocking my coffee over. I tell him I needed to take a break today, that I left the office. Serious little fellow. He looks so much like Astrid that sometimes it hurts just laying eyes on him. He wants to know when his mother will be back. I tell him Tuesday, for the funeral. I wonder, suddenly, whether the funeral is a good idea for him. Isn't he too young? Should he be there? He's only eleven. Pauline's funeral frightens even me. I ask him gently how he feels about it. He bites his lip. He says that if we are both there, Astrid and me, maybe he'll feel up to it. I say I'll talk it over with his mother. His small hand covers mine. His lower lip trembles. This is the first time he is confronted with death. Somebody he knew well, somebody he grew up with, as Pauline had spent countless summers and skiing vacations with us. Someone who was only three years older than he is now.

I try to comfort my son. Am I any good at this? When I was his age, my mother had died and no one had comforted me. Was that why I was useless at reaching out, offering tenderness and support? Are we not forever shaped by our childhood, its scars, its secrets, its hidden pain?

When Saturday comes around, Margaux is still with Patrick and Suzanne. It appears that she needs to be with them, they need to be with her. If Astrid had been here, would our daughter have stayed home? Is she not here because she feels I cannot comfort her, I cannot help her? I hate asking myself these questions, but I feel I need to. I have shied away from them long enough.

Arno goes out, as usual, mumbling something about a party tonight, coming back late. When I mention his low grades, his upcoming report card, that maybe he should be studying instead of partying, he sends a withering look my way, rolls his eyes, and slams the door. I instantly feel like grabbing him by the scruff of his neck and kicking his bony ass down the stairs. I have never hit my children. I have never hit anyone in my life. Does this make me a good person?

Lucas is subdued, and it worries me. I cook his favorite meal, steak, fries, and ketchup, followed by chocolate ice cream. He is even allowed Coca-Cola. I make him promise not to tell his mother. Being such a health food devotee, she would be horrified. For the first time that evening, he finally smiles. He likes the idea of sharing a secret with me. I watch him devour his dinner. We haven't been alone like this for a very long time. Dealing with Margaux and Arno is a constant battle, a never-ending wrestling match. Easy, flowing moments like these are precious nuggets I want to hoard and cherish.

As last night was a restless one, I decide to go to bed early. Lucas seems tired too, and for once, he doesn't complain when I suggest sleep. He asks if he can keep his door open and the light on in the hallway. He hasn't asked that for years. I comply. I sink into bed, praying I won't be plagued by last night's images. Pauline's dead face. Suzanne dressing her daughter's body. And now will it be my mother in the moonlit bedroom and the stranger in her arms? Surprisingly enough, sleep comes swift and fast.

THE PHONE WAKES ME, shrill in the dead of night. I fumble for the light, for the receiver. The alarm clock by the bed reads 2:47 a.m.

A man's voice, curt.

"Are you Arno Rey's father?"

I sit up in bed, my mouth dry.

"Yes—"

"Commissaire Bruno, police department, tenth arrondissement. You need to come in, sir. Your son is in trouble. As a minor, he cannot be released without your consent."

"What happened?" I ask, out of breath. "Is he all right?"

"He's in a sobering-up cell. Yes, he is all right now, but you need to come right away."

He gives me the address, 26 rue Louis Blanc, and hangs up. I stagger up, put my clothes on mechanically. Sobering-up cell. Does this mean he is drunk? Isn't that where they put drunk people? *Your son is in trouble* . . . What trouble? Should I call Astrid once again in Tokyo? What for? There is nothing she can do where she is now. *Oh yeah,* comes that inner voice again, that little voice I hate. *You're the one in charge, buddy, you're the one standing there in the front line. You're the one who has to go out there into the hurricane, you're the one who has to face the enemy, that's your job, buddy, you're the daddy. You're the father. Get on with it, man.*

Lucas! I can't leave him, can I? What if he wakes up and finds the place empty? I'll just have to bring him with me. *No,* says the inner voice, *you can't bring him. What if Arno is in a terrible state, imagine the damage. He's already upset by Pauline's death, you can't do this. You can't bring a fragile eleven-year-old into a police station in the middle of the night because his brother is in a drunk tank. Think again, Daddy.*

I pick up the phone, dial Mélanie's number. Her voice is so surprisingly clear that I wonder for a split second whether she was asleep. I briefly explain the situation about Arno. If I leave the key under the doormat for her, can she come over and spend the rest of the night in our apartment? I can't leave Lucas alone, and there is no one else I can call. She says of course, she'll be on her way. She'll take a taxi. Her voice is calm and reassuring.

The police station is somewhere behind the Gare de l'Est, near the Canal Saint-Martin. Paris is never empty on a Saturday night. There are crowds of people strolling along the place de la République and the boulevard de Magenta, despite the cold. It takes me a while to get there, to park. I tell the cop at the door I'm Arno Rey's father. He nods, lets me in. The place is as run-down and disheartening as the hospital morgue. A small, thin man with pale gray eyes comes up to me and introduces himself. Commissaire Bruno.

"Can you explain what happened?" I ask him.

"Your son was arrested with other teenagers."

"Why?"

His deadpan manner irritates me. He seems to enjoy taking his time, watching every muscle of my face.

"They ransacked an apartment."

"I don't understand."

"Your son gate-crashed a party tonight. With a couple of his friends. The party was given by a young girl called Émilie Jousselin.

She lives on the rue du Faubourg Saint-Martin, around the corner from here. Your son had not been invited. And once your son and his friends got there, they called more friends. Easy, with mobile phones. So a whole load of other friends turned up. Friends of friends. And so on and so forth. A hundred people at least. And everybody got drunk. They all had liquor with them."

"What did they do?" I ask, trying to keep my voice steady.

"The place was trashed. Somebody sprayed graffiti on the walls, broke china, cut up the parents' clothes. Stuff like that."

I gulp.

"I know it's a shock, sir. Believe it or not, it happens regularly. We have to deal with this kind of thing at least once a month. Nowadays parents leave for the weekend and don't even know their kids are planning to have a party. This young girl hadn't told her parents. She is fifteen. She just told them she was having a couple of girlfriends over."

"Is she from my son's school?"

"No. But she advertised her party on her Facebook page. And that's how it all started."

"How do you know my son was part of this?"

"We were called by neighbors who realized the party was getting out of hand. When my men got there, they arrested as many youths as they could. Most of them got away. But your son was very drunk. He could hardly move."

I look around for a chair to sit on. There isn't one. I glance down at my shoes. Regular leather loafers. My everyday shoes. My feet in my everyday shoes. Yet today my feet have carried me into the hospital morgue to view Pauline's dead body, then to Mélanie's apartment to hear the truth about what had caused the accident, then here, now, in the middle of the night, in a police station, about to confront my drunken son.

"Would you like a glass of water?" offers Commissaire Bruno.

So he is human, after all. I accept and watch his thin form walk away. He is back almost immediately, hands me a glass.

"Your son is coming now," he says.

A couple of minutes later two policemen appear, shouldering Arno, who shuffles along with the unsure gait of a drunkard. His face is pale, his eyes bloodshot. He doesn't look at me. I feel shame and anger shoot through me. How would Astrid react? What would she say to him now? Would she scold him? Soothe him? Shake him?

I sign a couple of papers. Arno can hardly stand up. He reeks of alcohol, but he is sober enough to know what is going on. Commissaire Bruno tells me I will probably need to find a lawyer, in case the young girl's parents press charges, which they probably will do. We leave the police station. I don't want to help my son. I let him shamble along behind me to the car. I have not said a single word to him. I don't even want to touch him. He repels me. For the first time in my life I am disgusted by my own flesh and blood. I watch him as he ineptly gets into the car. For a split second he looks so young, so frail, that I experience fleeting pity. But the revulsion takes over again. He fumbles with his seat belt, cannot buckle it. I do not move. I wait till he finally manages to secure it. He is breathing loudly through his mouth, the way he did when he was a kid. When he was a nice little boy. The little boy I carried around on my shoulders, who used to look up at me the way Lucas still does now. Not the lanky, supercilious teenager with the frosty sneer. I marvel ironically at what hormones do, how they transform our children overnight into beings we no longer recognize.

At nearly four o'clock in the morning, the streets are empty, Christmas lights glowing merrily in the cold darkness with nobody to see them. I still have not spoken to my son. What would my father have done in this situation? I cannot help smiling sardonically. Beaten me to a pulp? He did hit me, I recall. Stinging clouts across my face. Not often; I was a subdued teenager, not the defiant, uncouth sort sitting to my right.

The silence stretches between us. Does he find it uncomfortable? Does he have any idea of what happened tonight? Is he afraid of me? Of what I will say to him? The inevitable lecture? The consequences? No pocket money, no more going out, better grades, better behavior, writing to the parents to say sorry . . .

Slouched toward the car door, he appears to be falling asleep. When we arrive at rue Froidevaux, I give him a dig in the ribs that jolts him awake. He makes his hesitant, vacillating way up the stairs. I don't wait for him. Mélanie has left the keys under the mat, and as I open the door, I see her curled up on the sofa, reading. She gets up, hugs me, and we both observe Arno as he enters, swaying unsteadily. He takes in his aunt, and a lopsided grin broadens his face. But nobody smiles back at him.

"Aw, come on, you guys, give me a break," he whines.

My hand reaches back, and I slap him across the face with all my might. It happens fast, yet oddly I can see my gesture in slow motion. Arno gasps. The traces of my fingers are outlined on his cheek, bright red. I have still not uttered a single word.

He stares at me, outraged. I stare back. *Yes*, says the little voice, *that's right, you're the daddy. You're the father, and you are setting down the law, your law, whether this little asshole who happens to be your son likes it or not.*

My eyes bore into his like gimlets. I have never looked at my son this way before. At last he glances down.

"Come on, young man," says Mélanie briskly, grabbing his arm. "You are heading straight to the shower and then to bed."

She leads him out of the entrance, away from me. My heart is beating painfully. I am out of breath, although I have hardly moved. I sit down slowly. I hear the sound of the shower running, and Mélanie comes back. She sits next to me and lays her head against my shoulder.

"I don't think I've ever seen you so angry," she whispers. "You were intimidating."

"How's Lucas?"

"In the Land of Nod."

"Thank you," I murmur.

We sit there together. Her familiar, sisterly smell. Lavender and spice.

"Astrid has missed out on so much," she remarks. "Pauline's death. Arno, tonight. Our mother."

Strangely, it is not Astrid who comes to my mind right now. It is Angèle. It is her presence that I crave, her warm, supple body, her sarcastic laugh, her surprising tenderness.

"When you hit Arno, you looked so much like our father," Mélanie says softly. "The way he used to get angry with us."

"This is the first time I ever hit Arno."

"Do you feel bad about it?"

I sigh. "I don't know. All I feel is anger. You're right. I've never felt such anger."

I don't admit to Melanie that I am angry with myself because I feel Arno's behavior is somehow my fault. Why have I been such a limp, transparent father? Because I never put my foot down, never spelled out the rules the way my own father did? Because when Astrid left me, the one thing that scared me was this: that being bossy with my children would make them love me less?

"Stop thinking, Tonio," comes Melanie's comforting voice. "Go to bed. Get some rest."

I'm not even sure I feel sleepy anymore. Mélanie goes to Margaux's room. I stay up for a little while longer, looking at the old black-and-white photo album with all the Noirmoutier photos. I look at the photographs of my mother, and it is a stranger I see. I doze off into an uneasy slumber.

On Sunday morning Lucas and Mélanie go for brunch on the rue Daguerre. I shower and shave. When Arno finally emerges from his room, I still have absolutely nothing to say to him. He seems disconcerted by my silence. Bent over the *Journal du Dimanche* and a coffee, I don't even raise my head as he shuffles noisily around the kitchen. I don't have to look up to know he is wearing his wrinkled, unclean navy blue pajama bottoms, no T-shirt. Scrawny back, jutting ribs. A flock of red pimples between his bony shoulder blades. Long, greasy hair.

"Is there a problem?" he finally mumbles, crunching his cornflakes loudly.

I remain absorbed by my reading.

"You can at least, like, talk to me," he bleats.

I get up, fold my paper, and walk out of the room. I need to physically get away from him. I feel the same revulsion I experienced last night in the car. I never thought such a thing could be possible. You always hear about children being disgusted by their parents, not the other way around. Is this a taboo subject, something no one talks about? Am I the only parent to feel this way? Would Astrid ever feel this way? No, she couldn't. She gave birth to these kids. She carried them.

The doorbell rings. I glance at my watch. Getting on for noon. Too soon for Mel and Lucas to be back, they only just took off. Probably Margaux, who forgot her keys. I feel nervous about confronting my daughter. I don't know how to express my tenderness for her, all my concern at this fragile, difficult moment in her life. I open the door almost fearfully.

But it is not Margaux's slight figure waiting for me on the doorstep. It is a tall woman wearing a black Perfecto jacket, black jeans, and black boots, holding a helmet against her hip. I quickly gather her into my arms and crush her wildly against me. She smells of leather and musk, an intoxicating combination. I hear Arno's step on the creaking floorboards behind me, but I don't care. He has never seen me with any woman apart from his mother. "I thought you could do with a little sexual healing," she murmurs against my ear.

I draw her into the warmth of the apartment. Arno stands there stupidly. Gone is the impertinent teen. He cannot take his eyes off the Perfecto jacket.

"Hello. I'm Angèle. Your father's number one fan," says Angèle slowly, looking him up and down. She holds out her hand and bares her perfect white teeth in a wolfish smile. "I believe we met at the hospital this summer."

Arno's face is a perfect mixture of surprise, shock, discomfort, and delight. He shakes Angèle's hand and scuttles off like a shy bunny.

"Are you okay?" she says to me. "You look—"

"Like hell." I grimace.

"I've seen you look perkier."

"The past forty-eight hours have been—"

"Interesting?"

I take her in my arms again, nuzzling the top of her glossy head. "Devastating, is more like it. I don't know where to begin."

"Don't begin," she says. "Where's your room?"

"What?"

The slow, greedy grin.

"You heard me. Your room?"

AS I LIE IN BED, her scent still on my skin, I hear the muffled roar of the Harley cut through the Sunday-night silence. She is gone. She stayed for the entire day. But I know she will be back, and the mere thought of that comforts me. Angèle seems to propel a new vitality into me, the way the embalming fluid she pumps into her patients restores their lifelike color. I don't mean only the sex, which of course is an important and thrilling part of our affair. I also mean the matter-of-fact, down-to-earth manner she has of dealing with the agonizing issues of my life. We had gone over each different issue, in my bed, holding each other.

Margaux. Had she been seeing a grief counselor? Someone she could talk to about her best friend dying in front of her very eyes? That was absolutely necessary. I made a note of it. Angèle went on about the way teenagers dealt with death, how some of them were lost, upset, in shock, and how others, as she had all those years ago, grew up instantly but gained a certain hardness that would never wear off.

Arno. Slapping him probably made me feel better, but it was not going to help us communicate. There would come a time, she said, when I would have to sit down and talk to him, really talk to him. Yes, he needed limits, and yes, I was right to put my foot down, but

I would have to stick to this new inflexibility. I had smiled when she said that and stroked the curving softness of her naked hips. What did she know about teenagers? I murmured. Did she have one hidden somewhere that she had forgotten to mention? She had turned around to glare at me in the dim light. What did I know about her life, apart from her job? Nothing much, I admitted. Well, she had a sister, a little older, divorced, who lived in Nantes. Nadège had three unruly teenagers, eighteen, sixteen, and fourteen. Their dad had remarried and was no longer involved enough to give a hand in their upbringing. Angèle was the one who gave a hand. She held them on a tight rein, but she was honest and fair with them. Every week, she spent a night in Nantes at her sister's house. It was easy, as the Le Loroux-Bottereau hospital was only twenty kilometers away. She loved those kids, even if they were sometimes hell to deal with. So yes, she knew all about teenagers, thank you very much.

Clarisse. I had shown Angèle the photographs. "What a beautiful woman!" she exclaimed. "The spitting image of your sister." Then I told her why Mélanie lost control of the car. Her face sobered up instantly. I could tell she was trying to find the right words. She knew how to deal with death, she knew how to deal with teenagers, but this particular issue was a tough one to cope with. She remained silent for a couple of minutes. I tried to describe my mother, her straightforward simplicity, her rural upbringing we knew nothing about, the contrast between the prosperous Rey family and her country girl childhood, but I found myself faltering, powerless to summon her back, to explain to Angèle who my mother really was. Yes, that was it, that was the heart of it, the dark heart of it. Our mother was a stranger. And even more so since Mélanie's flashback.

"What are you going to do about this?" Angèle had asked.

"When I am ready, and I think I will be quite soon, after the funeral, after Christmas, I want to go see my grandmother, with Mélanie."

"Why?"

"Because I'm sure she knows something about my mother and this woman."

"Why can't you talk to your father?"

The question was so simple, so easy. I was taken aback.

"My father?"

"Yes, why not? Don't you think he knows about this? He was her husband after all."

My father. His aging face, his shrunken silhouette. His rigidity. His authority. The Commendatore's marble statue.

"I don't talk to my father."

"Oh well, I didn't speak to my dad either," she drawled. "But that's because he died."

I had to smile.

"You mean you had a fight and you're no longer on speaking terms?" she asked.

"No," I said, knowing full well how odd this would sound. "I have never talked to my father. I have never had a real conversation with him."

"But why?" she asked, baffled.

"Because that's the way it is. My father is not the kind of person you can have a conversation with. He never shows love, never shows affection. He wants to be the boss, every time."

"And do you let him?"

"Yes," I admitted, "I did let him, because it was the easy way out. Because he left me alone. Sometimes I admire my son's outbursts because I never dared confront my own father. No one talks to each other in my family. It's something we were not taught to do."

She kissed the side of my neck.

"Hmm, don't let that happen with your own kids, buddy."

It had been interesting watching her with Mélanie, Lucas, Arno, and Margaux, who finally came home later on. They could have been cold to her, could have resented her presence, especially at this thorny moment, where so many different, destabilizing events had sandwiched us with pain, fear, and anger. But Angèle's shrewd sense of humor, her directness, her warmth appealed to them, I could tell. When she said to Mélanie, "I'm the famous Morticia, and I'm very happy to meet you," there was a split second of awkwardness, but then Mélanie laughed outright and seemed genuinely pleased to lay eyes on her. Over a cup of coffee, Margaux had asked her about her job. I slipped out of the kitchen discreetly. The only person who did not seem seduced by Angèle was Lucas. I found him sulking in his room. I didn't need to ask him what was wrong, I sensed it intuitively. He was being loyal to his mother, and the sight of another woman in our house, a woman I was obviously smitten with, offended him. I didn't have the heart to talk to him about it straightaway. There was too much on my plate right now. I'd find a way. I'd talk to him. No, I would not be like my own father, putting a lid on everything.

When I came back into the kitchen, Margaux was crying silently and Angèle was holding her hand. I hovered at the door, unsure of what to do. Angèle's eyes met mine. Her golden eyes were sad and wise, almost like an elderly person's. I drew away again. In the living room, Mélanie was reading. I went to sit next to her.

"I'm glad she is here," said my sister after a while.

I was glad too. But I knew she would be leaving later on that night. The long and cold drive home to Vendée. And me counting the days until I'd be seeing her again.

ON MONDAY MORNING, the day before Pauline's funeral, I meet Xavier Parimbert, the boss of a renowned feng shui Internet site, at his office near the avenue Montaigne. This meeting has been scheduled for a while. I don't know the man personally, although I have heard of him. He is small and wiry, probably in his early sixties, with dyed hair like that of Aschenbach from *Death in Venice* and the spruce figure of one who watches his weight with an eagle eye. The same kind of man as my father-in-law—a kind I find I have waning patience with. He leads me into his vast silver and white office, waves off an obsequious assistant, sits me down, and gets straight to the point.

"I've seen your work, in particular the day-care center you designed for Régis Rabagny."

At another time in my life my heart would have sunk at such a sentence. Rabagny and I did not end our business collaboration in a happy fashion. I feel certain he has not spread good publicity for me. But since then, Pauline has died and is to be buried tomorrow, and a hard truth concerning my mother has come boomeranging back, not to mention Arno's little foray into insurgence. So I now find that Rabagny's name brushes off me like water off a duck's back, and I also find that I don't really care if this dapper sexagenarian is about to bad-mouth me.

However, he doesn't. He graces me with an astonishingly mellifluous smile.

"Not only is the day-care center impressive, but there's another point that is, in my opinion, most attractive."

"And what would that be? That it is feng shui?"

My irony triggers a polite chuckle.

"I am referring to the way you dealt with Monsieur Rabagny."

"Could you be more specific?"

"You are the only person I know, apart from me, who has told him to go to hell."

It is my turn to chuckle, as the memory of that day comes back. There had been a final, brutal onslaught on his part, once again about a matter that did not concern me or my men. Sickened by the sound of his voice, I had said very clearly into the phone, to Florence's amazement, "Now fuck off."

How Xavier Parimbert has any inkling of this escapes me.

He smiles again, as if to offer an explanation.

"Régis Rabagny happens to be my son-in-law."

"How unfortunate," I remark.

He nods. "I've often thought so myself. But my daughter loves him. And where love is concerned—"

The phone on his desk rings, and he reaches out an elegant manicured hand.

"Yes? No, not now. Where? I see."

As the conversation continues, I turn my eyes to the deceptively simple surroundings. I know nothing about feng shui, only that it is an ancient Chinese art about wind and water affecting our well-being. Something to do with how our surroundings influence us. This must be the tidiest office I have ever seen, no clutter, no paperwork, nothing to upset the eye. On one side, an aquarium takes up an entire wall. Strange, squiggly black fish languidly swim up and down among the bubbles. Luxuriant exotic plants stand in another corner. A cluster of burning incense sticks gives off a subtle, soothing aroma. On the board behind his desk, I see photograph after photograph of Parimbert with celebrities.

He at last puts the phone down and turns all his attention to me.

"Would you care for some green tea and bran scones?" he says cheerfully, as if proposing a special treat to a reluctant child.

"Sure," I reply, sensing that a refusal might not go down so well.

He rings a special buzzer on his desk, and a sleek Asian woman dressed in white comes in holding a tray. She bows, eyes downcast, and with practiced, graceful movements ceremoniously pours out the tea from a heavy, ornate pot. Parimbert watches with a placid expression. I am offered a stodgy-looking piece of pastry, which I assume is the bran scone. There is a moment of stillness while he eats and drinks in almost ecclesiastical silence. I bite into the scone and instantly regret it. It has the rubbery consistency of chewing gum. Parimbert takes great, swooping sips of his tea, smacking his lips with relish. I find the beverage far too hot to swallow with such enthusiasm.

"Now," he says with one last smack, "let's get to business."

A Cheshire cat smile. The tea has left an unfortunate green residue speckled across his teeth, as if a lush mini-jungle had suddenly sprouted from his gums. I want to burst out laughing, and I realize in the same aching moment that this is the first time I have felt like laughing since Pauline died. Culpability takes over. The laughing fit subsides.

"I have a plan," says Parimbert mysteriously. "And I honestly believe that you are the one who is going to carry out this plan."

He waits sententiously. I nod. He goes on.

"I want you to imagine a Think Dome."

He pronounces the last two words with tremulous awe, as if he had said "Holy Grail" or "Dalai Lama." I wait and nod, trying to understand what a Think Dome is and praying I don't look too dim-witted.

Parimbert gets up, hands thrust into his impeccably pressed gray trouser pockets, and paces across the polished floorboards. He pauses theatrically in the middle of the room.

"A Think Dome is a place where I would take only a handful of people—people selected very carefully—in order for us to gather and reflect in harmony. This place would be here, in these premises. I want it to resemble an Igloo of Intelligence. Do you understand?"

"Absolutely," I say. Once again, the impulse to snigger is irresistible.

"I have not spoken to anyone about this. I want you to have carte blanche. I know you are the perfect man for this. That is why you have been chosen. And you will be paid very well."

He mentions a sum that is on the generous side, although I still have no idea how large the Think Dome is supposed to be and in what material it should be completed.

"I want you to come up with thoughts. Just get them down on paper and come back to me with them. Let your positive energy flow. Be creative. Be daring. Go with your inner force. No need to be timorous here. The Think Dome has to be near my office. You will be sent a layout of this floor."

I take my leave and head down the avenue Montaigne. The luxury shops are in overdrive for Christmas. Elegant women laden with designer shopping bags totter past on high heels. The traffic roars. The sky is dark gray. As I make my way to the Left Bank, I think of Pauline. The funeral. Her family. I think of Astrid, on her way home right now, landing later on today. I think of how, despite the death of a teenager, Christmas still approaches, inexorable, women still shop on the avenue Montaigne, and men like Parimbert take themselves seriously.

I AM AT THE WHEEL, Astrid on my right, the boys and Margaux in the back. This is one of the first times since the divorce that we are all together in the Audi. Like the family we used to be. Ten o'clock in the morning, and the sky is as overcast as it was yesterday. Astrid is fighting jet lag. She has not spoken much. I went to pick her up at Malakoff earlier on. I had asked if Serge was coming and she said he was not.

It is a one-hour drive to Tilly, the small town where Suzanne's family owns a house. Pauline's entire class will be there. Lucas has decided he wants to come. His first funeral. What was my first after my mother's? Probably Robert's, my grandfather. Later on, a close friend who died in a car crash. Another who had cancer. I realize that this is also Margaux's first funeral, and Arno's. I glance at their faces in the rearview mirror. No iPods, I notice. Their faces are drawn and pale. They will remember today. They will remember today for the rest of their lives.

Since Saturday, Arno has been withdrawn. I still have not had my father-son talk with him. I know I need to schedule this, that there is no point avoiding it. Astrid does not know about Arno yet. It's my job to tell her. After the funeral.

After the funeral. Will it bring closure? How will Suzanne and

Patrick ever recover? Will Margaux be able to heal slowly? The country roads are empty and silent. Monotonous winter scenery. Leafless, lifeless trees. If only the sun could come out and light up the gloominess. I find myself craving that first morning sunlight, the warm touch of the rays on my skin, closing my eyes to it, basking in it. Please God, or whoever it is up there, please send some sun for Pauline's funeral. *I don't believe in God,* Margaux had said fiercely at the morgue. *God wouldn't let a fourteen-year-old die.* I think of my religious upbringing, Mass every Sunday at Saint-Pierre de Chaillot, my first Communion, Mélanie's. When my mother died, did I question God's existence? Did I resent Him for letting my mother die? When I think of those dark years, I find myself remembering so little. Only pain and sorrow come back. And yes, incomprehension. Maybe I did feel, as my daughter does today, that God had let me down. But the difference is that Margaux can say this to me. There was no way I could ever have voiced this to my own father. I would never have dared.

The little church is packed. The entire class is here, all Pauline's friends, all her teachers. But also her friends from other classes, from other schools. I have never seen such a young assembly at a funeral. Rows and rows of teenagers dressed in black, each holding a white rose. Suzanne and Patrick, standing at the door, greet every person coming in. Their bravery impresses me. I cannot help imagining Astrid and me in the same circumstances. I can tell that Astrid is thinking the same thing. She hugs Suzanne desperately. Patrick kisses her. Astrid is already in tears.

We sit just behind the first row. The noise of chairs grating the floor slowly abates. Then a woman's voice singing the purest and saddest hymn I have ever heard rises from somewhere. I cannot see the singer. The coffin comes in, carried by Patrick, his brothers, his father.

Margaux and I have seen Pauline's body. We know she is in that coffin, wearing her pink shirt, her jeans, her Converse sneakers. We know because we have seen her, we have seen the way her hair is brushed back, the way her hands are folded on her stomach.

The priest, a youngish man with a flushed face, begins to speak. I hear his voice, but I cannot make out his words. I find it unbearable being here. My heart begins a fast, thick thud that hurts. I watch Patrick's back, directly in front of me. How can he stand so straight? Where does he get his strength from? Is this what believing in God is all about? Is God the only way to help deal with this nameless awfulness?

The priest's voice drones on. We sit and stand. We pray. Then Margaux's name is called. I am startled. I did not know she was going to say something during the ceremony. Astrid glances at me questioningly. I shake my head.

Margaux stands near her friend's coffin. There is a moment of silence. I wonder fearfully whether she is going to make it. Whether she will be able to speak, to say anything at all. Then my daughter's voice rings out with a vigor that surprises me. Not the voice of a timid teenager. The voice of an assured young woman.

"'Stop all the clocks, cut off the telephone.'"

W. H. Auden. "Funeral Blues." She doesn't need to read from a piece of paper. She says the verses as if she had written the poem herself. Her voice is hard, deep, full of restrained anger and pain.

She continues with the same strength and conviction.

But then, for the first time, her voice falters. She closes her eyes. The church is absolutely quiet. Astrid holds my hand so tight it hurts. Margaux takes a deep breath, and her voice comes back, but it is a whisper now, so low we can barely hear it.

"She is telling us now about hopelessness."

When she returns to her chair, the church fills with a tense and poignant silence that seems to last forever. Astrid is holding Lucas. Arno has grabbed his sister's arm. The very air swells and vibrates with tears. Then the priest's voice buzzes on, and other teenagers come to speak, but again, I don't make out the words. I stare at the paved stoned floor and wait for it to be over, gritting my teeth. I find I cannot cry.

I remember the stream of tears that had gushed from me the day Pauline died. Now it is Astrid who is crying in the chair next to me. Crying as I did that day, crying her eyes out. I put my arm around her, hold her close. She hangs on to me for dear life. Lucas watches us. He hasn't seen us do that since before Naxos.

Outside, it appears that my prayers have been answered, because a whitish sun timorously shines from behind clouds. We slowly follow Pauline's coffin to the adjoining graveyard. We are quite a crowd. Villagers peer at us from their windows. So many young faces. Margaux has gone ahead to join her classmates. They are the first ones to see Pauline's coffin lowered into the grave. One by one they each throw a rose into the opening.

Most of them are crying openly. Parents and teachers silently wipe away tears. This too seems to last forever. A young girl collapses with a thin scream. There is a rush toward her. A teacher gently picks her up, carries her away. Astrid's hand finds her way into mine again.

After the burial, there is a gathering at the family house. But most people take their leave, eager to get back to their day, their life, their work. We stay on for lunch because Pauline was Margaux's best friend. Because we feel we need and have to be there. The dining room fills up with close friends and family. Most of them we know. The four teenagers here were Pauline's closest friends. Part of the tightly knit gang.

We are familiar with all these girls. Valentine, Emma, Bérénice, and Gabrielle. We know all their parents. I observe their mournful faces, and I can guess what they are thinking, what we are all thinking, each and every one of us. This could have been our daughter's funeral. This could have happened to us. That could be our daughter's body back at the small graveyard, in that grave, in that coffin covered with white roses.

In the late afternoon, as dusk is already darkening the sky, we leave. We are one of the last families to go. My children seemed drained, as after a long trip. Once in the car, they close their eyes and seem to fall asleep. Astrid remains silent too. She keeps her hand on my thigh, as she used to during those long drives to the Dordogne.

When we arrive at the major road, the one that leads to the highway, the car wheels skirt over a thick coat of mud. A squelching, hissing sound. I peer out at the road but cannot make out what is covering it. A stifling stench finds its way into the car and jolts the children awake. Something rotten, putrid. Astrid clamps a Kleenex to her nose. We drive on slowly, the wheels still churning. Then Lucas gives a little cry, points ahead. A lifeless form lies in the middle of the road, and the car in front of us swerves abruptly to avoid it. It is the meaty carcass of an animal. Now I see that the ground is strewn with viscera. Fighting the fetid stink, I keep my hands steady on the wheel. Lucas screams again. Another shapeless figure suddenly looms, the broken limbs of another animal. Police lights flash, slowing us down. We are told that a truck carrying waste animal remains from a nearby slaughterhouse has lost its entire load. Pails of blood riddled with organs, hides, skins, fatty tissue, guts, and remains of dead stock litter the road for another five kilometers.

It is like a vision from hell. We inch along. The smell of rot is unbearable. Finally the sign indicating the highway appears. Sighs of relief are heard. We speed toward Paris. I drive them to Malakoff, right up to the house on the rue Émile Zola. I leave the motor running.

"Why don't you stay for dinner?" suggests Astrid.

I shrug. "Why not?"

The children file out of the car. I hear Titus's joyful bark from the other side of the fence.

"Is Serge there?" I ask carefully.

"No, he's not."

I don't ask where he is. After all, I don't care. I'm just glad he is not there. I cannot get used to this guy in my house. Yes, it still feels like my house. My house, my wife, my garden. My dog. My old life.

We have dinner just like in the old days, in the open kitchen area that I designed with such care. Titus is beside himself with joy. He keeps putting his humid jaw on my knee, gazing up at me with incredulous ecstasy. The children stay with us for a while, then finally go up to bed. I wonder where Serge is. I keep expecting him to barge through the front door. Astrid does not talk about him. She talks about the children, about today. I listen. How can I explain that I feel I am light-years ahead? That I was there when all this took place?

As she goes on, I make a fire in the fireplace. I can tell that no one has done that for a long time. The grate is empty and dusty. The wood stock is the one I bought, years ago. No cozy tête-à-tête by the hearth for Serge and Astrid. I hold out my hands to the heat. Astrid comes to sit next to me on the floor, resting her head on my arm. I don't smoke, because I know she hates it. We watch the flames. If anybody passing by happened to glance through the window, they would see a happy couple. They'd assume a happy marriage.

I tell her about Arno. I describe the police station, Arno's state, and how cold I was the next morning. How he reacted. I say I have not yet talked to him, but I will. That we need to find a good lawyer. She listens, dismayed.

"Why didn't you call me?"

"I did think about it. But what could you have done from Tokyo? You were already in shock over Pauline's death."

She nods. "You're right."

"Margaux got her period," I say.

"I know about that. She told me. Said you dealt with it pretty well, for a dad."

I feel a glow of pride.

"Really? I'm glad. Because I didn't do too well when Pauline died."

"What do you mean?"

"I just couldn't find the right words. I couldn't comfort her. So I suggested we call you. And she was incensed."

I am on the verge of telling her about my mother. But I hold back. Not now. Now is for our own little family, for our children, for their respective problems. Astrid goes to fetch *limoncello* from the freezer and comes back with the tiny crystal glasses I bought years ago in the Porte de Vanves flea market. We sip in silence. I tell her about Parimbert and the Think Dome. I describe the feng shui office, the black fish, the green tea, the bran scones. She laughs. We both laugh.

Where is Serge? I wonder. Why is he not here? I want to ask her. I don't. We talk about Mélanie, how well she is healing. We talk about Astrid's job. About Christmas coming up. What about a joint Christmas at Malakoff, she suggests. Last year was so complicated, Christmas Eve with her, New Year's Eve with me. What about doing it together this year? Pauline's death has made everything so sad, so fragile. Yes, why not, I say. But what about Serge, I think, where will he be? I say nothing, but she must have sensed my inner questions.

She says, "Serge blew his top in Tokyo when you called."

"Why?"

"He is not the father of these children. They have no hold over him."

"What do you mean?"

"He is younger. He doesn't know how to deal with all this."

The fire crackles on merrily. Titus's mighty snore can be heard. I wait.

"He left. He needs to think things over. He's with his parents in Lyon."

Why don't I feel relief washing through me? Instead, I experience a cautious numbness that puzzles me.

"Are you okay?" I ask gently.

She turns her face to me. It is marked with tiredness and pain.

"Not really," she whispers.

This should have been my cue. The moment to take her into my arms, the moment I'd been waiting for, for so long, the moment to win her back. To win it all back.

The moment I used to dream about those first nights at rue Froidevaux when I'd get into that empty bed and feel that there was nothing left to live for. The moment I'd been watching for since Naxos, since she took off. The moment I had so clearly imagined.

But I say nothing. I cannot say what she wants me to say. I merely watch her and nod compassionately. She searches my face, my eyes. She doesn't find what she is looking for, and she breaks into tears.

I take her hand, kiss it softly. She sobs, wipes her cheeks. She whispers, "You know, sometimes I want it back. So badly."

"What is it you want back?" I ask.

"I want you back, Antoine. I want our old life back." Her face crumples up again. "I want it all back."

She plants feverish kisses over my face. Salty kisses. Her warmth, her scent. I want to cry with her and kiss her too, but I can't. Something stronger is holding me back. I clasp her to me. I finally do kiss her, but the passion has gone. The passion is dead. She strokes me, kisses my neck, my lips, and it feels as if the last time we did this was only yesterday, not two years ago. Desire stirs, for old times, for memories' sake, then fades away. Now I am holding her the way I would hold my daughter, my sister—the way I could have held my mother. I hold her steadfastly. I kiss her like a brother kisses a sister.

I feel an unhurried wonder creep though me. How is this possible? I no longer love Astrid. I care for her deeply, she is the mother of my children, but I no longer love her. There is tenderness, caring, respect, but I don't love her the way I used to. And she knows it. She feels it. She stops the kisses, the precise caresses. She draws back, faltering fingers covering her face.

"I'm sorry," she says, taking a deep, shaking breath. "I don't know what came over me."

She blows her nose. A long pause. I give her time. I hold her hand.

"Lucas told me about your girlfriend. The tall, dark one."

"Angèle."

"How long have you been seeing her?"

"Since the accident."

"Are you in love with her?"

I rub my forehead. Am I in love with Angèle? Of course I am. But there is no way I can say this to Astrid right now.

"She makes me happy."

Astrid smiles, a brave smile.

"That's good. Great. I'm glad." Another pause. "Listen, I'm awfully tired all of a sudden. I think I'll go up to bed. Will you let Titus out for his last pee?"

Titus is already waiting by the door, wagging his tail with anticipation. I put my coat on, and we head out into the biting cold. He waddles around the garden happily, lifting his leg. I rub my hands together, blow on them to keep warm. I want to get back into the warm house. Astrid has gone upstairs. As Titus flops down in front of the dying fire, I go up to say goodbye. Lucas's light is off. Arno's light is off. Margaux's is on. I hesitate to knock, but she hears my step. Her door creaks open.

"Bye, Dad." She flits to me like a little ghost in her white nightdress. Hugs me in a flash and takes off again. I go down the small corridor to what used to be my old bedroom. It hasn't changed much. Astrid is in the adjoining bathroom. I sit on the bed and wait for her. It was in this room that she told me she wanted a divorce. That she loved him. That she wanted to be with him. Not me. That she was so sorry. That she couldn't stand the lying any longer. I remember the shock and the hurting. Staring down at my wedding ring and thinking that this couldn't be true. Her going on about how our marriage had become something comfy and distended, like a slack pair of old slippers, and I had winced at the image. I knew what she meant. I knew exactly what she meant. But had it been entirely my fault? Is it always the husband's fault? Because I'd let the pizzazz fizzle out of our humdrum life? Because I didn't bring her flowers? Because I'd let a dashing, younger prince whisk her out of my reach? What did she see in Serge? I often wondered. His youth? His ardor? The fact that he wasn't a father? Instead of fighting for her, fighting like the devil, I had stepped back. A deflated balloon. One of my first, childish reactions had been to have a one-night stand with a colleague's assistant. It had done me no good. During our marriage I had not been the unfaithful kind. I wasn't good at that. Some men are. There had been one brief affair during a business trip with an attractive younger woman, just after Lucas was born. I had felt wretched. The guilt was too much for me to bear. I found adultery complicated. I gave it up. Then there had been that long, dry patch in our marriage, just before I found out about Serge. Nothing much went on in our bed anymore, and I'd been lazy about it, not bothering to delve into it. Maybe I didn't want to know. Maybe I already knew, deep inside, that she loved and desired another man.

Astrid comes out of the bathroom wearing a long T-shirt. She slips into bed with a weary sigh. She holds out her hand to me. I take it, lying down next to her, fully clothed.

"Don't go just yet," she murmurs. "Wait till I fall asleep. Please."

She turns off the bedside lamp. The room seems dark at first. Then I can make out the furniture, the dim streetlight filtering in through the curtains. I will wait till she drops off, then silently take my leave. A juxtaposition of images whirls. The carcasses on the road. Pauline's coffin. Xavier Parimbert and his smug smile. My mother and a woman in her arms. The next thing I know, an alarm is buzzing deafeningly in my ear. I can't understand what time it is, or where I am. A radio blares. France Info. It is seven a.m. I am in Astrid's room, in Malakoff. I must have fallen asleep. I feel her warm hands on me, on my skin, and it is too enjoyable a sensation to pull away. I am still dazed with slumber, incapable of opening my eyes. *No,* says the little voice, *no, no, no, don't do this, don't do this.* Her hands, pulling off my clothes. *No, no, no.* Yes, says the flesh, oh yes. *You'll regret this, this is the stupidest thing to do right now, it will hurt both of you.* Oh, the bliss of her familiar velvety skin. How I have missed it. *There is still time to stop, Antoine, still time to get up, put your clothes on, and get the hell out of here.* She knows exactly how to touch me. She hasn't forgotten. When was the last time Astrid and I made love? It was probably right here, in this very bed. Two years ago. *You stupid fool. You dumb idiot.* It happens fast, a quick flash of shuddering pleasure. I hold her tight, heart pumping. I say nothing, nor does she. We both know this is a mistake. I get up slowly, stroke her hair clumsily. I gather up my clothes, slip into the bathroom. When I leave the room, she is still in bed, her back to me. Downstairs, Lucas is having breakfast. He sees me, his face exploding into a delighted grin. My heart sinks.

"Dad! You spent the night!"

I smile back at him, flinching inwardly. I know that his dream is to see Astrid and me reunited again. He's never been shy about this. He has told Mélanie. Me. Astrid. He thinks it is still possible.

"Yes, I was tired."

"Did you sleep in Mom's room?"

Hope shining through his eyes.

"No," I lie, hating myself. "I slept down here on the sofa. I just went upstairs to use the bathroom."

"Oh," he says flatly. "Will you be coming back tonight?"

"No, little fellow. Not tonight. But you know what? We will be spending Christmas all of us together. Right here. Like in the old days. How about that?"

"Great!" he says. And he does seem happy about it.

It is still dark outside, and Malakoff appears fast asleep as I drive down the rue Pierre Larousse, then straight into Paris, up the rue Raymond Losserand, which will take me to the rue Froidevaux. I don't want to think about what just happened. It is like a defeat, no matter how agreeable it was. By now, even the enjoyment has faded. There is nothing left but a bittersweet pang of regret.

Christmas eve at Malakoff had been a success, and Astrid pulled it off beautifully. Mélanie came, and so did my father, not looking his best, perhaps even more weary, as well as Régine and Joséphine. I hadn't seen so many Reys in the same room for a very long time.

Serge was not there. When I tactfully asked Astrid how things were going with him, she sighed. "It's complicated." After we had cleared up the meal, opened the presents, and everyone was chatting in the living room in front of the fire, Astrid and I went up to Serge's study to have a talk about the children. About what they were turning into, how we felt we had no control over them. That what we got back from them was disdain, no respect, no affection, no love. Margaux seemed swathed in continuous mute contempt, refusing to see the grief counselor we found. And as we had foreseen, Arno was expelled from the lycée. We enrolled him in a dour boarding school near Reims. The lawyer looking after his case expected the matter to boil down to a sum of money handed over to the Jousselin family for damages. What that sum should amount to, we did not yet know. Luckily, we were not the only parents involved. All this was no doubt normal, part of modern adolescence and its hazards, but even the thought of that did not make it easier to bear. For either of us. I felt relief that she was going through the same turmoil and tried to convey this to her. "You don't understand," she said. "It's worse for me. I gave birth to them." I tried to describe the repugnance I experienced the night of Arno's arrest. She nodded, her face a peculiar blend of alarm and wit. "I see what you mean, Antoine, but it is worse for me. These kids came out of me"—she placed her palm on her stomach—"and I can still feel that. I gave birth to them, they were lovely for years, and now this." I could only add, feebly, "I know, I was there when they were born." She had smirked.

Early January, the no-smoking ban hits France. Funnily enough, submitting to it is easier than I thought. And there are so many people like me puffing away in the freezing cold in front of restaurants and offices that I feel I am part of a conspiracy. A blue-fingered one. I hear that Serge has returned. Lucas tells me he is home. I can't help wondering if Astrid ever told him about us, about that night after Pauline's funeral. And how he took it. Back at the office, Parimbert proves to be a troublemaker, just like his obnoxious son-in-law. Beneath the bland exterior and the beguiling smile, he rules with an iron fist. Negotiating with him is a punishing task that leaves me drained of vitality.

The only bright light in my bleak existence was the surprise birthday party thrown for me by Hélène, Didier, and Emmanuel. This took place at Didier's apartment. Didier is a colleague, but the difference between him and me is that we started out roughly at the same time and he has gravitated to another galaxy of success and prosperity. He never became bigheaded about it. He could have. The only thing we now have in common is that his wife left him for a younger man, some arrogant Eurotrash banker from the city. His ex-wife, whom I was quite fond of, became Posh Spice's clone. Her remarkable Grecian nose now looks like an electrical plug. Didier is a tall, emaciated fellow with long, thin hands and a startling howl of a laugh. He lives in a spectacular loft in the twentieth arrondissement, near Ménilmontant, converted from a vast old warehouse tucked away between two dilapidated buildings. When he bought it all those years ago, we'd sniggered, hooting that he'd freeze his ass off in the winter and bake during the summer. But he ignored us and slowly transformed the place into a centrally heated air-conditioned glass-and-brick glory that had us all green with envy.

I had not given much thought to my upcoming forty-fourth birthday. There was a time when, as a family man, it was endearing to receive presents from my children—those clumsy drawings and lopsided ceramic creations. But I was no longer a family man. And I knew I would spend my birthday evening alone. As I had last year. That morning, I received a text message from Mélanie and one from Astrid. And one from Patrick and Suzanne, who had gone off on a long trip east. I think I would have done just that if I had lost my daughter. My father usually never remembered my birthday. But surprisingly, he called me at the office. How soft and tired his voice sounded, I thought. Not at all the trumpetlike, bossy tone of yesterday.

"Do you want to come over for a bite for your birthday?" he said. "It will be just you and me. Régine has a bridge dinner."

The avenue Kléber. The orange and brown seventies dining room with overbright lighting. My father and me, face-to-face at the oval table. His spotted, trembling hand pouring out the wine. *You should go, Antoine. He's an old man now, he's probably lonely. You should make an effort, do something for him for once. For once.*

"Thanks, but I have other plans for tonight."

Liar. Coward.

When I hung up, guilt took over. I should call him back, say that I could make it finally. I uneasily turned to my computer, back to the Think Dome. The Think Dome, no matter how it had made me chortle in the beginning, was taking up a lot of energy, but in a surprisingly motivating way. This was the first time in ages I found myself working on a project I enjoyed, that egged me on, that stimulated me. I had researched igloos, their history, their specificity. I had looked up domes, remembered the beautiful ones I had visited in

Florence, in Milan. I sketched page after page, drew shapes and forms I never imagined I could think up, hatched ideas I never thought I could possibly conceive.

A little beep signaled an incoming e-mail. It was from Didier: "Need your advice about an important business deal. A guy you worked with. Can you drop in tonight at around eightish? Urgent."

I e-mailed back: "Yes, of course."

So when I turned up on Didier's doorstep, I was not expecting anything at all. He greeted me, let me in, poker-faced. I followed him into the huge main room, which I found oddly silent, as if a hush had fallen over it, and all of sudden, screams and shouts exploded from all around me. Bewildered, I discovered Hélène and her husband, Mélanie, Emmanuel, and two women I did not know, who ended up being Emmanuel's and Didier's new ladies. Music was turned on full blast, champagne was produced, pâté and tarama, salads, sandwiches, fruit, and a chocolate cake, followed by a shower of presents. I was delighted. For the first time in what seemed ages, I relaxed, enjoyed the champagne, enjoyed being the center of attention.

Didier kept looking at his watch, I couldn't think why. When the doorbell rang, he rushed to his feet.

"Ah," he announced, "the pièce de résistance."

And he opened the door with a flourish.

She glided in, wearing a long white dress, an astounding dress for the middle of winter, just like that, out of nowhere, her chestnut hair tied back, a mysterious smile hovering on her lips.

"Happy birthday, Mister Parisian," she whispered, à la Marilyn Monroe, and she came to kiss me.

Everybody clapped and cheered. I caught Mélanie and Didier exchanging triumphant glances and guessed they had rigged all this up behind my unsuspecting back. Nobody could take their eyes off Angèle. Emmanuel gawked and discreetly gave me a jovial thumbs-up. I could tell that the ladies—Hélène, Patricia, and Karine—were longing to ask Angèle about her job. I imagined she was used to this.

She was most likely questioned like this every day. When the first timid question came, something like, "How can you handle dead people all day long?" she answered, without being flippant, "Because it helps other people stay alive."

It was a wonderful evening. Angèle in her white dress, like a snow princess. The beauty of Didier's loft, the skylight opening out onto the night's cold darkness. We laughed, we drank, we even danced. Mélanie proclaimed it was the first time she had danced in a very long time. We all clapped again. I felt dizzy, a mixture of champagne and joy. When Didier asked me how Arno was, I replied flatly, "A disaster." His hyena-like laugh burst out, which got everybody going. I then told them about the man-to-man conversation I'd finally had with my son when he was expelled from school. The talking-to I'd given him, my heart sinking as I realized how much I sounded like my own father, admonishing, rebuking, finger wagging. Then I got up and aped Arno's languid slouch, his disgruntled scowl. And even took on his voice, raspy, drawling, immediately identifiable as that of a hip teenager: "C'mon, Dad, when you were my age, there was, like, no Internet, no mobile phones, you guys were living in the Middle Ages. I mean, come on, you were born in the sixties, what do you understand of today's world?" This triggered another round of hoots. I felt elated, egged on by something I'd never experienced. I was making people laugh. I had never achieved that in my life. Astrid used to be the bubbly, funny one. She cracked the jokes, she had everyone in stitches. I was the silent onlooker. Until tonight.

"You've got to hear about my new boss, Parimbert," I said to my new audience. They had of course heard of him. He had just about plastered himself on every poster on every street corner, and you couldn't turn on the TV or your computer without being confronted with his Cheshire cat smile. I imitated how he marched around a room, fists deep in his pockets, shoulders hunched up, and his peculiar grimace—which I'd mastered to a *T*—as if to convey how hard, how powerfully he was thinking, an old ladyish pout followed by the rapid intake of his upper and lower lip, making him look like a dried-out prune. And then his way of orally capitalizing certain words to give them emphasis, sotto voce: "Now, Antoine. Remember how strong the Mountain must be in your Back. Remember how each Particle around you is Alive, full of Energy and Intelligence. Remember that Purifying your Inner Space is Absolutely necessary."

I told them about the Think Dome, the nightmarish yet incredibly inspiring complication of the affair, Parimbert peering over my rough copies, too vain to wear glasses. He never seemed to be pleased or displeased by my creations, merely puzzled, as if they triggered colossal concern. I began to suspect that he had no idea what the Think Dome was supposed to be. He just very much liked the *idea* of it. "Now, Antoine, remember, the Think Dome is a Bubble of Potential, a Liberating cell, a Closed Space that in fact knows how to set us Free." They were hysterical with laughter. Hélène was wiping away tears. I told them about the seminar Parimbert had invited me to, where for an entire day, in a modern complex in the chic western suburbs, I had been introduced to his team. His associate was a terrifying Asian personage with a cadaverous mask-like face, whose gender was difficult to determine. All the people who worked with Parimbert seemed either about to collapse or on drugs, sporting glassy, intoxicated expressions. They all wore black or white. Some were very young, barely out of college. Others were seriously getting on. Nobody looked remotely normal. At one o'clock, stomach rumbling, I had been looking forward to lunch. But as the minutes ticked by, to my dismay, no lunch was announced. Standing at the head of the room, screens flashing behind him, Parimbert was droning on about the website's success and how he was Expanding through the Entire World. I discreetly asked the haggard but elegant-looking lady next to me about lunch. She stared at me as if I had said "sodomy" or "gang bang." "*Lunch?*" she repeated with a revolted whisper. "We don't have lunch. Ever." Distressed, I had asked, "Why not?" belly gurgling away all the more. She had not deigned to answer me. At four o'clock, green tea and bran scones were imperially ushered in. But my stomach balked. And I had spent the rest of the day feeling dangerously faint and had rushed to the nearest *boulangerie* as soon as I could to wolf down an entire baguette.

"You were so funny," said Mélanie as we took our leave. Didier, Emmanuel, and Hélène agreed. A mixture of admiration and surprise. "I had no idea you could be so funny."

Later, when I fell asleep, holding my snow princess close to me, I felt happy. A happy man.

SATURDAY AFTERNOON. MÉLANIE AND I stand outside the enormous wrought-iron door that leads into our grandmother's building. We telephoned this morning, informed the placid, good-natured Gaspard that we were coming to visit Blanche. I haven't been here since before the summer. More than six months. Mélanie types out the digital code, and we walk into the huge, red-carpeted hall. The concierge peers at us from behind the lace curtain of her *loge,* nods at us as we go past. Nothing much has changed here. The carpet may look a touch more threadbare, perhaps. An iron and glass, surprisingly silent elevator has recently replaced the creaky old-fashioned one.

Our grandparents lived here for more than seventy years. Since their marriage. Our father and Solange were born here. In those days, most of the imposing Haussmanian building belonged to Blanche's grandfather, Émile Fromet, a well-off property owner who possessed several residences in the Passy area of the sixteenth arrondissement. We were often told about Émile Fromet in our childhood. There was a portrait of him above a mantelpiece, an unyielding-looking man with a redoubtable chin that Blanche luckily did not inherit but passed on to her daughter, Solange. We knew, very young, that Blanche's wedding with Robert Rey had been a grand event, the faultless union between a dynasty of lawyers and a family of doctors and property owners. A cluster of respectable, highly regarded, influential wealthy people with the same upbringing, the same origins, the same religion. Our father's marriage to a rural southerner had probably caused a certain commotion back in the sixties.

Gaspard opens the door to us, his asymmetrical face flushing with contentment. I cannot help feeling sorry for the man. He must be five years older than I am at the most, and he looks as if he could be my father. No family, no children, no life apart from the Reys. Even when he was young, he seemed wizened, shuffling about the place in his mother's tow. Gaspard has been living here forever, in a room up under the roof, devoted to the Reys, like his mother, Odette. Odette had slaved for our grandparents till the day she died. She terrorized us when we were small, forced us to wear felt slippers so as not to mat the freshly polished parquet floor, urging us to keep our voices down, as "Madame" was resting and "Monsieur" was reading the *Figaro* in his office and did not want to be disturbed. No one knew who Gaspard's father was. No one asked. When Mélanie and I were small, Gaspard did odd jobs around the apartment, errands of all sorts, and did not seem to spend much time at school. His mother died ten years ago, and he took over the upkeep of the place. It had given him a new importance he was proud of.

Mélanie and I greet him. Our arrival is the highlight of his week. When Astrid and I brought the children in to see their great-grandmother back in the good old Malakoff days, he was ecstatic.

As ever, when I enter this place, I am struck by the darkness of it. The northern exposure does not help. The 450-square-meter apartment never catches a glimmer of sun. Even in the middle of summer it harbors a sepulchral gloom. Solange, our aunt, is on her way out. We have not seen her for a long time. She says hello briefly, not unkindly, pats Mélanie on the cheek, does not ask about our father.

Brother and sister live in the same vicinity, he on the avenue Kléber, she on the rue Boissière, five minutes away, but they never see each other. They never got along. They never will. It's too late.

The apartment is a continuous succession of great rooms with molded ceilings. *Grand salon* (which was never used, too big, too cold), *petit salon*, dining room, library, office, four bedrooms, two old-fashioned bathrooms, and the out-of-date kitchen far away at the back. Every day, Odette used to wheel a squeaky table laden with food along the never-ending corridor from the kitchen to the dining room. I can still remember the sound of those wheels.

On our way here, we discussed how we were going to tackle our grandmother. We couldn't exactly come out with "Did you know your daughter-in-law was having affairs with women?" Mélanie suggested that we look around the place. What did she mean? I asked. Did she mean to snoop? Yes, she meant to snoop, and her expression was so comical I had to smile. I felt oddly excited, as if she and I were embarking on some new and strange adventure. But what about Gaspard? I had asked. He watched over the place like a hawk. Mélanie had waved a nonchalant hand. Gaspard would not be a problem. The problem was where to look.

"Hey, guess what?" she had said with a sprightly voice as I parked the car along the avenue Henri-Martin.

"What?"

"I met a guy."

"Another old lech?"

She had rolled her eyes.

"No. Actually, he's a little younger than I am. He's a journalist."

"And?"

"And."

"Is that all you have to say?"

"For the moment."

The nurse on duty today is one we have never seen. But she seems to know all about us, greeting us by our first names. She informs us that our grandmother is still asleep and that it is not wise to wake her now, as she had a bad night. Can we wait another hour or so? Maybe have a coffee somewhere or do a spot of shopping? she suggests with a bright smile.

Mélanie turns in order to locate Gaspard. He is not far off, giving orders to a cleaning lady. She whispers to me, "I'm going to snoop. Keep him busy."

She slips off. For what seems like ages I listen to Gaspard's woes about the difficulty of finding the right staff, the soaring prices of fresh fruit, the new neighbors on the fourth floor who make so much noise. Mélanie at last comes back and spreads her hands, as if to say, "Found nothing."

We decide to return in an hour. As we head to the door, Gaspard says in a rush that he's very happy to make tea or coffee for us. We can go sit in the *petit salon* and he'll bring it to us. It's cold outside today, we can stay cozily here. He seems so eager to have us stay that we feel we can't refuse. We wait for him in the *petit salon*. A cleaning lady is dusting along the corridor. She nods to us as she passes.

This is the room that brings back the most memories. The French windows looking out to the balcony. The dark green velvet sofa and chairs. A large, low glass table. My grandfather's silver cigarette box is still there. This is where my grandparents gathered for their coffee or to watch television. This is where we played charades. Listened to the grown-ups talk.

Gaspard comes back with a tray, coffee for me, tea for Mélanie. He pours out our cups carefully, hands us milk and sugar. He sits on a chair facing us, fists on his knees, his back very straight.

We ask him how our grandmother has been recently. Not too good, he says, her heart has been acting up again and she spends most of her days sleeping. The medication knocks her out.

"You remember our mother, don't you?" says Mélanie unexpectedly, sipping her tea.

His smile lights up his face.

"Oh, your mother! *Petite* Madame Rey. Yes, of course I remember her. Your mother was unforgettable."

Clever girl, I think.

Mélanie goes on. "What do you remember about her?"

Gaspard's smile stretches even wider.

"She was such a lovely, kind person. She gave me little presents, new socks, and chocolates—and flowers, sometimes. I was devastated when she died."

The apartment around us is silent all of a sudden. Even the cleaning lady dusting in the *grand salon* is going about her chores noiselessly.

"How old were you?" I ask.

"Well, Monsieur Antoine, I'm five years older than you, so I was fifteen. Such sadness."

"What do you remember about the day she died?"

"It was terrible, terrible . . . Seeing her carried out . . . on that stretcher . . ."

He seems uncomfortable all of a sudden, twisting his hands, shuffling his feet. He has stopped looking at us. He looks down at the carpet.

"Were you at the avenue Kléber when it happened?" asked Mélanie, surprised.

"Avenue—Kléber?" he stutters, confused. "I don't remember, no. It was such a horrible day. I don't remember."

He rushes to his feet, leaves the room hastily. After a split second we get up and follow him.

"Gaspard," says Mélanie firmly, "can you please answer my question? Why did you say you saw her being carried out?"

We are standing in the entrance, just the three of us, in the shadow of the dark place. The tall bookshelves seem to lean forward; the pale faces in the old paintings above us have expectant, watchful expressions. The marble bust on the writing table next to us waits too.

Gaspard is tongue-tied, his cheeks flushed. He is trembling. His forehead glistens with a sudden sweat.

"What is wrong?" asks Mélanie quietly.

He swallows audibly, his large Adam's apple bobbing up and down.

"No, no," he whispers, backing off, shaking his head. "I can't."

I grab him by the shoulder. His upper arm feels bony and weak beneath the cheap fabric of his suit.

"Is there something you need to tell us?" I say, using a firmer voice than my sister's.

He shudders, wipes his brow with the back of his hand, steps away again.

"Not here!" he manages to croak.

Mélanie and I exchange glances.

"Where, then?" she asks.

He is already halfway down the corridor, his skinny legs quivering. He whispers, "In my room. On the sixth floor. In five minutes."

He disappears. The vacuum cleaner is abruptly turned on, startling us. We look at each other for a moment. Then we leave.

THE WAY TO THE SERVICE ROOMS is up a narrow, snaking staircase that has no elevator. This is where the poorer residents of the prosperous building live, slogging up those steep steps every day. The higher you go, the flakier the paint. The stronger the smell. The stench of minuscule, airless rooms, promiscuity, the lack of proper bathrooms. The unpleasant reek of a common toilet on the landing. I have never been up here. Neither has Mélanie. There is an uncomfortable contrast between the opulence of the grand apartments and this squalid, overcrowded area tucked away under the roof.

Six stories to climb. We do so in silence. We have not said a word to each other since we left Blanche's place. Questions whirling round and round in my head, and in Mélanie's too, I know.

When we get to the top floor, it is like another world. Bare floorboards, a winding passageway lined with dozens of numbered doors. The whine of a hair dryer. Loud, metallic TV voices. People quarreling in a foreign language. A mobile phone twittering. A baby's squeal. A door opens, and a surly woman stares out at us. The room behind her has a slanting, blotched ceiling, grimy carpets, grubby furniture. Which one is Gaspard's door? He did not tell us. Is he hiding? Is he scared? Somehow I know he is waiting for us, twisting his hands, trembling. He is plucking up his courage.

I watch Mélanie's small, square shoulders underneath her winter coat. Her step is sturdy and sure. She wants to know. She is not afraid. Why am I afraid, and not my sister?

Gaspard stands at the end of the passageway, his face still flushed. He lets us in quickly, as if he does not want us to be seen. His confined little room is stifling after the chilly stairway. The electric heater is on full blast, letting out a faint humming noise and the smell of burned hair and dust. The room is so small that he, Mélanie, and I bump into one another. The only thing to do is to sit on the narrow bed. I look around, taking in the scrupulously clean surfaces, the crucifix on the wall, the cracked washbasin, the makeshift cupboard area with a plastic curtain. Gaspard's life exposed in all its wretchedness. What does he do with himself when he comes back up here after leaving Blanche with the night nurse? No TV. No books. On a small shelf, I notice a Bible and a photograph. I look at it as discreetly as possible. With a jolt, I realize it is a photograph of my mother.

Gaspard stands, as there is no place for him to sit. He waits for us to speak, his eyes darting from Mélanie to me. I can hear a radio in the next room. The walls are so thin I can make out every single word of the news.

"You can trust us, Gaspard," says Mélanie. "You know that."

He puts a quick finger to his lips, his eyes round with fear.

"You must talk quietly, Mademoiselle Mélanie," he whispers. "Everyone here can hear!"

He comes closer to us. I smell the rank odor of his armpits. Instinctively, I shrink back.

"Your mother . . ." he murmurs. "She was my only friend. She was the only person who really . . . understood me."

"Yes," says Mélanie, and I marvel at her patience. I'm not interested. I want him to get to the point, fast. She puts a soothing hand on my arm, as if she knows exactly what I am thinking.

"Your mother was like me. She came from a humble background, from the south, and she wasn't complicated and fussy. She was a simple, good person. She never thought only about herself. She was generous, warm."

"Yes," says Mélanie again, while I clench my fists with impatience.

The radio in the next room is turned off, and silence fills up the little place. Gaspard starts to get that sweaty, anxious look again. He keeps glancing toward the door, wringing his hands. Why is he so uneasy? He ducks down and pulls a small transistor radio from under the bed, fumbles to switch it on. Yves Montand's sultry voice: "'*C'est si bon, de partir n'importe où, bras dessus bras dessous . . .*'"

"You were going to tell us about the day our mother died," I say finally, ignoring Mélanie's pacifying gesture toward me.

Gaspard gathers up enough courage to look me fully in the face.

"You must understand, Monsieur Antoine. This is . . . difficult for me—"

"'*C'est si bon . . .* '" hums Montand, debonair, insouciant.

We wait for Gaspard to go on. He does not.

Mélanie puts a hand on his arm.

"You have nothing to fear from us," she whispers. "Nothing at all. We are your friends. We have known you since we were born."

He nods, the flesh on his cheeks wobbling like jelly. His eyes brim over. To our horror, his face crumples up and he starts to sob without a sound. There is nothing else to do but to wait. I avert my eyes from the sorry spectacle of Gaspard's pasty, ravaged face. The Montand song finally ends. Another tune starts, a familiar one. I can't remember who sings it.

"What I am about to say, I have told no one. No one knows. No one knows, and no one has talked about it since 1974."

Gaspard's voice is so low that we have to lean forward. The bed creaks as we do so.

A stealthy chill. Is it my imagination, or do I really feel it creeping up my spine? Gaspard is crouched on the floor. I can see the top of his head, the bald spot crowning it.

Gaspard's whisper is heard again. "The day she died, your mother had come to see your grandmother. It was early. Your grandmother was still having her breakfast. Your grandfather was away that day."

"Where were you?" inquires Mélanie.

"I was in the kitchen, helping my mother. I was making orange juice. Your mother loved fresh orange juice. Especially mine. It reminded her of the Midi." A touching, pathetic smile. "I was so happy to see your mother that morning. She did not come often. In fact, she hadn't been to see your grandparents for a long time, since Christmas. When I opened the door, it was like sunshine on the landing. I did not know she was coming. She had not called. My mother was not warned. She was annoyed, my mother. She made a fuss about *petite* Madame Rey turning up just like that. She was wearing her red coat, and how beautiful she was with her long black hair, her pale skin, her green eyes, such a beauty. Like you, Mademoiselle Mélanie. You are so much like her, sometimes it hurts to look at you." The tears well up once more. But he manages to hold them back. He breathes slowly, taking his time. "I was in the kitchen, cleaning up. It was a lovely winter day. I had many chores to do, and I did them thoroughly. And then my mother rushed in, her face white. She was holding a hand over her mouth like she was going to vomit. I knew then that something dreadful had happened. I was only fifteen years old, but I knew."

The chill creeps along my chest, my thighs, which begin to tremble. I dare not look at my sister. But I can sense how stiff her presence is next to me.

A silly tune comes on. I wish Gaspard would turn it off.

"'*Pop pop pop muzik, pop pop pop muzik. Talk about pop muzik . . .*'"

"My mother could not speak for a moment. Then she screamed, 'Call Dr. Dardel, quick! Look up his number in Monsieur's address book in the study. Tell him to come right now!' I rushed to the study, and I made that phone call, trembling all over, and the doctor said he'd be right there. Who was ill? What had happened? Was it Madame? She had high blood pressure, I knew that. She had recently been given new medication. All sorts of pills to take during her meals."

Dr. Dardel is a familiar name. He was my grandparents' closest friend and personal doctor. He died in the early '80s. A stocky, white-haired man. Much respected.

Gaspard pauses. What is he trying to tell us? Why is it so long-winded?

"'*New York London Paris Munich everybody talk about pop muzik.*'"

"For God's sake, get on with it," I mutter, teeth clenched.

He nods hurriedly.

"Your grandmother was in the *petit salon,* still wearing her dressing gown. She was pacing up and down. I couldn't see your mother. I couldn't understand. The door to the *petit salon* was ajar. And then I saw part of the red coat. On the floor. Something had happened to *petite* Madame Rey. Something that nobody wanted to tell me."

Footsteps are heard creaking past the door. He stops, waits till they fade away. My heart is thumping so hard I am certain they can both hear it.

"Dr. Dardel was there in a flash. The door to the *petit salon* closed. Then I heard an ambulance. Sirens right outside the building. My mother would not answer any of my questions. She told me to shut up, and she boxed my ears. They came to get *petite* Madame. That was the last time I ever saw her. She looked like she was asleep, her black hair around her face. She was very pale. They carried her away on a stretcher. Later on that day, I was told she was dead."

Mélanie gets up awkwardly, knocking the radio with her foot. It turns off. Gaspard stumbles up as well.

"What are you talking about, Gaspard?" she snaps, forgetting to lower her voice. "Are you saying our mother had the aneurysm here?"

He looks petrified. He stammers, "I—was ordered by my mother never to mention that *petite* Madame had died here."

Mélanie and I gape at him.

"But why?" I manage to say.

"My mother made me swear not to tell. I don't know why. I don't know. I never asked." He seems about to cry again.

Mélanie whimpers, "What about our father? Our grandfather? And Solange?"

He shakes his head.

"I don't know what they know, Mademoiselle Mélanie. This is the first time I have ever talked about it to anyone." His head droops like a wilting flower. "I'm sorry. So sorry."

"Do you mind if I smoke?" I say abruptly.

"No, no, of course, please."

I go and stand near the small window, light up. Gaspard picks up the photograph on the shelf.

"Your mother confided in me, you see. I was young, only fifteen, but she trusted me." He says this with infinite pride. "I think I was one of the only people she trusted. She used to come up here in this room to see me and talk to me. She didn't have any friends in Paris. So she talked to me."

"What did she tell you when she came up to see you?" Mélanie asks.

"So many things, Mademoiselle Mélanie. So many wonderful things. She told me all about her childhood in the Cévennes. The little village where she used to live, near Le Vigan, that she had never been back to since her marriage. She told me that her father and her mother sold fruit at the market. She lost her parents when she was still young. Her father had an accident and her mother a bad heart. She was raised by her older sister, who was a hard woman and did not like it when she married your father, a Parisian. She was lonely sometimes. She missed the south, the simple life there, the sun. She was lonely because your father was very often away for his business. She talked about you and Mademoiselle Mélanie. She was so proud of you. You were the center of her world."

A pause.

"She said that having you two made everything worth it. How you must miss such a mother, Mademoiselle Mélanie, Monsieur Antoine. How you must miss her. I had a mother who never showed me any affection. Your mother was all love. She gave us all the love she had."

I don't need to look at him to guess that his eyes are full of tears. I don't need to look at Mélanie either. I finish my cigarette and toss it out of the window into the courtyard. Icy air comes blasting in. In the next room, music comes on, startlingly loud. I glance at my watch. It is getting on for six o'clock, and night has fallen.

"We need you to let us back into our grandmother's apartment," says Mélanie, her voice still shaky.

Gaspard nods humbly. "Of course."

During the entire way down, no one breathes a word.

THE NURSE LEADS US into the large, shuttered bedroom, where we can barely make out a hospital bed, its back slightly upright, and the diminutive form of our grandmother on top of it. We politely ask the nurse to leave, as we need to talk to our grandmother in private. She obeys.

Mélanie turns the bedside lamp on, and we can at last see our grandmother's face. Blanche has her eyes closed, and her eyelids flutter when she hears Mélanie's voice. She looks old and tired, and fed up with life. Her eyes open slowly and they linger on Mélanie's face and then mine. No reaction. Does she even remember who we are? Mélanie takes her hand, talks to her. Again the eyes, going from Mel to me silently. A thick necklace of wrinkles along her shriveled neck. Getting on for ninety-four, I calculate.

The room around us has not changed either. Heavy ivory curtains, thick carpets, a bookshelf, a *coiffeuse* in front of the window, with the familiar objects that have been there forever: a Fabergé egg, a gold snuffbox, a small marble pyramid, and the same photographs that gather dust in their silver frames: our father and Solange as children, Robert, our grandfather, then Mel, Joséphine, and me. A couple of photos of my children when they were babies. None of Astrid. Nor of Régine. And none of our mother.

"We want to talk to you about our mother," says Mélanie clearly. "About Clarisse."

The eyelids flicker again and close. This looks like a dismissal.

"We want to know about the day she died," Mélanie goes on, ignoring the closed eyelids.

The parched eyelids quiver open, and Blanche looks at both of us in silence for a long time. I am certain she is not going to say a word.

"Can you tell us what happened here on February twelfth, 1974, Grand-mère?"

We wait. Nothing. I want to tell Mélanie this is hopeless. Not going to work out. But all of a sudden Blanche's eyes seem to open even wider, and there is a peculiar expression in them, something almost reptilian, which disturbs me. I watch her dried-up chest heave laboriously. The eyes don't blink, staring out at us, glowering at us, defiant, dark spots in a deathly, skull-like countenance.

As the minutes crawl by, I begin to understand that my grandmother will never speak, that she will take what she knows to her grave. And I loathe her for it. I loathe every inch of her repulsive, crumpled skin, every inch of what she is, Blanche Violette Germaine Rey née Fromet, from the sixteenth arrondissement, born to wealth, born to prosperity, born to excellence.

We stare at each other, my grandmother and I, for what seems an eternity, causing Mélanie to glance from her to me, taken aback. I make sure Blanche receives the entirety of my abhorrence, that she gets the full blast of it, up front, spilling out onto her immaculate nightdress. My disdain for her is such that it has me shaking from head to toe. My hands itch to grab one of the embroidered pillows and smother the white face, to snuff out the arrogance in those blazing eyes.

It is a fierce, silent battle between her and me, and it lasts forever. I can hear the ticktock of the silver alarm clock on the bedside table, the footsteps of the nurse just behind the door, the subdued roar of the traffic along the tree-lined avenue. I can hear my sister's nervous breathing, the wheeze of Blanche's old lungs, my own heart thumping the way it did in Gaspard's room, moments ago.

Finally the eyes close. Very slowly, Blanche's gnarled hand creeps over the coverlet like a desiccated insect and presses on a bell. A strident ring is heard.

The nurse instantly steps in.

"Madame Rey is tired now."

We leave in silence. Gaspard is nowhere to be seen. As I go down the stairs, ignoring the elevator, I think of my mother being carried out right here, on a stretcher, wearing her red coat. My chest feels tight.

Outside, it is colder than ever. Mélanie and I find we cannot talk to each other. I am shattered, and by the pallor of her face, I know Mélanie is too. I light up a cigarette while she turns to her phone, checks it. I offer to drive her home. From the Trocadéro to the Bastille, the traffic is dense on a Saturday evening, as usual. We don't speak, but I know she is thinking exactly the same thoughts.

The truth about our mother's death. Something so monstrous that for the moment, not talking about it keeps it at bay.

PARIMBERT'S PERSONAL ASSISTANT IS a beefy woman called Claudia who hides her excess fat beneath a billowing black dress that looks like a cassock. She talks to me in a patronizing, irritatingly amicable way. First thing on Monday morning she is already on the phone, harassing me about the Think Dome deadline. The project has been accepted by Parimbert, but a new delay has come from one of my suppliers, who is not on time delivering the special luminous screens I ordered, which changed color constantly and formed the dome's entire interior. On another day, at another point, I would have submissively sat back and let this woman haggle. Not anymore. I think of her caffeine-stained teeth, her furry upper lip, her patchouli perfume, her Mozartean Queen of the Night screeches, and my disgust, impatience, and annoyance bubble up with just enough energy to detonate with the efficient precision of a pressure cooker. It does me so much good it almost feels like the aftermath of sex. I can hear Florence gasping in the next room.

I slam down the phone. Time for a quick smoke in the chilly courtyard. I slip into my coat. Then my phone rings. It is Mélanie.

"Blanche is dead," she announces flatly. "Passed away this morning. Solange just called me."

Blanche's death does nothing to me. I did not love her. I will not miss her. The detestation I felt at her bedside on Saturday is still fresh. Nevertheless, she was my father's mother, and I think of him. I know I should call him. I should call Solange. I don't. I go smoke my cigarette out in the cold. I think of the difficult days ahead concerning Blanche's inheritance and how Solange and my father will fight. It will get ugly. It already did a couple of years ago, and Blanche wasn't even dead yet. We were kept out of it. Nobody told us, but we knew there were conflicts and complications between brother and sister. Solange felt that her brother, François, was the favorite sibling, that he had always been advantaged. After a while she stopped seeing him. And us.

Mélanie asks if I want to come by later and see Blanche's body. I tell her I will think about it. I sense a tiny distance between my sister and me, a new one—one that wasn't there before, one I have never felt. I know she didn't approve of my aloofness toward Blanche, the way I stared down at her on Saturday, the way I showed her my true feelings. Mélanie asks if I have called our father yet. I say I will. Again, she sounds as though she disapproves. She tells me she is on her way to see our father. And the way she says it hints that I should be doing that as well. Fast.

When finally I get to my father's place, it is evening. Margaux is silent during the drive, earphones in her ears, eyes riveted to her cell phone, fingers flying as she texts message after message. Lucas is in the back, engrossed by his Nintendo. I feel as if I am alone in the car. Modern kids are the most silent brand ever.

Mélanie opens the door to us. Her face is pale and sad. Her eyes are tearful. Did she love Blanche? I wonder. Will she miss her? We hardly saw our grandmother anymore. What did she mean to Mélanie? But Blanche was the only grandmother we had, I realize. Clarisse's parents died when she was young. Our grandfather passed away years ago, when we were teenagers. Blanche is our last link to our childhood, and that is why my sister is crying.

My father is already in bed. I am surprised to hear this. I glance at my watch. Seven thirty. Mélanie says in a low voice that our father is very tired. Is there reproach in her voice, or am I imagining things? I ask her what is wrong with him, but she brushes me away as Régine appears, overly made up and glum. She hugs us in a distracted, off-hand fashion, offers drinks and crackers. I explain that Arno is at his boarding school, that he'll be back for the funeral.

"Don't talk to me about the funeral," Régine groans, pouring herself a hefty glass of whiskey with an unsteady hand. "I don't want to deal with all this. I never got on with Blanche. She never liked me, and I don't see why I should have anything to do with her funeral, for God's sake."

Joséphine comes in, looking rather more graceful than usual. She kisses us and sits down next to her mother.

"I just spoke to Solange," says Mélanie, her voice firm. "She will be making all the arrangements for the funeral. You don't have to worry, Régine."

"Well, if Solange takes over, then there is nothing any of us will need to do. Your poor father either. He's far too tired to face Solange right now. Blanche and Solange were always rude to me, looking me up and down because I didn't have the right figure, because my parents weren't as rich." Régine goes on, pouring more whiskey and knocking it back viciously. "Always made me feel like I wasn't good enough for François, that I wasn't proper enough to be a Rey. Ghastly Blanche and her even ghastlier daughter."

Lucas and Margaux exchange surprised glances. Joséphine exhales noisily. It occurs to me that Régine is more than tipsy. Only Mélanie keeps her eyes to the ground.

"No one is ever good enough to be a Rey," slobbers Régine, lipstick smudging her teeth. "They made bloody sure we all knew that. Even if you come from a high-quality family with fine money. Even if you come from a family of decent people. Never good enough to be a fucking Rey."

She starts to bawl, her empty glass clattering to the table. Joséphine rolls her eyes and gently but firmly pulls her mother up. I can tell by her routine gestures that this happens often. She hauls the weeping Régine away.

Mélanie and I look at each other. I think of what lies ahead. The candlelit bedroom on the avenue Henri-Martin where Blanche's body awaits me.

But it is not the sight of my dead grandmother that frightens me tonight. She was practically dead when I saw her two days ago, apart from the dreadful, glaring eyes.

What frightens me is having to go back there. Back to the place where my mother met her death.

MÉLANIE TAKES MY CHILDREN back home. She has already been to see Blanche's body with Solange and our father earlier today. I turn up alone at my grandmother's house. It is late. Nearly eleven. I am worn-out. But I know Solange is waiting for me. The only son. It is my duty to be there.

The *grand salon* is surprisingly full of elegant strangers sipping champagne. Friends of Solange, I suppose. Gaspard, dressed in an austere gray suit, explains that yes, they are indeed her friends, and they've come to comfort Solange tonight. He adds in a low voice that he needs to talk to me about something important. Can I wait for him before I leave? I say I will.

I always thought my aunt was a lonely, reclusive person, but when I see tonight's turnout, I guess I am wrong. But what do I know about my aunt? Nothing. She never got on with her older brother. She never married. She led her own life, and we saw little of her after our mother's death and the Noirmoutier summers. She did, however, look after Blanche a great deal, especially after Robert—her father, my grandfather—passed away.

Solange comes toward me as I stand in the entrance. She is wearing a pearl necklace and an ornate embroidered dress that seems a trifle glamorous for the occasion. She seizes my hand. Her face is swollen, her eyes fatigued. I wonder what her life will be like now, without her mother to look after, the hiring of nurses, that enormous apartment to run. She takes me to Blanche's room, and I can only follow her. There are people standing around the bed, praying. I don't know them. A candle is lit. I gaze at the silent form on the bed. But the only thing I imagine is her terrible eyes glaring out at me. I look away.

My aunt leads me this time to the empty *petit salon*. The chatter and low voices of her guests can hardly be heard here. She closes the door. Her face, which reminds me so much of my father's, with a larger chin, seems rigid all of a sudden, less forthcoming. I am aware that this may not be a pleasant moment. Being in this room is already uncomfortable. I keep glancing down at the carpet. This is where my mother's body fell. Right here, by my feet.

"How is François tonight?" she asks, toying with the pearl necklace.

"I didn't see him. He was asleep."

She nods. "I hear he is being brave."

"About Blanche?" I ask.

A small stillness. The pearls click.

"No. About his cancer."

I remain rooted to the spot. Cancer. Of course. Cancer. My father has cancer. For how long? Cancer of what? How bad is it? No one in this family ever talks.

Silence is preferred. Slow, chloroformed silence. Stealthy silence, covering everything up like a deadly, smothering avalanche.

I wonder if she knows. If she can guess, just by watching my face, that this is the first time I am told about my father's illness. The first time it has been named.

"Yes," I say, unsmiling. "You're right. He's being brave."

"I must be getting back to my guests," she says finally. "Goodbye, Antoine. Thank you for coming."

She leaves, her back stiff. As I walk to the entrance, Gaspard comes out of the *grand salon* carrying a tray. I make a sign to him, indicating that I will be waiting for him downstairs. I go down and light up a cigarette, just outside the building.

Gaspard turns up a few minutes later. He seems composed, a little weary. He gets straight to the point.

"Monsieur Antoine, I need to tell you something."

He clears his throat. He looks calmer. Not like the other day in his room.

"Your grandmother is dead now. I was afraid of her—so afraid, you understand? Now she cannot scare me anymore." He pauses, pulls on his tie. I decide not to rush him. "A couple of weeks after your mother died, a woman came here to see Madame. I opened the door to her. An American lady. When your grandmother saw her, she lost control. She shouted at the lady and told her to leave right away. She was furious. I had never seen her so infuriated. There was no one at home that day except for your grandmother and me. My mother was out shopping, and your grandfather was away."

A stylish woman wearing a mink coat walks up to where we are standing. Whiffs of Shalimar. We remain silent as she enters the building. Then Gaspard goes on, moving closer to me.

"The American lady spoke good French. She screamed back at your grandmother. She said she wanted to know why your grandmother had never answered her calls, why your grandmother had her followed by a private detective. And then she yelled this at the top of her voice, 'You better tell me how Clarisse died, right now!'"

"What did she look like, this American?" I ask, my pulse quickening.

"She was in her forties, long blond hair that was almost white, tall, the sporty type."

"And then what happened?"

"Your grandmother told her that if she did not leave at once, she would call the police. Then she ordered me to show the lady out. She left the room, and I was alone with the American lady. She said something in English that sounded horrible, and she slammed the door without once looking at me."

"Why didn't you tell us this the other day?"

He blushed. "I couldn't bring myself to tell you anything until your grandmother was no longer here. This is a good job, Monsieur Antoine. I have been doing it all my life. The pay is decent. I respect your family. I didn't want any trouble."

"Is there anything else you need to tell me?"

"Yes, there is." He nods eagerly. "When the American lady talked about the detective following her, I suddenly remembered a couple of phone calls for your grandmother from an agency. I don't have a curious nature, and I hadn't found those calls strange, but with the quarrel, it all came back to me. And then I found something—er—helpful in your grandmother's wastepaper basket the day after the American lady came."

His face goes even redder. "I hope you don't think—"

I smile.

"No, of course I don't think you were doing anything wrong, Gaspard. You were just emptying her trash can, right?"

He looks so relieved I almost chuckle.

"I have kept this for all these years," he whispers, and hands me a crumpled piece of paper.

"Why did you keep this, Gaspard?"

He draws himself up to his full height. "For your mother's sake. Because I revered her. Because I want to help you, Monsieur Antoine."

"Help me?"

His voice remains steady. His eyes are very solemn.

"To help you understand what happened. The day she died."

I smooth the paper out slowly. It is an invoice, addressed to my grandmother from the Viaris Agency, Private Investigators, on rue d'Amsterdam, in the ninth arrondissement. Quite a hefty sum, I note.

"Your mother was a lovely person, Monsieur Antoine."

"Thank you, Gaspard," I say. I shake his hand. It is a clumsy moment, but he seems content.

I watch him go into the building, his twisted back, his skinny legs. I drive home as swiftly as I can.

A quick check on the Internet confirms what I feared. The Viaris Agency no longer exists. It merged with a larger group called Rubis Détective: Professional Investigation Services, "surveillance, shadowing, undercover operations, activity checks, credit standing." I had no idea this sort of business still existed. And theirs is flourishing, according to the stylish, modern website with ingenious plug-ins. Their offices are near the Opéra. I notice an e-mail address. I decide to write to them, to explain the situation. That I would need the results of the investigation my grandmother, Blanche Rey, commissioned in 1973. I include the invoice number on my grandmother's bill. Could they get back to me as soon as possible? Urgent, thank you. I include my mobile number.

I want to call Mélanie about all this, and nearly do, but it is getting on for one o'clock in the morning. I lie in bed for a long time, tossing and turning, before sleep finally sinks in.

My father's cancer. My grandmother's upcoming funeral. The tall, blond American.

You better tell me how Clarisse died, right now.

THE NEXT MORNING, WHEN I get to the office, I look up Laurence Dardel's number. She is Dr. Dardel's daughter, probably in her mid-fifties now, I presume. Her father was the close friend, the family doctor who signed my mother's death certificate as, according to Gaspard, he was the first to arrive at the avenue Henri-Martin on that fateful day in February 1974. Laurence became a doctor herself, taking on most of her father's clientele and their families. I hadn't seen her in years. We were not particularly friendly. When I call her office, I am told that she is tending to patients at the hospital where she works. The only thing to do, it appears, is to book an appointment. The next possible slot with Dr. Dardel is in a week. I say thank you and hang up.

I remember that her father lived on the rue Spontini, not far from the rue de Longchamp. He had his medical office there. Hers is on the avenue Mozart, but I am quite certain she still lives in the rue Spontini apartment, which she inherited from her father. I remember going there as a boy, after my mother's death, to have tea with Laurence and her husband. There were children, much younger than we were. I have little recollection of them. Laurence Dardel married a man whose name I cannot recall. She kept her maiden name for work purposes. There is no way I can check if she still lives on the rue Spontini without going there myself.

After a morning of steady work I call my father at lunchtime. I get Régine on the phone, and she tells me he is with his sister, organizing Blanche's funeral, which will take place at Saint-Pierre de Chaillot church, as expected. I inform her that I will call back tonight, not too late. In the late afternoon I have a meeting, one of the last ones, with Parimbert at his office. The Think Dome is in the process of being installed, and minor details need to be ironed out.

When I arrive, I note with alarm that Rabagny, his insufferable son-in-law, is also there. I am even more astounded when the man scrambles up to shake my hand with a smile, one I have never seen him use, exposing an unappetizing expanse of gum, telling me what a fantastic job I did on the Think Dome. Parimbert looks on with his customary self-satisfied smirk, and I can almost hear him purr. Rabagny is all worked up; his face is sweaty, just about puce. To my astonishment, he actually stutters. He is convinced that the Think Dome and its structure of light panels changing color is a revolutionary concept of the utmost artistic and psychological significance, and he wants to develop it, with my permission. "This could be huge," he breathes. "This could go worldwide." He's got it all planned out, he's been giving a lot of thought to it. I need to sign a contract, get my lawyer to look at it of course, but this should be moving fast, and if all goes well, I will soon be a billionaire. He too. There is nothing much else to do but wait till he stops to draw breath, which he does eventually, spluttering and purple around the gills. I remain aloof, pocket the proffered contract, and tell him frostily that I will give it some thought. The colder I am, the more he grovels. After a terrifying moment when he hovers near me like an over-affectionate puppy and I fear he is actually going to kiss me, he finally leaves.

Parimbert and I get to work. He is not wholly satisfied with the sitting areas, which are too comfortable in his opinion, not suitable for the immense intellectual exertion that will take place within the dome. He would prefer hard, ascetic seating in which one is forced to sit bolt upright, as if in the classroom of an inflexible teacher. No subsiding into tantalizing indolence.

No matter how soft-voiced he is, Parimbert is a demanding client, and I leave his office much later than I had anticipated, feeling bludgeoned. I decide to drive straight to the rue Spontini. The traffic at this hour is slow, but it shouldn't take me more than twenty minutes to get there. I park the car near the avenue Victor-Hugo and go into a café to wait a little while more. I still have not heard from the Rubis agency. I toy with the idea of calling my sister and telling her what I plan to do, but as I take out my phone, it starts ringing. Angèle. My heart leaps, as always, whenever she calls. I am on the verge of telling her about my visit to Laurence Dardel's home, but at the last minute I hold back. I want to keep this to myself, this quest, or whatever it is. This mission for the truth. I talk about something else, about our next weekend together, which is coming up.

I then call my father. His voice sounds feeble. Not at all like him. As usual, our conversation is brief and dispassionate. It seems my father and I are separated by a towering, hefty wall. We converse with each other, but nothing is exchanged, no tenderness, no affection. No closeness. And it has been like this all our lives. Why should it ever change? I wouldn't even know how to begin. Ask him about his cancer? Tell him I know? Tell him I care? Impossible. He has not programmed me to do that. And as usual, like every time I hang up after talking with my father, hopelessness rears its weary head.

It is now nearly eight o'clock. Laurence Dardel is most probably at home: 50 rue Spontini. I don't have the code to get in, and I wait outside, smoking, pacing up and down to keep warm, until a person finally walks out of the building. The list outside the concierge's door informs me that the Fourcade-Dardel family lives on the third floor. These dignified, red-carpeted Haussmanian buildings all have the same odor, I think as I go up—savory wafts from cooking pots, beeswax polish, flowery interior fragrances.

My ring is answered by a young man in his twenties who is wearing headphones. I explain who I am and ask him if his mother is there. Before he can answer me, Laurence Dardel appears. She peers at me and says, smiling, "You're Antoine, aren't you? François's son?"

She introduces me to her own son Thomas, who wanders off with his headphones, and takes me into the living room. She hasn't changed much with the passing of time. Her face is as I remembered it, small, sharp, and pointed, her eyelashes sandy, her hair drawn back in a neat ponytail. She offers me a glass of wine, which I accept.

"I read about your grandmother's death in the *Figaro*," she says. "You must all be upset. We will of course be at the funeral."

"I wasn't particularly close to her," I say.

She raises an eyebrow.

"Oh. I thought you and Mélanie doted on her."

"Not exactly."

There is a silence. The room we are sitting in is conventional and bourgeois. There is nothing out of place here. Not a spot on the pale gray carpet, not a speck of dust to be seen. Traditional furniture, unimaginative paintings, rows and rows of medical books. Yet this apartment could be made into a gem, I note, as my expert eye singles out ungainly false ceilings, superfluous paneling, unwieldy doors. My nose picks up a persistent cooking odor. It is dinnertime, I realize.

"How is your father?" Laurence asks politely.

She is a doctor, after all. I don't need to pretend.

"He has cancer."

"Yes," she says.

"You know that, don't you?"

"I've known for a while."

"How long have you known?"

She puts a hand under her chin, purses up her mouth. "My father told me."

I feel a slight wrench in my chest.

"But your father died in the early eighties."

"Yes," she says, "1982."

She has the same stocky build as her father, the same stubby hands.

"You mean my father was already ill in 1982?"

"Yes, he was. But he pulled through with treatment. Then he was all right, I believe, for a while. Until recently."

"Are you his doctor?"

"No, but my father was until he died."

"He seems very tired," I say. "Exhausted, even."

"That's because of the chemo," she says. "It knocks you out."

"Is it working?"

She looks at me levelly. "I don't know, Antoine. I'm not his doctor."

"Then how did you know he was ill again?"

"Because I saw him recently, and I could tell."

So she too, like Dr. Besson, had noticed it.

"My father has not told Mélanie nor me that he is ill. His sister knows—God knows how, because they hardly speak to each other. I don't even know what sort of cancer he has. We know nothing. He will say nothing."

She nods but makes no comment. She finishes her glass of wine and puts it down.

"Why are you here, Antoine? Can I help you?"

Before I can answer her, the front door clicks and a burly, balding man comes in. I vaguely recognize her husband. Laurence tells him who I am.

"Antoine Rey. It's been a while! You look more and more like your father."

I hate it when people say that. His name comes back to me—Cyril. After a couple of minutes of small talk in which he expresses his condolences for Blanche's death, he leaves the room. I notice Laurence glancing at her watch.

"I won't take up too much of your time, Laurence. And yes, I do need your help." I pause.

She looks at me expectantly. She has a vigorous, capable look that lends her a certain toughness. Almost like a man.

"I want to look at my mother's medical file."

"May I ask why?"

"There are a couple of things I want to check. Like her death certificate, for example."

Her eyes narrow. "What do you need to know exactly?"

I lean forward and say with a purposeful tone, "I need to know exactly how and where my mother died."

She seems taken aback. "Is this necessary?"

Her attitude jars me. I let it show.

"Is there a problem?"

My voice comes out a lot sharper than I had planned.

She jumps back as if I had poked her.

"There is no problem, Antoine, no reason to get angry."

"Then can I have the file?"

"I have to look for it. I'm not quite sure where it is. It may take a while."

"What do you mean?"

She looks at her watch again.

"My father's files are all here, but I don't have time to get it for you right now."

"And when will you have the time?"

Once again, my voice has a nasty undertone that I can't help. There is a mounting tension between us, a palpable hostility that surprises me.

"I will find it as soon as possible. I will call you when I have done so."

"Fine," I say, getting up hastily.

She rises too, her pointed face red. She looks up at me.

"I remember your mother's death well. It was a terrible moment for your family. I was about twenty years old, I had just met Cyril, and I was studying to be a doctor. I remember my father calling me and telling me that Clarisse Rey had died of an aneurysm. That she was dead by the time he got to her, that there was nothing he could do."

"I still need to look at that file," I say firmly.

"Going back into the past never does any good. You are old enough to know that."

I say nothing. Then I find one of my cards in my pocket. I hand it to her.

"Here is my number. Please call me as soon as you have located the file."

I walk out as fast as I can, not saying goodbye, my cheeks burning. I close the door behind me and scuttle silently down the stairs. I don't even wait till I'm outside to light a cigarette.

Despite the resentment, the fear of what I don't know and don't understand, as I run to my car in the cold darkness, I feel close to my mother, closer than I have felt in years.

THE RUBIS AGENCY CALLS ME at the end of the following day. A charming, efficient woman called Delphine. No problem giving me the file. It has been thirty-odd years after all. All she needs is for me to drop by at their bureau. She'll check my ID and have me sign a piece of paper.

It takes me a while to get from Montparnasse to the Opéra. Trapped in heavy traffic, I listen to the radio, take deep breaths, try not to let my unease take over. I haven't slept well for the past weeks. Sleepless nights, endless questions. Feeling dwarfed by something I cannot comprehend. I keep meaning to call my sister, tell her all I have learned, but I hold back, still. I want to know the whole story for myself. I want to have all the cards in my hand. The Rey dossier the Rubis agency is about to give me. Dr. Dardel's medical file concerning my mother. And then it seems to me I shall know what to do and how to tell Mélanie.

Delphine keeps me waiting for a good ten minutes in a fancy ivory and crimson waiting room. Is this where spouses suspecting their other halves of adultery wait with anticipation and angst? There is no one around at this late hour. Delphine at last appears, a womanly creature dressed in ruby red, flourishing a warm smile. Private detectives don't look like Columbo these days.

I sign a release form, show her my *carte d'identité*, and she hands me a large beige envelope that has been sealed with a thick wad of wax. This has not been opened in years, I can tell. "REY" is typed out in big black letters. I am told that what is inside is the originals of what was sent to my grandmother. I long to open it as soon as I get into the car, but I force myself to wait.

At home, I make coffee, light a cigarette, and sit down at the kitchen table. I draw a deep breath.

There is still time to put the envelope away. To never open it. To never know. I look around the familiar room. The boiling kettle, a scattering of crumbs on the counter, an unfinished glass of milk. The apartment is quiet, Lucas is no doubt asleep, and Margaux is in front of her computer. I wait, still. I wait for a long time.

Then I seize a knife and slit the envelope open. The seal gives way, cracks in two. It is done.

The first items that tumble out are a couple of black-and-white press clippings from *Vogue* and *Jours de France* magazines. My parents at cocktail parties, social events, races—1967, 1969, 1971, 1972. Monsieur and Madame François Rey. Madame wearing Dior, Jacques Fath, Schiaparelli. Were these dresses lent to her? I don't remember her ever wearing them. How gorgeous she looked. So fresh, so pretty.

More press clippings, this time from *Le Monde* and *Le Figaro.* My father and the Vallombreux trial, the one that made him famous in the early seventies. I find two more small clippings: the announcement of my birth and of Mélanie's in the *Figaro*'s *Carnet du Jour.* I then find a large manila envelope. Inside are three black-and-white photographs, two color ones. Bad quality, grainy close-ups. But I have no trouble recognizing my mother. She is with a tall, platinum-haired woman who seems older than she. Three of the photographs are shot in Paris, in the streets. My mother is looking up and smiling at the woman. They are not holding hands, but they are evidently close. It is fall or winter—they both have coats. The two color photos are taken in a restaurant or a hotel bar. They are sitting at a table. The blond woman is smoking. She is wearing a purple blouse and a pearl necklace. My mother's face is somber, downcast eyes and tight mouth. In one photograph the woman is stroking my mother's cheek.

I lay all the photographs out on the kitchen table carefully. I look at them for a while. A mosaic of my mother and this stranger. I know this is the woman Mélanie saw in our mother's bed. This is the American Gaspard mentioned.

Inside the envelope is a typed letter addressed to my grandmother from the Agence Viaris. The date is January 12, 1974. A month before my mother died.

Dear Madame Rey,

As per your instructions and according to our contract, here is the information you requested concerning Clarisse Rey née Elzyère and Miss June Ashby. Miss Ashby, of American nationality, born in 1925 in Milwaukee, Wisconsin, has an art gallery in New York City on West 57th Street. She comes to Paris every month for business and stays at the Régina Hotel on the place des Pyramides in the first arrondissement.

Miss Ashby and Madame Rey, during the course of the weeks from September to December 1973, met every time Miss Ashby came to Paris, which totals five times. Madame Rey each time came to the Régina Hotel in the afternoons and went directly up to Miss Ashby's room. Madame Rey came down again a couple of hours later. On one occasion, December 4, Madame Rey came after dinner and did not leave the hotel till the next morning at dawn.

Please find our invoice enclosed.

Agence Viaris, Private Investigators

I look closely at the photographs of June Ashby. A striking woman. Her eyes seem dark, but the photographs are not good, I can't really tell. She has high cheekbones, the wide shoulders of a swimmer.

She doesn't look "butch." There is even something intensely feminine about her—her long, slender limbs, the bead necklace around her neck, dangling earrings. I wonder what she said in English the day she came to confront Blanche, which sounded so horrible according to Gaspard. I wonder where she is now. I wonder how she remembers my mother.

I feel a movement and quickly turn. Margaux is standing directly behind me, wearing her dressing gown. Her hair is pulled off her face, making her look like Astrid.

"What is all this, Dad?"

My first reaction is to shamefacedly hide the photos, cram them back into the envelope, and invent some story about sorting out old documents. But I do not move.

It is too late to lie. Too late to be silent. Too late to pretend I don't know.

"This was given to me tonight."

She nods.

"The brunette. She looks so much like Mélanie . . . Isn't that your mother?"

"Yes, that is my mother. And the blond lady is . . . her friend."

Margaux sits down and examines each photograph with interest.

"What is all this about?"

No more lies. No more silence.

"My grandmother was having my mother and this woman followed by a private investigator."

Margaux stares at me.

"Why would she do that?" Then it hits her. She is only fourteen, after all. "Oh," she says slowly, her face flushing. "They were lovers, right?"

"Yes, they were."

A pause.

"Your mother was having an affair with this lady?"

"That's right."

Margaux scratches her head thoughtfully. She whispers, "Is this like some kind of huge family secret that nobody ever talks about?"

"I guess so."

She picks up one of the black-and-white photographs.

"She looked so much like Mélanie. It's amazing."

"She did."

"Who is the other lady, her friend? Did you ever meet her?"

"An American. This happened a long time ago. If I ever met her, I don't remember her."

"What are you going to do with all this, Dad?"

"I don't know," I reply truthfully.

I unexpectedly have a vision of the Gois passage being lapped away by tongues of seawater. Soon, only the rescue poles indicate that a road lies deep beneath the surface. An uneasy feeling washes over me.

"Are you okay, Dad?"

Margaux's hand grazes my arm. The gesture is such a rare one coming from her that it both startles and moves me.

"I'm okay, honey. Thanks. You get to bed now."

She lets me kiss her. She slips away.

There is only one thing left in the envelope, a thin sheet of paper that has been crumpled and smoothed out. It is written on the Hotel Saint-Pierre stationery. The date reads August 19, 1973. The shock of my mother's handwriting strikes me like a blow. I read the first lines with a thumping heart.

You have just left your room, and I am slipping this under your door, not leaving it in our usual safe hiding place, and I pray you get it before you catch your train back to Paris . . .

MY HEAD SEEMS A little clearer, although I feel my heart still thrumming painfully, as it did in Gaspard's room a couple of days ago. I go to the computer and type out "June Ashby" on Google. The first item that pops up is the art gallery that bears her name on Fifty-seventh Street in New York City. Specializes in modern and contemporary art by women. I search for data about her, but there is none on the site.

I go back to Google, scroll down the page. Then I see it.

> June Henrietta Ashby died in May 1989 of respiratory failure at Mount Sinai Hospital in New York City. She was 64 years old. Her renowned art gallery on 57th Street, founded in 1966, focuses on modern European art by women, which she introduced to American art lovers. It is now run by her associate, Donna W. Rogers. Miss Ashby was a gay rights activist, cofounder of the New York lesbian social club and advocacy group Daughters of Hope.

I feel a piercing sadness learning that June Ashby is dead. I would have liked to know this woman, the woman my mother loved, whom she had met in Noirmoutier in the summer of 1972. The woman she had loved in secret for more than a year. The woman my mother was ready to face the world with, the woman she wanted to raise us with. I am too late. Nineteen years too late.

I print out the entry and clip it to the other documents in the envelope. I look up Donna W. Rogers and Daughters of Hope on Google. Donna is a weathered-looking woman in her seventies, with an astute face and cropped copper hair. The lesbian social club has a rich and interesting website. I surf through it, reading about meetings, concerts, gatherings. Cooking lessons, yoga, poetry seminars, political conferences. I forward the link to Mathilde, an architect I worked with a couple of years ago. Her girlfriend, Milèna, has a hip bar I often go to in the Latin Quarter. Despite the lateness of the hour, Mathilde is in front of her computer and e-mails me right back. She is curious as to why I sent her that link. I explain that the social club was cofounded by a woman who had been my mother's lover. Then my cell phone rings. It is Mathilde.

"Hey! I didn't know your mother was a *goudou*," she says.

"Neither did I."

A silence, but not an uncomfortable one.

"When did you find out?"

"Not long ago."

"How are you feeling?"

"Odd, to say the least."

"And does she know you know? Did she tell you?"

I sigh. "My mother died in 1974, Mathilde. I was ten years old."

"Oh, I'm sorry," she says quickly. "Forgive me."

"Forget it."

"The fact that she was a lesbian—did your father know?"

"I don't know. I don't know what my father knows."

"Do you want to pop over to the bar so we can have a drink and chat?"

I'm half tempted. I enjoy Mathilde's company, and her girlfriend's bar is an amusing nightspot. But exhaustion weighs me down tonight and I tell her so. She makes me promise to come by soon. I do.

Later, in bed, I call Angèle. I get her voice mail. I don't leave a message. I try the home number. No answer. I struggle not to let this annoy me, but it does. I know she sees other men. She is discreet about it. I want to tell her not to. I decide to tell her soon. But what will she come back with? That we are not married? That she's allergic to fidelity? That she lives in Clisson and I live in Paris, and how are we going to work that one out? Yes, how? There is no way she would ever move to Paris. She hates its pollution, its noise, and do I see myself being buried in that small provincial town? And she might even ask me (for she has probably guessed it) if I had slept with Astrid recently and not told her.

I miss her tonight as I lie there in my empty bed, so many questions whirling around in my head. I miss her astuteness, the fast way her brain works. I miss her body, the scent of her skin. I close my eyes and quickly make myself come, thinking of her. It gives me some sort of release, but it doesn't make me feel any happier. I feel lonelier than ever. I get up to smoke a cigarette in the dark silence.

June Ashby's fine features come back to me. I can see her ringing the Rey doorbell, tall and formidable in her fury, her grief. She and Blanche, face-to-face. The New World versus *la vieille* Europe, embodied by Paris's sixteenth arrondissement.

You better tell me how Clarisse died, right now.

I have never heard her voice and I never will, but it seems to me that I can hear it tonight, a deep, strong voice, the American accent coming out thick and strong through the polished French. I can hear her pronouncing "Clarisse" the way Americans say it, emphasizing the final syllable, softening the *r*.

You better tell me how Clarisse died, right now.

Later, when I finally fall asleep, the disquieting vision of seawater closing hermetically over the Gois never leaves my troubled dreams.

IT IS DONE. BLANCHE lies in the Rey family grave at the Trocadéro cemetery. We stand by the tomb under a surprisingly blue sky, a small group of us—my children, Astrid, Mélanie, Solange, Régine, Joséphine, close friends, faithful servants, and my frail father, leaning on a cane I have never seen him use. I notice how his illness has gradually taken over. His skin, sickly and yellow, has a waxlike consistency. He has lost most of his hair, even his lashes and brows. Mélanie is at his side, and I observe how she never leaves him, holding his arm, looking across at him with solace like a mother comforting a child. I know my sister has a new boyfriend, Eric, a young journalist I have not yet met, but despite this new man in her life, she now appears to be thoroughly taken up by our father and his well-being. During the ceremony in the cold and dark church, her hand was always on our father's shoulder. I can tell how concerned she is, how he moves her. Why is it that I am not moved? Why is it that my father's vulnerability triggers only pity? As I stand there, it is not my father I think of. Nor my grandmother. I think of my mother, whose coffin lies in that grave a few feet below me. Did June Ashby ever come here? Did she ever stand where I am standing now, looking down at the tombstone that bears Clarisse's name? And if she did, was she overcome by the same questions that are now tormenting me?

After the burial we gather at the avenue Henri-Martin for a party in Blanche's honor. Several of Solange's friends turn up. The same elegant, well-to-do throng that was here the night Blanche died. Solange asks me to help her carry flowers into the *grand salon*, which has been opened especially for the occasion. Gaspard and a couple of employees have laid out a tasty buffet, and I observe Régine, cheeks caked with rouge, starting on the champagne. Joséphine is too busy chatting up a rubicund, oily gentleman to notice. My father, very quiet, sits in a corner with Mélanie.

I am alone with Solange in the office, helping her find vases for the sickly sweet–smelling lilies that keep pouring in every time the doorbell chimes. On the spur of the moment I tackle her as she is concentrating on arranging the flowers.

"Do you remember a woman called June Ashby?" I ask point-blank.

Her carefully made-up face does not move a muscle.

"Very vaguely," she murmurs.

"An American woman, blond, tall—she had an art gallery in New York."

"Rings a bell."

I watch her hands hovering over the white petals, her pudgy, bejeweled fingers, her scarlet nail varnish. She was never a pretty woman, Solange. It could not have been easy for her, having a sister-in-law who had Clarisse's looks.

"June Ashby spent a couple of summers in Noirmoutier at the Hotel Saint-Pierre. While we were there."

"I see."

"Do you remember she was friendly with my mother?"

She finally looks at me. Nothing warm in those brown eyes.

"No. I don't remember."

A waiter comes in carrying a tray of glasses. I wait till he leaves.

"What do you remember about her and my mother?"

Again the stony look.

"Nothing. I remember nothing about her and your mother."

If she is lying, she is an accomplished liar. Her eyes look right at me, unwavering. Her entire self is composed, unruffled. The message she is sending my way is clear: "Don't ask any more questions."

She walks away, her back as stiff as ever, carrying lilies. I return to the *grand salon*, noting that the room is full of people I have never met. I greet them politely.

Laurence Dardel, wearing a black suit that makes her look years older, unobtrusively hands me a brown envelope. The medical file. I thank her and put it away next to my coat, but I am itching to tear it open. Mélanie's eyes follow me from afar, and I feel a pang of guilt. Soon, I tell myself, soon I will share all this with her. About June Ashby, the scrap with Blanche, the detective report.

I notice Astrid watching me as well, no doubt wondering why I look on edge. She is busy consoling Margaux, who was miserable during the funeral, for it brought back painful, fresh memories of Pauline.

Arno comes to stand next to me. He is home from boarding school to attend his great-grandmother's funeral. His hair is shorter, cleaner, and he has shaved.

"Hey, Dad."

He reaches out and pats my shoulder, goes over to the table where drinks and petits fours are laid out, and pours out a fruity beverage. After a longish spell of not talking to each other at all, apart from minimal conversation, our relationship has thawed out somewhat. I suspect the boarding school, with its strict hours, bracing hygiene, and vigorous, compulsory sports program, is doing him good. Astrid thinks so as well.

He leans toward me and whispers, "You know, those photographs. Margaux told me."

"About my mother?"

"Yup. She explained. About the letter from the agency and everything. Heavy stuff."

"How do you feel about it?"

He grins. "You mean about having a *gay* granny?"

I can't help grinning too.

"Kinda cool when you think of it," he says, "although I guess it wasn't so cool for Grand-père."

"No, I guess it wasn't."

"Kinda hard on a man's pride, I'd say. You know, like, to have a wife who prefers girls?"

Coming from a sixteen-year-old, I find his observation both mature and relevant. How would I have reacted if Astrid was having an affair with a woman? Isn't that the ultimate snub for a man? The most humiliating form of adultery? The true way to make a man feel anything but virile? But when I think of Serge and his hairy buttocks on Astrid's camera, I somehow feel that nothing could be worse.

"How are things with Serge?" I inquire, keeping well out of Astrid's range.

Arno wolfs down an entire chocolate éclair.

"Travels a lot."

"And your mother? How is she?"

Arno peers at me, munching away. "Dunno. Ask her. She's looking right at us."

I pour myself some champagne as Gaspard rushes to assist me.

"When are you seeing Angèle again?" Arno asks.

The champagne tastes icy and bubbly on my tongue.

"In a couple of weeks." And I nearly add, "I can't wait."

"Does she have kids?"

"No. She has a couple of nephews and nieces who are your age, I think."

"Are you going to Nantes?"

"Yes. She doesn't much like coming to Paris."

"That's a pity."

"Why?"

He blushes. "She's cool."

I laugh and rumple his hair the way I used to when he was a kid. "You're right. She's cool."

The minutes tick by. Arno discusses his school, his new friends. I listen and nod. Then Astrid comes to talk to us. After a while Arno takes off for more food, and she and I are left *en tête à tête.* She seems happier. It appears that Serge and she have made a new start. I'm glad to hear it. I say so. She wants to know about Angèle, she is curious about her. She has heard so much about her from the children. Why don't I bring her to Malakoff one evening for dinner? Sure, I say, but Angèle doesn't come to Paris often. She likes to stick to her beloved Vendée.

And all of a sudden, despite the pleasant conversation with my wife, the kind of conversation I haven't had with her for a while, it seems absolutely impossible not to peek right now, this very minute, at my mother's medical file. There is no way I can wait till I get home.

I murmur something about going to the bathroom, back away, and inconspicuously pick up the envelope, slip it under my jacket, and dash to the large bathroom down the long corridor. Once inside, the door locked, I open it feverishly. Laurence Dardel has written a note.

> Dear Antoine, please find enclosed your mother's complete medical dossier. These are photocopies, as you may notice, but nothing has been omitted. My father's notes are all there. I do feel this is not useful for you in any way, but you have a right, as Clarisse Rey's son, to look at this file. If you have any further questions, please get back to me. All best, LD.

"Snobbish bitch," I find myself muttering out loud. "Never liked her."

The first document is the death certificate. I pore over it, turning the light on to see it better. Our mother indeed died at avenue Henri-Martin. Not avenue Kléber. "*Cause of death: Aneurysm.*" An unexpected thought comes to me. "Wait a minute . . ." I mumble aloud to myself. "Wait a minute . . ." February 12, 1974 . . . we came home from school with the au pair in the afternoon . . . I was told, as soon as we arrived, by our father, that Clarisse suddenly died, that her body was at the hospital. . . . I didn't ask *where* she died. I naturally assumed she died at avenue Kléber. So I never asked. Neither did Mel.

I know I am right. *Mélanie and I were not told, because we never asked.* We were so small. We were in shock. I distinctly remember our father explaining about the aneurysm, how it happened, a vein bursting in the brain, how Clarisse had died, very quick, very fast, painlessly, but that's all he ever said about her death. And if Gaspard had not committed that slip of the tongue, we would have gone on thinking that our mother died at avenue Kléber.

As I flip through the pages of the file, the doorknob rattles and startles me.

"Coming!" I say hastily, folding up the sheets of paper and hiding them under my jacket. I flush the toilet, turn on the tap, and wash my hands. When I open the door, Mélanie is waiting for me, her fists on her hips.

"What are you up to?" she asks. Her eyes dart around the room.

"Just thinking. About a couple of things," I say, drying my hands busily.

"Are you hiding anything from me?"

"Of course not. I'm working on something, for both of us. I'm piecing it all together."

She steps into the bathroom, closes the door quietly behind her. Once again I am struck by her resemblance to our mother.

"Listen to me, Antoine. Our father is dying."

I stare at her. "He told you? About his cancer?"

She nods.

"Yes. He told me. Recently."

"You never said anything to me."

"He asked me not to."

I gape at her, stunned. Then I hurl the towel to the ground, anger sparking through me.

"This is outrageous. I'm his son, for Christ's sake."

"I know how you must feel. But he cannot talk to you. He doesn't know how. And you aren't good at that with him either."

I lean back against the wall and fold my arms across my chest. The anger bubbles up inside me. Fuming, I wait for her to speak.

"He hasn't got much time, Antoine. He has stomach cancer. I spoke to his doctor. The news isn't good."

"What are you trying to tell me, Mélanie?"

She goes to the basin, opens the tap, passes her hands under the running water. She is wearing a dark gray wool dress, black tights, black patent leather flats with gold buckles. Her silvery streaked hair is tied back with a black velvet bow. She bends to retrieve the towel, wipes her hands.

"I know you're on the warpath."

"The warpath?" I repeat.

"I know what you've been doing. I know you asked Laurence Dardel to give you our mother's medical file."

I am silenced by the seriousness in her voice.

"I know Gaspard gave you a document. He told me. I know you probably know who the blond woman was. And I overheard you questioning Solange just now."

"Wait, Mélanie," I blurt out, my face reddening with mortification at the idea of her thinking I could be hiding such important details from her. "You must understand that I was going to tell you all this. I—"

She holds up a slender, white hand.

"Just listen to me."

"Okay," I say, unnerved, smiling uneasily. "I'm all ears."

She doesn't smile back. She leans forward, her green eyes inches from mine.

"Whatever you find out, I don't want to know."

"What?" I breathe.

"You heard me. I do not want to know."

"But why? I thought you did. Remember? The day you remembered why we had the crash. You said you were ready to face the pain of knowing."

She opens the door without answering, and I fear she is about to slip off without another word. But she whips around, and when she faces me once more, her eyes are filled with such sorrow I want to take her into my arms.

"I've changed my mind. I'm not ready. And when you do find out—whatever it is—don't talk to our father. Don't ever tell him."

Something in her voice breaks, and she dashes away, face lowered. I stand there, unable to move. How is it that a brother and a sister can be so dissimilar? How is it that Mélanie prefers silence to the truth? How can she live, not knowing? Not wanting to know? Why does she want to protect our father so?

As I stand there, disconcerted, my shoulder against the door frame, my daughter emerges from the long corridor.

"Yo, Dad," she says. Then she sees my face. "Bad day?"

I nod.

"Me too," she says.

"So that makes two of us."

And to my wonder, she hugs me, hard. I hug her back, kissing the top of her head.

It is not till later, much later, when I am back home, that the idea comes to me.

My mother's note to June Ashby is in my hands, and I am reading it for the umpteenth time. Then I glance at the article I printed out about June Ashby's death. The name of her associate, Donna W. Rogers. I know what I want to do. It is very clear to me. I find the telephone number on the June Ashby Gallery website. I look at my watch.

Five o'clock in the afternoon in New York City. *Do it,* says the little voice. *Just do it. You have nothing to lose. She may not even be there, she may not remember a thing about your mother, she may not even take your call, but just do it.*

After a couple of rings a masculine voice says breezily, "June Ashby Gallery, how may I help you?"

My English feels rusty; I haven't spoken the language in months. I hesitatingly ask for Madame Donna Rogers.

"May I ask who is calling?" says the amiable voice.

"Antoine Rey. I am calling from Paris, France."

"And may I ask what this is about?"

"Please tell Madame Rogers that this—this is a very personal matter."

My French accent comes out so strongly it makes me squirm. He asks me to hold on.

Then a woman's firm tones are heard, and I know it must be Donna Rogers. I feel tongue-tied for a couple of seconds. Then I blurt out, "Yes, hello . . . My name is Antoine Rey. I'm calling you from Paris."

"I see," she says. "Are you one of my clients?"

"Um, no," I reply awkwardly. "I am not a client, Madame. I'm calling you about something else. I'm calling you about . . . about my mother . . ."

"Your mother?" she asks. Then she says courteously, "Excuse me, what did you say your name was?"

"Rey. Antoine Rey."

A pause.

"Rey. And your mother's name . . ."

"Clarisse Rey."

There is such a long silence on the other end of the line that I fear I have lost her.

"Hello?" I say tentatively.

"Yes, I'm still here. You are Clarisse's son."

This is statement, not a question.

"Yes, I am her son."

"Can you hold on, please?"

"Of course."

I make out a couple of muffled words, some rustling and crumpling. Then the man's voice: "Hold on, sir, I'm transferring you to Donna's office."

She finally says, "Antoine Rey."

"Yes."

"You must be in your forties, I presume?"

"Forty-four."

"I see."

"Did you know my mother, Madame?"

"I never met her."

I am puzzled by her answer, but my English is too stilted for me to react fast enough.

She goes on. "Well, you see, June told me all about her."

"What did she tell you about my mother? Can you tell me?"

There is a long hush. Then she says quietly, so quietly I have to strain my ears to make out her words, "Your mother was the love of June's life."

FROM WHERE I SIT, the countryside scuttles by, a drab blur of gray and brown. The train is too swift for raindrops to settle on the windowpanes, but I know it is raining. It has been wet for the past week. Sodden, end of winter weather at its worst. I crave Mediterranean luminosity, the blue and white of it, the scorching heat. Oh, to be somewhere in Italy, on the Amalfi coast, where I went years ago with Astrid, the dry, powdery scent of pines swaying on rocky coves, the sun-kissed, salty breeze strong on my face.

The high-speed train to Nantes is jam-packed. It is Friday afternoon. Mine is a studious passenger car, people reading books or magazines, working on their laptops, listening to music from their earphones. In front of me, a young woman writes zealously in a black Moleskine notebook. I can't help looking at her. She is outstandingly attractive. Perfect oval of a face, luxuriant chestnut hair, fruitlike mouth. Her hands are exquisite too, long, tapered fingers, graceful wrists. She does not look up at me once. It is only when she glances outside from time to time that I can glimpse the color of her eyes. Amalfi blue. Next to her is a fleshy guy dressed in black who is engrossed in his BlackBerry. And by my side is a seventy-year-old woman reading poetry from a small book. She looks impossibly British, a mop of silver hair, aquiline nose, toothy smile, and immense hands and feet.

From Paris to Nantes is barely a two-hour trip, but I am counting the minutes, which seem to be crawling by at a snail's pace. I haven't seen Angèle since she turned up for my birthday in January, and the yearning for her seems bottomless. The lady next to me gets up and comes back from the bar with a cup of tea and crackers. She flashes a friendly smile at me, and I smile back. The pretty girl is still scribbling away, and the man in black finally puts his BlackBerry down, yawns, and rubs his forehead jadedly.

I think of the past month. Mélanie's unforeseen warning after Blanche's funeral: *Whatever you find out, I don't want to know.* Solange's hostility when I mentioned June Ashby's name: *I remember nothing about her and your mother.* And the emotion in Donna Rogers's voice: *Your mother was the love of June's life.* She had asked me for my address in Paris, that day, on the telephone. A couple of things she could send me that June had kept and that maybe I would like.

I had received the parcel a few weeks later. It contained a stack of letters, some photographs, and a small reel of Super 8 film. And a card from Donna Rogers.

Dear Antoine,

June kept these preciously till she died. I am sure she would be happy thinking they are now in your keep. I don't know what the little film reel is, she never told me, but I'd rather you find out for yourself.

All best to you,
Donna W. Rogers

As I opened the letters with slightly trembling fingers and started reading, I thought fleetingly of Mélanie, wishing she could be there with me, sitting next to me in the privacy of my bedroom, sharing these precious vestiges of our mother's life. The date read "July 28, 1973. Noirmoutier, Hotel Saint-Pierre."

> Tonight I waited for you on the pier, but you did not come. It grew cold, and after a while I left, thinking maybe it was difficult for you to get away this time. I told them I just needed a quick walk on the beach after dinner, and I wonder if they believed me. She always looks at me like she knows something, although I am sure, perfectly sure, that nobody knows. Nobody knows.

My eyes teared up, and I sensed I could no longer go on reading. It didn't matter. I could always read them later. When I felt stronger. I folded the letters away. The photographs were black-and-white portraits of June Ashby taken by a professional photographer. She looked rather beautiful—strong, arresting features, piercing eyes. On the back of the photographs was my mother's round, childish handwriting: *"My sweet love."* There were other photographs, a color one of my mother wearing a blue and green evening dress I had never seen, standing in front of a full-length mirror in a room I did not recognize. She was smiling into the mirror at the person taking the photo, who I assumed was June. In the next photograph, my mother was in the same pose, but stark naked. The dress lay at her feet, a crumpled blue and green heap. I sensed my face growing red, and I quickly averted my eyes from my mother's body, a body I had never seen in the nude. I felt like a Peeping Tom. I did not want to look at the other photographs. Here was my mother's love affair exposed in all its blatancy. Would it make any difference if June Ashby had been a man? I forced myself to think about this, hard. No, I did not think so. At least not for me. Was the fact that she was having a lesbian affair more difficult to stomach for Mélanie? Was it worse for my father? Was that why Mélanie did not want to know? I felt relieved that my sister was not here with me after all, that she had not seen the photographs. I then picked up the small Super 8 reel. Did I really want to know what was on it? What if it was intolerably intimate? What if I regretted watching it? The only way to find out was to have the film converted to a DVD. It was easy to locate a place on the Internet that did just that. If I sent the film first thing next morning, I would receive my DVD in a couple of days.

The DVD is now in my backpack. I got it just before I left to catch the train, and I have not yet had time to view it. "5 minutes," reads the data printed on the cover. I take it out of my bag and finger it nervously. Five minutes of what? The expression on my face must be overwrought; I feel the pretty girl watching me. Her eyes are inquisitive, not unkind. She looks away.

The daylight dims as the train dashes forward, swaying slightly as it reaches its full speed. Another hour to go. I think of Angèle waiting for me at the Nantes station, and then the wet ride on the Harley to Clisson, thirty minutes away. I hope the rain will have abated. But she never seems bothered by rain. She has all the right gear.

I take my mother's medical file out of my bag. I have read it carefully but have learned nothing from it. Clarisse started seeing Dr. Dardel just around the time of her marriage. She often had colds and migraines. She measured 1 meter 58, smaller than Mélanie. She weighed 48 kilos. A tiny wisp of a woman. All her vaccines were in order. Her pregnancies were supervised by an obstetrician, Dr. Giraud, at the Belvédère Clinic, where Mélanie and I were born.

All of a sudden a loud, ominous thwack is heard, and the train lurches sideways violently, as if its wheels have struck branches or a tree stump. Several people cry out in shock. My mother's file slinks to the ground and the English lady's tea spills all over the table. She exclaims, "Oh dear!" and dabs at the mess with a napkin. The train slows down instantly and comes to a shuddering halt. We all wait in silence, looking at one another. The rain beats down on the windowpanes. Some people get up, try to peer outside. Panicked murmurs arise from each side of the coach. Nothing happens for a while. A child whimpers. Then a cautious voice is heard on the loudspeaker: "Ladies and gentleman, our train is blocked due to technical difficulty. More information to come. Apologies for the delay." The stout man in front of me lets out an exasperated sigh and grabs his BlackBerry. I text Angèle and describe what has happened. She texts back almost instantly, and her message makes my blood run cold.

I hate to tell you this, but that's not a technical difficulty. That's a suicide.

I get up, startling the English lady, and walk toward the head of the train. Our coach is situated in the front, near the engine. Passengers in the adjoining carriages are just as restless and impatient. Many of them are using their phones. The noise level gets increasingly louder. Two ticket inspectors appear in their dark uniforms. Their faces are positively morose.

With a sinking heart, I know Angèle is right.

"Excuse me," I say, cornering them in the small space between two coaches, near the toilets. "Can you tell me what's going on?"

"Technical problems," mumbles one of them, wiping his damp forehead with a shaking hand. He is young, and his face seems awfully white.

The other man is older and perceptibly more experienced.

"Was it a suicide?" I ask.

The older guy nods grimly. "It was. And we'll be here for a while. Some folks aren't going to like it."

The younger guy leans against the toilet door, his face paler than ever. I feel sorry for him.

"It's his first time." The older guy sighs, taking off his cap and running his fingers through thinning hair.

"Is the person . . . dead?" I manage to ask.

The man looks at me quizzically.

"Well, when a high-speed train is going that fast, that's usually what happens," he grunts.

"It was a woman," whispers the younger man, his voice so low I can hardly hear him. "The driver said she was kneeling on the tracks, facing the train, her hands clasped as if in prayer. There was nothing he could do. Nothing."

"Come on now, kid, get a grip," says the elder man firmly, patting his arm. "We need to make an announcement. There are seven hundred passengers on this train tonight, and they'll be here for another couple of hours."

"Why does it take so long?" I inquire.

"The body remains have to picked up one by one," says the older inspector wryly, "and they're usually stretched along the tracks for several kilometers. From what I just saw, with the rain and everything, it's not looking good at all."

The younger man turns away as if he is going to be sick. I thank the other man and stagger back to my seat. I find a small bottle of water in my bag and drink hastily. But my mouth still feels dry. I text Angèle.

You were right.

She texts back:

Those are the worst suicides. The messiest kind. Poor person. Whoever it was.

The announcement finally comes. "Due to a suicide on the railway, our train will experience considerable delay."

People around us groan and sigh. The English lady stifles a little cry. The fat man bangs his fist down on the table. The pretty girl had her earphones in and didn't hear the announcement. She digs them out.

"What happened?" she asks.

"Somebody committed suicide and now we're stuck here in the middle of nowhere," whines the man in black. "And I have a meeting in an hour."

She stares at him with her perfect sapphire eyes.

"Excuse me. You just said somebody committed suicide?"

"Yeah, that's what I said," he drawls, brandishing his BlackBerry.

"And you're complaining we're going to be late?" she hisses in the coldest voice ever.

He stares back at her.

"I have an important meeting," he mutters.

She looks at him scathingly. Then she gets up, and as she heads to the bar, she turns around and says, just about loud enough for the entire carriage to hear, "Asshole."

THE ENGLISH LADY AND I share a drink at the bar, some Chardonnay to cheer us up. It is dark now, and the rain has stopped. Huge floodlights illuminate the tracks, revealing the gruesome ballet of policemen, ambulances, firemen. I can still feel the thwack of the train hitting that poor woman's body. Who was she? How old was she? What despair, what lack of hope could have led her here tonight, waiting in the rain, kneeling on the tracks, her hands joined?

"Believe it or not, I'm on my way to a funeral," says the English lady, whose name is Cynthia. She gives a dry chuckle.

"How sad!" I exclaim.

"An old friend of mine. Gladys. Tomorrow morning. She had all sorts of grisly health complications, but she was terribly brave about it. I admired her very much."

Her French is excellent, just a trace of a British accent. When I comment on it, she smiles again.

"I've been living in France all my life. Married a Frenchman." She winks.

The pretty girl comes back into the bar coach and sits not far from us. She is talking on her phone, waving her hands about. She looks agitated.

Cynthia goes on, "And just as we hit that poor person who decided to put an end to his or her life, I was in the middle of choosing a poem to read at Gladys's funeral."

"Did you find your poem?" I ask.

"I did, indeed. Have you ever heard of Christina Georgina Rossetti?"

I grimace. "I'm not very good with poetry, I'm afraid."

"Nor am I. But I wanted to choose one that was neither morbid nor sad, and I think I have at last found it. Christina Rossetti was a Victorian poet, totally unknown in France, I believe, and wrongly so, for most talented in my opinion. Her brother Dante Gabriel Rossetti stole the limelight. He was rather more famous. You may have seen his paintings. Pre-Raphaelite stuff. Rather good."

"Not very good at paintings either."

"Oh, come on now, I'm sure you've seen his work. Those somber, sensuous ladies with flowing auburn hair, full mouths, and long dresses."

"Perhaps." I shrug, smiling at the expressive way her hands suggest abundant bosoms. "What about the sister's poem? Can you read it to me?"

"I will. And we shall think about the person who just died, shall we not?"

"It was a lady. The ticket inspectors told me."

"Then I shall read this poem for her. Bless her soul."

Cynthia takes the poetry book out of her bag, slides her oversize owl-like glasses over her nose, and begins to read in a loud, theatrical voice. Everybody in the bar coach turns around.

"When I am dead, my dearest,
Sing no sad songs for me;
Plant thou no roses at my head,
Nor shady cypress tree:
Be the green grass above me

With showers and dewdrops wet;
And if thou wilt, remember,
And if thou wilt, forget."

Her voice goes on, soaring through the sudden hush, above the grating, scraping noises of whatever is going on outside, which I don't want to think about. It is a poignant poem, beautifully simple, and somehow it fills me with hope. When she finishes reading, some people murmur their thanks, and the pretty girl's face is tearful.

"Thank you," I say.

Cynthia nods. "I'm glad you like it. I think it is fitting."

The girl comes up to us timidly. She asks Cynthia for the author of the poem and writes it down in her notebook. I ask her to join us, and she sits down gratefully. She says she hopes we didn't think she was rude—what she said to the man in black earlier on.

Cynthia scoffs. "Rude? My dear, you were remarkable."

The girl smiles ruefully. She is unusually good-looking. Her figure is exceptional, swelling breasts only just visible under a loose, dark sweater, long line of hip and leg, round buttocks under tight Levi's.

"You know, I can't help thinking about what happened," she whispers. "I almost feel responsible, as if I killed that poor person myself."

"That's not what happened," I tell her.

"Perhaps, but I can't help it. I keep feeling that bump." She shivers. "And I keep thinking about the man who was driving the train . . . Can you imagine? And with these high-speed trains, I guess there's no way you can brake fast enough. And this person's family. I heard you saying it was a woman. . . . I wonder if they've been told by now. Has she even been indentified? Maybe nobody knows. Maybe her loved ones have no idea that their mother, sister, daughter, wife, whatever, is dead. I can't bear it." She starts to cry again, very softly. "I want to get off this awful train, I want this to never have happened, I want this person to be still alive!"

Cynthia takes her hand. I don't dare. I don't want this lovely creature to think I'm coming on to her.

"We all feel the same," says Cynthia soothingly. "What happened tonight was dreadful. Horrible. How can anyone not be upset?"

"That man . . . That man who kept saying he was going to be late," she sobs, "and there were others too. I heard them."

I too will be haunted by that *thwack*. I don't tell her, because her awesome beauty is stronger than the hideous power of death. Tonight I am swamped by death. Never in my life has death hovered to such an extent around me, like the buzz of a persistent black moth. The cemetery my apartment gives onto. Pauline. The carcasses on the road. My mother's red coat on the *petit salon* floor. Blanche. Angèle's feminine hands handling corpses. That faceless, desperate woman waiting for the train under the drizzle.

And I am glad, so glad, relieved even, to be but a man, a mere man who in the face of death feels more like reaching out and groping this gorgeous stranger's breasts than breaking into tears.

I NEVER TIRE OF Angèle's exotic-looking bedroom, with its saffron gold ceiling and its warm, cinnamon red walls that make such an interesting contrast with the morgue she works in. The door, window frames, and baseboards are painted midnight blue. Orange and yellow silk embroidered saris hang over the windows, and small Moroccan filigree lanterns cast a flickering, candlelit glow on the bed, which is covered with fawn linen sheets. Tonight there are rose petals scattered over the pillows.

"What I like about you, Antoine Rey," she says, fumbling with my belt (and I with hers), "is that underneath that romantic, well-behaved, charming exterior, those clean jeans and crisp white shirts, those lovat green Shetland sweaters, you are nothing but a sex fiend."

"Aren't most men?" I ask, struggling with her knee-high black leather motorcycle boots.

"Most men are sex fiends, but some of them even more than others."

"There was this girl on the train . . ."

"Mmmh?" she says, unbuttoning my shirt.

Her boots at last clunk to the floor.

"Amazingly attractive."

She grins, slipping out of her black jeans.

"You know I'm not the jealous kind."

"Oh, yes, I know that. But thanks to her, I was able to get through those three excruciating hours waiting on the train while they were scraping the poor lady off the wheels."

"And how did you get through those three hours thanks to this amazingly attractive girl, may I ask?"

"By reading Victorian poetry."

"Sure."

She laughs, that low, sexy, throaty laugh I love so much, and I grab her, press her to me, kiss her avidly. I fuck her as if there is no tomorrow. The fragrant rose petals get mixed up in her hair and in my mouth and taste bittersweet. I feel like I cannot get enough of her, as if this is our last time. I am frantic with lust. I yearn to tell her I love her, but no words pass my mouth, only sighs, moans, and groans.

"You know, you should spend more time on trains," she mutters dizzily as we lie on the crumpled linen sheets, spent.

"And I feel sorry for all those dead people you fiddle with. They have no idea what a good lay you are."

It is later, much later, after we have showered, after a late-night snack of cheese, Poilâne bread, a few glasses of Bordeaux, and a couple of cigarettes, and after we have installed ourselves in the living room, with Angèle comfortably laid out on the couch, that she finally says, "Tell me. Tell me all about June and Clarisse."

I take the medical file, the photographs, the letters, the detective report, and the DVD out of my bag. She watches me, glass in hand.

"I don't know where to begin," I say slowly, feeling confused.

"Imagine you are telling a story. Imagine I know nothing, nothing whatsoever. I have never met you, and you have to explain it all, very carefully, with all the right details. A story. Once upon a time . . ."

I reach out and take one of her Marlboros. I don't light it, I just keep it between my fingers. I stand up, facing the old fireplace, with its dying blaze, embers gleaming red through the darkness. I like this room too, its size, its beams, its walls lined with books, the antique square wooden table, the quiet garden beyond that I cannot see, for the shutters are closed for the night.

"Once upon a time, in the summer of 1972, a married woman goes to Noirmoutier island with her parents-in-law and her two children. She is on holiday for two weeks, and her husband will join her on weekends if he's not too busy. She is called Clarisse, she is lovely and sweet, and not a sophisticated Parisienne . . ."

I pause. It feels strange talking about my mother in the third person.

"Go on," urges Angèle. "That's fine."

"Clarisse comes from the Cévennes, and her parents were simple, rural people. But she married into a wealthy, well-to-do Parisian family. Her husband is a young maverick lawyer, François Rey, well known for the Vallombreux trial in the early seventies."

My voice wavers. Angèle is right, it is a story. My mother's story. And I have never told it to anyone. After a pause, I go on.

"At the Hotel Saint-Pierre, Clarisse meets an American woman called June, who is older than she. How do they meet? Perhaps coming down for drinks one evening. Perhaps on the beach one afternoon. Maybe at breakfast, at lunch, at dinner. June has an art gallery in New York. She is a lesbian. Was she there with a girlfriend? Was she alone? All we know is—Clarisse and June fall in love that summer. This is not . . . just an affair, a summer fling. . . . This is not just sex. This is love. A hurricane-like, unexpected, twister of a love. . . . Real love—the kind that comes once in a lifetime—"

"Light that cigarette," orders Angèle. "It will help."

I comply. I inhale deeply. She's right. It does help.

"Of course, nobody must know," I continue. "There is too much at stake. June and Clarisse see each other when they can during the rest of 1972 and the beginning of 1973, which is not very often, because June lives in New York. But she comes to Paris for business every month or so, and that's how they meet, at June's hotel. And then, during the summer of 1973, they plan to spend time together again, at Noirmoutier. And things aren't as easy, as simple, that summer for June and Clarisse. Even if Clarisse's husband is not often there, because he works and travels, one day the mother-in-law, Blanche, has a horrible, niggling suspicion. She knows. And that day she makes up her mind."

"What do you mean?" says Angèle, alarmed.

I don't answer. I continue my story, concentrating, taking my time.

"How does Blanche know? What does she see? Is it a fleeting glance of longing that lasted a trifle too long? A tender hand caressing a bare arm? Is it a forbidden kiss? Is it a silhouette she spied in the night, flitting from one room to another? Whatever Blanche saw, whatever it was, she kept it to herself. She did not tell her husband. She did not tell her son. Why? Because the shame was too great. The horror and the shame of her daughter-in-law, now a Rey, now a mother, having an affair—and to crown it all, an affair with a woman. The Rey family name could not be soiled. Not over her dead body. She had worked too hard for this. She had not been brought into the world for this. She, a Fromet from Passy, married to a Rey from Chaillot—no, it was unthinkable. It was monstrous. It had to be ended. Fast."

Oddly enough, I am very calm as I tell the story, my mother's story. I do not look at Angèle's face, because I know it must be stricken. I know what my words sound like to her, their reach, their potency. I have never uttered this story, never pronounced that precise sequence of sentences, never said what I am now saying, and each word coming out is like a birth, the shock of cold air on a fragile, naked body slithering out of the womb.

"Blanche confronts Clarisse in Noirmoutier, at the hotel. Clarisse cries, she is upset. There is a scene in Blanche's room on the first floor. Blanche warns her. She is frightening, ominous. Blanche threatens her, says she will reveal the affair to her husband, her son. She says she will take the children away from her. Clarisse sobs, yes, yes, of course, she will never see June again. But she cannot. It is beyond her control. She sees June again and again, and she tells her all this, but June laughs it off. She is not afraid of a snob of an old lady. The day June leaves for Paris to fly back to New York, Clarisse slips a love letter under June's door. But June never gets it. It is intercepted by Blanche. And that's when the trouble truly begins."

Angèle gets up to stir the embers of the fire, as the room is getting cold. It is late now—how late, I don't know. I am aware of a leadlike weariness weighing on my eyelids. But I know I need to go to the very end of the story, the part I am dreading, the part I don't want to have to say out loud.

"Blanche is aware that Clarisse and June are still lovers. In the letter she stole, she learns that Clarisse dreams of a future with June and the children. Somehow, somewhere. She reads this with loathing and revulsion. No, there is no future for June and Clarisse. No future is possible for them. Not in her world. And there is no way her grandchildren, Reys, will have anything to do with this. She goes to a private detective in Paris and explains that she wants her daughter-in-law followed. She pays a lot of money for this. Again, she never tells her family. Clarisse thinks she is safe. She is waiting for the day she and June will be free. She knows she has to leave her husband, she knows what this entails. She is afraid for her children, but in her mind, she is in love, and she believes love will find a way. Her children are the most precious beings to her, and so is June. She likes to imagine a place, a safe place, where she can live one day with June and the children. June is older, wiser. She knows. She knows that two women cannot live together like a couple and be treated normally. This may occur in New York, perhaps, but not in Paris. Not in 1973. Certainly not in the kind of society the Rey family live in. She tries to explain this to Clarisse. She says they need to wait, to take their time, that things can happen quietly, slowly, with less difficulty. But Clarisse is younger and more impatient. She doesn't want to wait. She doesn't want to take her time."

The pain is setting in at last, like a familiar, dangerous friend you let in with apprehension. My chest feels constricted, too small to contain my lungs. I stop and take a couple of deep breaths. Angèle comes to stand behind me. Her warm body presses against mine. It gives me the strength to carry on.

"That Christmas is a dreadful one for Clarisse. Never has she felt lonelier. She misses June desperately. June has her busy, active life in New York, her gallery, her society, her friends, her artists. Clarisse has only her children. She has no friends apart from Gaspard, the son of her mother-in-law's maid. Can she trust him? What can she tell him? He is only fifteen, barely older than her son, a nice, simple-minded young boy. What can he understand? Does he know two women can fall in love? That it doesn't necessarily make them evil, immoral sinners? Her husband is dedicated to his work, his trials, his clients. Maybe she tries to tell him, maybe she drops clues, but he is too busy to hear. Too busy climbing the social ladder. Too busy paving his way to success. He plucked her out of nowhere, she was just a girl from Provence, so unsophisticated it made his parents reel. But she was beautiful. She was the loveliest, freshest, most charming girl he had ever met. She didn't care about his fortune, the family name, the Reys, the Fromets, the real estate, the property, the establishment. She made him laugh. No one ever made François Rey laugh."

Angèle's arms snake their way around my neck, and her hot mouth kisses the back of my neck. I steady my shoulders. I am coming to the end of the story.

"Blanche receives the file from the detective in January 1974. It is all there. All of it. How many times the women met, where, when. Photographs and all. It repels her. It drives her mad. She nearly tells her husband. She nearly shoves it under his nose, she is so outraged, so disgusted, so appalled. But she doesn't. June Ashby notices that they are being followed. She traces the detective back to the Rey residence. She calls Blanche to order her to mind her own *fucking business*, but Blanche never takes her calls. June gets the maid or the maid's son. June tells Clarisse to be careful, she tries to warn her, to explain that it all needs to die down a bit, that they should lie low, that they should wait. But Clarisse can't stand it. Clarisse can't stand the idea of being followed. She knows Blanche is going to call her in, to show her the incriminating photos. She knows Blanche will force her to never see June again, that she will threaten to take the children away from her. And so one morning, one cold, sunny winter morning in February, Clarisse waits till her children are on their way to school, she waits till her husband has gone to his office, and she puts on her pretty red coat and walks from the avenue Kléber to the avenue Henri-Martin. It is a short walk, one she has often done with the children, with her husband, but not recently, not since Christmas, not since she knows that Blanche wants June out of her life. She walks quickly until she is breathless, until her heart pumps too hard, too fast, but she walks on, heedless, intent on getting there as soon as possible. She walks up the stairs and rings the bell with a trembling finger, and Gaspard, her friend, her only friend, opens up and smiles. She says she needs to see Madame right away. Madame is in the *petit salon*, finishing her breakfast. Odette asks if she wants some tea, some coffee. She says no, she won't be a minute, she just has something to say to Madame and she'll be gone. Is Monsieur there? No, Monsieur is not here today. Blanche is sitting down reading her mail. She is wearing her silk kimono and she has curlers in her hair. When she looks up at Clarisse, she does not look happy to see her. She orders Odette to close the door and to leave them. Then she gets up. Wielding a document under Clarisse's nose, she snarls, 'Do you know what this is, have you any idea?' 'Yes, I know,' says Clarisse quietly. 'These are photographs of June and me, you had us followed.' Blanche feels an unprecedented gush of fury. Who does this peasant think she is? No upbringing. No breeding. From the gutter. Uncouth, slatternly, coarse little peasant. 'Yes, I have photos of your disgusting affair. I have it all here, let me show it to you. See? It's all here, *when* you see her, *where* you see her. And now this shall go straight to François so that he knows who his wife really is, so that he sees she is not fit to be the mother of his children.' Clarisse replies, very calmly, that she is not afraid. Blanche can do just that, Blanche can show it to François, to Robert, to Solange. Blanche can show it to the entire world. 'I love June and she loves me, and we want to spend the rest of our lives together with the children. This is exactly what should happen, no more hiding, no more lies. I will tell François myself. There will be a divorce. We will explain it to our children as gently as possible. François is my husband, and I should tell him myself because I respect him.' Blanche's venom swells, huge, bloated, out of proportion. 'What do you know about respect? What do you know about family values? You are nothing but a slut. And I will not have you tarnishing our name with your revolting lesbian business. You will stop seeing that woman as of right now, and you will do exactly as you are told. You will maintain your rank—'"

I stop, my voice now a mere croak. My throat is parched. I go into the kitchen and pour myself a glass of water with shaking hands. I drink it down in a gulp, the glass rattling against my front teeth. When I go back to Angèle, the most unexpected and uncomfortable image jumps to my eyes, like a slide being propped there against my will.

I see a woman kneeling on rail tracks at dusk, and I see the train zooming up to her at a very fast pace. The woman is wearing a red coat.

"ODETTE IS STANDING JUST outside the closed door. She has been standing there since Madame ordered her to leave, her ear glued to the panel, although that isn't necessary, as Madame is shouting so loudly. She has heard it all, the entire wrangle. She now hears Clarisse's firm, 'No. Goodbye, Blanche,' and then there is a skirmish, the echo of a brief struggle, the sharp intake of breath, an exclamation, but whose voice is it, she can't make out, and then a dull thud, something heavy falling to the floor. Madame's voice saying, 'Clarisse! Clarisse!' and then, 'Oh, my God.' The door opens, Madame's face is haggard, she seems petrified. She looks utterly silly with the rollers bobbing up and down on her head, and it takes her a couple of minutes to talk, to actually speak to Odette. 'There's been an accident. Call Dr. Dardel, fast. Hurry!' What accident? thinks Odette as she rushes to get her son, orders him to call Dr. Dardel immediately, and comes running back to the *petit salon* on her squat legs, where Madame is waiting, prostrate on the couch. What accident? What happened? 'There was an argument,' moans Madame, her voice strangled. 'She was going to leave, and I held her back. I hadn't finished with what I was telling her, and I grabbed her sleeve, and she stupidly fell, she fell forward, and she banged her head on the table corner right there, look, where it is at its sharpest.' And Odette looks and sees the sharp corner, the glass corner, and she sees how still Clarisse is lying on the carpet, no movement, no breathing, her face drained of all color, and she says, 'Oh, Madame, she is dead.' Then Dr. Dardel arrives, the reliable family doctor, the old, faithful friend. He examines Clarisse, and he says the same words, 'She is dead.' Blanche wrings her hands, she sobs, she tells the doctor it was all a frightful accident, such a stupid, monstrously stupid accident. He looks at Blanche as he signs the death certificate, pen poised, and he says, 'There is only one thing to do. There is only one solution, Blanche. You must trust me. Let me do what I have to do.'"

I stop. That is the end of the story.

Angèle gently turns me around so I can see her face. She puts both hands on my cheeks and looks at me for a long time.

"Is that how it happened, Antoine?" she says very softly.

"I will never know the truth. That is the closest I can get to it."

She goes to the fireplace, leaning her forehead against the smooth wood of it, then glances back at me.

"Did you ever manage to talk to your father about this?"

My father. How can I begin to tell her? How can I describe our last talk, a few days ago? I felt compelled that evening, as I left the office, to confront him. No matter what Mélanie said. No matter how hard she had tried putting me off for reasons of her own. I needed to talk to him then. There would be no more waiting. No more guesswork. What exactly did he know about Clarisse's death? What had he been told? Did he know about June Ashby?

When I turned up, my father and Régine were having dinner in front of the television. They were watching the news. The upcoming American presidential elections. The tall, thin man, barely older than I am, the one people were calling "the black Kennedy." My father was silent, tired. Little appetite. Loads of pills to swallow. Régine whispered that next week he was scheduled to stay at the hospital for a while. A bad patch was coming up. She shook her head despondently. When the meal was over and Régine was on the phone with a friend in another room, I said to my father, hoping he'd tear his eyes away from the television, that I would like to talk to him if he didn't mind. He nodded and gave a sort of grunt, which I assumed was a positive response. But when he finally turned his eyes to me, they were so full of weariness that I was instantly silenced. The eyes of someone who knew he was dying, who could not bear being on the face of this earth any longer. There was sheer misery in those eyes, as well as a quiet submission that stirred me. Gone was the maverick lawyer. Gone was the dictatorial father. Gone was the arrogant censor. I was looking at an old, sick, foul-breathed man who was ready to die, and who didn't want to listen to me, or to anyone else, anymore.

It was too late. Too late for me to reach out and tell him I cared, too late for me to tell him that I knew he had cancer, that I knew he was dying, too late to ask him about Clarisse and June, too late to risk myself in that territory with him. He blinked slowly, not even puzzled. He waited for me to speak, and when I finally did not, he shrugged weakly and looked back at the television. He did not even ask me what I wanted. I felt as if he had dropped a curtain onto a stage. The show was over. *Come on, Antoine, this is your father. Reach out, take his hand, make sure he knows you're there, even if you can't bring yourself to do it, make an effort, tell him you do care, tell him before it is too late. Look at him, he is dying, there is not much time. There is no time.*

I remembered when he was young, his smile shining out like a beacon in his otherwise severe face, when his hair was dark and thick, not the meager, scanty roots of today. I remembered when he would take us into his arms and kiss us lovingly, when Mélanie used to ride on his shoulders at the Bois de Boulogne, when his protective hand at the small of my back, propelling me ahead, made me feel I was the most powerful boy in the world. I remembered, after my mother's death, how he clammed up, how the tender kisses stopped, how he became demanding, inflexible, how he criticized, how he judged, how he made me feel wretched. I wanted to ask him why life had made him so acrimonious, so hostile. Was it losing Clarisse?

Losing the only person who ever made him happy? Was it finding out she had been unfaithful? That she loved someone else? That she loved a woman? Was it that, that final humiliation, that had broken my father's heart, broken his soul?

But I asked him nothing. Nothing at all. I got up. He did not move. The television blared on. So did Régine's voice next door.

"Goodbye, Father."

He grunted again, not even looking at me. I left, closing the door behind me. On the stairs, I could no longer contain the bitter tears of remorse and pain that seemed to sear into my flesh.

"No, I could not talk to my father. I couldn't do it."

"Don't blame yourself, Antoine. Don't make it even harder on yourself."

The urge to sleep takes over like a heavy blanket thrown over my head. Angèle leads me to bed, and I marvel at the gentleness of her hands, those respectful, caring hands that deal with death every day. I drop into an uneasy sleep, like sinking into a bottomless, murky sea. Such strange dreams come to me, my mother kneeling in her red coat facing the train, my father with his happy smile of long ago, climbing a treacherously steep, snowy peak, his face burned by the sun, Mélanie, wearing a long black dress, floating on the surface of a black swimming pool, arms outstretched, sunglasses perched on her nose, and me striding through a thick, overgrown forest, bare feet on muddy, insect-ridden soil.

When I wake up, morning has broken, and for a panic-stricken second I don't know where I am. Then I remember. Angèle's place. In her remarkably renovated nineteenth-century house that used to be a small primary school. Situated by a river in the heart of Clisson, that quaint historical town near Nantes I had never heard of before I met her. Ivy creeping up granite walls, two broad chimneys overlooking the tiled roof, and an enchanting walled garden, the pupils' old playground. I am in Angèle's comfortable bed. But she is not lying next to me. The space next to me is cold. I get up, patter downstairs. The appetizing aroma of coffee and toast greets me. A pale, lemony sunshine pours through the windowpanes. Outside, the garden is covered with a delicate sprinkling of frost, like icing on a cake. From where I stand, I can just glimpse the top of the ruins of Clisson's medieval castle.

Angèle is sitting at the table, hugging one knee, deeply immersed in a document. Her open laptop is nearby. As I come closer, I see that she is studying my mother's medical file. She glances up, and by the circles under her eyes, I can tell she hasn't slept much.

"What are you doing?" I ask.

"I was waiting for you. I didn't want to wake you."

She rises, pours me a cup of coffee, hands it to me. I see that she is dressed for the day, wearing her customary black jeans, boots, and black turtleneck.

"You look like you haven't had much sleep."

"I read your mother's medical file."

Something about the way she says it makes me look at her more closely.

"Did you notice anything?"

"Yes," she says. "I did. Sit down, Antoine."

I sit next to her. It is warm and sunny in the kitchen, and after that troubled sleep, those disturbing, vivid dreams, I don't think I can face anything distressing. I brace myself.

"What did you notice?"

"I'm not a doctor, you know that. But I work in a hospital and I see death every day. I read medical files too, I talk to doctors. I examined your mother's file while you were asleep. I took notes. And I did some research on the Internet, as well as sending a couple of e-mails to friends of mine who are doctors."

"And?" I ask, suddenly unable to drink my coffee.

"Your mother had been having migraines two years before she died. Not very often, but strong ones. Do you remember them?"

"One or two. She had to lie down in the dark, and Dr. Dardel would come to see her."

"A few days before she died, she had a migraine, and she saw her doctor. Look, you can read it here."

She hands me the photocopied note. Dr. Dardel's crooked handwriting. I had seen this before. It was the last entry in his notes before Clarisse died. *"February 7, 1974. Migraine, nausea, vomiting, eye pain. Double vision."*

"Yes, I saw that," I say. "What of it?"

"What do you know about brain aneurysms, Antoine?"

"Well, I know an aneurysm is a like a small bubble or a tiny blister that forms on the surface of a brain artery. I know the aneurysm has a thin wall compared with the thicker wall of a normal brain artery. And the danger is when that weaker wall bursts."

"That's pretty clear. Good."

She pours out some more coffee.

"Why are you asking me this?"

"Because I do think your mother may have died of a ruptured brain aneurysm."

I look at her in dismayed silence. Finally I mumble, "You don't think there was a fight with Blanche?"

"I'll tell you what I think happened. But when I do, it will still be up to you, Antoine. You will have to believe what you think is true."

"You think I'm exaggerating the story? That I'm imagining things? That I'm being paranoid?"

She puts an appeasing hand on my shoulder.

"Of course not. Keep your hair on. Your grandmother was a homophobic old bitch. Just listen to me, okay? February seventh, 1974. Dr. Dardel sees your mother at the avenue Kléber. She has a severe migraine. She is in bed, in the dark. He gives her the usual medicine, and it clears up a day later. So he thinks. So she thinks. So everybody thinks. But the bad news about a brain aneurysm is that it can swell, slowly, surely, and maybe your mother had it for a while in her brain, but nobody knew, and her occasional migraines came from there. When an aneurysm swells up, before it bursts, before it bleeds, it puts pressure on the brain or on places near the brain, like optical nerves, for instance, or face and neck muscles. '*Migraine, nausea, vomiting, eye pain. Double vision.*' If Dr. Dardel had been a little younger and perhaps a little more dynamic, with those symptoms, he should have had your mother sent to the hospital right away. My two doctor friends confirmed this to me by e-mail. Maybe Dr. Dardel had a busy schedule that day, maybe his mind was on other urgent matters, maybe he wasn't worried. But the aneurysm in your mother's brain grew and swelled. And on February twelfth, 1974, a couple of days later, it ruptured."

"Tell me how you think it happened."

"It happened while she was with your grandmother, that very morning of February twelfth. The story is the same, your mother in her red coat, walking to the avenue Henri-Martin. But your mother probably doesn't walk that fast, because she is not feeling well at all. She is still nauseous, and maybe she even vomited that morning. She feels dizzy, and her step is unsure. Perhaps, most probably, there is a stiffness in her neck. But she wants to confront your grandmother, and for her, this is just the tail end of her migraine. She is not worried about her health. She is much more worried about June. And facing your grandmother."

I bury my face in my hands. The idea of my mother toiling up the avenue Henri-Martin in pain, her arms and legs weighing a ton, going to face Blanche like a brave little soldier heading out to battle is unbearable.

"Go on."

"The story continues, similar to yours. Gaspard opens the door, maybe he notices how ashen she is, how short of breath she is, but she has only one goal, tackling your grandmother. Maybe your grandmother notices something too, that Clarisse's face is alarmingly pale, that her speech is slurred, that she doesn't seem to stand up straight, as if she were tipsy. The conversation is the same, Blanche flaunts the photos, the detective's report, and Clarisse says she will stand her ground, that she will never stop seeing June, loving June. And then it happens. Suddenly. Like lightning. The worst pain ever. Like a shot aimed at the back of her head. Clarisse lurches, puts her hand to her temples, and she falls right there and then. Maybe she does knock her head on the table corner, but she's already dead. There is nothing your grandmother can do. There is nothing the doctor can do. When he comes, he knows. He knows he made a mistake by not sending her to the hospital a few days before. He probably carried that guilt all his life."

Now I understand why Laurence Dardel was bothered about me asking for that file. She knew a medical eye could easily pick out her father's malpractice.

Angèle comes to sit on my knees, which is not easy, considering how long-legged she is.

"Does this help you? At all?" she asks softly.

I put my arms around her, nestling my chin in the crook of her neck.

"I don't know. What hurts is not knowing what really happened."

She strokes my hair.

"When I came back from school that day, the day my father shot himself, there was no note. He left nothing. It drove us mad. It drove my mother mad. Just before she died, a couple of years ago, she told me how dreadful it was, not knowing why he had killed himself even after all those years. There was no other woman. No financial problems. No health problems. Nothing."

I hold her tight, thinking of her at thirteen discovering her dead father. No note. No explanation. I shudder.

"We never knew. We had to live with that. I learned to. It wasn't easy, but I did."

And it dawns on me that this is precisely what I am going to have to do.

"It's time," says Angèle vigorously. We are having our coffee after lunch, and the sun is so exceptionally warm that we are sitting outside on the patio, in front of the kitchen. The little garden is slowly coming to life. Spring is not far. I can smell it tickling my clogged-up Parisian nose. Grassy, humid, fresh, and pungent. Delicious.

I glance at her, surprised. "Time for what?"

"Time to go."

"Where?"

She smiles. "You'll see. Put something warm on. The wind can be tricky."

"What are you up to?"

"Wouldn't you like to know."

I used to be edgy, at first, riding behind her on the Harley-Davidson. I wasn't used to motorcycles. I never knew which side to lean on during a turn, and as a city boy, I was convinced that bikes were too dangerous to be trusted. I had never driven one in my life. And I had never ridden behind anyone, let alone a woman. Angèle drove her Harley every day from Clisson to the hospital at Le Loroux, rain or shine, sleet or snow. She hated cars, being stuck in traffic jams. She bought her first Harley when she was twenty years old. This was Harley number four.

A pretty woman on a vintage Harley gets noticed, I soon discovered. The distinctive throaty exhaust roar of the Harley turns heads, but so does the black leather–clad, curvaceous creature sitting atop it. Riding behind her was much more pleasant than I had anticipated, as I am stuck to her in a quasi-sexual posture, my thighs engulfing her, my crotch glued to her stupendous ass, my stomach and chest fixed to her hips and back.

"Come on, Mister Parisian, we haven't got all day!" she yells, throwing me my helmet as the Harley growls invitingly.

"Are we expected?"

"Well, yes, we are!" she says exultantly, checking her watch, "and if you don't get a move on, we'll be late."

We weave down bumpy country roads lined with fields touched by the first magical promise of spring. The sun is positively warm, but the bite of the air stays nippy. We drive for what I guess must be an hour or so, but it doesn't seem long at all. It is in fact heavenly to be tucked snugly behind Angèle, the Harley's rumbling vibrations strong in my loins, the sun caressing my back.

It is not till I see the signposts for the Gois that I understand where we are. I had never realized how close Clisson was to Noirmoutier. The scenery strikes me as completely different in the wintertime, browner tones, no green. The sand on the shore appears darker too, earthier, but no less beautiful. The first rescue poles seem to greet me, and the gulls circle overhead with piercing cries as if they remember me. The beach stretches far away, dark brown, touched with gray. The dark blue sea sparkles under the sun, and I can see the black, uneven lines of conches, shells, seaweed, rubble, cork, and pieces of wood.

There are no more cars on the Gois, and the tide is closing over from the right, the first lathered sheets of water already covering the causeway. The place is nearly deserted, not like in summer, when thick crowds gather to watch the sea conquer the land. Angèle does not slow down. In fact she drives even faster, and I tug at her jacket to draw her attention, as I cannot be heard through my helmet and hers. She ignores me superbly, gearing the Harley up, and the few people who are parked on land point at us with startled expressions as we rocket past. I can almost hear them exclaim, "Hey, are they going to cross the Gois?" I pull on her jacket, harder this time. Somebody honks loudly to warn us, but it is too late. The Harley's wheels send impressive sprays of seawater gushing up on either side of us as they hit the paved causeway. I hope to God Angèle knows what she is doing. I read too many stories as a boy about accidents on the Gois at high tide not to know this is a crazy feat. At least thirty people have died here in the past hundred years. And God knows how many more before that. I hold on to her for dear life, praying the Harley doesn't skid and send us plunging headfirst into the sea, praying the engine doesn't get swamped by one of those frothy waves that seem larger by the minute. Angèle drives those four kilometers smoothly and with such cocksure self-assurance that I guess this is not her first time.

It is a wonderful, exhilarating ride. And I suddenly feel safe, gloriously safe, safer than I have felt since knowing the touch of my father's protective hand on my back as a boy. Safe, with my body clasped against hers as we seem to glide over water, over what is no longer a road, for it can no longer be seen. Safe, as I look up at the island ahead, at the familiar rescue poles dotting our way through the sea's glittering surface, beckoning us as a lighthouse leads a ship to security in the harbor. And I wish this moment could last forever, that the beauty and perfection of it would never leave me. We pull in on land amid the clapping and cheering of passersby who are standing near the cross guarding the mouth of the Gois.

Angèle stops the engine and takes off her helmet.

"I bet you were scared shitless." She chuckles, a broad smile on her face.

"No!" I gasp, putting my helmet on the ground so I can kiss her wildly, more cheering and clapping going on behind us. "I wasn't scared. I trusted you."

"You can. First time I did that, I was fifteen years old. On a friend's Ducati."

"You drove a Ducati at fifteen?"

"You'd be surprised at what I did at fifteen."

"I'm not interested," I say airily. "How are we getting back? The Gois is closing over."

"We'll take the bridge home. Less romantic, though."

"Much less romantic. Wouldn't I love to get stranded on one of those rescue poles with you. I can think of all sorts of things to do to you."

The huge sweep of the bridge can be seen from where we stand, although it is more than five kilometers away. The road has gone now, entirely swallowed by the water. The sea has regained its supremacy, immense and shimmering.

"I used to come here with my mother. She loved the Gois."

"And I used to come here with my dad," she says. "We spent a couple of summers here too, when I was a kid. But not at the Bois de la Chaise, that was too chic for us, Monsieur! We went to the beach at the Guérinière. My father was born at La Roche-sur-Yon. He used to know this spot like the back of his hand."

"So maybe we both came to the Gois on the same day when we were small."

"Maybe we did."

We sit down on the grassy hill near the cross. We sit shoulder to shoulder, sharing a cigarette, near where I sat with Mélanie on the day of the accident. I think of my sister, wrapped up in a bubble of ignorance by her own will. I think of everything I now know that she never will unless she asks me. I take Angèle's hand and kiss it. I think of the long line of *ifs* that led me to this hand, to this kiss. If I hadn't decided to organize a surprise for Mélanie's fortieth birthday.

If Mélanie hadn't had that flashback. If there had been no accident. If Gaspard hadn't had that slip of the tongue. If he hadn't kept that invoice. But another *if* surfaces. What if Dr. Dardel had sent my mother to the hospital on February 7, the day she had the bad migraine? Could she have been saved? Would she still be alive today? Would she have left my father? Would she and June be living together? In Paris? In New York?

"Stop that," comes Angèle's voice.

"Stop what?"

She puts her chin on her knees and looks oddly young all of a sudden, gazing out to the sea, the wind whipping at her hair. Then she says in a low voice, "Antoine, I looked everywhere for that note. As my father lay there, his blood and brains scattered all over the kitchen, before I called for help, I looked for that note, shrieking at the top of my lungs, tears streaming down my face, trembling from head to toe. I looked for it high and low, I combed that goddamn house for it, the garden, the garage. I kept thinking my mother was going to come home any minute from the clerk's office she worked in, and I had to find that note before she arrived. I never did. There was no note. And then this monstrous *why* loomed up. Was he that unhappy? What was it we hadn't seen? How could we have been so blind, my mother, my sister, and I? And what if I *had* noticed something, and what if I had come home from school earlier that day, or what if I hadn't gone to school at all? Would he have killed himself? Or would he still be here today?"

I can see what she is getting at. She goes on. Her voice is stronger now, but I pick up a vibrant note of pain that moves me.

"My dad was the calm, quiet type, like you, not talkative, much more silent than my mother. His name was Michel. I look like him. The same eyes. He never seemed depressed, he didn't drink, he was healthy, athletic. He liked to read. All those books in my house are his. He admired Chateaubriand, Romain Gary, nature, the Vendée, and the sea, and he seemed a tranquil, happy fellow, or at least so we thought. The day I found him dead, he was dressed in his best gray suit, one that I saw him wear only on special occasions, Christmas or New Year's Eve. And he had a tie on, and his best black shoes. He never dressed like that every day. He worked in a bookstore, and he wore corduroys and sweaters. He was sitting at the table when he shot himself. I thought maybe the note was trapped under his body, as he had slumped forward after the shot, but I hadn't dared touch him. I was afraid of dead bodies then, not like now. But when they came to get him, there was no note under him. Nothing. Then I hoped a letter might come in the mail, that perhaps he had posted us a note the day he died, but nothing turned up. It was only when I began my job as a mortician, and when I got my first suicide cases that the healing process slowly began in an unexpected way. But this was later, years later, ten years later at least. I recognized my anguish and my despair when I met the families of those who'd killed themselves. I listened to their stories, I shared their grief, sometimes I even cried with them. Many of them told me why their loved ones had chosen to die, many of them knew. Broken hearts, illness, desperation, anguish, fear—there were so many reasons. And then it hit me one day as I was tending to the body of a man who was my dad's age. He had shot himself because the pressure at his job was too great. This man was dead, and so was my father. This man's family knew why he had pulled the trigger, whereas we didn't. But what difference did it make? Only death was left behind. A dead body to embalm, to put in a coffin, and to bury. Prayers to be said and grieving to begin. Knowing would never bring my father back. Knowing would never make the grieving any easier. Knowing never makes death easy."

There is a tiny teardrop quivering at the side of her eye, and I gently wipe it away with my thumb.

"You are a wonderful woman, Angèle Rouvatier."

"Don't get mushy on me, Antoine," she warns. "I hate that. Let's go. It's getting late."

She gets up and walks to the Harley. I watch her put on her helmet and her gloves and deftly kick-start the engine. The sun seems less strong now, and a chill is setting in.

WE COOK A LEISURELY dinner together, she and I, side by side. Vegetable soup (leeks, carrots, and potatoes), lemon and thyme (from the garden), roasted chicken with basmati rice, apple crumble. A cool bottle of Chablis keeps us company. The house is welcoming and warm, and I become conscious of how much I enjoy its peace and quiet, its size, its bucolic simplicity. I never thought an urbanite like me would revel in such a rustic setting. Could I possibly live here with Angèle? Nowadays, with computers, mobile phones, and high-speed trains, it was technically feasible. I think of my future workload. Rabagny was in the process of clinching a lucrative deal for me concerning the Think Dome patent. I would soon be busy again for him and Parimbert, for a highly ambitious, exciting European project that would bring money rolling in. And it seemed there was nothing I couldn't do for them right here. It was merely a matter of organization and clever planning.

But would Angèle want me here? *I'm not the marrying kind. I'm not a family person. I'm not the jealous type. Don't get mushy on me, Antoine.* Maybe Angèle's tantalizing spell spawns from the fact that I know I will never fully possess her. I can fuck her blind, which she obviously enjoys, and no doubt she is truly moved by my mother's story, but she will never want to live with me. She is like the cat in the *Just So Stories* by Kipling. The cat that walked by itself.

After dinner I suddenly remember the DVD made from the Super 8 reel. How could I have forgotten it? It is in the living room with the photographs and letters. I rush to fetch it and hand it to Angèle.

"What is this?" she asks.

I explain that it was sent to me by Donna Rogers from New York. June Ashby's partner. She slides it into her laptop's DVD drive.

"I think you need to watch this by yourself," she murmurs, caressing my hair, and before I can make up my mind whether I need her presence or not, she swings the Perfecto jacket over her shoulders and slips out into the dark garden amid a whoosh of cold country air.

I sit down in front of the computer and anxiously wait. The first image to flicker on the screen is my mother's face in the sunlight, filmed from close up. She has her eyes closed as if in sleep, but a tiny smile plays around her lips. Very slowly, she opens her eyes, shades them with her hand, and with a spasm of mixed pain and joy, I look into them, incredulous. How green they were, greener than Mélanie's, how soft and gentle they were, such serene, luminous, loving eyes.

I had never seen a film of my mother. Here she is on the screen of Angèle's computer, miraculously resuscitated, and I can barely breathe, fraught with exhilaration and emotion. Sudden tears trickle down my cheeks and I wipe them away hurriedly. I am amazed at the fine quality of the film. I was expecting coarse, poorly colored images. Now she is walking on a beach, and with a quickening pulse I recognize the Plage des Dames, the pier, the lighthouse, the wooden cabins, and her fuzzy orange bathing suit. I experience the strangest sensation. Somehow I know I am right around the corner building a sand castle, calling out to her, but June, who is no doubt filming, is not interested in a little boy's sand castle. The film then jumps to the rescue poles and the long stretch of the Gois passage, and I see my mother far away, a tiny silhouette, walking along the edge of the causeway at low tide on a gray and stormy day, wearing a red sweater and shorts, her black hair blowing in the wind. She seems far away at first, hands in pockets, but she walks closer and closer with her unforgettable dancer's walk, feet turned outward, back and neck straight. So graceful, so nimble. She is walking exactly where Angèle and I drove that very afternoon, heading to the island as we were, toward the cross. Her face is still a blur. Then it becomes clearer, and I see she is smiling. She breaks into a run, right up to the camera, laughs, clears a strand of hair from her eyes. Her smile is full of love, brimming over with it. Then she puts one of her small tanned hands to her chest, exactly over her heart, kisses it, and places her palm on the camera. The pink flesh of her palm is the last image of the film. The last image I see.

I click on the video to start it over again, awestruck by the images of my mother alive, moving, walking, breathing, smiling. I don't know how many times I watch it. Over and over again. Until I know it by heart, until I feel I was there. Until I can watch it no more because my agony is unbearable. Until my eyes are so full of tears I can no longer see the screen. Until I miss my dead mother so much I want to lie down on the uneven stone floor and weep. My mother will never know my children. My mother will never know who I am now. What I have grown into. Her son. A man leading his life the best way he can, a man doing his best, whatever that best may be. Something inside me is unleashed, snaps, lets go. I feel it go. I feel the agony go. In its place, a dull ache remains, and I know it will have a hold on me forever.

I stop the video and eject the DVD. I put it back into its cover. The door to the garden is ajar, and I slip outside. The air is sweet and cool. The stars twinkle. A dog howls in the distance. Angèle is sitting on a stone bench looking up at the stars.

"Do you want to talk about it?" she asks.

"No."

"Are you all right?"

"Yes."

She leans close to me. I put an arm around her shoulders, and we share the quiet cold of the night, the occasional faraway yelp of the dog, the starry radiance that shines down on us. I think of my mother's pink palm covering the camera. I think of the Harley gliding over the Gois. I think of Angèle's supple back against my chest, her confident gloved hands on the wide handlebar. And I feel sheltered, as I did that afternoon, knowing that this woman, whom I may or may not spend the rest of my days with, this woman who may send me packing tomorrow morning or take me in forever, this extraordinary woman whose job is death, has given me the kiss of life.

Acknowledgments

Thank you:

Nicolas, my husband, for his patience and his help.
Louis and Charlotte, our children, for being the great people they have blossomed into.
Laure, Catherine, and Julia, my first readers.
Abha, for her feedback and advice.
Sarah, for her beady eye.
Erika and Catherine, for helping me imagine Angèle.
Lauren and Jan, for their help on the U.S. edition.
Chantal, for giving me that space on the rue Froidevaux.
Guillemette and Olivier, for introducing me to Noirmoutier.
Mélanie and Antoine Rey, for letting me borrow their names.
Héloïse and Gilles, for trusting me again.

Last but certainly not least, to the fabulous St. Martin's team and, in particular, Sally, George, Matthew, Jennifer, Lisa, Anne, Sarah, and Mike.

A SECRET KEPT

by Tatiana de Rosnay

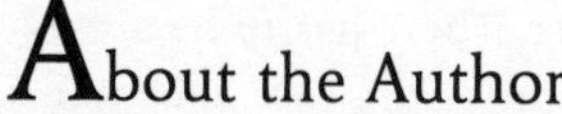

About the Author

• A Conversation with Tatiana de Rosnay

Behind the Novel

• "How Writing *Sarah's Key* Changed My Life"
An Original Essay by the Author

Keep on Reading

• Recommended Reading
• Reading Group Questions

A
Reading
Group Gold
Selection

For more reading group suggestions,
visit www.readinggroupgold.com.

ST. MARTIN'S GRIFFIN

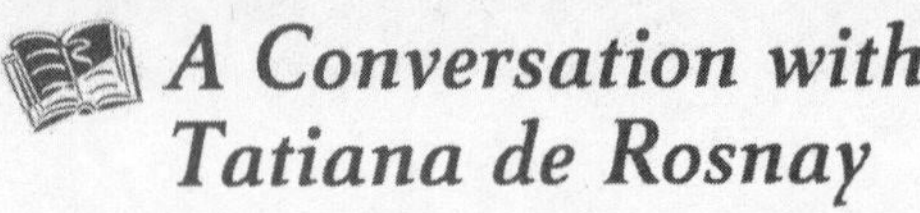

A Conversation with Tatiana de Rosnay

The first chapter of *A Secret Kept* really hooks you in. Is that the most difficult part to get right?

I find that—and this goes for my tastes as a reader, not only as a writer—I love being hooked into a book immediately. The opening lines of a book are so important. You really need to somehow charm your reader. If you can't get her attention in the first pages you may have lost her. There has to be an ambience. Not necessarily the entire cast of characters but something that is planted into the reader's mind so she'll say "What's going to happen?"

"I...know a lot more about men than I used to."

Was it hard writing from a male perspective?

It wasn't the first time I'd done it but it was the first time I did it with such honesty and lucidity. Previously I'd written a couple of novels where men were heroes but I did it tongue in cheek, making fun of men in not a very nice way but I was a lot younger in those days. Now, as I'm approaching fifty, I probably know a lot more about men than I used to. I think Antoine comes out as a very realistic character. Most of my readers think he really does exist and I've modelled him after somebody but he's an imaginary figure. My next book—the one I'm going to write this summer—will have a male hero.

Is that the ultimate compliment, when someone assumes the characters are real?

Yes. I get very touching e-mails from my male readers who say "thank you for writing this book and you've recognized something—you obviously know men quite well."

As someone who is truly bilingual do you ever find it hard to write completely in one language?

It's a complicated process. Sometimes it's a mere word or sentence that comes to me, if I'm writing the book in English, in French. It's not always easy to

deal with. Sometimes even during an interview somebody can ask me a question in English that I want to answer in French and vice versa—that's the story of my life!

You're very active on Facebook and Twitter—is that vital to success nowadays?

I was active on social media before I was a successful author. Don't forget that before *Sarah's Key* I sold 2,000 copies of each of my books in a good year. I had a blog at that point, I was already on Facebook. I wasn't on Twitter yet because that's only three years old. I've always been a geek so I've always used the Internet. Perhaps at first for self-promotion, as many authors do. Now I don't really need that anymore but it's a fantastic way to talk to my readers and let them know what I'm doing. I find it very useful.

I completely understand that some writers don't like it and shy away from that kind of thing but look at Joanne Harris. I met her on Twitter and have always adored her work. And now we're giving a talk together here in London next month. She actually tweets such funny things, she cracks me up! I sometimes don't have time to be so witty in my tweets. I tweet a lot about what I'm doing and where I am or if I'm unhappy or happy about something but I would never post anything personal. I've learned that.

And you sometimes have Facebook interactions with your characters?

It was my husband's idea to create Angèle Rouvatier's Facebook page and that was a huge success. She's such a powerful woman: She's a mortician; she drives a Harley-Davidson; she smokes Marlboros. It was so easy to create her Facebook page—she belongs to the Marlboro group, the Harley-Davidson group, she lives in the Vendée. We had no idea it would be such a success. The press really picked up on that in

France. Then, to my surprise, I started getting friendship requests from characters from my books! These are fans creating Facebook pages and completely respecting the code of each character. I find that a wonderful mark of sympathy for my books and what I do for them. It's a fun way of making the characters live on.

Are you tempted to incorporate these Facebook interactions into your writing?

Yes. In my next novel—the book I haven't started to write yet—it will be about a young male writer. I'm not going to tell you any more but quite a bit about the social networks and how we writers use them and the pitfalls. Sometimes disturbed people contact you and there are things you need to learn how to avoid as a writer. My young writer will make a couple of mistakes.

"Writing Sarah's Key *I learned the truth about a certain part of my country's history...and I still feel a scar."*

Your Twitter biography describes you as Franco-British with a zest of Russian. Do you identify with one more than the others?

I'm such a melting pot. My name comes from my Russian grandmother. She fled the Russian Revolution and she was an incredible character. She was the most ungrandmotherly grandmother you can imagine but such a fantastic optimist. I really miss her. It sounds corny to say you miss your grandmother but I really miss her.

The problem with being such a mix of nationalities is you don't feel you're one in particular. I was born in France but I don't really feel French. Technically I'm half English, and I was raised in America. I'd say I feel a little bit of everything.

About the Author

You've got such an amazing family tree. Have you considered writing your memoirs? (Tatiana is the great-great-granddaughter of Isambard Kingdom Brunel; granddaughter of Lord Jebb, Churchill's right-hand man, and painter Gaëtan de Rosnay; and daughter of scientist Joël de Rosnay.)

For the moment, no. I'm really into fiction and I don't think I could write anything else. But Isambard Kingdom Brunel, who is my great-great-great-grandfather, is unknown in France for some obscure reason. One of my plans would be to write about him. It would have to be a novel because there are so many books that exist here about him, after all he's a famous figure of this country—the only novelty I could give would be to track down the French connection. He is *franglais* like me—his father was French and his mother was British like me. I'm very interested in what he did and his life so one day something might come out of there but I'm not sure. It's circling 'round in my head but I have to really pinpoint it and work on it.

Who do you curl up with and read in the evening?

I read a lot of French and English writers but there are two writers that I really enjoy reading: one of them is Tracy Chevalier. I met her quite recently. I really enjoy her work. And my absolute British idol is Ian McEwan. Once I saw him fleetingly in a book fair in Oslo and I nearly died! I didn't muster up the courage to go up and speak with him but I was given the pen that he signed with all afternoon and I still have it, which goes to show how warped I am where he's concerned! I think he's brilliant.

Excerpted from an interview with Philippa Warr for MyDaily UK, www.mydaily.co.uk © AOL (UK) Limited 2011

An Original Essay by the Author

"How Writing *Sarah's Key* Changed My Life"
by Tatiana de Rosnay

The idea for *Sarah's Key* came to me by linking two stories: Sarah's story, seen through the eyes of a little Parisian girl forced to wear a yellow star, and whose life dramatically changed in July 1942, and Julia's story, set in the present, an American married to a Frenchman. Because Julia is commissioned by her magazine to write about the Vel d'Hiv's anniversary, she plunges into the horror of July '42. In this way I could reveal the taboos and scars that the Vel d'Hiv has left in France, more than sixty years later.

"[A]s a writer, seeing your work becoming a film is an amazing and exciting event."

I started to write *Sarah's Key* in a way I had never written anything before. I guess you can say I wrote it with my guts. Some of the passages were hard to write because I knew this is how it had happened. This is what happened to those children, to those families.

After I'd written about twenty pages, I gave them to my husband, Nicolas, to read, as he is my first reader. I noticed he was taking a long time reading them and I wondered why. Then he said to me when he had finished: "This is good, very powerful, you must go on." And then he said: "Why did you write it in English?" (He is French and not bilingual like me!) I hadn't even noticed I had written it in my mother tongue. But I knew why. Being half-French, half-English, I felt I had to retreat into my English side to write about this dark part of French history. So I went on writing *Sarah's Key* in English, although my previous published books were all in French. Also, having an American heroine, Julia, made it impossible for me to envisage her speaking in French.

When the book came out in France in 2007, I was worried about how the French Jewish community would react to it. How would they feel about a non-

Jewish woman writing about this highly sensitive part of France's past? And that's when the letters and e-mails started to come in. More and more each day. So moving that they made me cry. I met several Vel d'Hiv survivors who had read my book. They have become friends. They are in their seventies and eighties, but when I look at them, I see the children they used to be.

This book has now become a movie. I attended the filming of several scenes. It is a French movie, but parts of it are in English. Mélusine Mayance is the extraordinary actress who plays ten-year-old Sarah. When I first laid eyes on her, I couldn't believe it. Here was my Sarah, in real life! The Vel d'Hiv scenes were hard to watch. It was both sobering and moving to see 400 extras dressed in 1940s style, wearing the yellow star.

I then met Kristin Scott Thomas who plays Julia Jarmond. I think she is the perfect actress to play this role. She has been living in France for twenty years and told me she felt very close to Julia in spirit.

Many of my readers think I'm Julia Jarmond. Well, I'm not. I am French, she is American, her husband is not mine, thank God! But I guess Julia and I share the same horror, the same emotion, concerning the fate of the Vel d'Hiv children. I chose an American heroine because in a way I wanted to pay homage to the three years I spent in the United States as a child, when my father taught at MIT.

Writing *Sarah's Key* has changed my life. I learned the truth about a certain part of my country's history. I learned it late and I learned it hard, and I still feel a scar when I think about those children. I am French, and this happened in my country, sixty-nine years ago, in my city, just ten minutes from where I live.

I also wrote *A Secret Kept* directly in English. *A Secret Kept* is the story of a modern man confronted with a dark family truth, who will meet love in an unexpected way. It is about love (a first for me!), death, parents, children, and secrets—a very personal novel, as it comes close to my life in many ways. It is also the story of our modern lives today, as parents, as children, as siblings. It is about watching our parents become old people while our children become teenagers, both of which are not always easy. It is about caring and loving, and learning to communicate within a family.

I got the idea for this book thanks to my husband. He and I had invited his sister to Dinard in Brittany to surprise her for her fortieth birthday, where they had not been in thirty years. The whole weekend, memories kept coming back to them and as a writer it was fascinating to see. Memories of the beach, their grandparents, family meals, learning how to swim....On the way home I told them, "I think you gave me an idea for my next book." They said, "Oh that's great, but don't you need something more? Something stronger or darker?"

So I knew I had their story as a starting point—a story of a brother and sister going down memory lane, revisiting a place they went to as children—but I needed to have that extra twist. So I decided that the sister would have a disturbing flashback, which readers would discover throughout the book. I set the story not in Dinard, but in Noirmoutier, which is a beautiful island in Vendée, on the west coast of France. There is a submersible road there called the Gois Passage, which you can only use to get on the island at low tide, and it is a very Romanesque place. That road has a special significance in my novel and its symbolism and imagery play an impor-

tant part through the entire story. If you ever get to Noirmoutier, you need to see it.

A Secret Kept is about love—its secrets and its power, its magic, and I suppose its surprises. There is the love affair between Antoine and Angèle, but there is also the invisible love story you discover through the love letters in the book. I found it incredibly moving to write those letters. The sexy scenes between Antoine and Angèle were tricky to write, because I had to think from a man's point of view. But it was an enriching experience; writing about love is something that people have been doing for so many years, we will never tire of it.

My children are now nineteen and twenty-one, no longer really teenagers, but when I wrote this two or three years ago, I was drawing from my experience as a parent, understanding the issues that teens face and the limits and communication they need.

A Secret Kept is dedicated to my son's best friend who passed away suddenly at a young age. I asked my son if I could use his story as part of my book, and, although the details and characters are different, the emotions and how we came together as a family during this time are all there.

I worked very hard on creating Antoine. I worked hard to capture him as a lover, a husband, an ex-husband, a brother, a son, a father. I feel like I knew him intimately. If he walked into a room, I think I would recognize him and say hello. It was interesting to create the character of Angèle, because usually in my books, the women are more fragile and searching for something. Angèle was the first female character I imagined who wasn't searching for anything—instead, she was the helping hand to Antoine. I wanted to portray a man in that more fragile role. Yes, men have midlife crises too!

Angèle Rouvatier is a special character for me. I loved imagining her. She is strong, intelligent, sassy, beautiful. She rides a Harley, wears a black leather jacket, and she has a rather special job. She is a mortician. She knows a lot about life, and a lot about death. We often talk about midwives who bring us into this world, and we never talk about those who tend for us when we die.... I interviewed three female morticians to imagine Angèle's character and I was struck by the generosity and humanity of these women.

Angèle Rouvatier lives on on Facebook and has 3,000 friends. People often ask me if she actually exists and if I wrote about a real person in the book. Angèle is a fictional character, but she will respond to any messages and posts. It's a very fun way to interact with fans and it's given a lot of other writers I know similar ideas for creating their characters on Facebook.

A Secret Kept is going to become a movie in France, which is exciting news. I can't wait to see who will play Angèle and Antoine, and Mélanie. I think that, as a writer, seeing your work becoming a film is an amazing and exciting event.

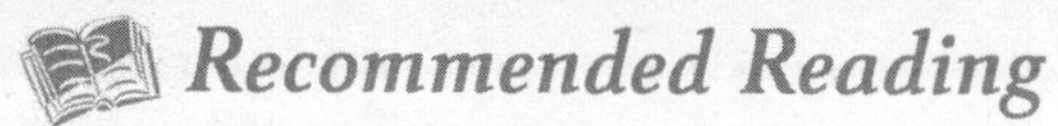

The Pursuit of Happiness
Douglas Kennedy

Charlotte Gray
Sebastian Faulks

Reservation Road
John Burnham Schwartz

My Dream of You
Nuala O'Faolain

Sophie's Choice
William Styron

Suite Française
Irène Némirovsky

After You'd Gone
Maggie O'Farrell

Resistance
Anita Shreve

Reading Group Questions

1. Discuss the different narrative structures employed in *A Secret Kept*. What do you think the author intended to achieve with each? Do you prefer one over the others?

2. How does the author describe the classic, wealthy 16th arrondissement of Paris—where Blanche Rey's apartment and the avenue Kléber one are located—as opposed to where Antoine lives, on the Left Bank? What does this tell you about the Rey family?

3. Part of the novel takes place on Noirmoutier Island, which is connected to the west coast of France by the Gois Passage. Why is Antoine so attached to the Gois Passage? Do you see any parallels between the author's descriptions of this place and the story as a whole?

4. What was your impression of Antoine at the beginning of the book? What about at the end? Over the course of the novel, how does he change and what does he learn about himself?

5. Discuss the different themes and imagery of death that come up in the novel and that Antoine has to face. Did you find them morbid? Or realistic?

6. Did you like the character of the sexy, streetwise mortician Angèle Rouvatier? What makes her different from other heroines and what do you think she represents? In what ways does she have a hand in the changes in Antoine's character?

7. François and Antoine Rey are two opposite personalities, as fathers, husbands, brothers, and sons. Discuss specific differences you see. Do you believe Antoine will ever get through to his father? What exactly do you think François knows about Clarisse, her life, her death?

8. Clarisse Rey is the invisible woman of this book. Yet her letters, photos, and the film that Antoine watches at the end, as well as Gaspard's confession, gradually expose her. What kind of woman was she? What do we learn about her? Compare her to Angèle, Mélanie, and Astrid.

9. How do Mélanie and Antoine react differently when they discover the truth about their mother and her death? Why do you think that Melanie chooses not to remember? Do you think you would react more like Mélanie or Antoine?

10. This novel explores taboo subjects and family secrets in a conservative French bourgeois society. Discuss those subjects and whether they would be taboo if the novel were set in the United States. What do you think really happened the day Clarisse went to confront Blanche?

11. Do you personally believe that family secrets should be revealed or hidden forever? In cases like the novel's, do you think the truth is more painful than lying?

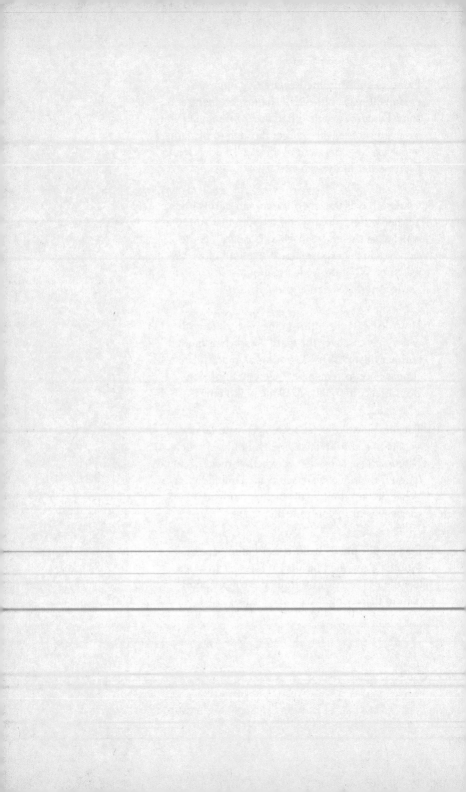

Turn the page for a sneak peek at Tatiana de Rosnay's new book

The House I Loved

Available February 2012

Paris slashed with saber cuts, its veins opened.

—ÉMILE ZOLA, *The Kill,* 1871

The old Paris is no more (the shape of a city changes faster, alas! than the human heart).

—CHARLES BAUDELAIRE, "The Swan," 1861

I wish for all this to be marked on my body when I am dead. I believe in such cartography—to be marked by nature, not just to label ourselves on a map like the names of rich men and women on buildings.

—MICHAEL ONDAATJE, *The English Patient*

Author's Note

Born and bred a Parisian, I love my city like most Parisians do. I have always been fascinated by its richness and history. Napoleon III and Baron Haussmann, between 1852 and 1870, gave Paris a new and much-needed modernity. They shaped the city into what it is today.

But I often wondered what it must have been like, as a Parisian, to witness those changes. And what it must have meant to lose a beloved house, like Rose does. Those eighteen years of "embellishments," before the Commune insurrection stormed the city, were no doubt hell for Parisians. Zola artfully described it, and criticized it, in *The Kill*. Victor Hugo and Baudelaire also voiced their discontent, as did the Goncourt brothers. But however much Haussmann was resented, his work remains essential to the creation of a truly modern Paris.

I have taken very few liberties with dates and places in this novel. The rue Childebert, the rue Erfurth, the rue Taranne and the rue Sainte-Marguerite did exist, 140 years ago, within Saint-Germain-des-Prés. So did the place Gozlin, the rue Beurrière, the passage Saint-Benoît and the rue Sainte-Marthe.

The next time you walk along the boulevard Saint-Germain, go to the corner of rue du Dragon, just in front of the Café dé Flore. You will notice an entire line of ancient buildings, miraculously standing between Haussmannian ones. Those are the vestiges of one side of the old rue Taranne, where the fictitious Baronne de Vresse used to live. A famous American designer has a flagship store there that could very well have been the Baronne's home. Have a look inside.

When you walk up the rue des Ciseaux, toward the church, try to ignore the noisy boulevard in front of you, and imagine the small and narrow rue Erfurth leading you straight to the rue Childebert, which used to be exactly where the metro station of Saint-Germain-des-Près now stands, on the left. And if ever you glimpse a coquettish silver-haired sexagenarian with a tall brunette on her arm, then you may just have seen Rose and Alexandrine on their way home.

TR
Paris, April 2011

My beloved,

I can hear them coming up our street. It is a strange, ominous rumble. Thuds and blows. The floor aquiver under my feet. There are shouts too. Men's voices, loud and excited. The whinny of horses, the stamp of hooves. It sounds like a battle, like in that hot and dreadful July when our daughter was born, or that bloody time when the barricades went up all over the city. It smells like a battle. Stifling clouds of dust. Acrid smoke. Dirt and rubble. I know the Hôtel Belfort has been destroyed, Gilbert told me. I cannot bear to think about it. I will not. I am relieved Madame Paccard is not here to see it.

I am sitting in the kitchen as I write this to you. It is empty, the furniture was packed up last week and sent to Tours, with Violette. They left the table behind, it was too bulky, as well as the heavy enamel cooker. They were in a hurry and I loathed watching that being done. I hated every minute of it. The house stripped of all its belongings in one short moment. Your house. The one you thought would be safe. Oh, my love. Do not be afraid. I will never leave.

The sun peeks into the kitchen in the mornings, I've always appreciated that about this room. So dismal now, without Mariette bustling about, her face reddened by the heat of the stove, and Germaine grumbling, smoothing back wisps of hair into her tight chignon. If I try, I can almost pick up the enticing wafts of Mariette's ragout weaving its slow path through the house. Our once-cheerful kitchen is sad and bare without the gleaming pots and pans, kept scrupulously clean by Germaine, without the herbs and spices in their little glass bottles, the fresh vegetables from the market, the warm bread on its cutting board.

I remember the morning the letter came, last year. It was a Friday. I was in the sitting room, reading *Le Petit Journal* by the window, and drinking my tea. I enjoy that quiet hour before the day begins. It wasn't our usual postman. This one, I had never seen. A tall, bony fellow, his hair flaxen under the flat green cap. His blue cotton blouse with its red collar appeared far too large for him. From where I was sitting, I saw him jauntily touch his cap and hand the mail over to Germaine. Then he was gone, and I could hear his soft whistle as he marched up the street.

It was early still, I'd had my breakfast a while ago. I went back to my newspaper after a sip of tea. It seemed the Exposition Universelle was all they could talk about these past months. Seven thousand foreigners pouring through the boulevards every day. A whirl of prestigious guests: Alexander II from Russia, Bismarck, the Vice King of Egypt. Such a triumph for our Emperor.

I heard Germaine's step on the stairs. The rustle of her dress. I do not get much mail. Usually a letter from my daughter, from time to time, when she feels dutiful.

Or maybe from my son-in-law, for the same reason. Sometimes a card from my brother Émile. Or from the Baronne de Vresse, in Biarritz, by the sea, where she spends her summer. And the occasional bills and taxes.

That morning I noticed a long white envelope. Closed with a thick crimson seal. I turned it around. Préfecture de Paris. Hôtel de Ville.

And my name, printed large, in black lettering. I opened it. The words leaped out. At first I could not understand them. Yet my reading glasses were perched on the end of my nose. My hands were shaking so hard I had to place the sheet of paper on my lap and inhale a deep breath. After a while I took the letter into my hand again and forced myself to read it.

"What is it, Madame Rose?" whimpered Germaine. She must have seen my face.

I slipped the letter back into its envelope. I stood up and smoothed my dress down with the palms of my hands. A pretty frock, dark blue, with just enough ruffle for an old lady like me. You would have approved. I remember that dress, and the shoes I was wearing that day, mere slippers, sweet and feminine, and I remember Germaine's cry when I told her what the letter said.

It was not until later, much later, alone in our room, that I collapsed on the bed. Although I knew this would happen one day, sooner or later, it still came as a shock. That night, when the household was asleep, I fetched a candle and I found that map of the city you used to like to look at. I rolled it out flat on the dining-room table, taking care not to spill any wax. Yes, I could see it, the inexorable northern advance of the rue de Rennes sprouting straight from the Montparnasse railway station to us, and the boulevard Saint-Germain, a hungry monster, creeping westwards from the river. With two trembling fingers I traced their paths until my flesh met. Right over our street. Yes, my love, our street.

It is freezing in the kitchen, I need to go down to get another shawl. Gloves as well, but only for my left hand, as my right hand must go on writing this for you. You thought the church and its proximity would save us, my love. You and Père Levasque.

"They will never touch the church, nor the houses around it," you scoffed fifteen years ago, when the Prefect was appointed. And even after we heard what was going to happen to my brother Émile's house, when the boulevard de Sébastopol was created, you still were not afraid: "We are close to the church, it will protect us."

I often go to sit in the church to think of you. You have been gone for ten years now. A century to me. The church is quiet, peaceful. I gaze at the ancient pillars, the cracked paintings. I pray. Père Levasque comes to see me and we talk in the hushed gloom.

"It will take more than a Prefect or an Emperor to harm our neighborhood, Madame Rose! The church is safe, and so are we, its fortunate neighbors," he whispers emphatically. "Childebert, the Merovingian King, the founder of our church, watches over his creation like a mother would a child."

Père Levasque is fond of reminding me of how many times the church has been looted, plundered and burnt down to the ground by the Normans in the ninth century. I believe it is thrice. How wrong you were, my love.

The church will be safe. But not our house. The house you loved.

Experience the novel that has touched millions of readers....

"NOTHING SHORT OF MIRACULOUS."*

More than two years on the *New York Times* bestseller list—the timeless masterpiece from the author of *A Secret Kept*.

"A shocking, profoundly moving, and morally challenging story…nothing short of miraculous. It will haunt you, it will help to complete you."—*Augusten Burroughs

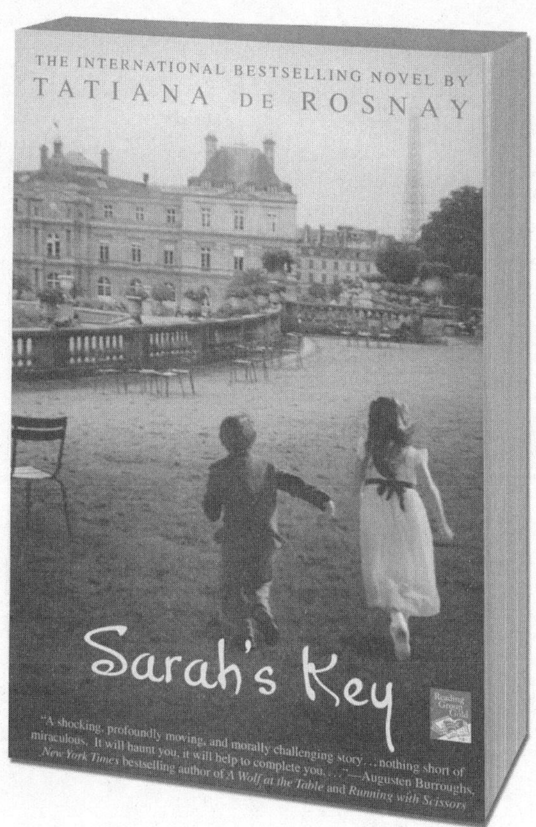

"It will make you cry—and remember."—Jenna Blum

Sarah's Key • A Secret Kept

Available on CD and for digital download

Praise for *Sarah's Key*:

"The story is heart wrenching, and Polly Stone gives an excellent performance. De Rosnay's novel is captivating, and the powerful narration gives it even greater impact."
— *Publishers Weekly* (starred review)

"Polly Stone's delivery of Sarah's story is riveting with its spare emotional power."
— *AudioFile* magazine

Praise for *A Secret Kept*:

An iTunes Best Audiobook of 2010 • An *AudioFile* Best of 2010 Selection

"Simon Vance is an ideal performer for this tightly plotted and beautifully made story about a French family whose stress fractures have widened into chasms. A performance to savor." — *AudioFile* magazine, an Earphones Award winner

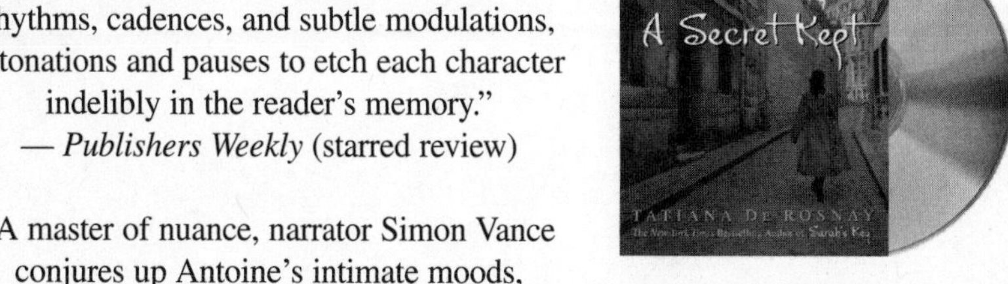

"[Simon] Vance is a reader's reader, and he narrates de Rosnay's novel with nuanced tones, rhythms, cadences, and subtle modulations, intonations and pauses to etch each character indelibly in the reader's memory."
— *Publishers Weekly* (starred review)

"A master of nuance, narrator Simon Vance conjures up Antoine's intimate moods, melancholy, regret, and the blossoming of possibility." — *BookPage*

Don't miss Tatiana de Rosnay's next audiobook, *The House I Loved*, available February 2012.

Visit www.macmillanaudio.com for audio samples and more!
Follow us on Facebook and Twitter.